Cucumber QUEST 4

The Flower Kingdom

Gigi D.G.

:01
First Second
New York

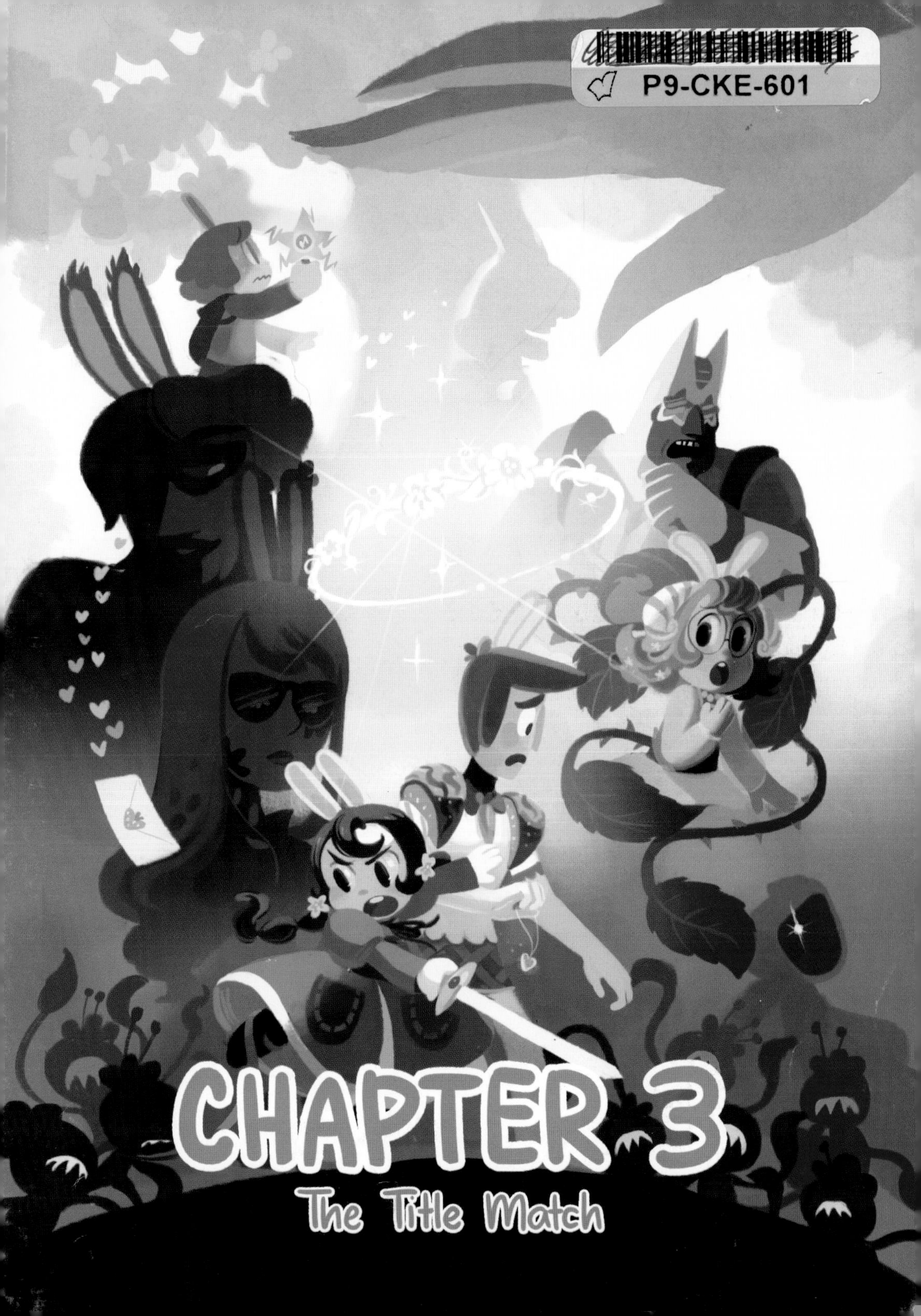

CHAPTER 3

The Title Match

And now...

The moment you've all been waiting for...

Buon appetito!!

This...!!

...would probably be **really good** if I were in the mood for pizza.

Right?

Thank you anyway, dearest pizza friends.

Though...

now that I look at you...

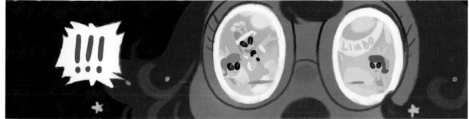

!!!

LIMBO

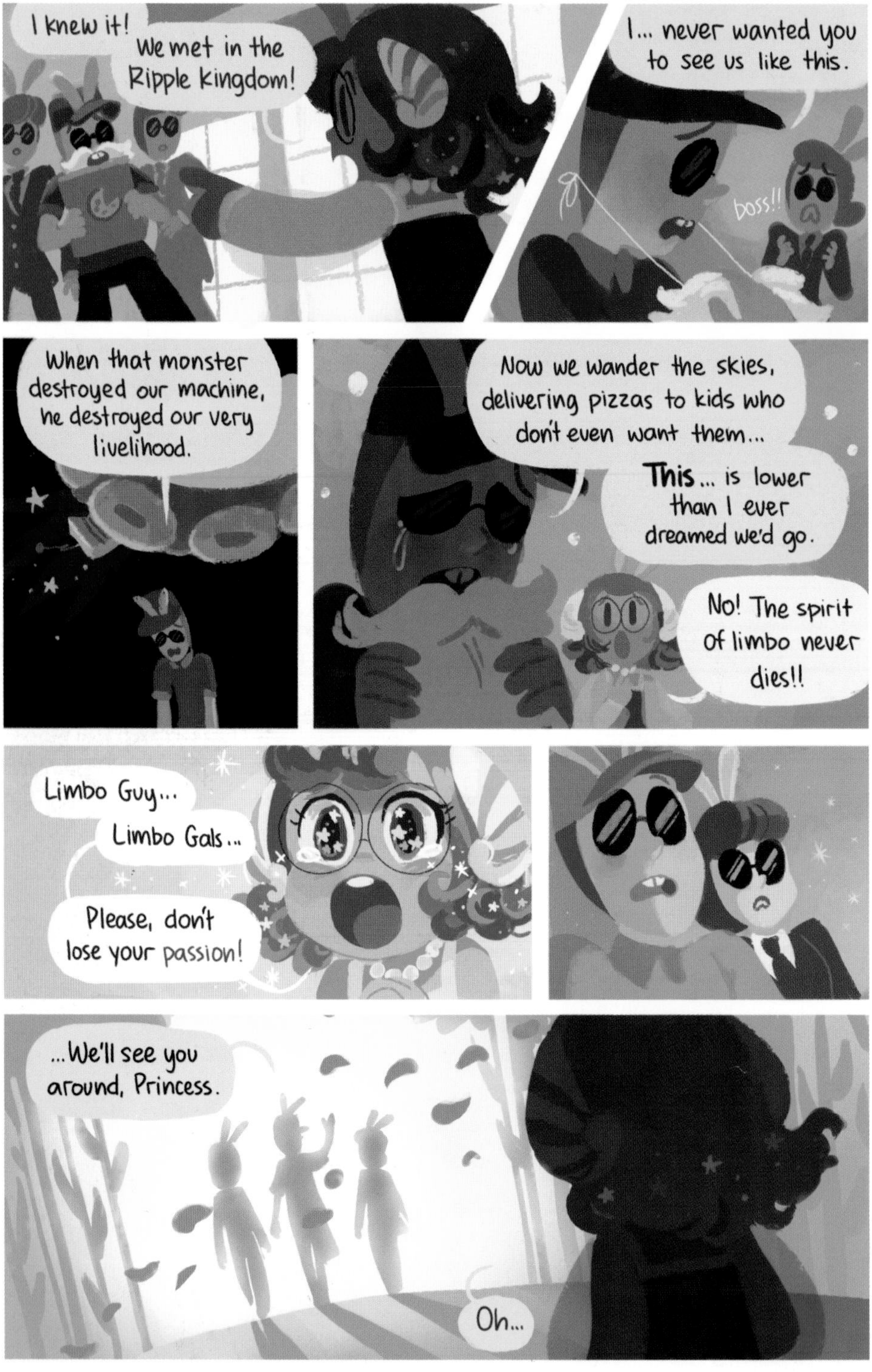
I knew it!
We met in the Ripple Kingdom!
I... never wanted you to see us like this.
boss!!
When that monster destroyed our machine, he destroyed our very livelihood.
Now we wander the skies, delivering pizzas to kids who don't even want them...
This... is lower than I ever dreamed we'd go.
No! The spirit of limbo never dies!!
Limbo Guy...
Limbo Gals...
Please, don't lose your passion!
...We'll see you around, Princess.
Oh...

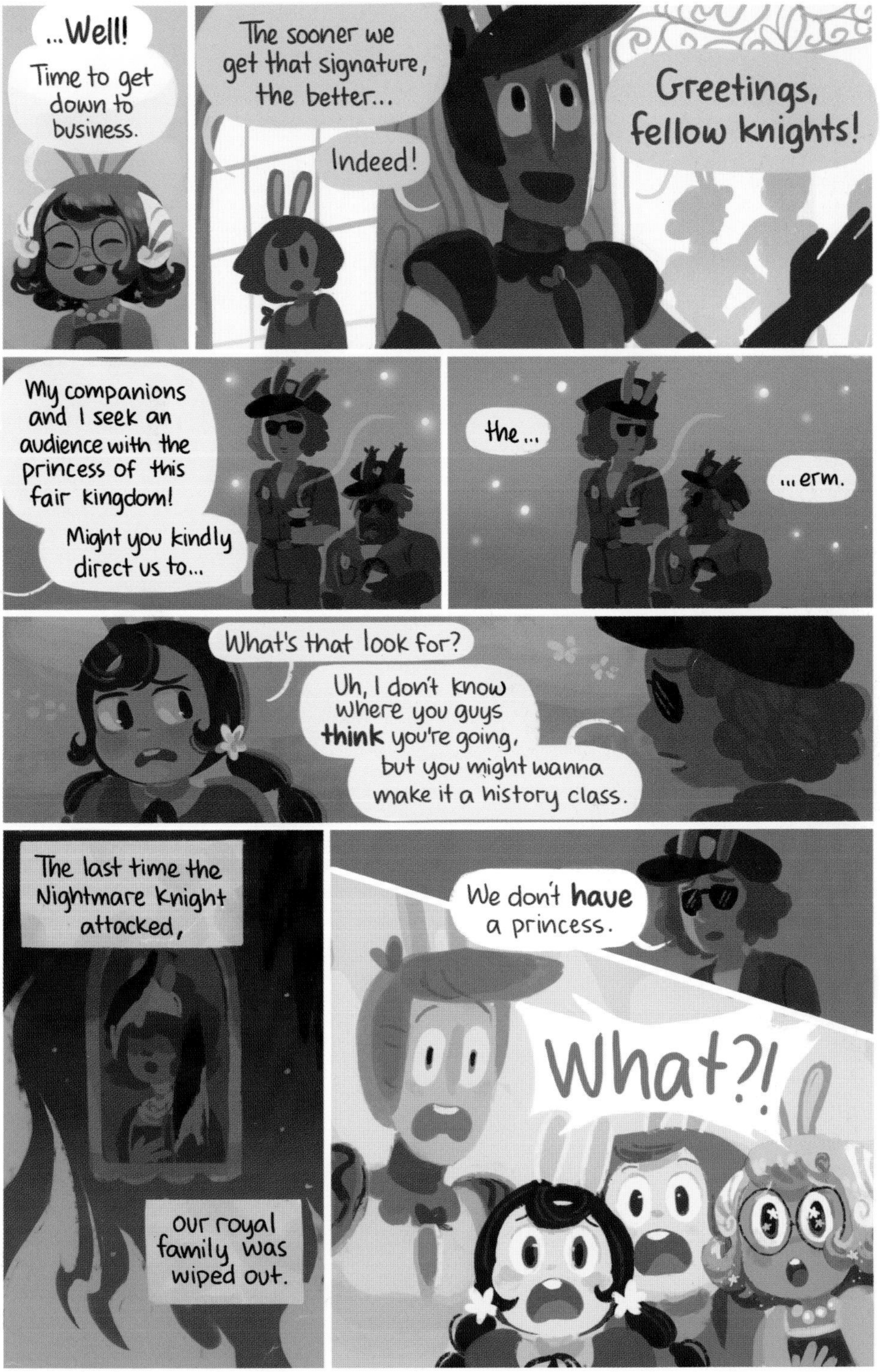
...Well!
Time to get down to business.
The sooner we get that signature, the better...
Indeed!
Greetings, fellow knights!
My companions and I seek an audience with the princess of this fair kingdom!
Might you kindly direct us to...
the...
...erm.
What's that look for?
Uh, I don't know where you guys **think** you're going,
but you might wanna make it a history class.
The last time the Nightmare Knight attacked,
our royal family was wiped out.
We don't **have** a princess.
What?!

The heroes approach.

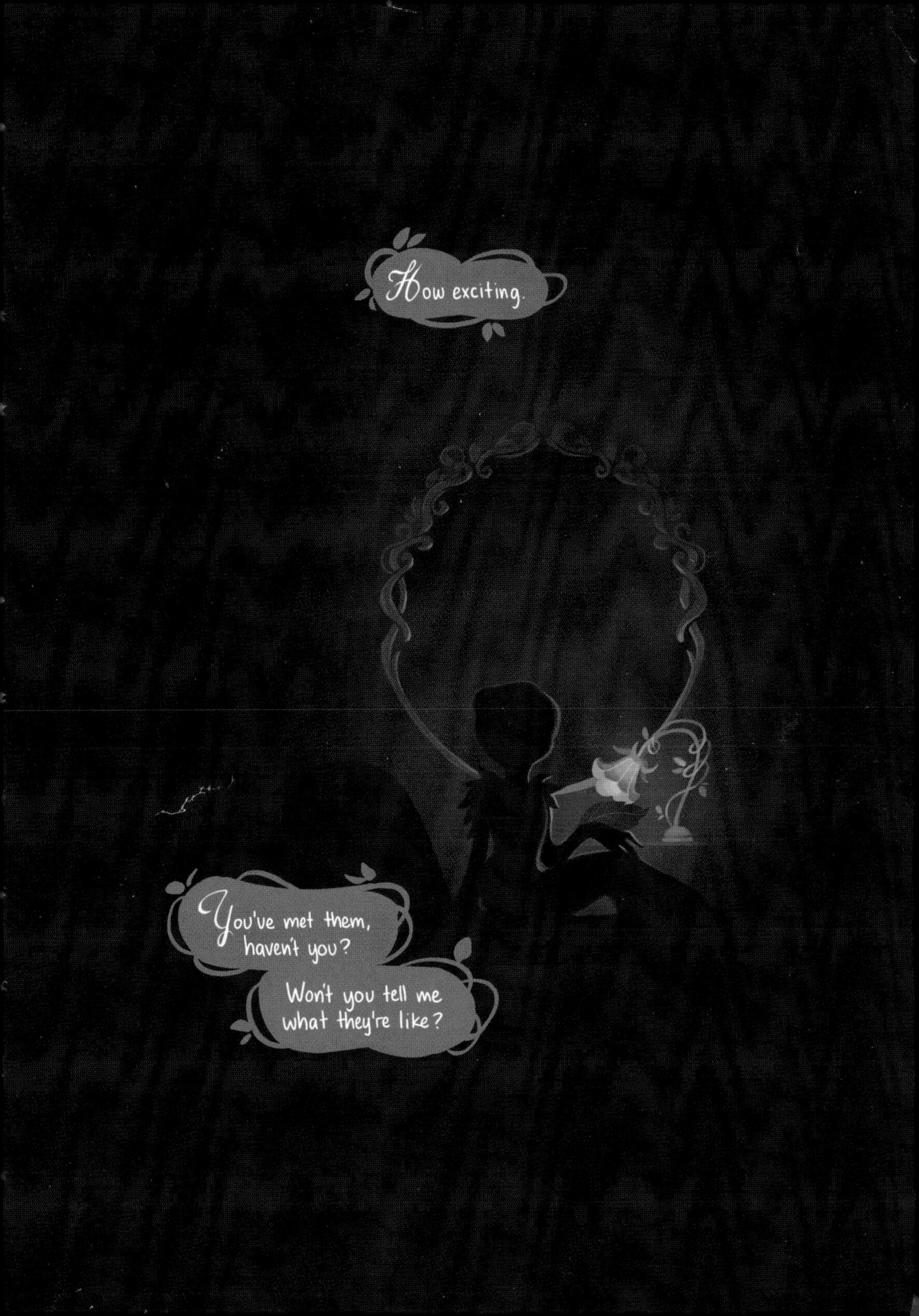
How exciting.
You've met them, haven't you?
Won't you tell me what they're like?

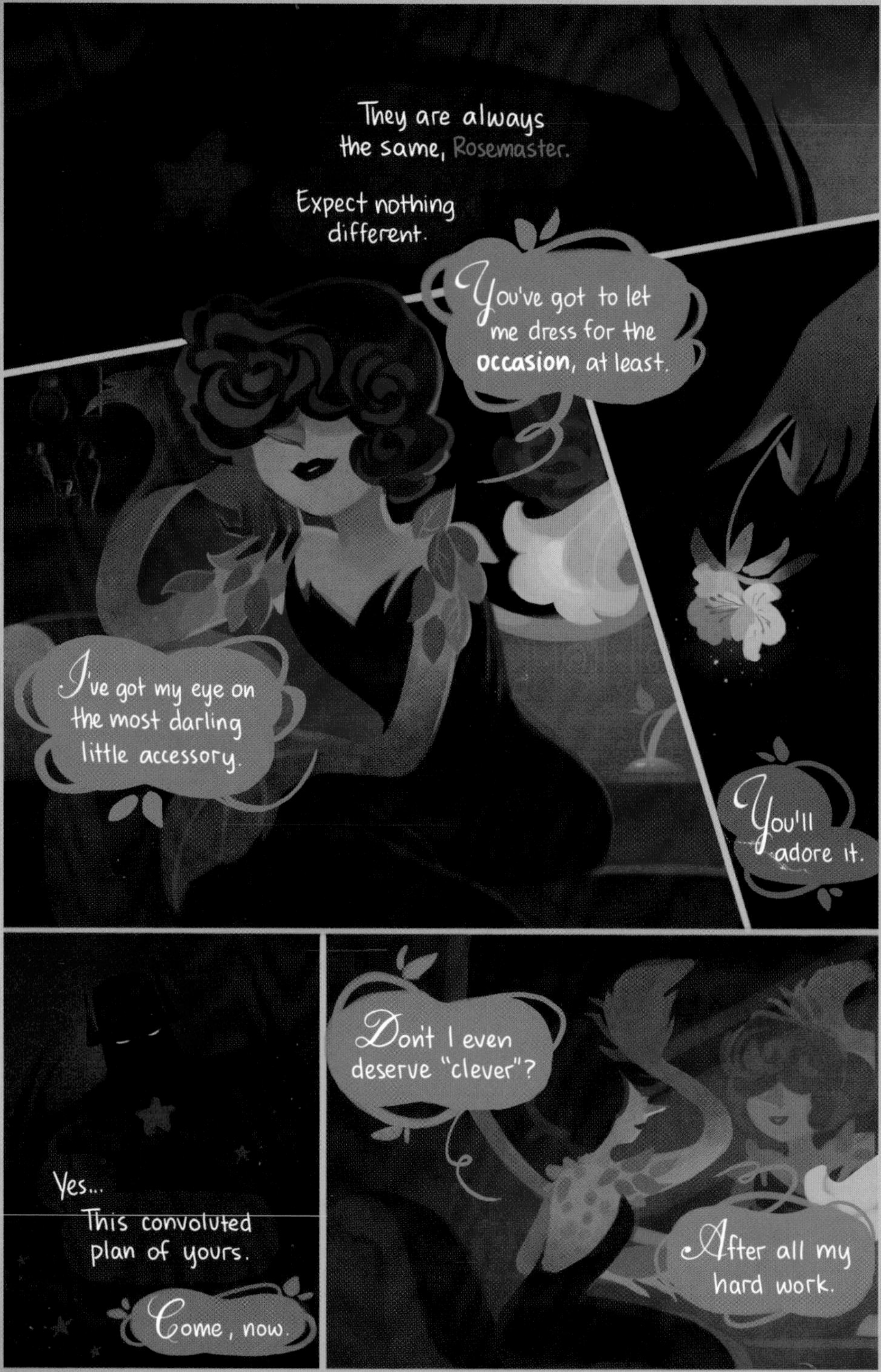
They are always the same, Rosemaster.
Expect nothing different.
You've got to let me dress for the occasion, at least.
I've got my eye on the most darling little accessory.
You'll adore it.
Yes...
This convoluted plan of yours.
Come, now.
Don't I even deserve "clever"?
After all my hard work.

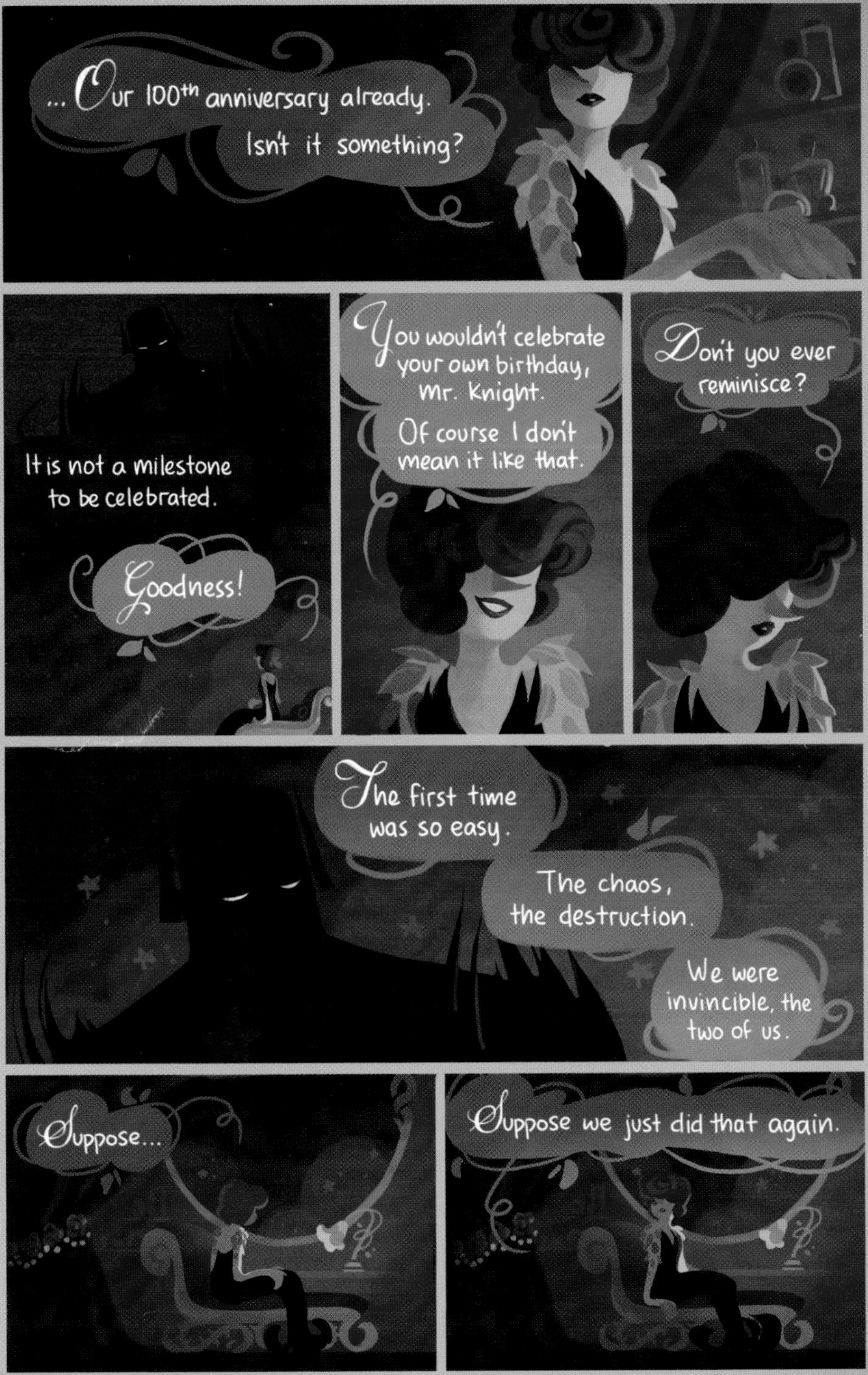
...Our 100th anniversary already.
Isn't it something?
It is not a milestone to be celebrated.
Goodness!
You wouldn't celebrate your own birthday, Mr. Knight.
Of course I don't mean it like that.
Don't you ever reminisce?
The first time was so easy.
The chaos, the destruction.
We were invincible, the two of us.
Suppose...
Suppose we just did that again.

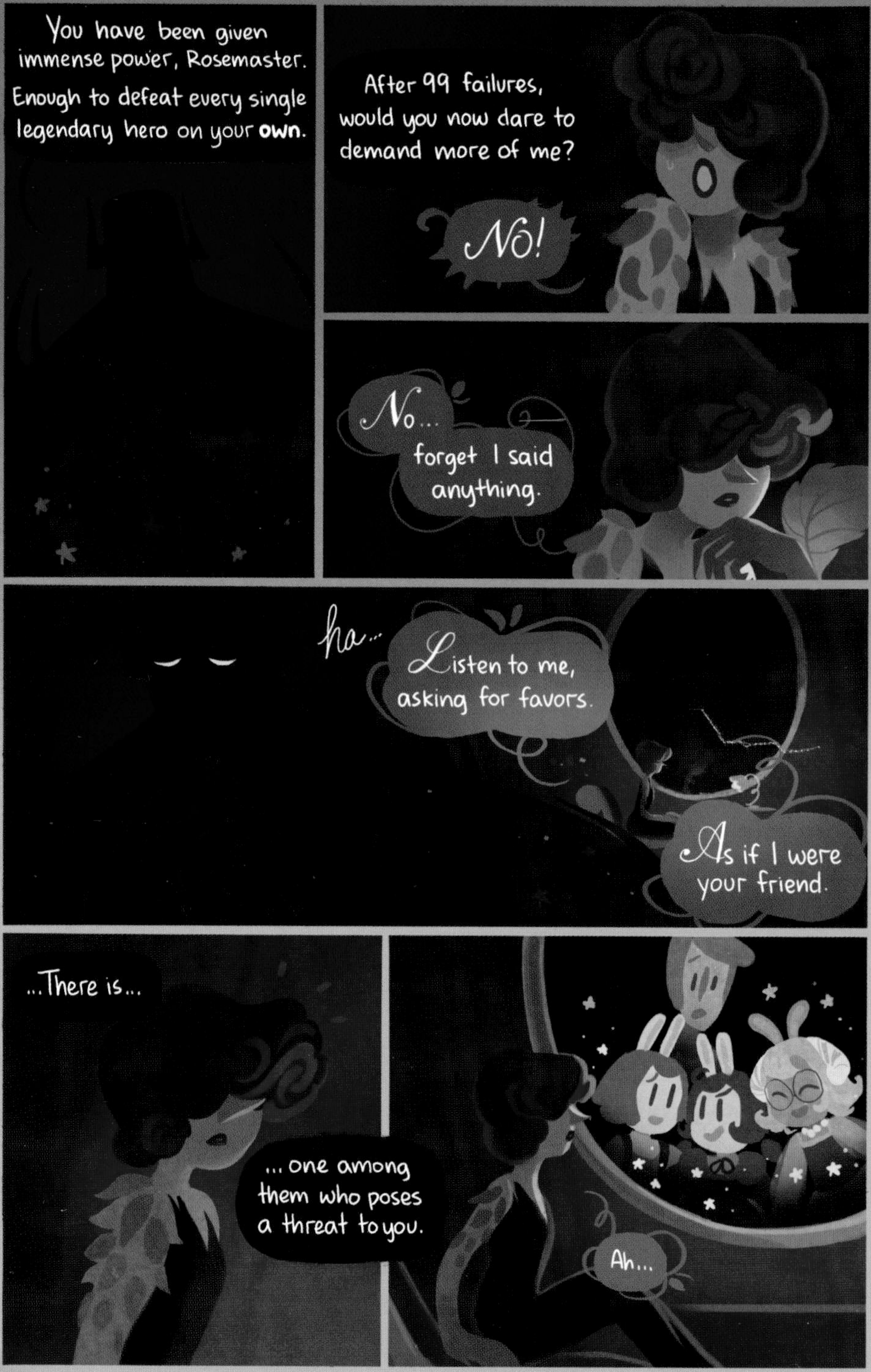
You have been given immense power, Rosemaster.
Enough to defeat every single legendary hero on your **own**.
After 99 failures, would you now dare to demand more of me?
No!
No...
forget I said anything.
ha...
Listen to me, asking for favors.
As if I were your friend.
...There is...
...one among them who poses a threat to you.
Ah...

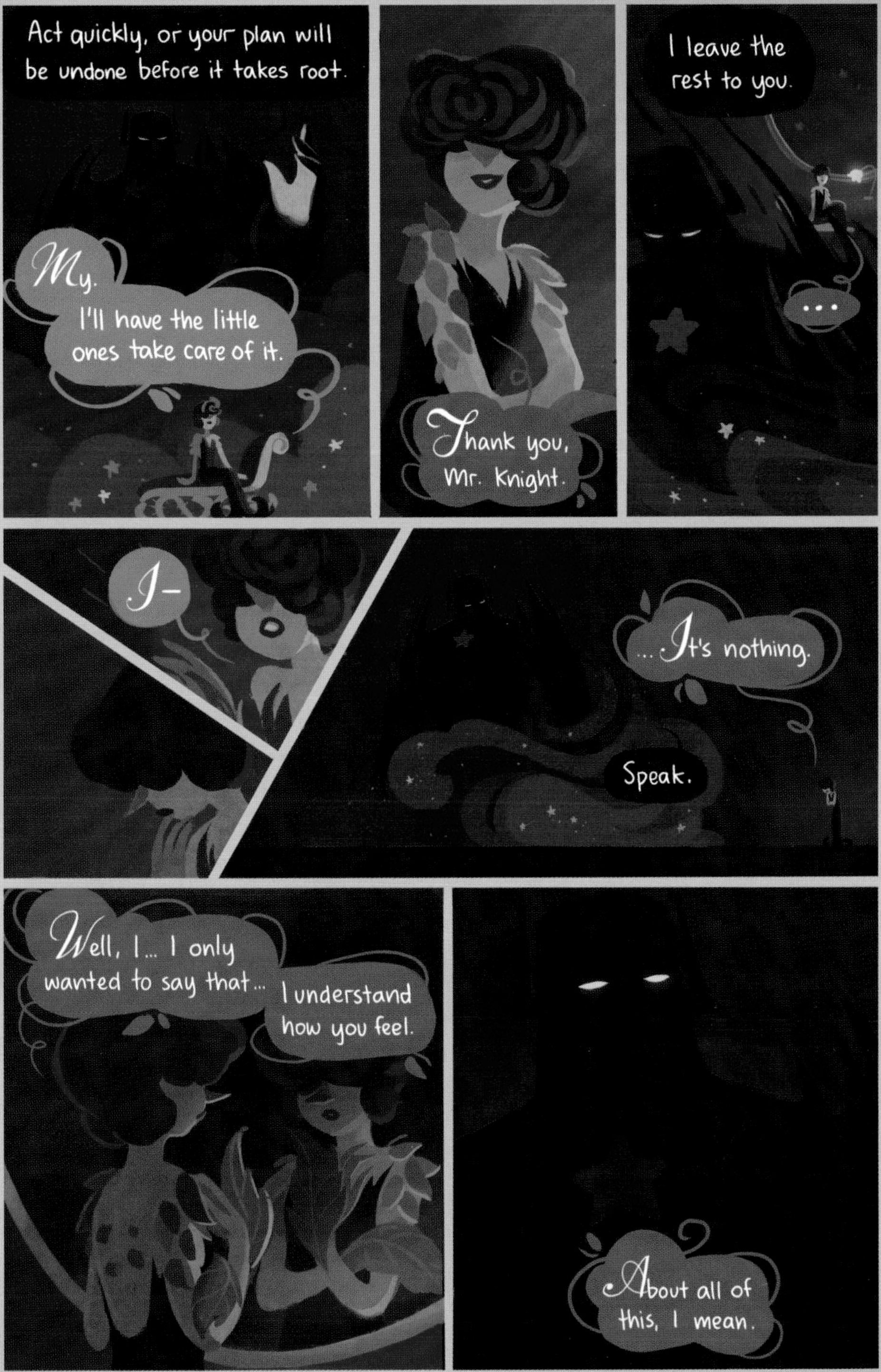
Act quickly, or your plan will be undone before it takes root.
My.
I'll have the little ones take care of it.
Thank you, Mr. Knight.
I leave the rest to you.
...
I–
...It's nothing.
Speak.
Well, I... I only wanted to say that...
I understand how you feel.
About all of this, I mean.

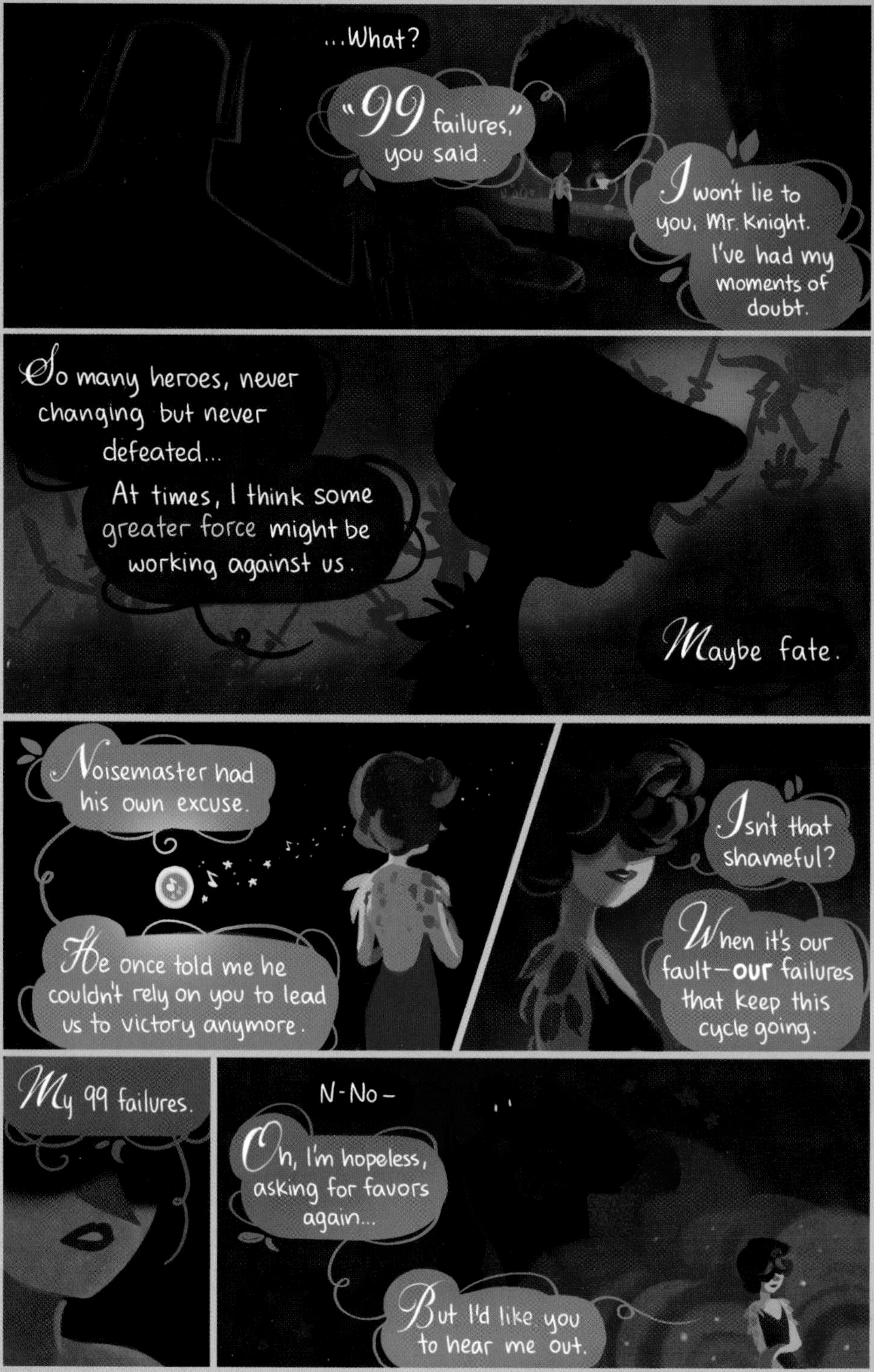
...What?
"99 failures," you said.
I won't lie to you, Mr. Knight. I've had my moments of doubt.
So many heroes, never changing but never defeated...
At times, I think some greater force might be working against us.
Maybe fate.
Noisemaster had his own excuse.
He once told me he couldn't rely on you to lead us to victory anymore.
Isn't that shameful?
When it's our fault—**our** failures that keep this cycle going.
My 99 failures.
N-No-
Oh, I'm hopeless, asking for favors again...
But I'd like you to hear me out.

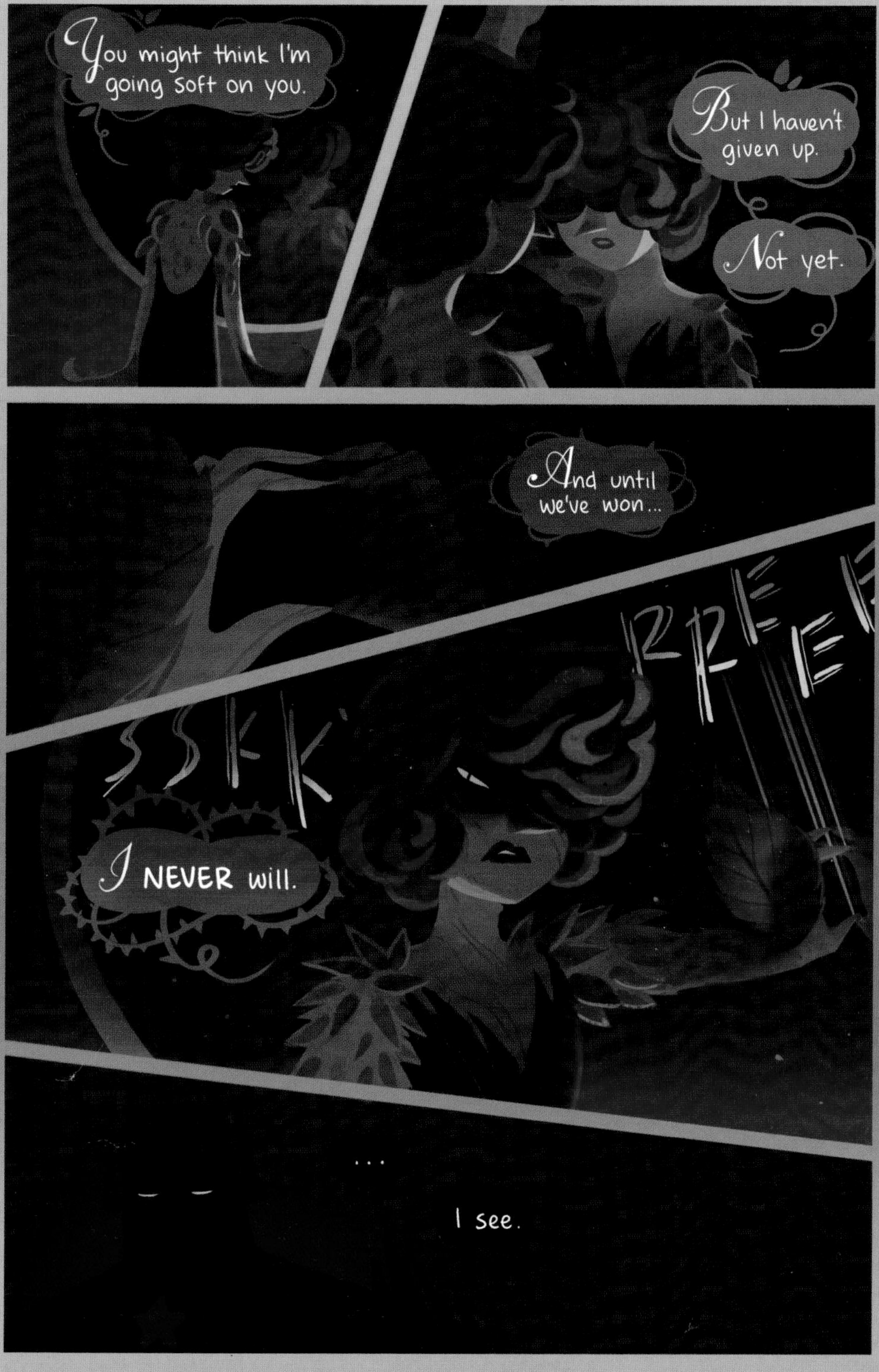
You might think I'm going soft on you.
But I haven't given up.
Not yet.
And until we've won...
RREEE
SSKK
I NEVER will.
...
I see.

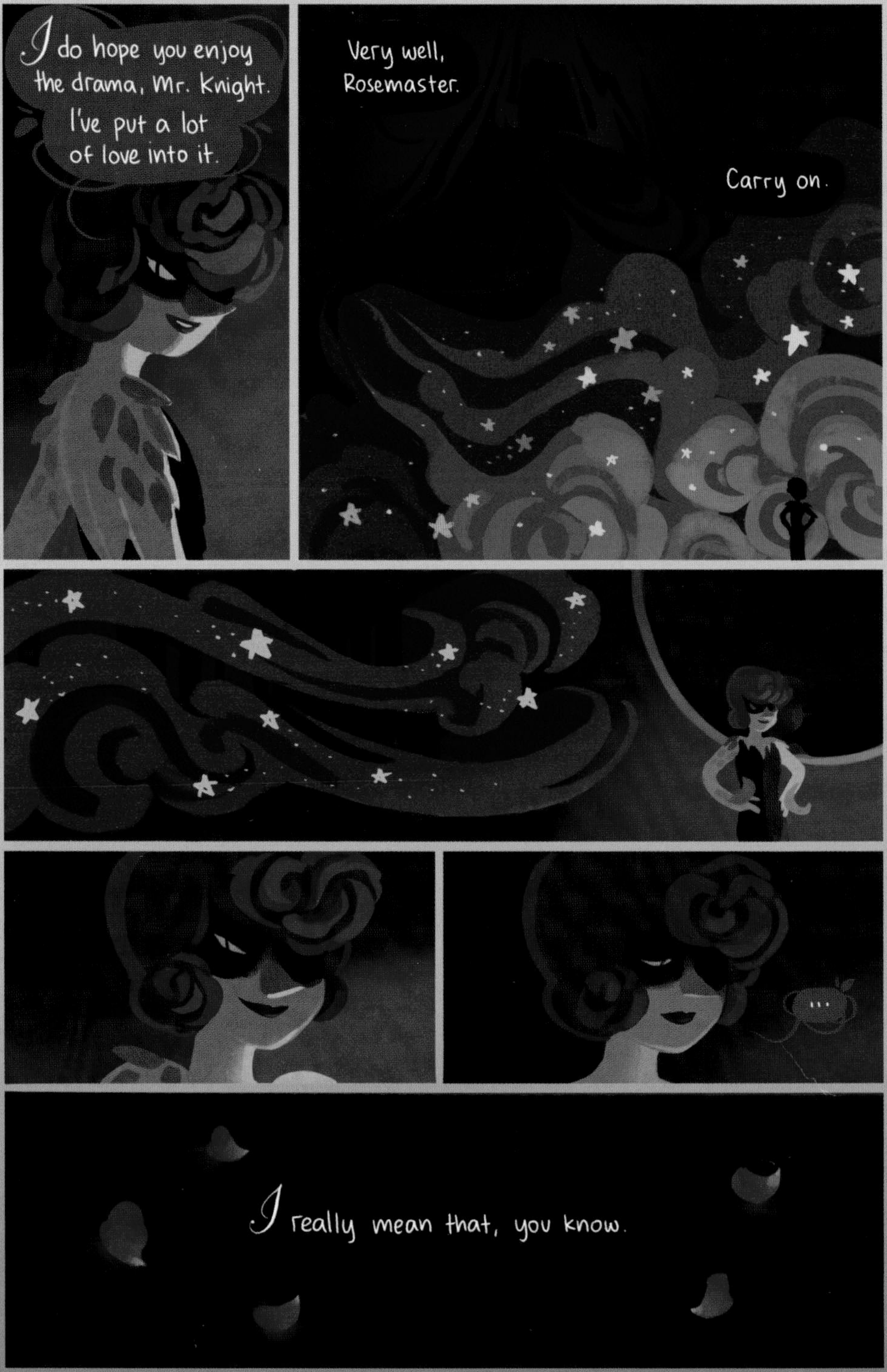
I do hope you enjoy the drama, Mr. Knight. I've put a lot of love into it.
Very well, Rosemaster.
Carry on.
...
I really mean that, you know.

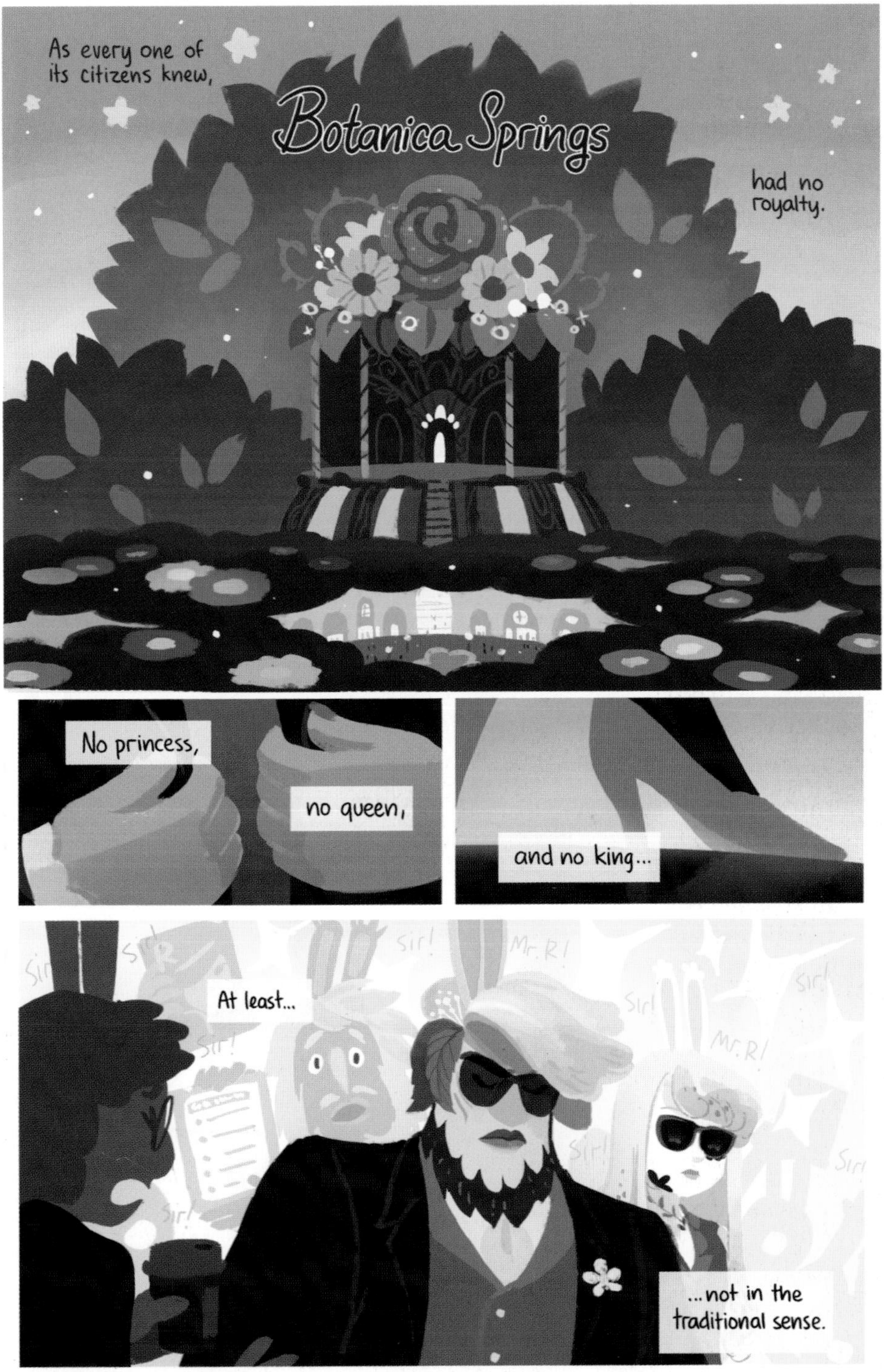
As every one of its citizens knew,
Botanica Springs
had no royalty.
No princess,
no queen,
and no king...
At least...
Sir!
Sir!
Mr. R!
Sir!
Mr. R!
Sir!
Sir!
Sir!
...not in the traditional sense.

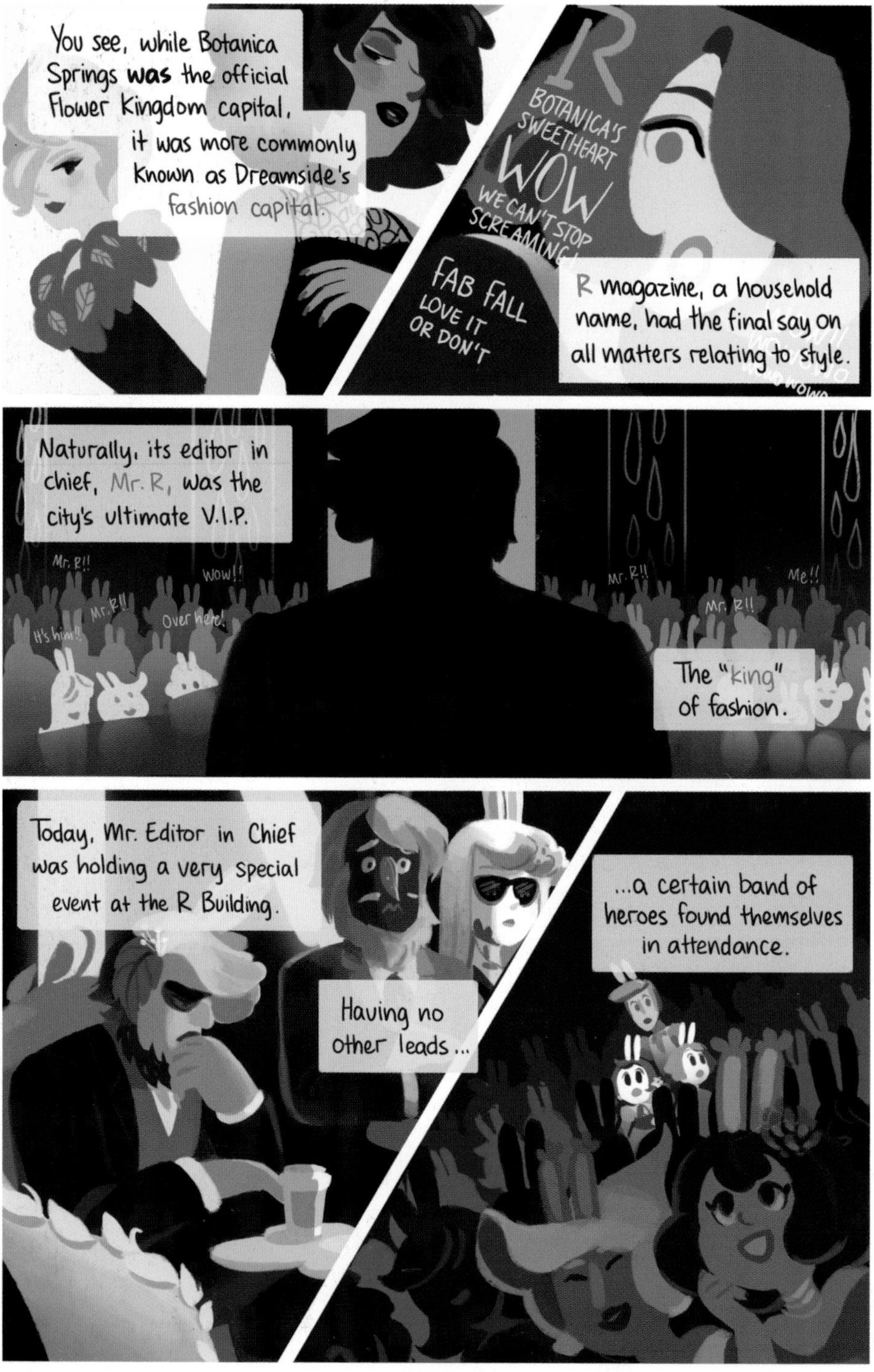

You see, while Botanica Springs **was** the official Flower Kingdom capital,
it was more commonly known as Dreamside's fashion capital.
R
BOTANICA'S SWEETHEART
WOW
WE CAN'T STOP SCREAMING!
FAB FALL
LOVE IT OR DON'T
R magazine, a household name, had the final say on all matters relating to style.
Naturally, its editor in chief, Mr. R, was the city's ultimate V.I.P.
Mr. R!!
Wow!!
Mr. R!!
It's him!!
Over here!
Mr. R!!
Me!!
Mr. R!!
The "king" of fashion.
Today, Mr. Editor in Chief was holding a very special event at the R Building.
Having no other leads...
...a certain band of heroes found themselves in attendance.

What is this **about?**

I feel a bit underdressed...

Look.

I think they're starting...

siiii...siighhh

Ahem... Mr. R is very distressed.

A-As you know, the new face of R magazine will be chosen tonight...

But he's lacking inspiration.

siiighhhhhhh

He needs a "vision," he says.

Something "fab."

Wait, that's it!

What's what?

What those officers said has been bugging me...

How the royal family was wiped out "last time."

We're the only ones who know the Nightmare Knight keeps coming back, which means they meant the first time.

And if there were no princesses after that...

Who could have signed the Dream Sword for every other legendary hero?

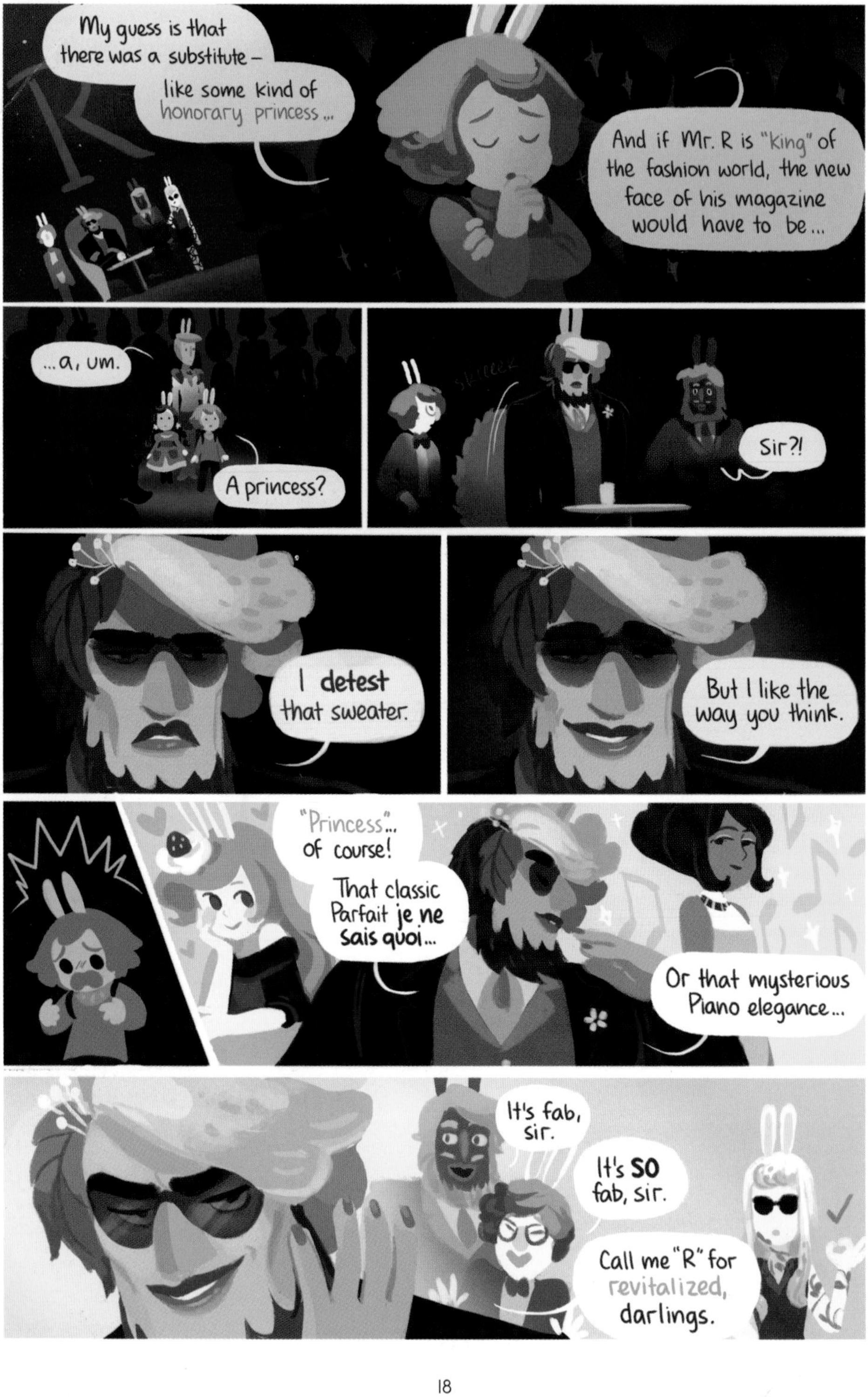

My guess is that there was a substitute –
like some kind of honorary princess…
And if Mr. R is "King" of the fashion world, the new face of his magazine would have to be…
…a, um.
A princess?
Sir?!
I detest that sweater.
But I like the way you think.
"Princess"… of course!
That classic Parfait je ne sais quoi…
Or that mysterious Piano elegance…
It's fab, sir.
It's SO fab, sir.
Call me "R" for revitalized, darlings.

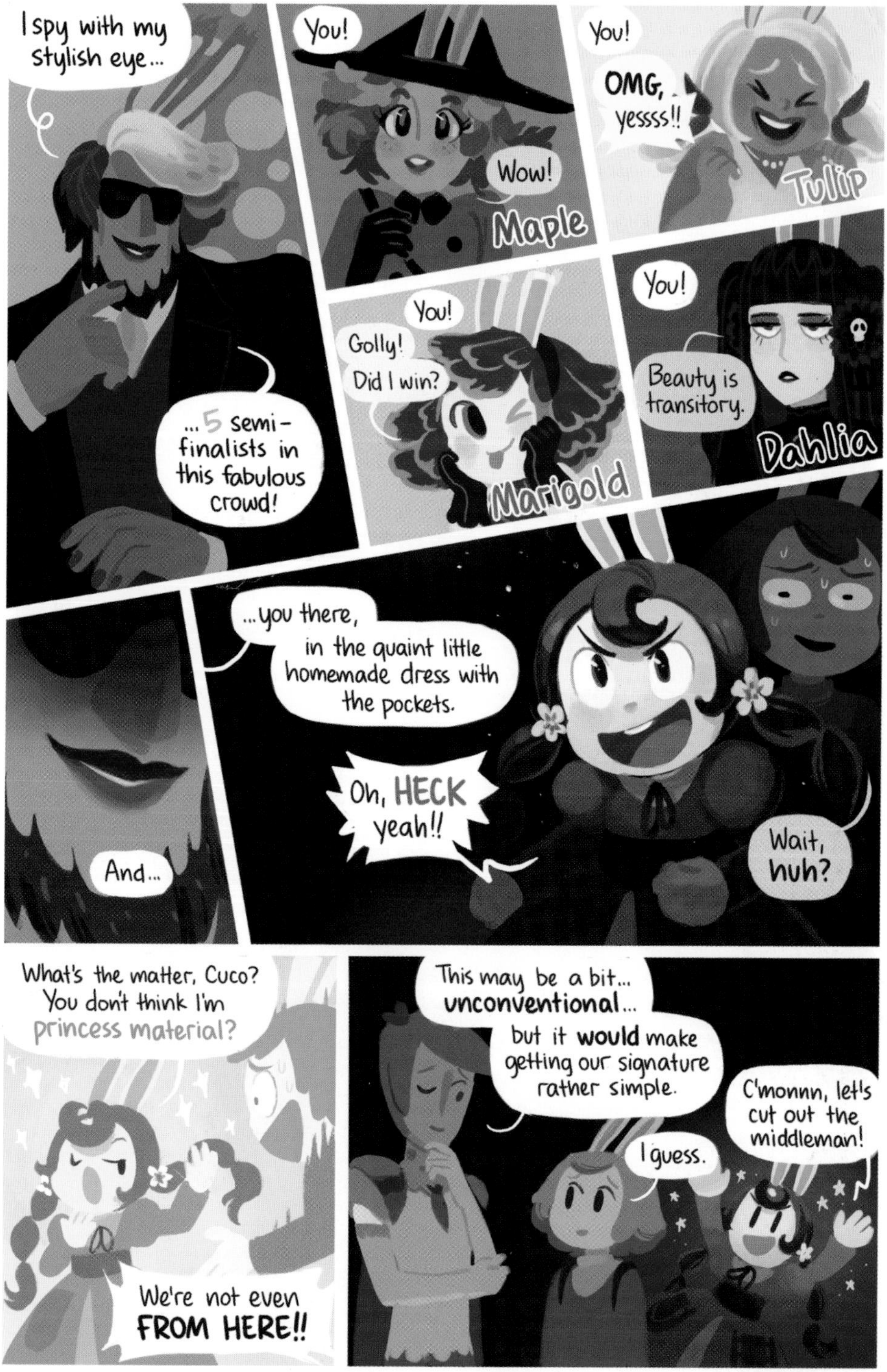

I spy with my stylish eye...
...5 semi-finalists in this fabulous crowd!
You!
Wow!
Maple
You!
OMG, yessss!!
Tulip
You!
Golly! Did I win?
Marigold
You!
Beauty is transitory.
Dahlia
And...
...you there, in the quaint little homemade dress with the pockets.
Oh, HECK yeah!!
Wait, huh?
What's the matter, Cuco? You don't think I'm princess material?
We're not even FROM HERE!!
This may be a bit... unconventional...
but it would make getting our signature rather simple.
I guess.
C'monnn, let's cut out the middleman!

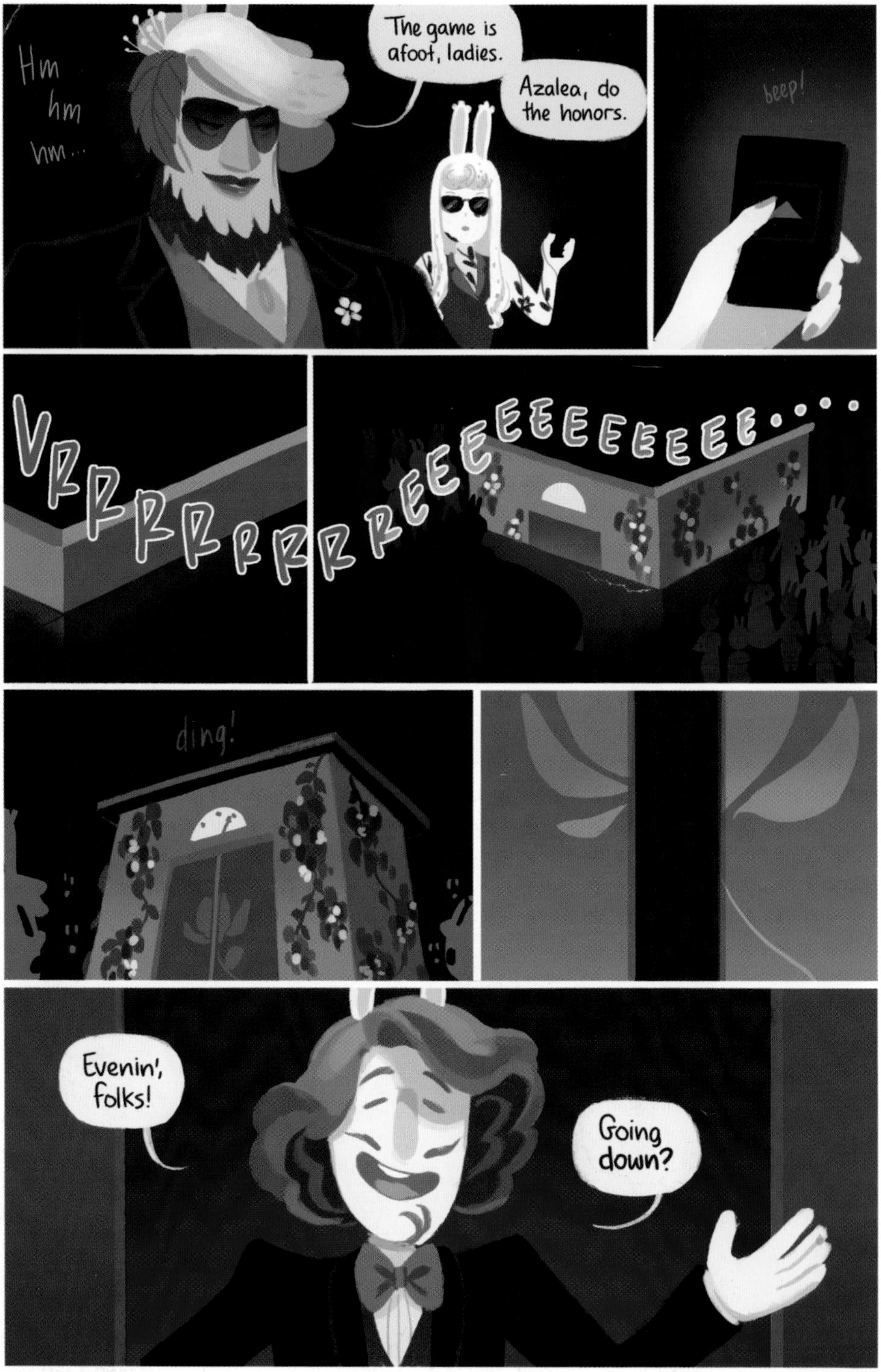

Hm hm hm...
The game is afoot, ladies.
Azalea, do the honors.
beep!
VRRRRRRRREEEEEEEEEEEE....
ding!
Evenin', folks!
Going down?

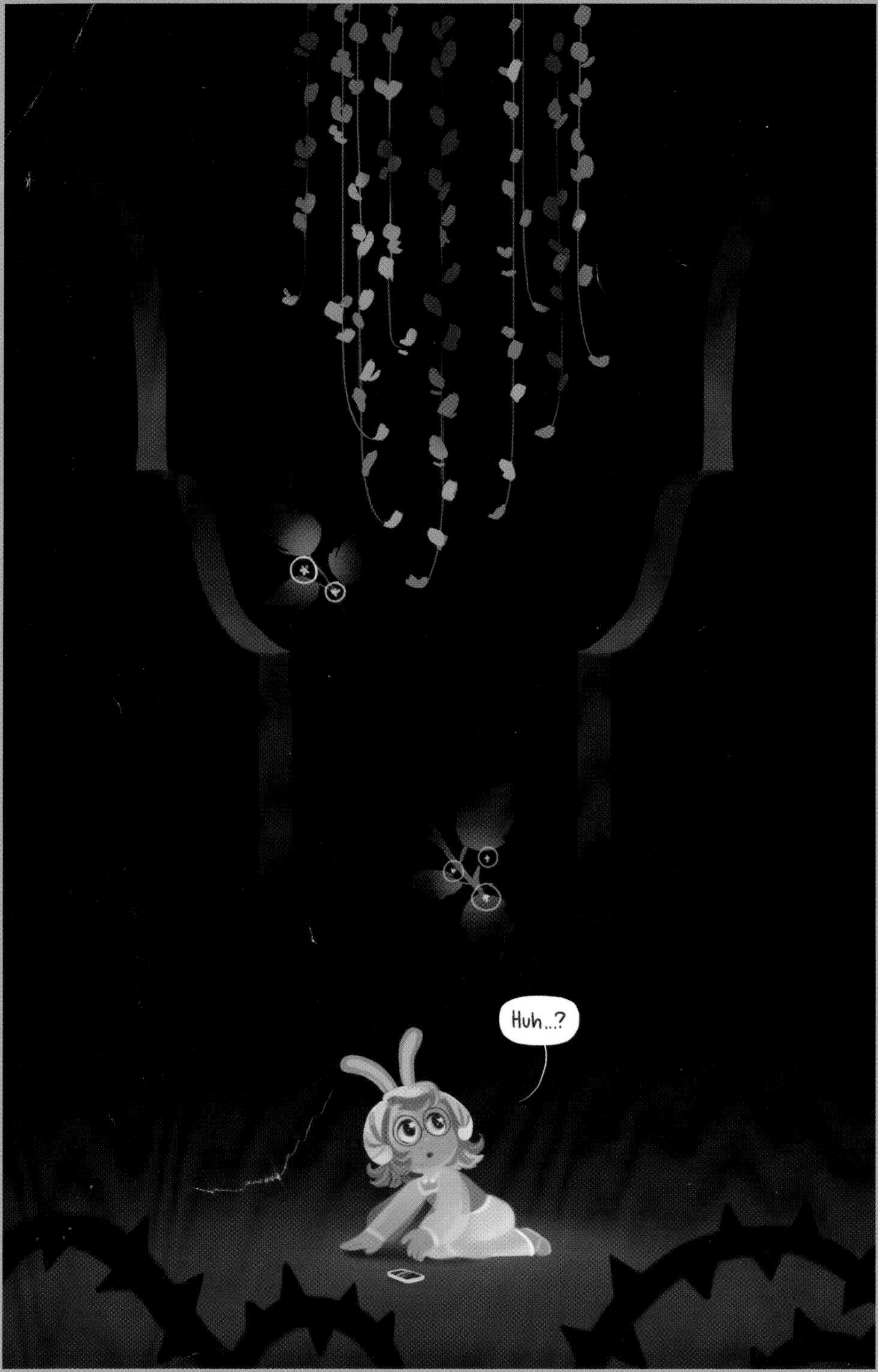
Huh...?

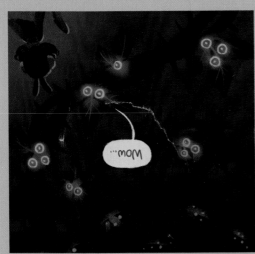

Wow...

—I

I'm sorry, Liquis! I can't control my cravings!

...to be honest, I could **really** go for that pizza right about now.

Well, I **would**, but...

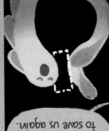

"...Hm?"

Oh, you think I should summon the Pizza Guy and Gals to save us again.

And where is everyone else?

But... where **is** her?

Those monsters must have brought us here...

Liquis!

Oh, thank goodness you're still with me.

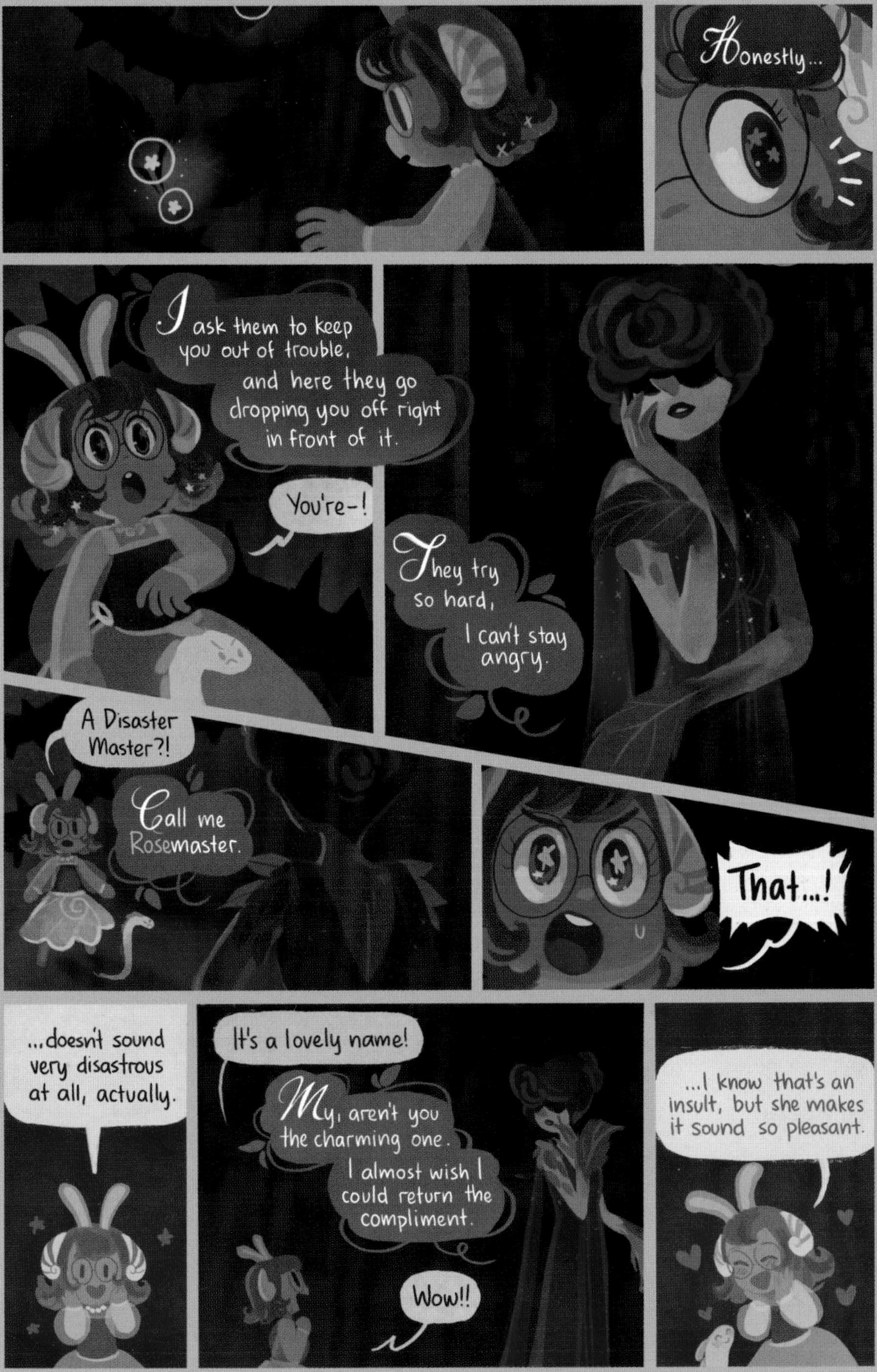
Honestly...
I ask them to keep you out of trouble, and here they go dropping you off right in front of it.
You're-!
They try so hard, I can't stay angry.
A Disaster Master?!
Call me Rosemaster.
That...!
...doesn't sound very disastrous at all, actually.
It's a lovely name!
My, aren't you the charming one.
I almost wish I could return the compliment.
Wow!!
...I know that's an insult, but she makes it sound so pleasant.

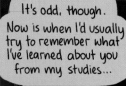

It's odd, though. Now is when I'd usually try to remember what I've learned about you from my studies...

...but I'm certain I've never heard **anything** about a Rosemaster before.

How tragic. I imagine you must be familiar with Thornmaster, then.

gasp! That's the one!

Thornmaster— I know I've seen **his** name in the legends!

And what do you think, now that you've met her?

Well, she's much more elegant than I was expecti—

Ohh.

You mean...

I'm not fond of legends, Princess.

Never was terribly fond of that name, either.

I-I'm so sorry!

It's good to meet you, Rosemaster! I hope we can get along—

WAIT A SECOND

What have you done with my friends? **I DEMAND** answers!

They must be so worried...

ha ha.

Oh no, I think they'll be just fine.

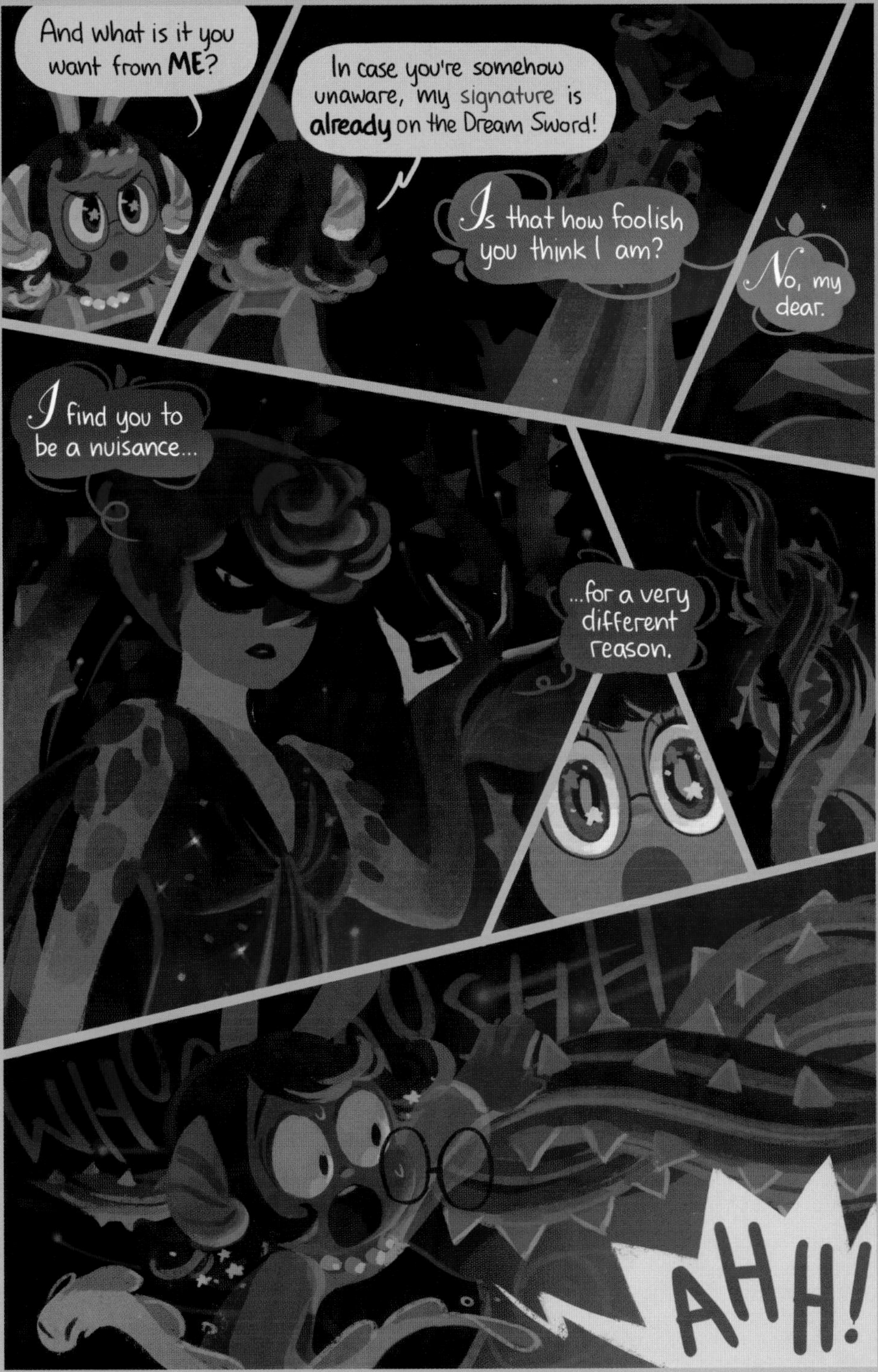

And what is it you want from **ME**?
In case you're somehow unaware, my signature is **already** on the Dream Sword!
Is that how foolish you think I am?
No, my dear.
I find you to be a nuisance...
...for a very different reason.
AHH!

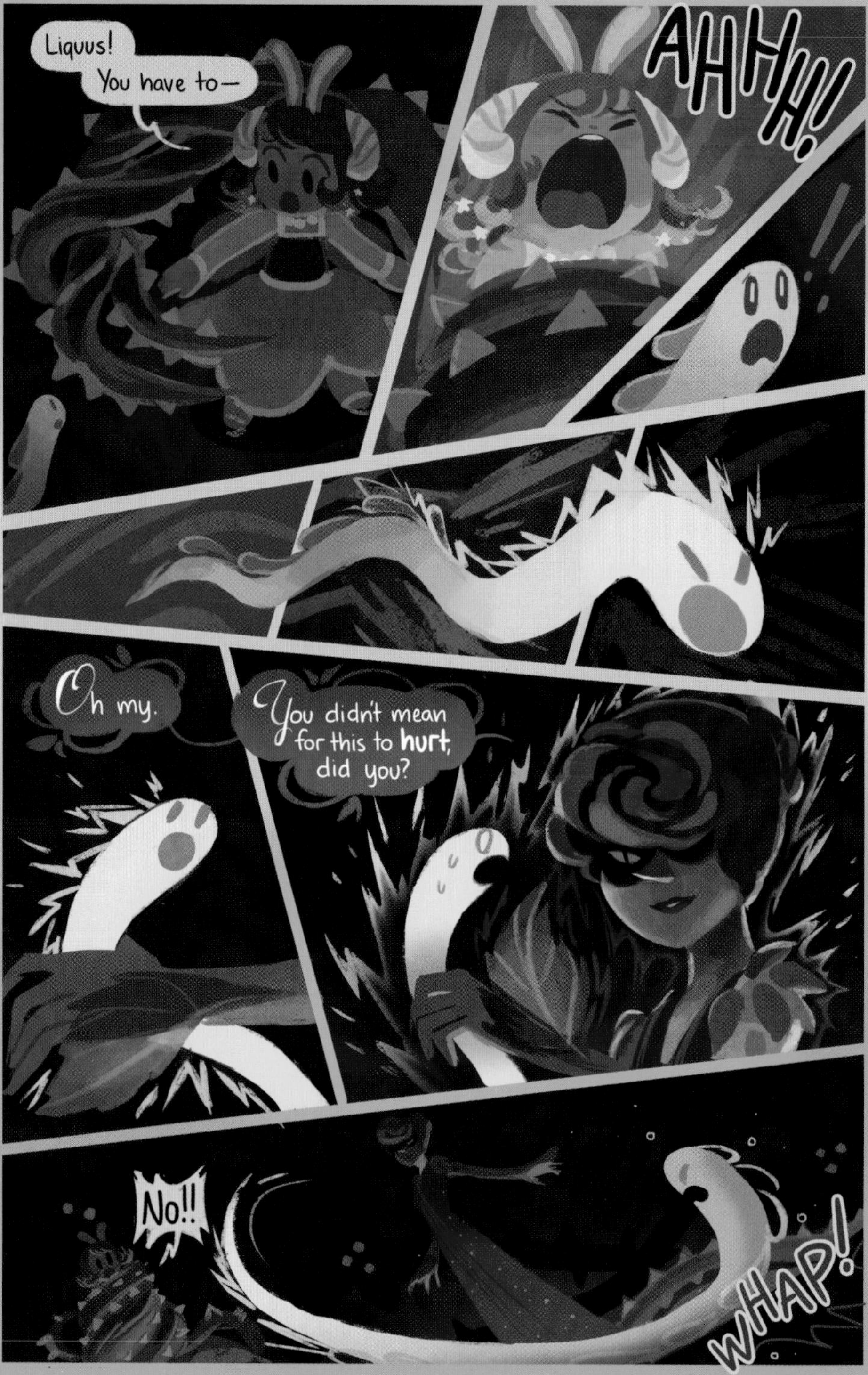

Liquus!
You have to—
AHHH!
Oh my.
You didn't mean for this to **hurt**, did you?
No!!
WHAP!

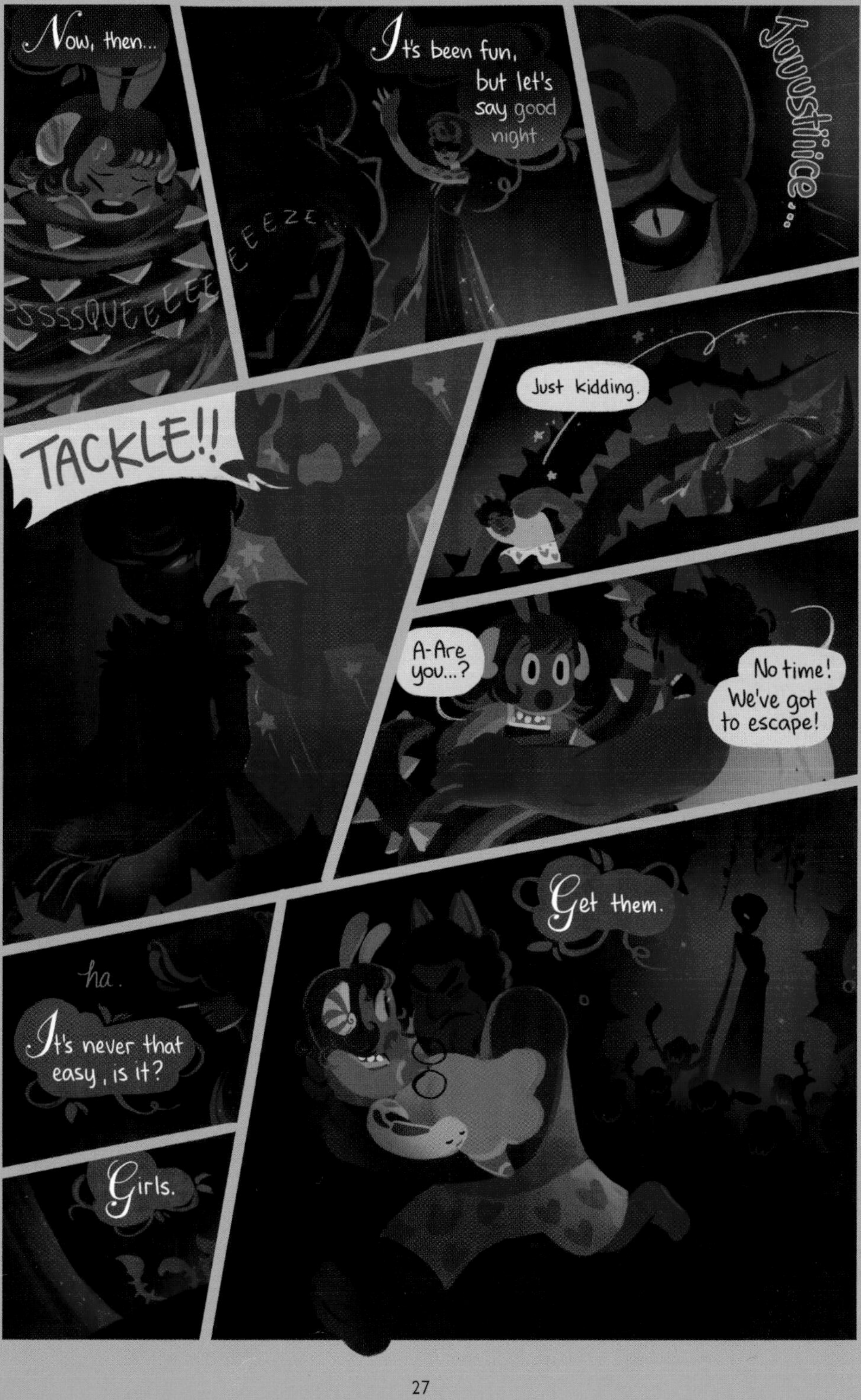
Now, then...
SSSSQUEEEEEE
EEEEZE...
It's been fun, but let's say good night.
Juuustiiice...
TACKLE!!
Just kidding.
A-Are you...?
No time! We've got to escape!
ha.
It's never that easy, is it?
Girls.
Get them.

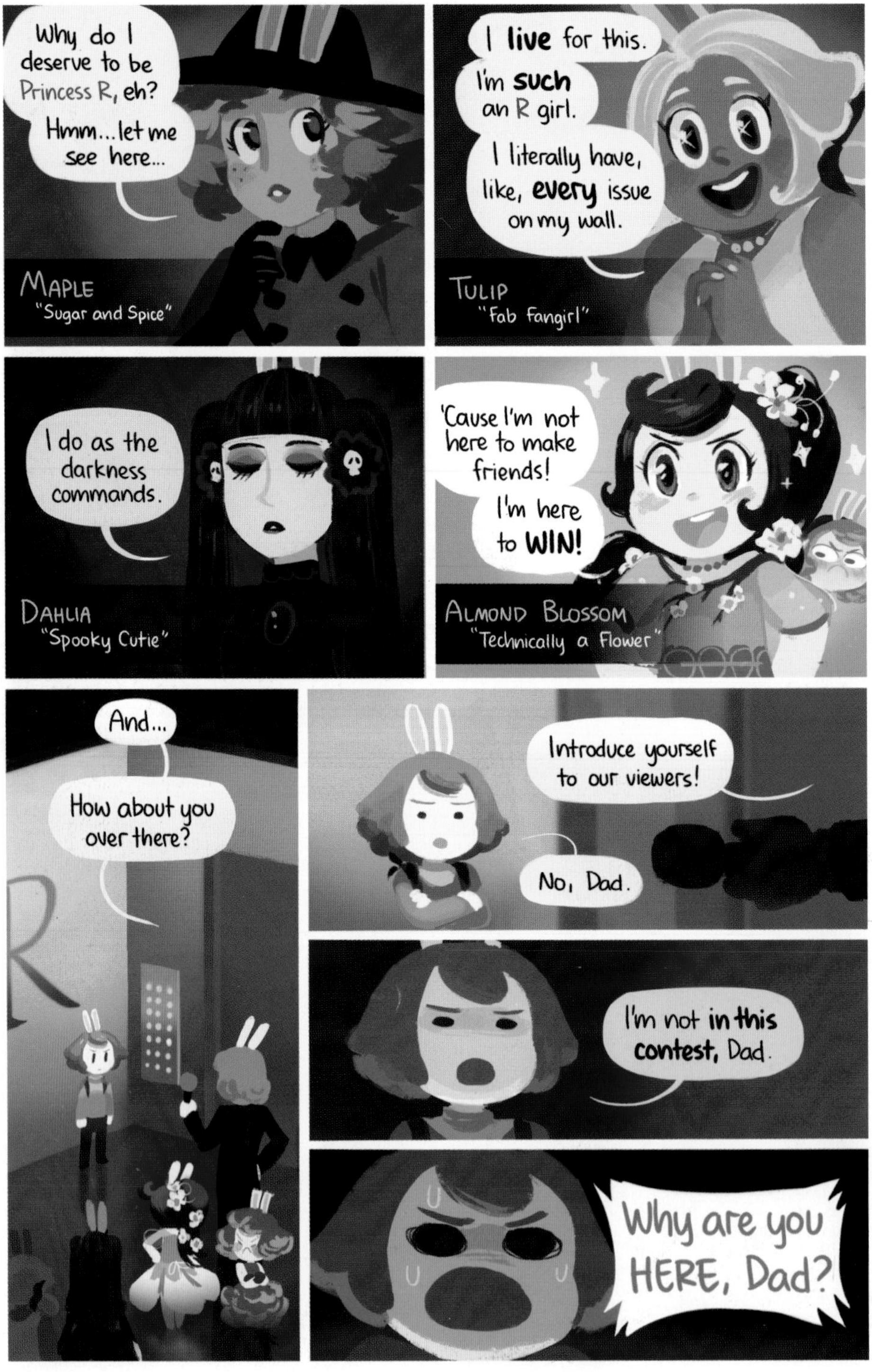
Why do I deserve to be Princess R, eh?
Hmm...let me see here...
MAPLE
"Sugar and Spice"
I live for this.
I'm such an R girl.
I literally have, like, every issue on my wall.
TULIP
"Fab Fangirl"
I do as the darkness commands.
DAHLIA
"Spooky Cutie"
'Cause I'm not here to make friends!
I'm here to WIN!
ALMOND BLOSSOM
"Technically a Flower"
And...
How about you over there?
Introduce yourself to our viewers!
No, Dad.
I'm not in this contest, Dad.
Why are you HERE, Dad?

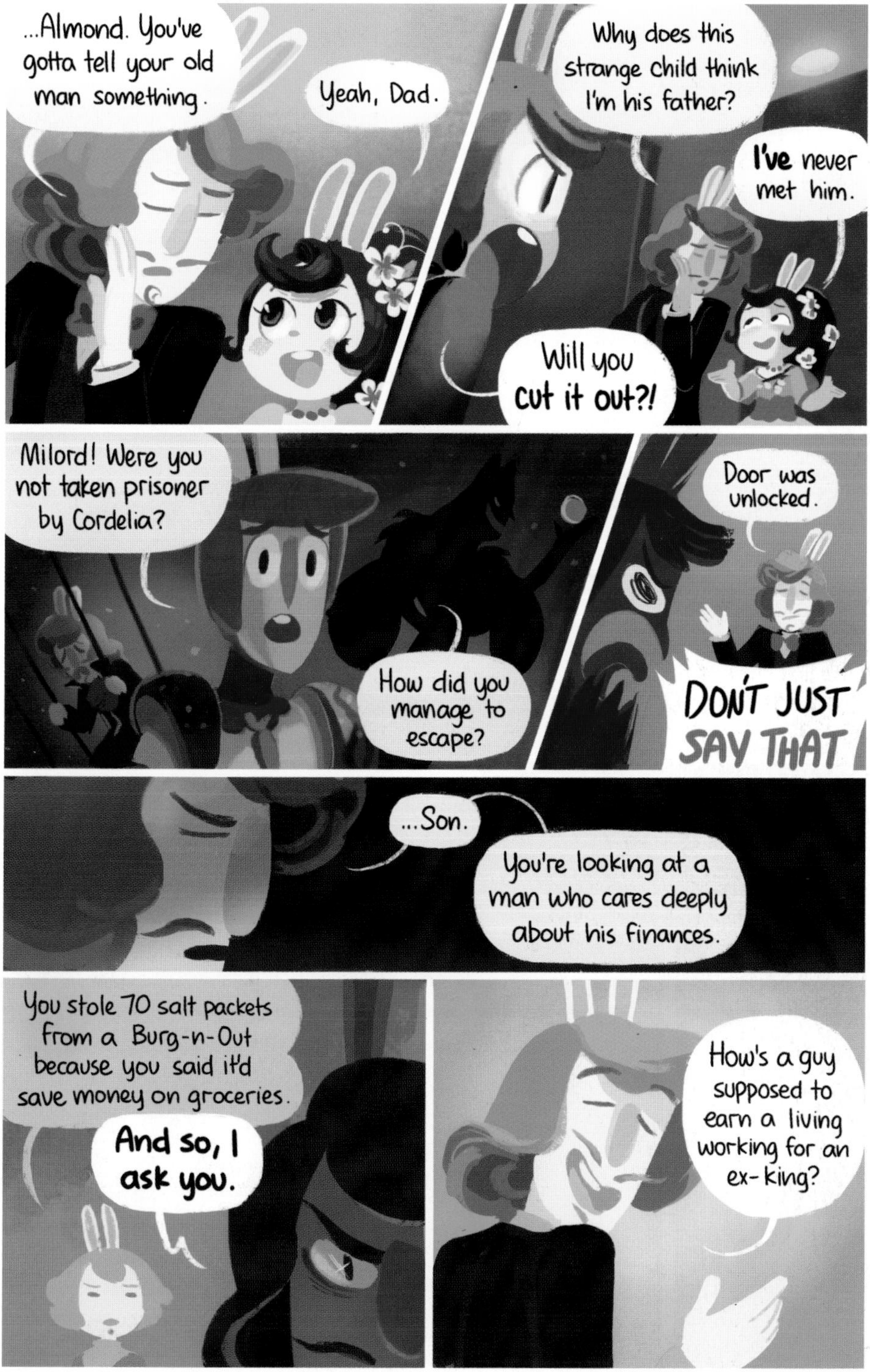
...Almond. You've gotta tell your old man something.
Yeah, Dad.
Why does this strange child think I'm his father?
I've never met him.
Will you **cut it out?!**
Milord! Were you not taken prisoner by Cordelia?
How did you manage to escape?
Door was unlocked.
DON'T JUST SAY THAT
...Son.
You're looking at a man who cares deeply about his finances.
You stole 70 salt packets from a Burg-n-Out because you said it'd save money on groceries.
And so, I ask you.
How's a guy supposed to earn a living working for an ex-king?

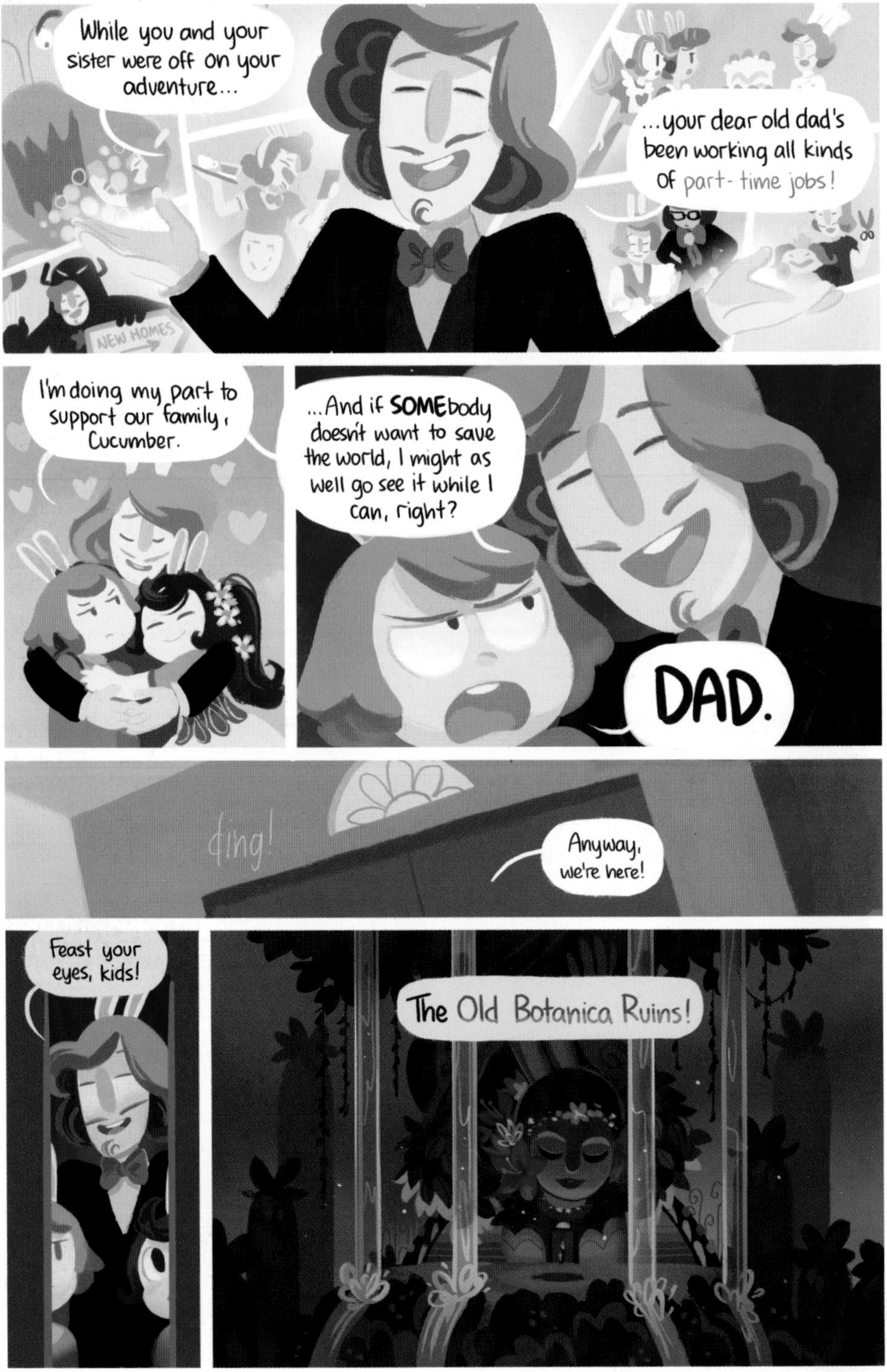
While you and your sister were off on your adventure...
...your dear old dad's been working all kinds of part-time jobs!
NEW HOMES
I'm doing my part to support our family, Cucumber.
...And if SOMEbody doesn't want to save the world, I might as well go see it while I can, right?
DAD.
ding!
Anyway, we're here!
Feast your eyes, kids!
The Old Botanica Ruins!

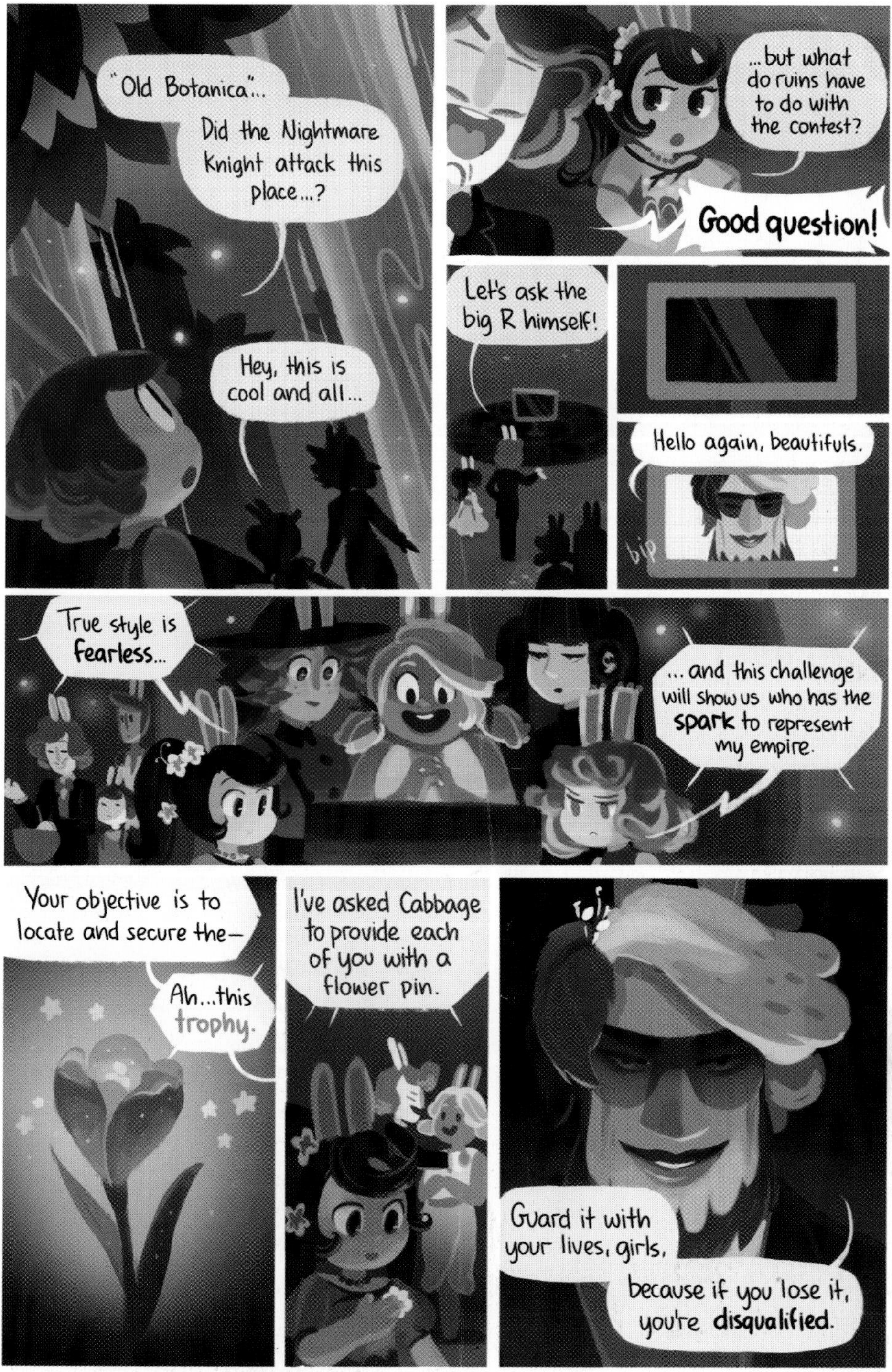
"Old Botanica"...
Did the Nightmare Knight attack this place...?
Hey, this is cool and all...
...but what do ruins have to do with the contest?
Good question!
Let's ask the big R himself!
Hello again, beautifuls.
bip
True style is **fearless**...
...and this challenge will show us who has the **spark** to represent my empire.
Your objective is to locate and secure the—
Ah...this trophy.
I've asked Cabbage to provide each of you with a flower pin.
Guard it with your lives, girls,
because if you lose it, you're **disqualified**.

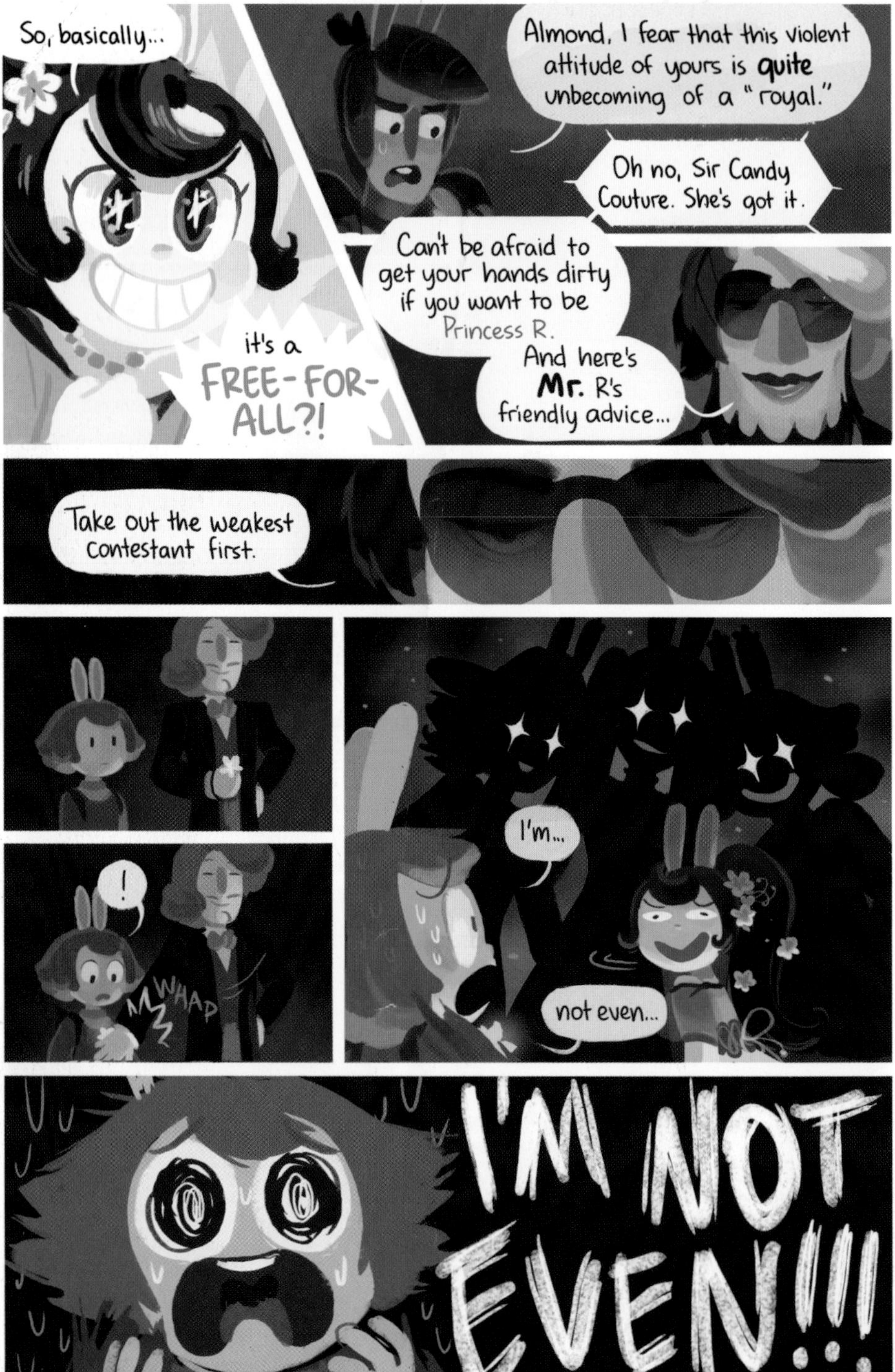

So, basically...
it's a FREE-FOR-ALL?!
Almond, I fear that this violent attitude of yours is **quite** unbecoming of a "royal."
Oh no, Sir Candy Couture. She's got it.
Can't be afraid to get your hands dirty if you want to be Princess R.
And here's **Mr.** R's friendly advice...
Take out the weakest contestant first.
!
WHAP
I'm...
not even...
I'M NOT EVEN!!!

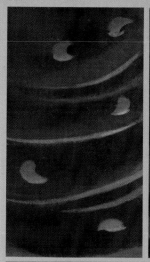

Oh.

Look who's back already.

Tell me you've got good news.

M-Miss Rosie... W-We...

We lost the intruder!!

Please forgive us! We're looking, but this place has too many rooms... They could be anywhere!

We're so—!!

Don't look so pathetic, dear. You're breaking my heart.

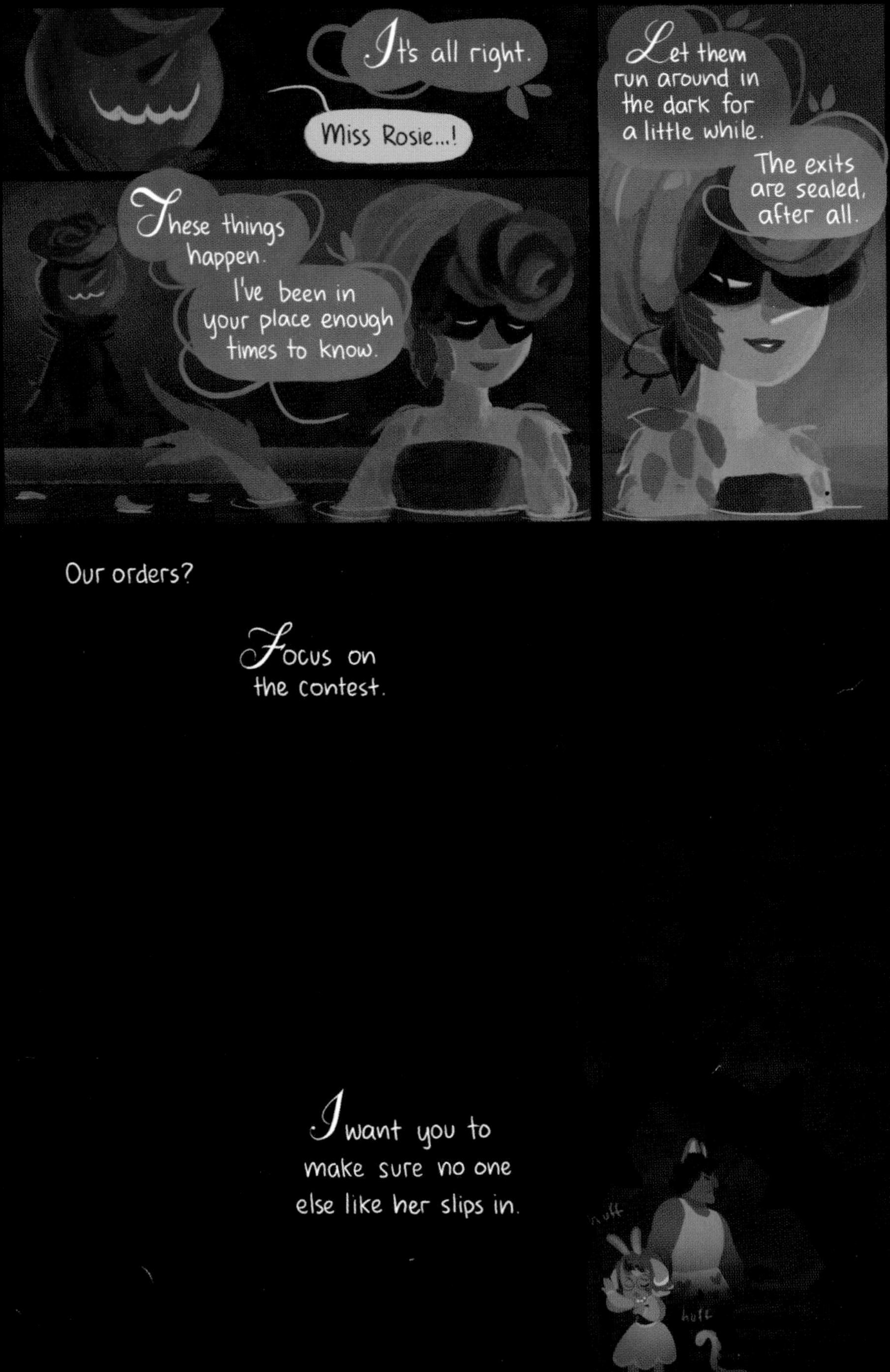
It's all right.
Miss Rosie...!
Let them run around in the dark for a little while.
The exits are sealed, after all.
These things happen.
I've been in your place enough times to know.
Our orders?
Focus on the contest.
I want you to make sure no one else like her slips in.
huff
huff

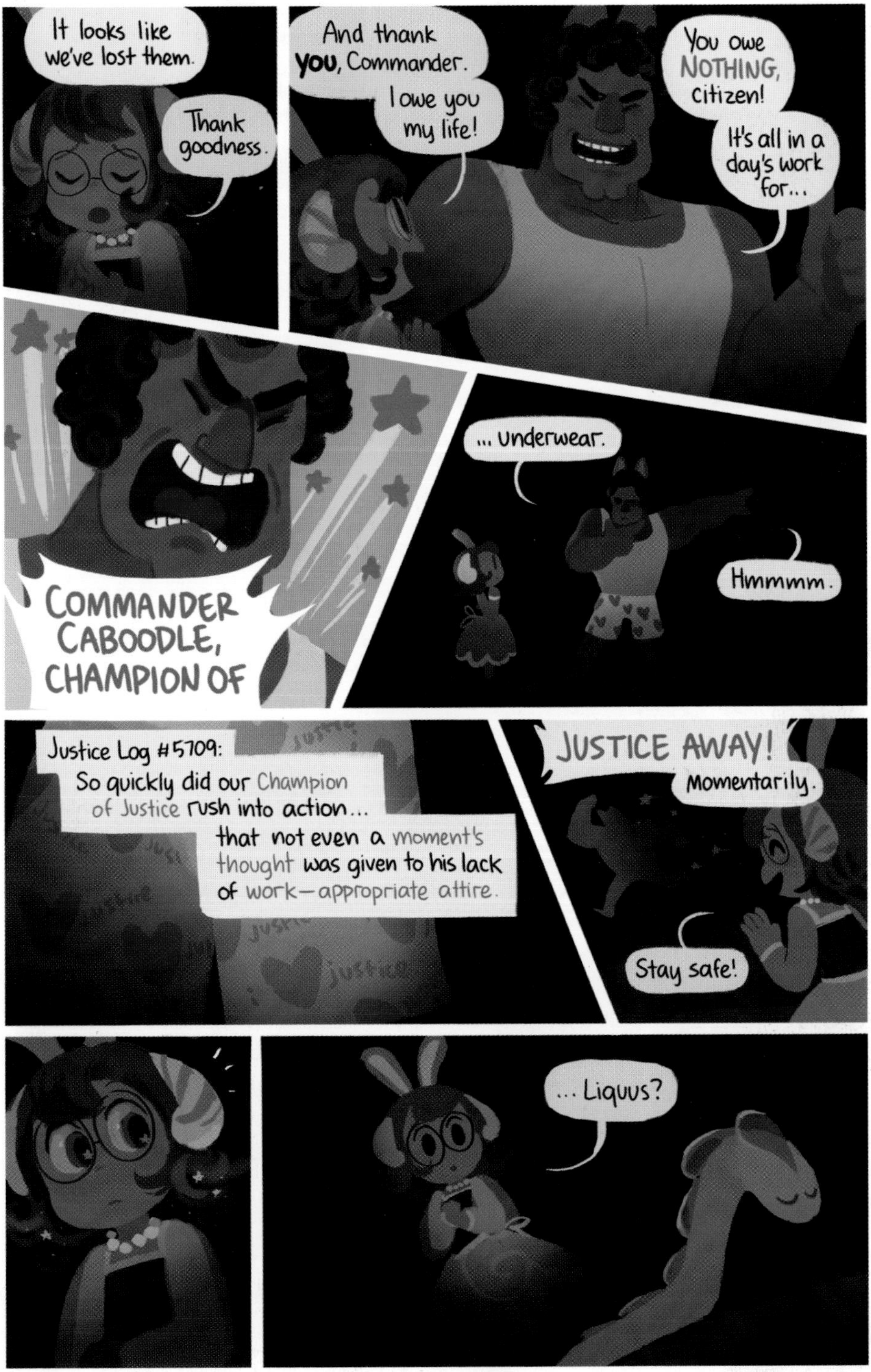
It looks like we've lost them.
Thank goodness.
And thank YOU, Commander.
I owe you my life!
You owe NOTHING, citizen!
It's all in a day's work for...
COMMANDER CABOODLE, CHAMPION OF
... Underwear.
Hmmmm.
Justice Log #5709:
So quickly did our Champion of Justice rush into action...
that not even a moment's thought was given to his lack of work—appropriate attire.
JUSTICE AWAY!
Momentarily.
Stay safe!
... Liquus?

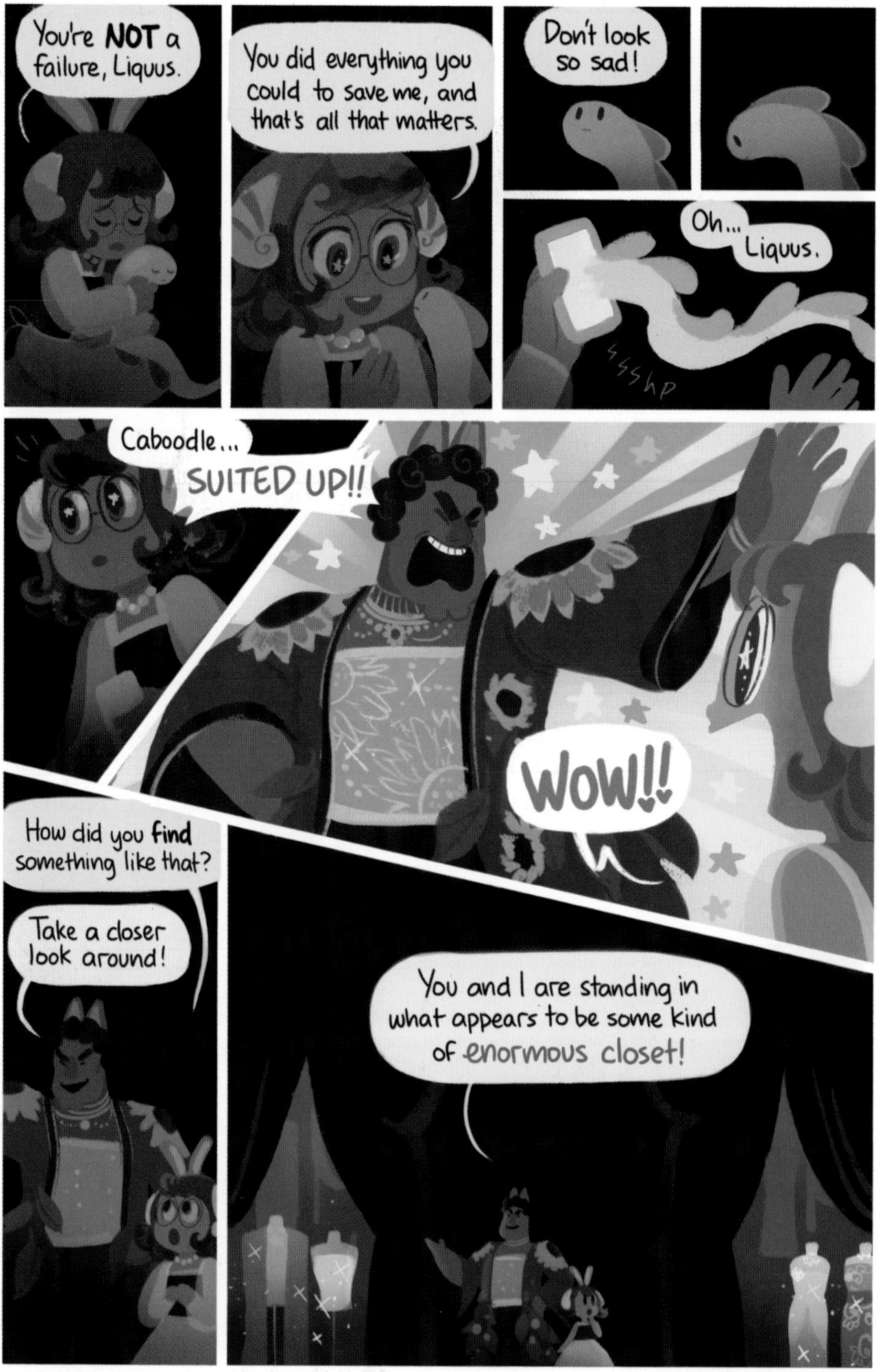
You're NOT a failure, Liquus.
You did everything you could to save me, and that's all that matters.
Don't look so sad!
Oh... Liquus.
ssshp
Caboodle...
SUITED UP!!
WOW!!
How did you find something like that?
Take a closer look around!
You and I are standing in what appears to be some kind of enormous closet!

You're right...

And it's all such well-made clothing, too...!

I almost feel like I've seen it somewhere...

And this...

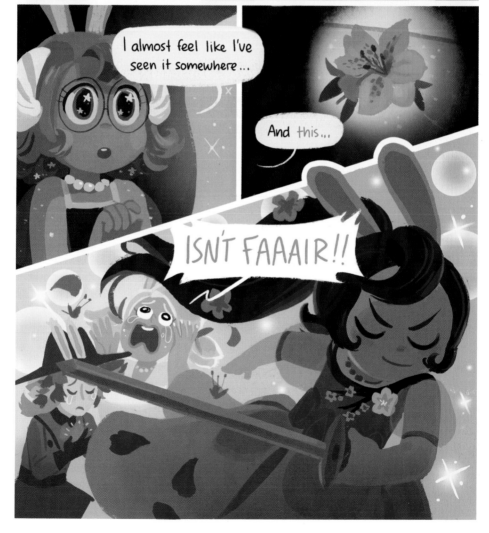

ISN'T FAAAIR!!

37

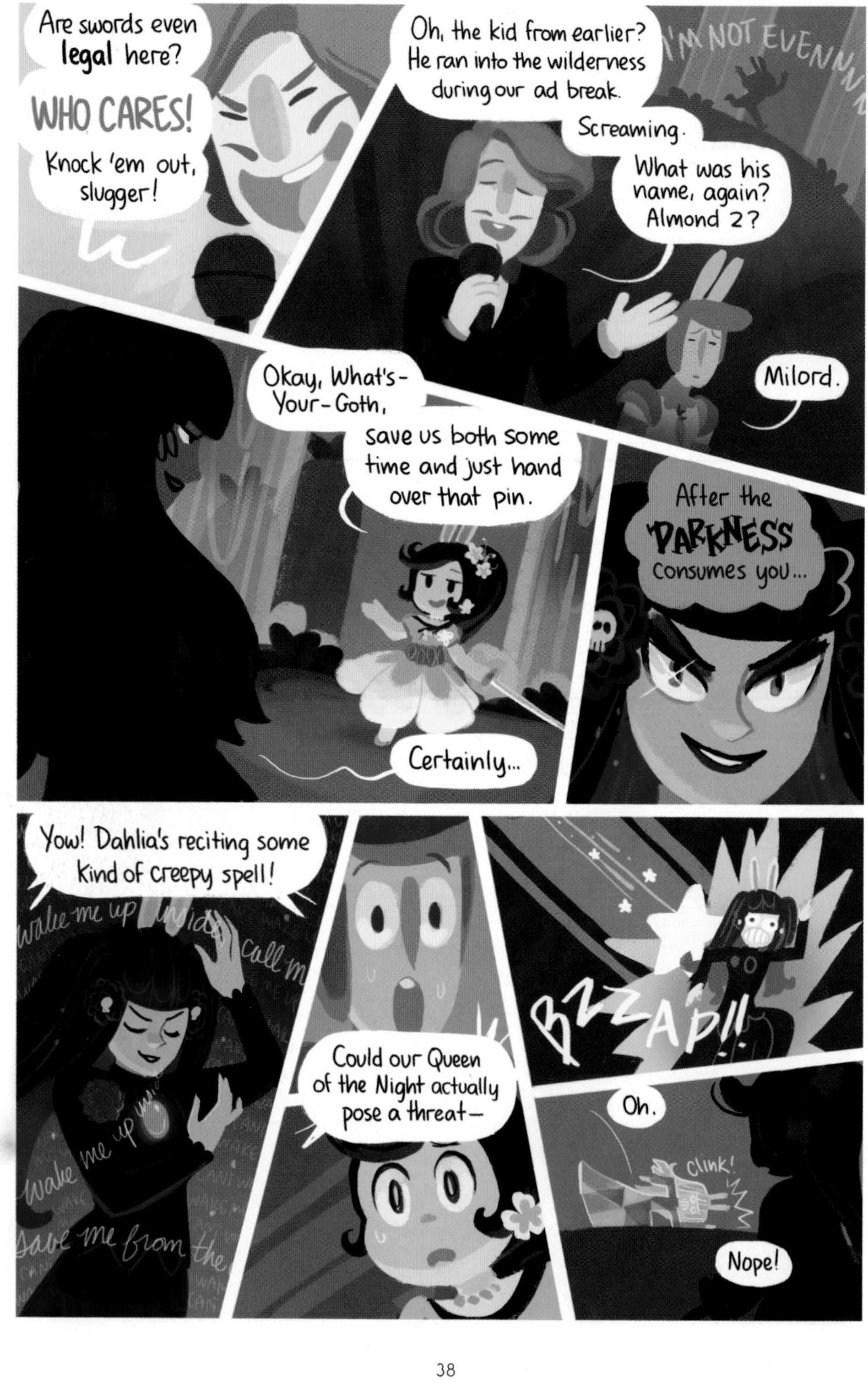
Are swords even **legal** here?
WHO CARES!
Knock 'em out, slugger!
Oh, the kid from earlier? He ran into the wilderness during our ad break.
Screaming.
What was his name, again? Almond 2?
I'M NOT EVENN
Milord.
Okay, What's-Your-Goth,
save us both some time and just hand over that pin.
Certainly...
After the DARKNESS consumes you...
Yow! Dahlia's reciting some kind of creepy spell!
wake me up inside
call m
wake me up
save me from the
Could our Queen of the Night actually pose a threat—
BZZZAP!!
Oh.
clink!
Nope!

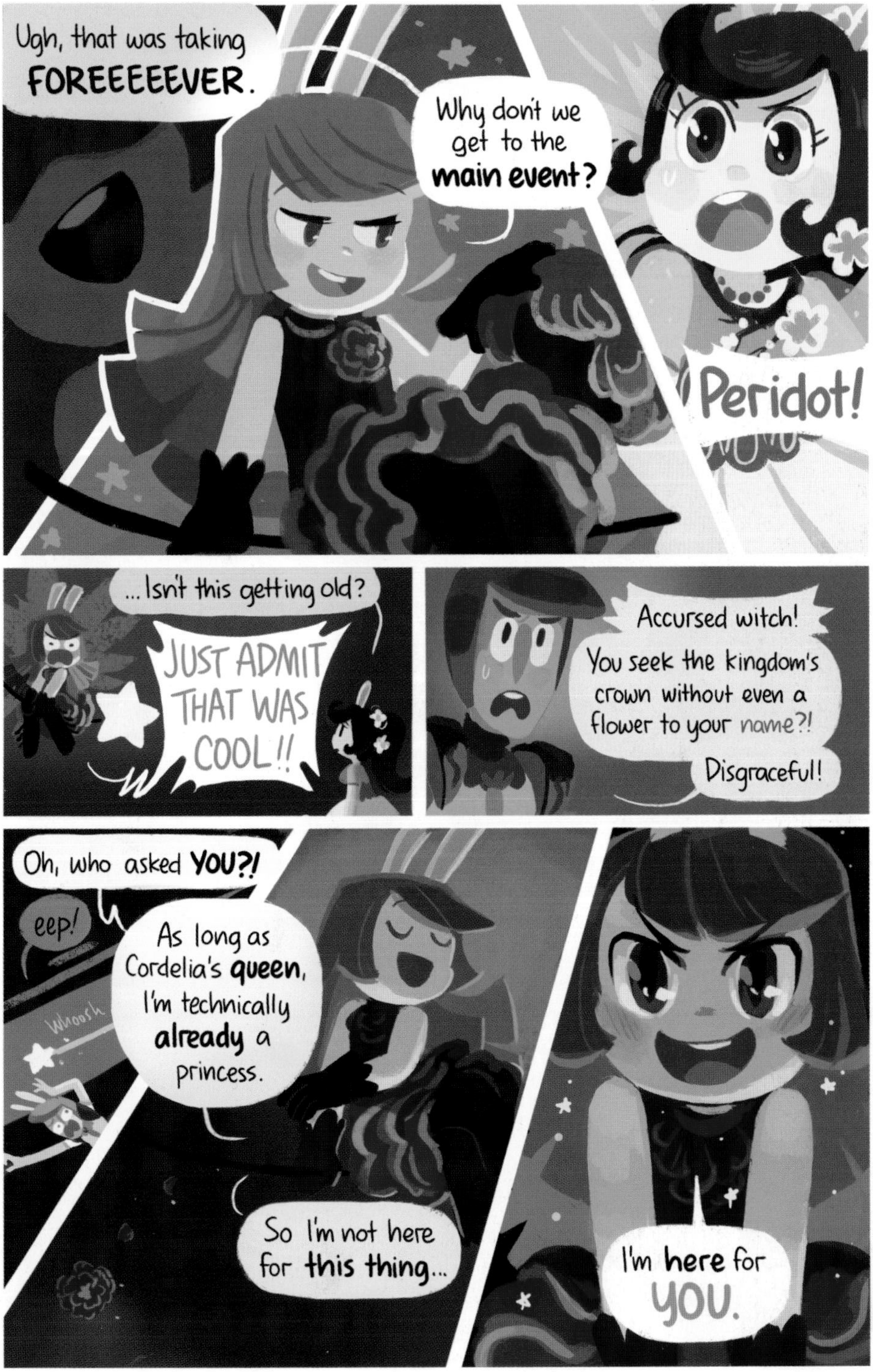
Ugh, that was taking FOREEEEEVER.
Why don't we get to the main event?
Peridot!
...Isn't this getting old?
JUST ADMIT THAT WAS COOL!!
Accursed witch!
You seek the kingdom's crown without even a flower to your name?!
Disgraceful!
Oh, who asked YOU?!
eep!
As long as Cordelia's queen, I'm technically already a princess.
whoosh
So I'm not here for this thing...
I'm here for YOU.

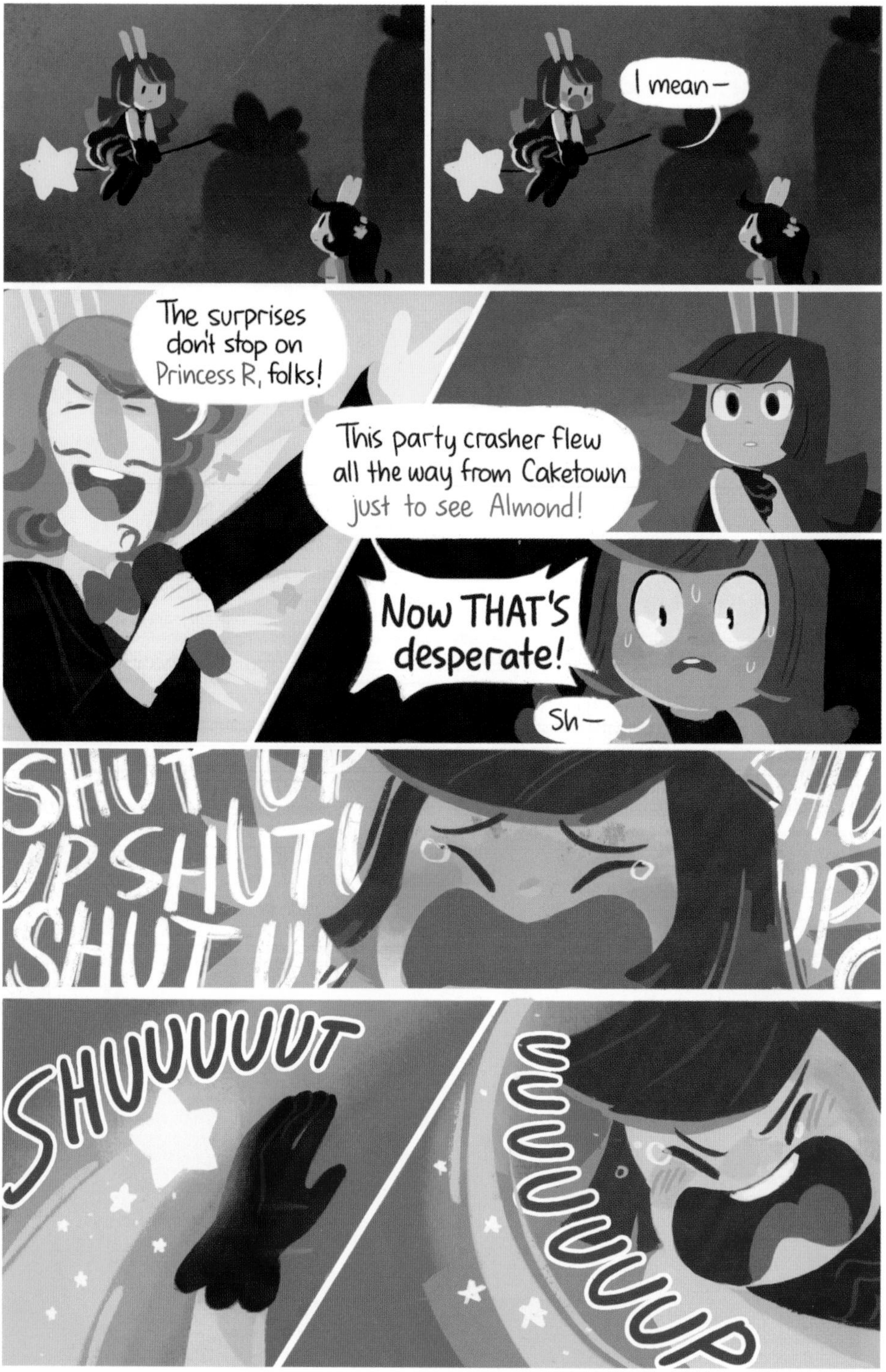

I mean—
The surprises don't stop on Princess R, folks!
This party crasher flew all the way from Caketown just to see Almond!
Now THAT'S desperate!
Sh—
SHUT UP
SHUT UP
SHUT UP
SHUUUUUT UUUUUUUP

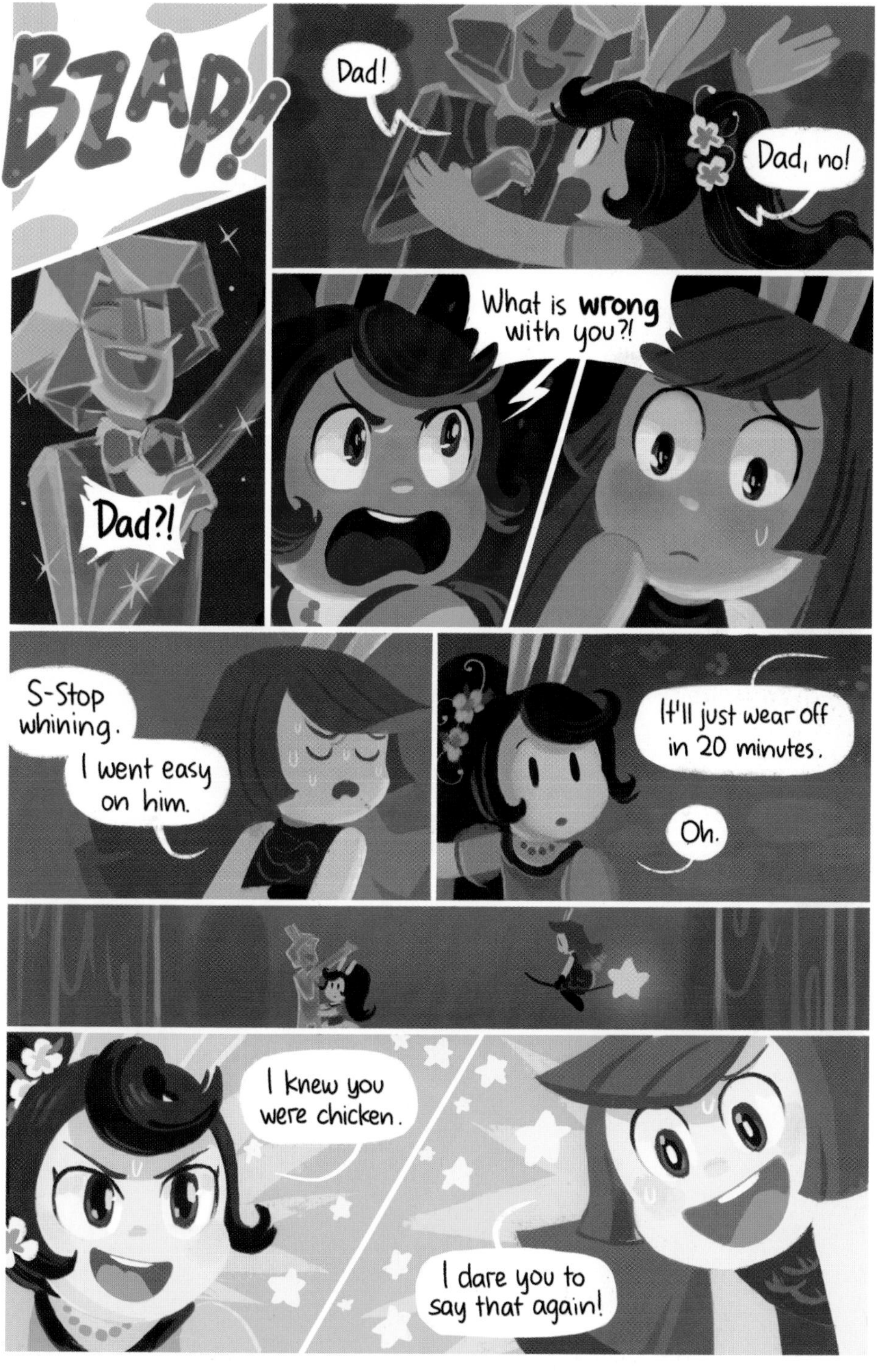
BZAP!
Dad!
Dad, no!
Dad?!
What is **wrong** with you?!
S-Stop whining.
I went easy on him.
It'll just wear off in 20 minutes.
Oh.
I knew you were chicken.
I dare you to say that again!

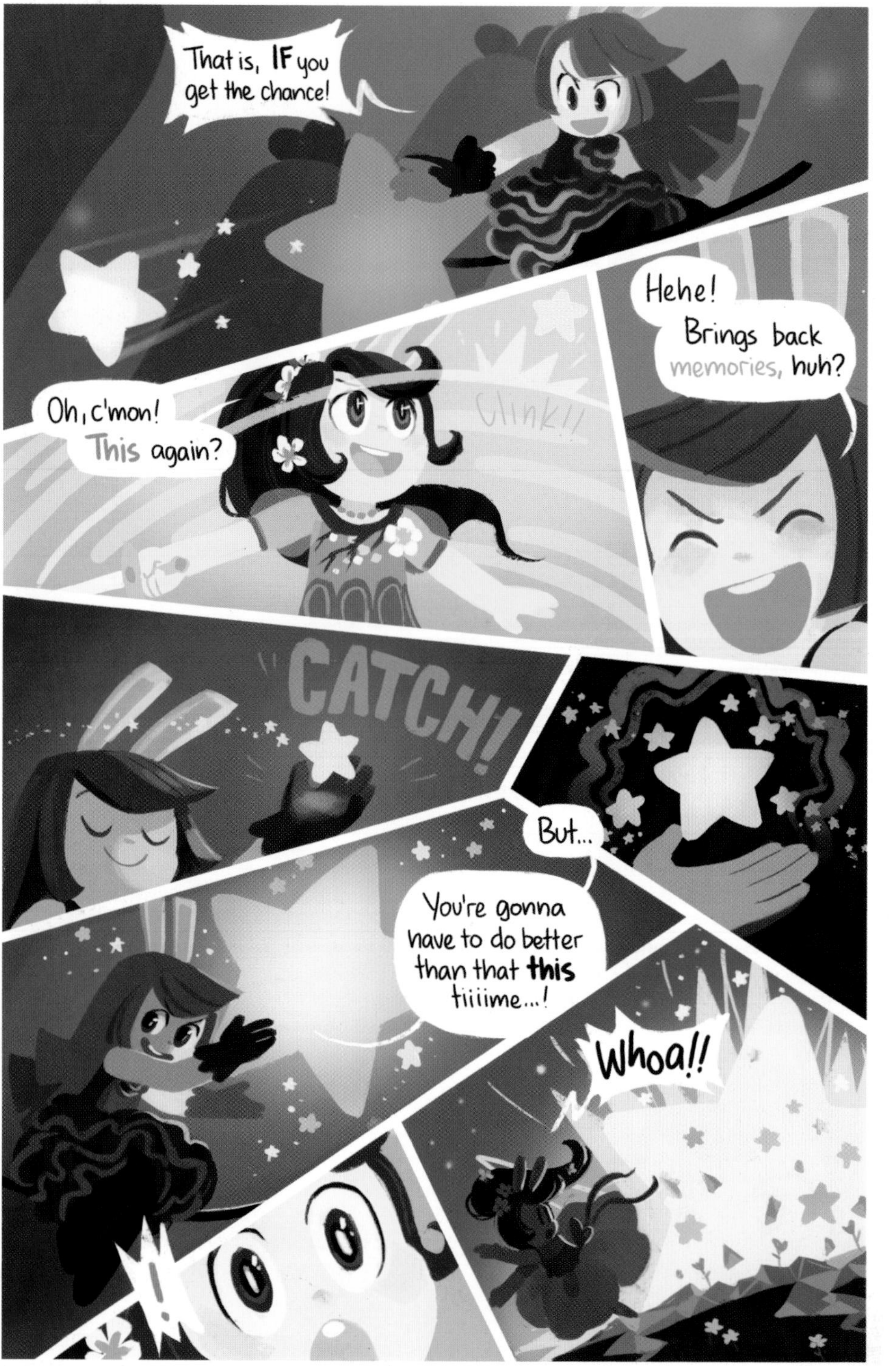
That is, IF you get the chance!
Oh, c'mon! This again?
Clink!!
Hehe! Brings back memories, huh?
CATCH!
But...
You're gonna have to do better than that this tiiiime...!
!
Whoa!!

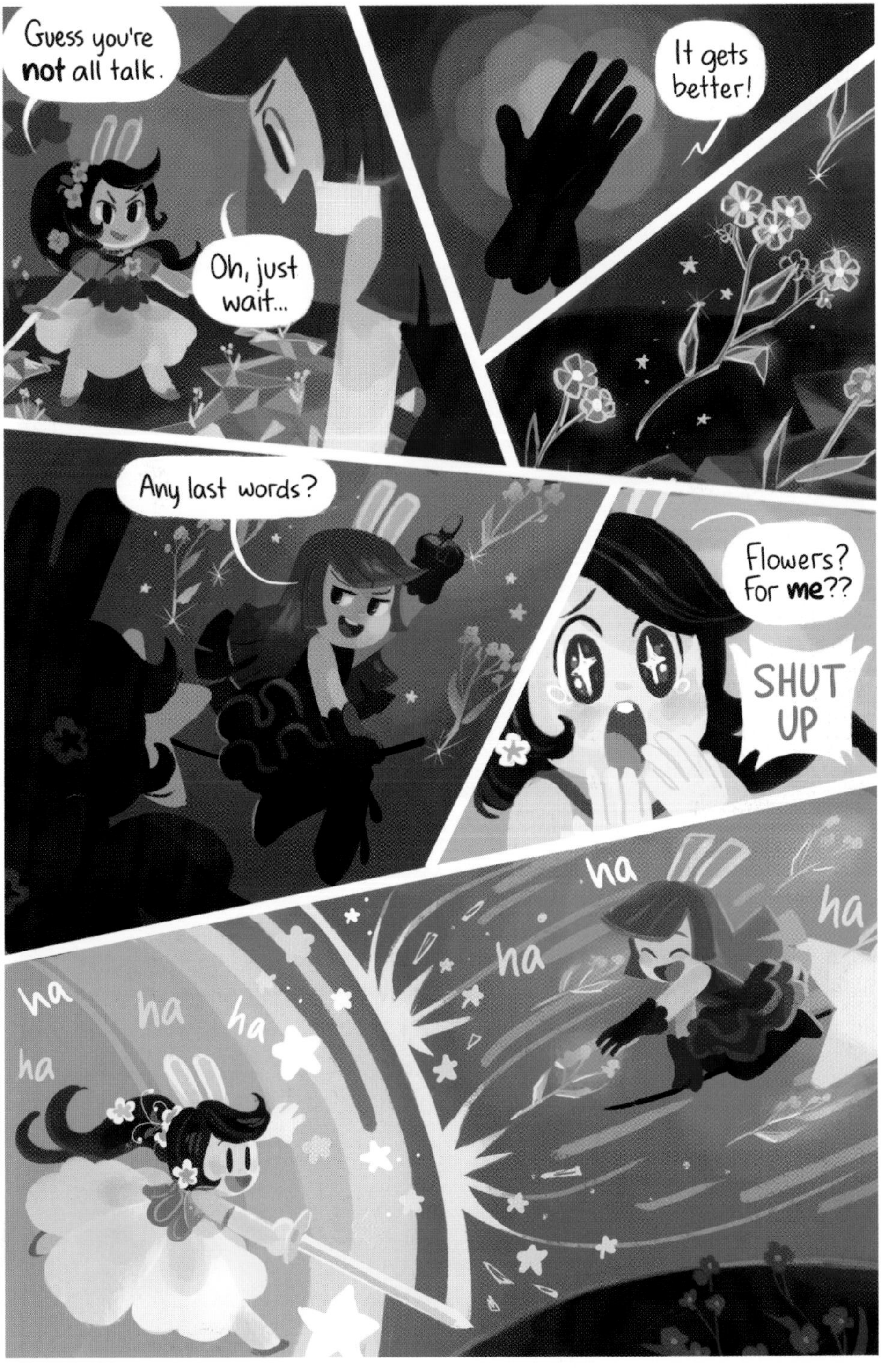
Guess you're **not** all talk.
Oh, just wait...
It gets better!
Any last words?
Flowers? For **me**??
SHUT UP
ha
ha
ha
ha
ha
ha
ha

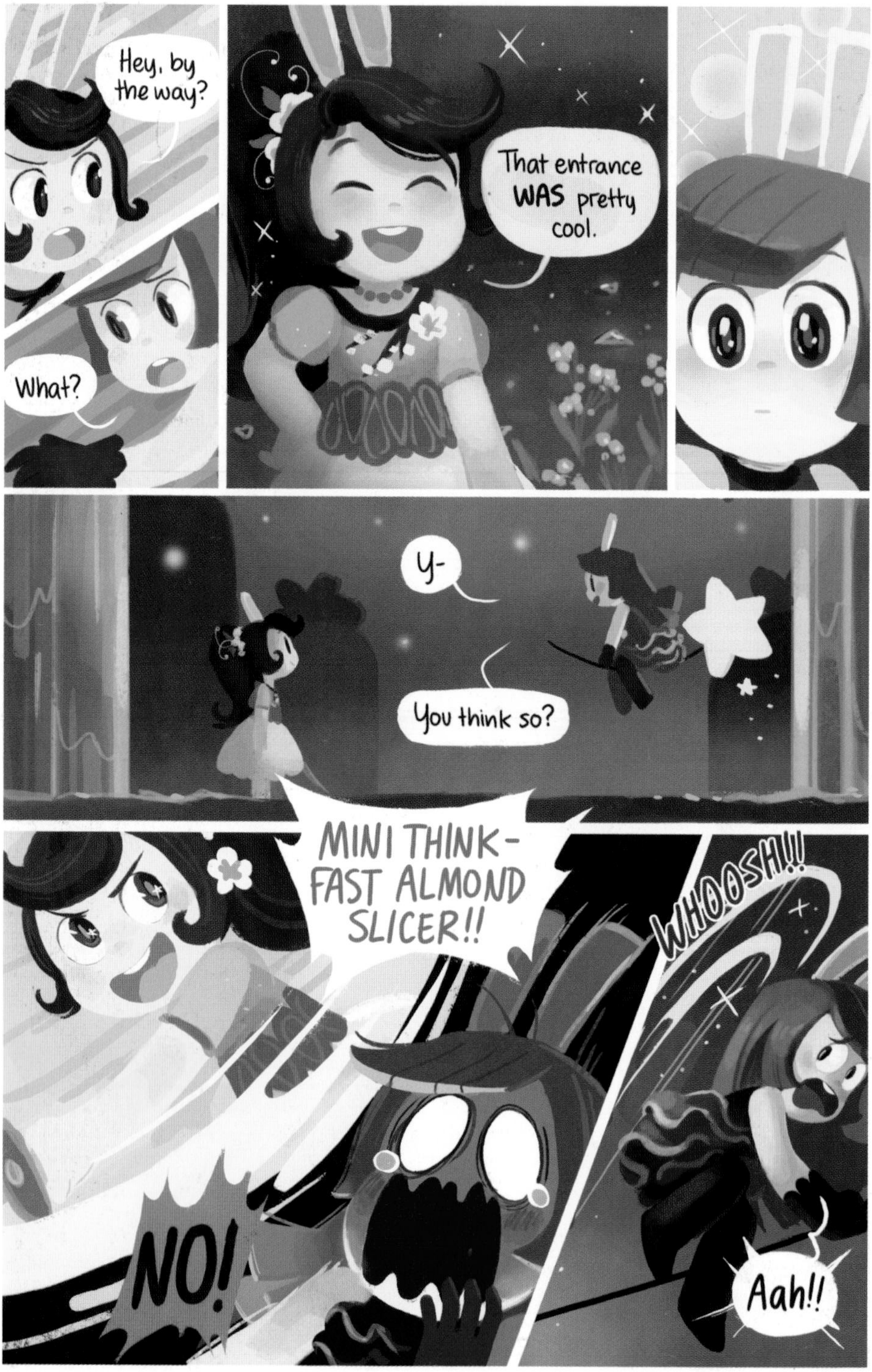

Hey, by the way?
What?
That entrance **WAS** pretty cool.
Y-
You think so?
MINI THINK-FAST ALMOND SLICER!!
WHOOSH!!
NO!
Aah!!

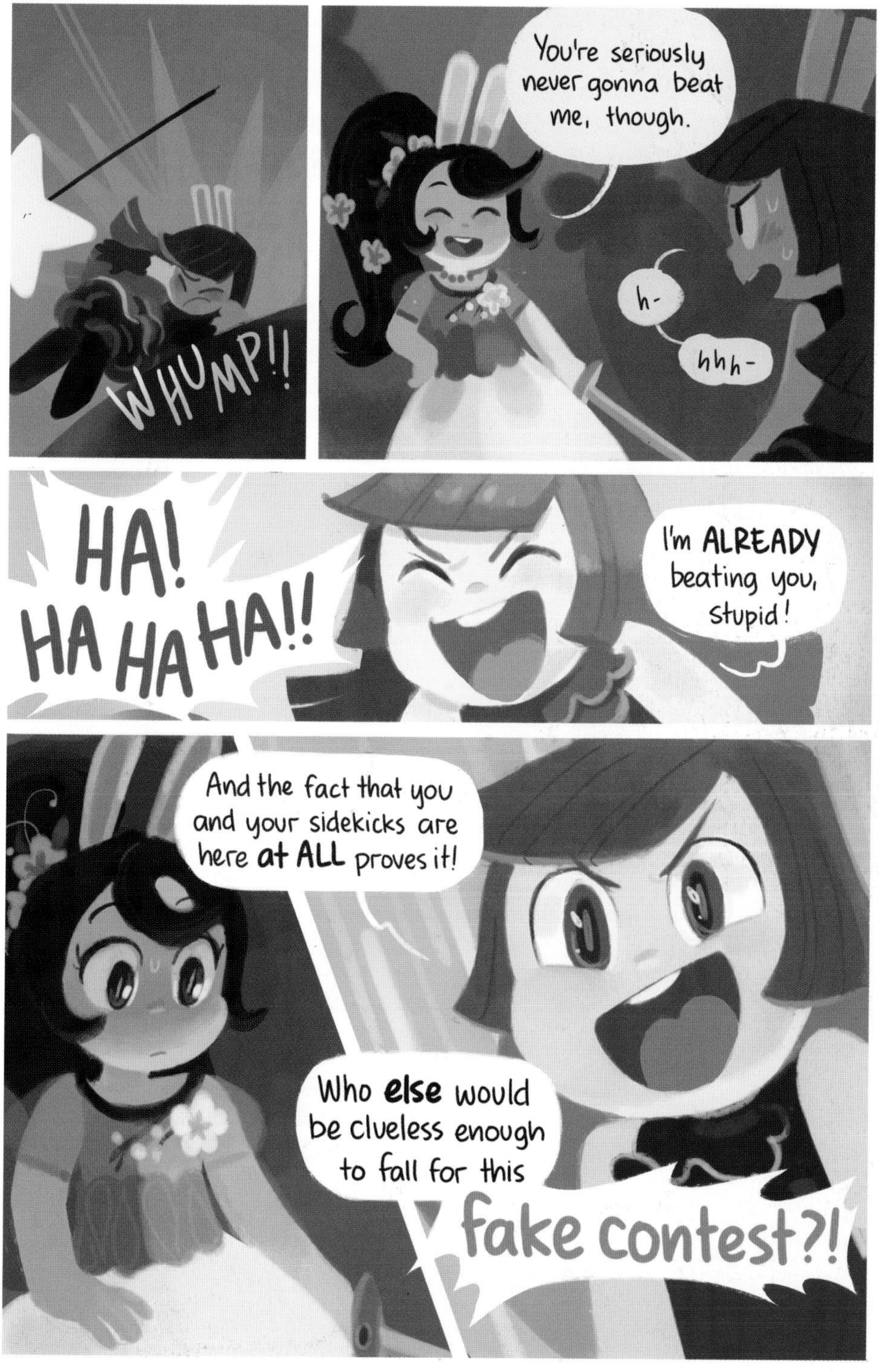
WHUMP!!
You're seriously never gonna beat me, though.
h-
hhh-
HA! HA HA HA!!
I'm **ALREADY** beating you, stupid!
And the fact that you and your sidekicks are here **at ALL** proves it!
Who **else** would be clueless enough to fall for this
fake contest?!

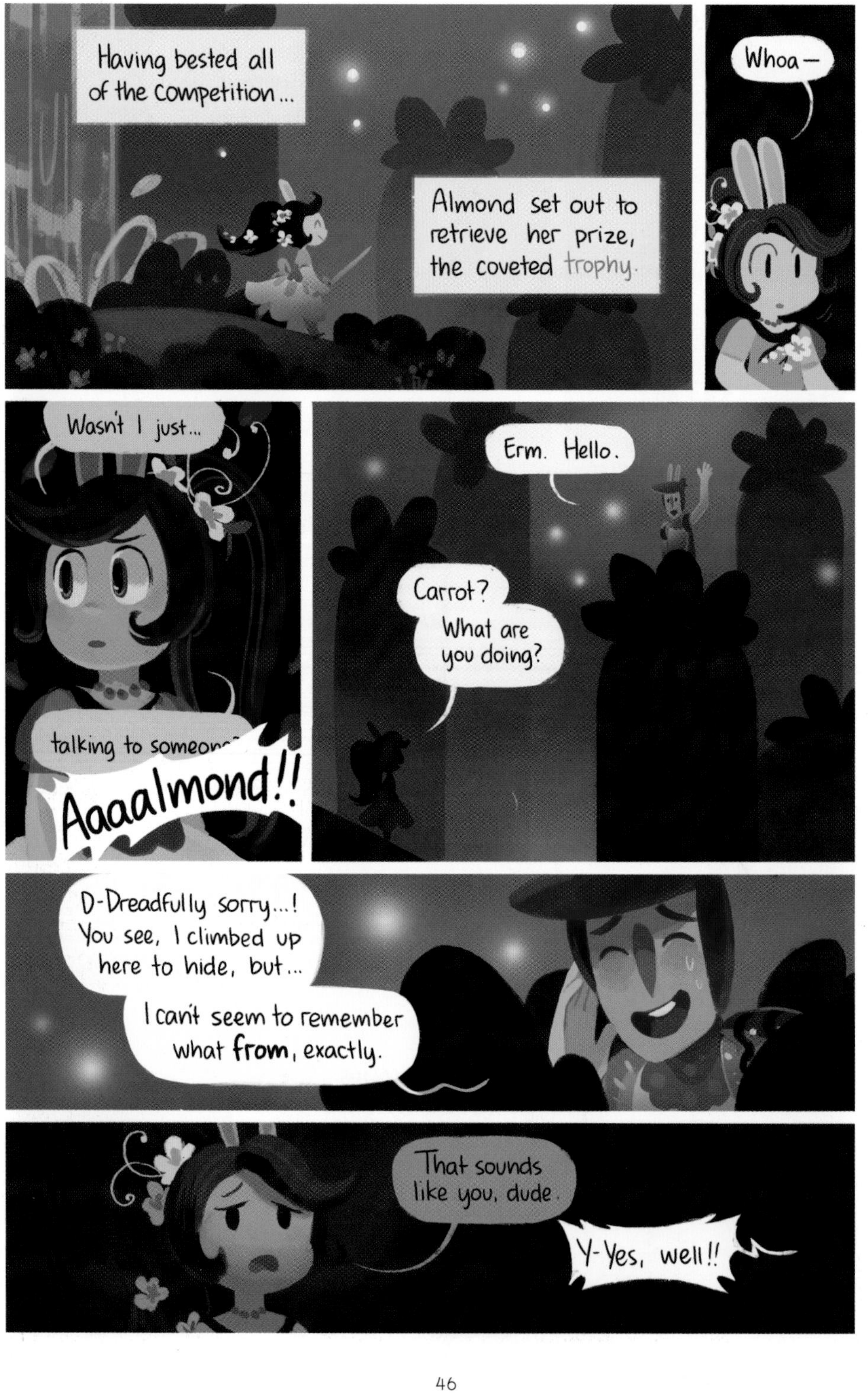

Having bested all of the competition...
Almond set out to retrieve her prize, the coveted trophy.
Whoa—
Wasn't I just...
talking to someone
Aaaalmond!!
Erm. Hello.
Carrot? What are you doing?
D-Dreadfully sorry...! You see, I climbed up here to hide, but...
I can't seem to remember what from, exactly.
That sounds like you, dude.
Y-Yes, well!!

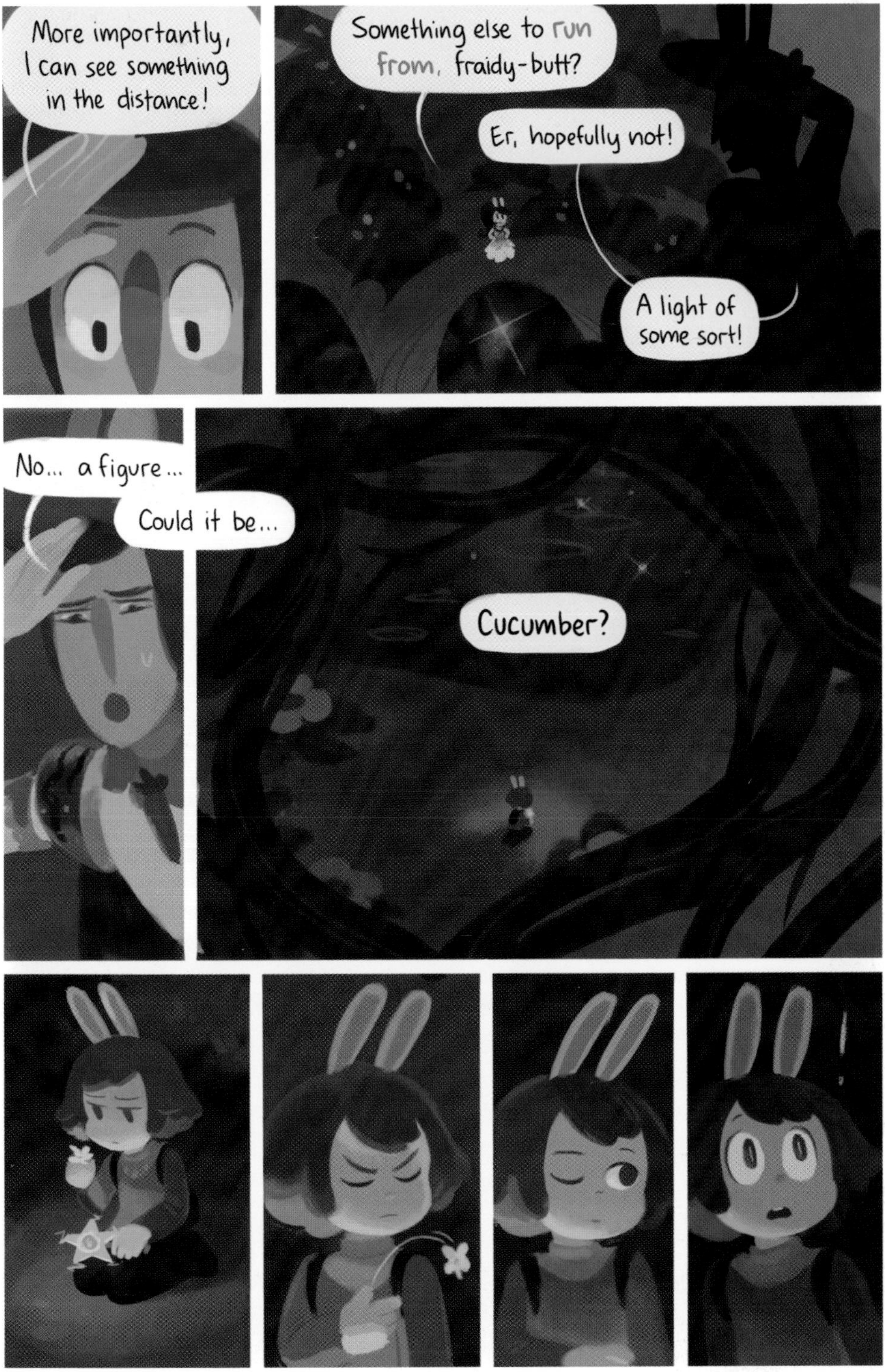
More importantly, I can see something in the distance!
Something else to run from, fraidy-butt?
Er, hopefully not!
A light of some sort!
No... a figure...
Could it be...
Cucumber?
!

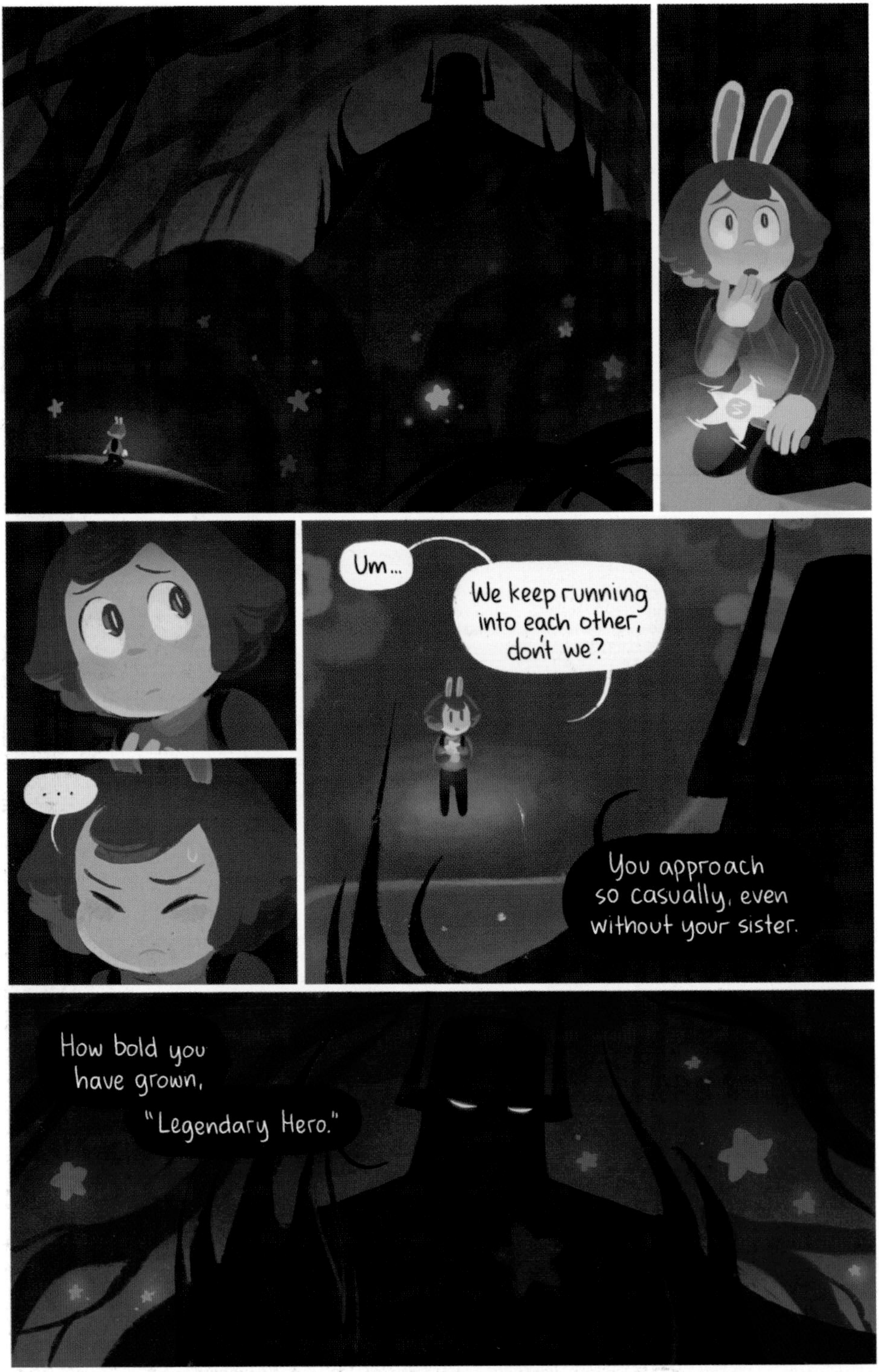

Um...
We keep running into each other, don't we?
. . .
You approach so casually, even without your sister.
How bold you have grown,
"Legendary Hero."

UM,
NO,
ACTUALLY.
I'm still completely terrified! Especially after, uh...
...th-the last time we...um...
It was not an act of pity that spared your life then.
Make no mistake of that.
U-Uh, yeah...
I wasn't really going to.
...
P-
Please, just listen...
I don't believe this has to end with violence.
If we just talk, there's got to be **some** way we can come to an understanding.
I-I think...
after this long, even you know that.

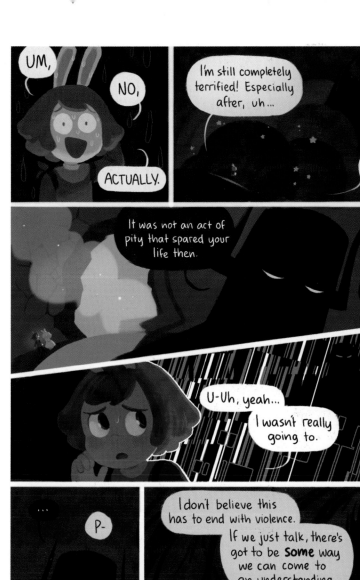

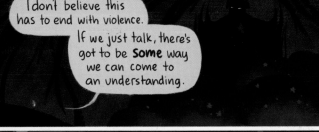

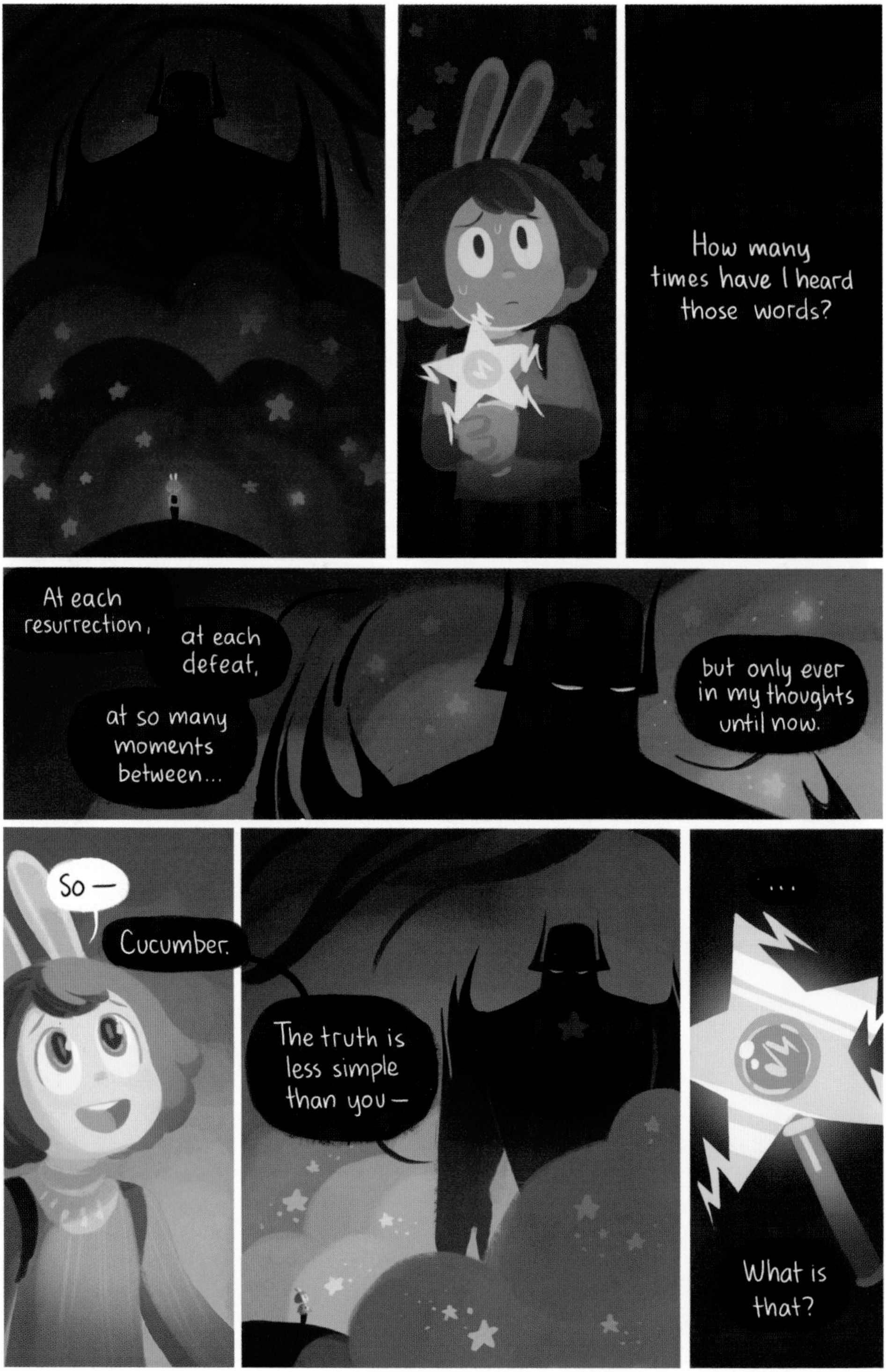
How many times have I heard those words?
At each resurrection,
at each defeat,
at so many moments between...
but only ever in my thoughts until now.
So —
Cucumber.
The truth is less simple than you —
...
What is that?

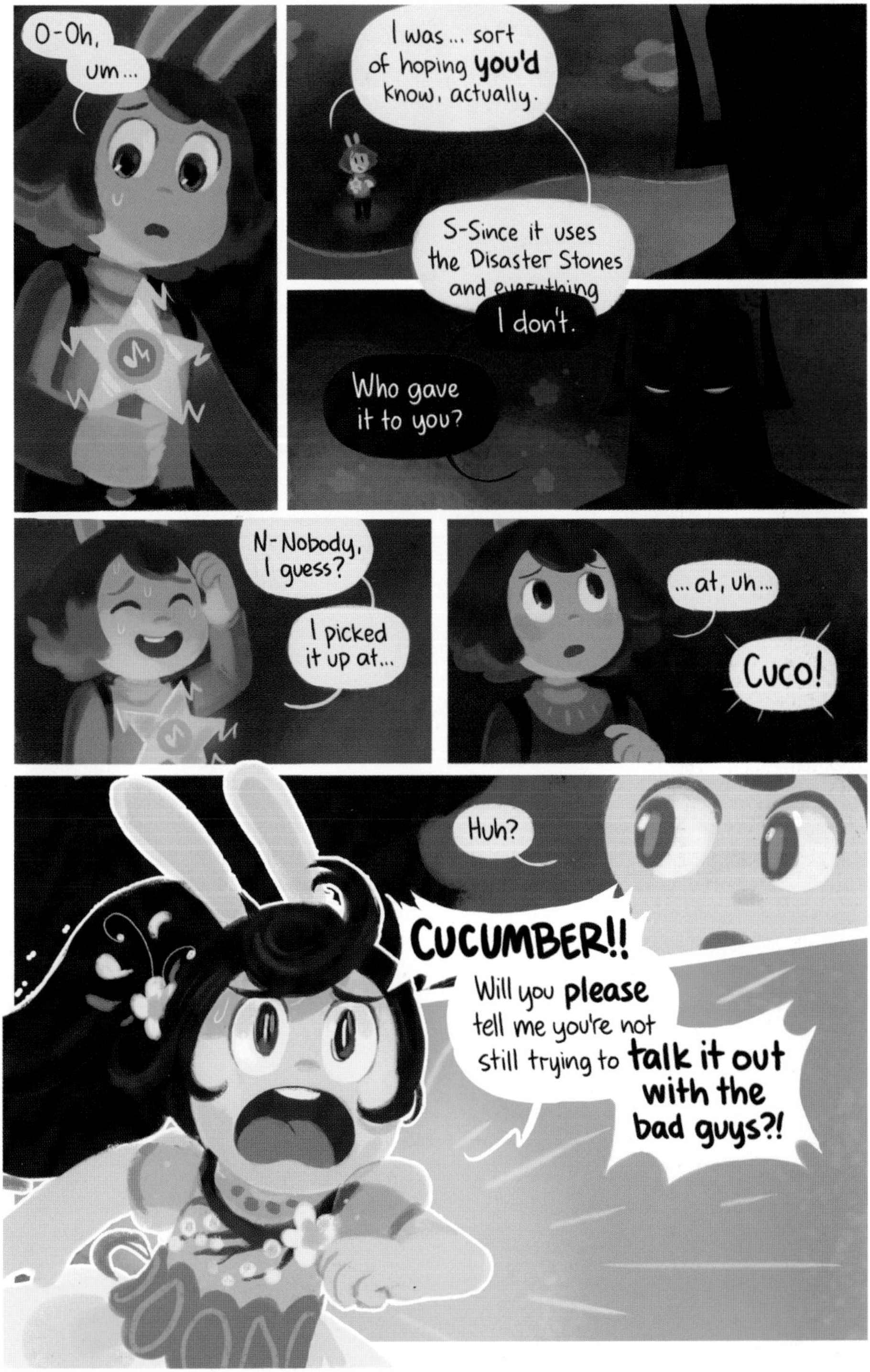
O-Oh, um...
I was... sort of hoping you'd know, actually.
S-Since it uses the Disaster Stones and everything
I don't.
Who gave it to you?
N-Nobody, I guess?
I picked it up at...
...at, uh...
Cuco!
Huh?
CUCUMBER!!
Will you please tell me you're not still trying to talk it out with the bad guys?!

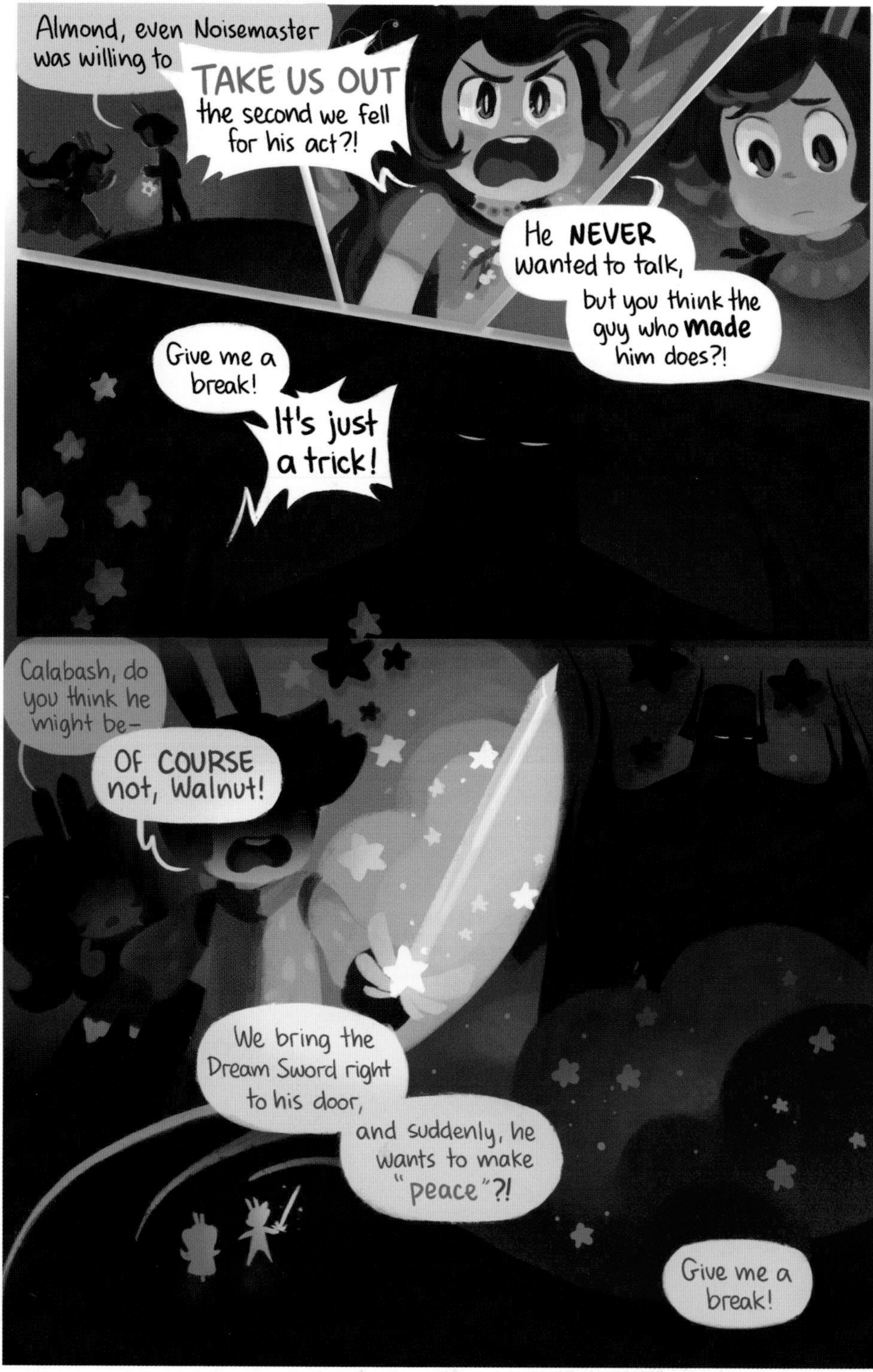
Almond, even Noisemaster was willing to
TAKE US OUT the second we fell for his act?!
He NEVER wanted to talk,
but you think the guy who made him does?!
Give me a break!
It's just a trick!
Calabash, do you think he might be–
OF COURSE not, Walnut!
We bring the Dream Sword right to his door,
and suddenly, he wants to make "peace"?!
Give me a break!

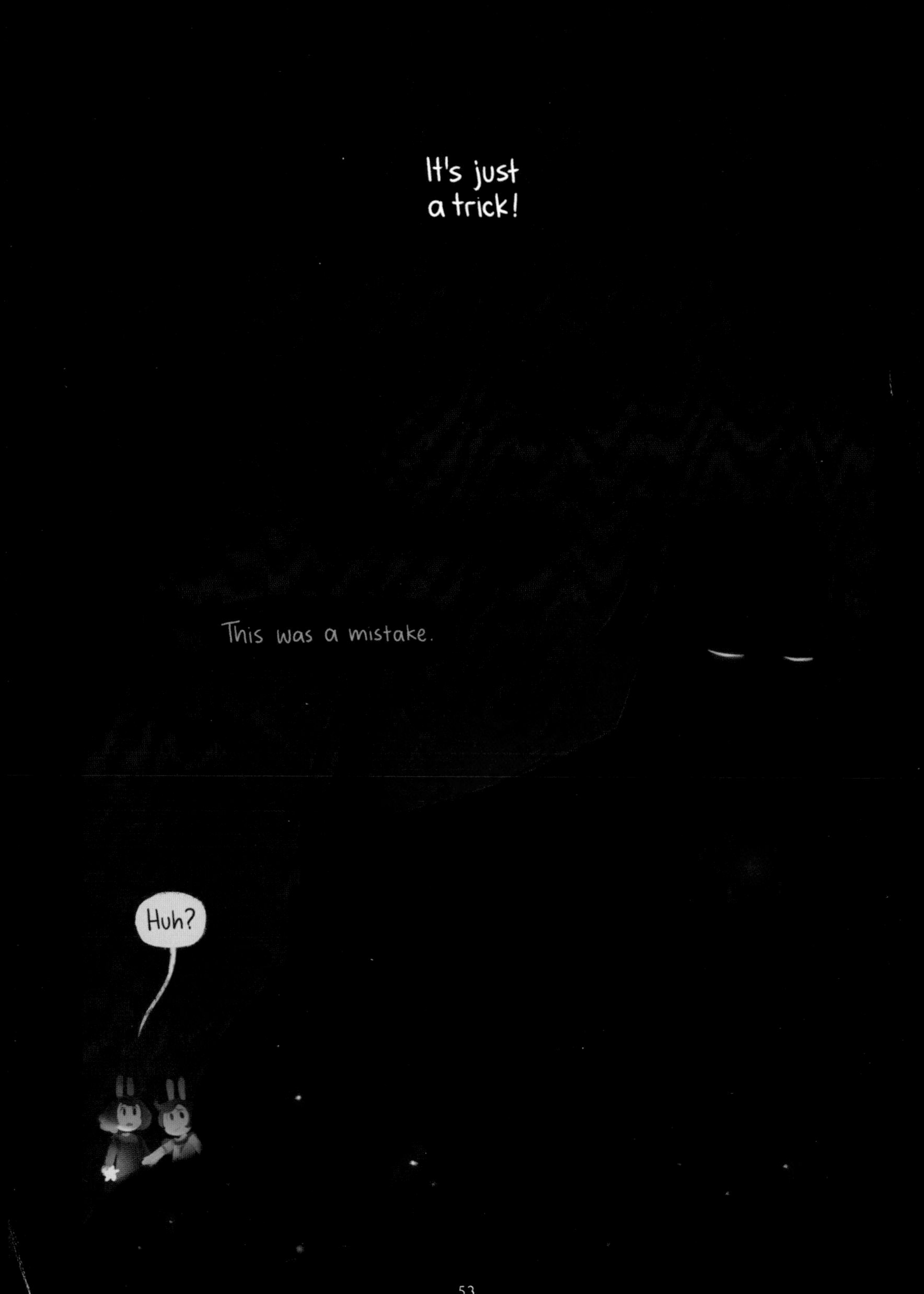
It's just a trick!
This was a mistake.
Huh?

Heed your sister's warning, "Hero."
You have forgotten what I am.
What?!
But you just—
If I must **remind** you, so be it.
AAAAAAH!!

Aaalmooond!!
Almond!
I understand the urgency...
...but surely you could have waited just a moment for
me...
to...
erm.
Carrot!
DO SOMETHING!!
I-
ahh-

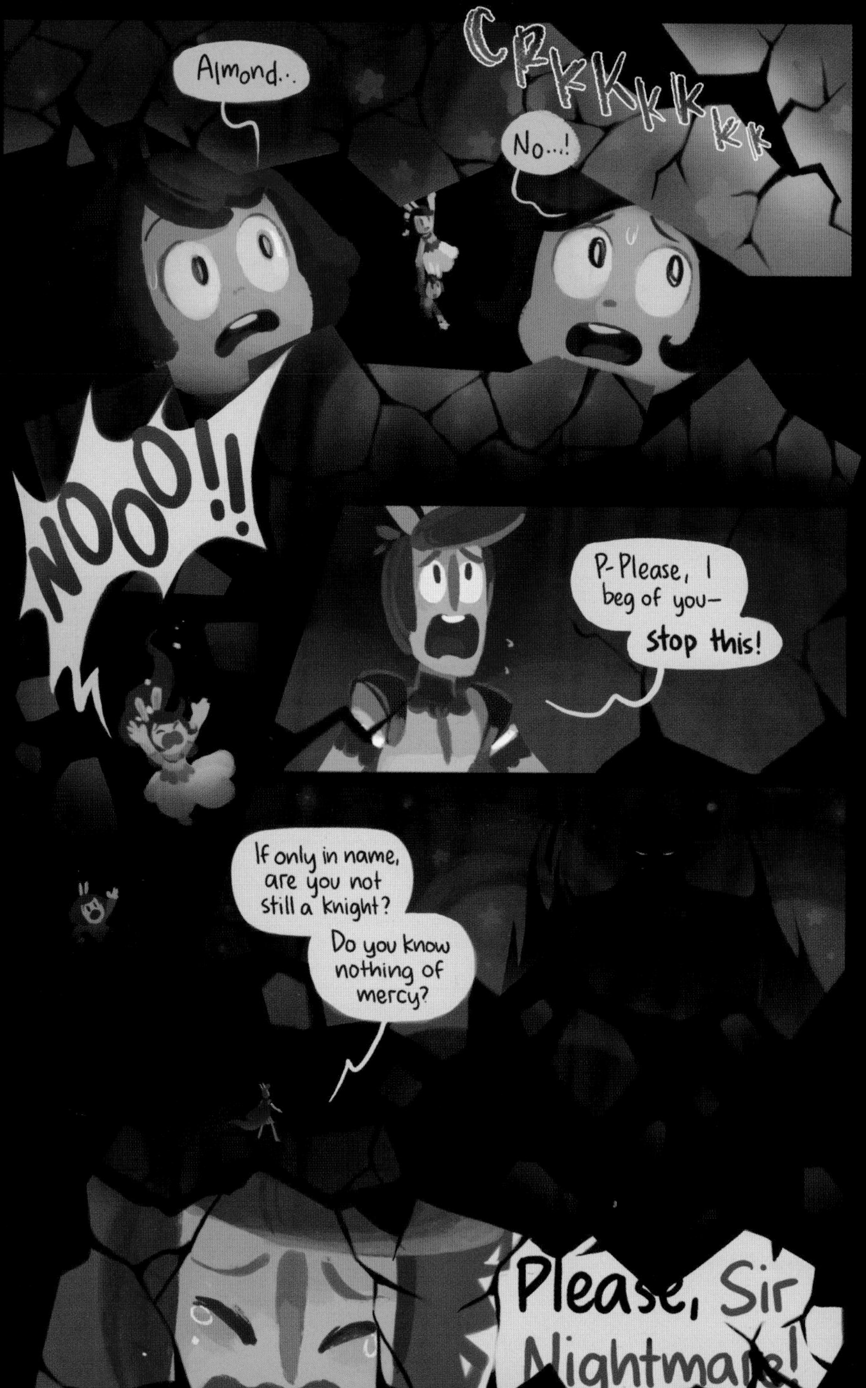
Almond..
CRKKKKKKK
No...!
NOOO!!
P-Please, I beg of you— stop this!
If only in name, are you not still a knight?
Do you know nothing of mercy?
Please, Sir Nightmare!

...ugh...
...huh...?
Carrot.
!!
I had heard rumors,
but to think that **tears** could be your only weapon...
You are more pitiful than I imagined.

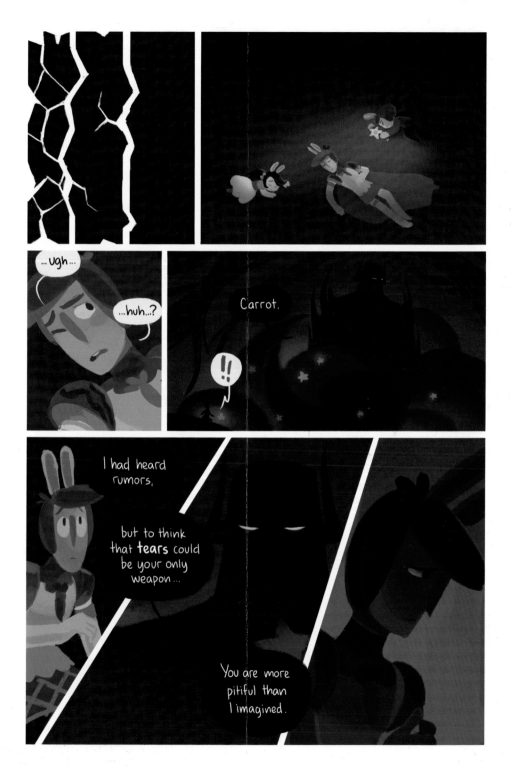

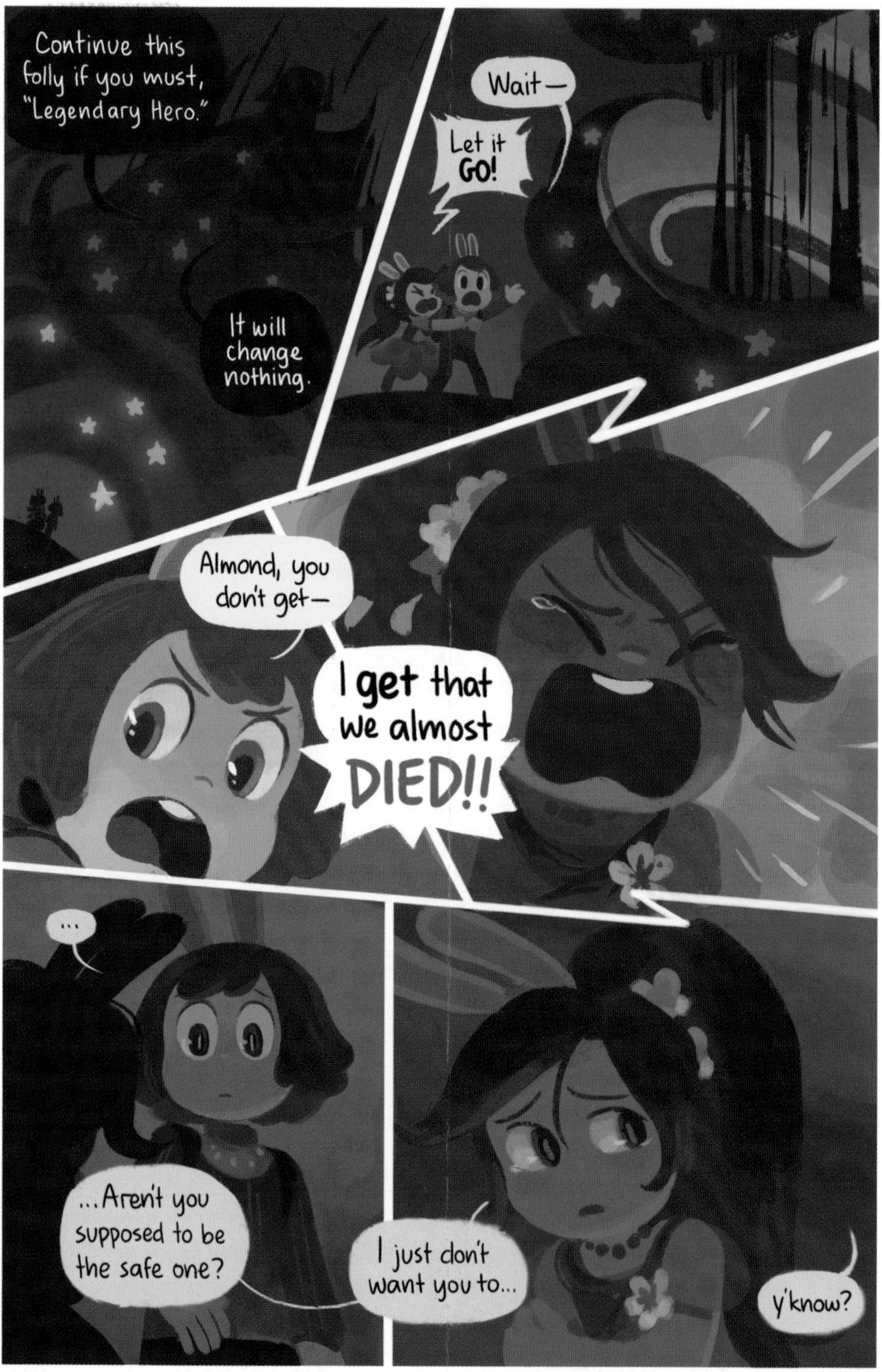

Continue this folly if you must, "Legendary Hero."
It will change nothing.
Wait—
Let it GO!
Almond, you don't get—
I get that we almost DIED!!
...
...Aren't you supposed to be the safe one?
I just don't want you to...
y'know?

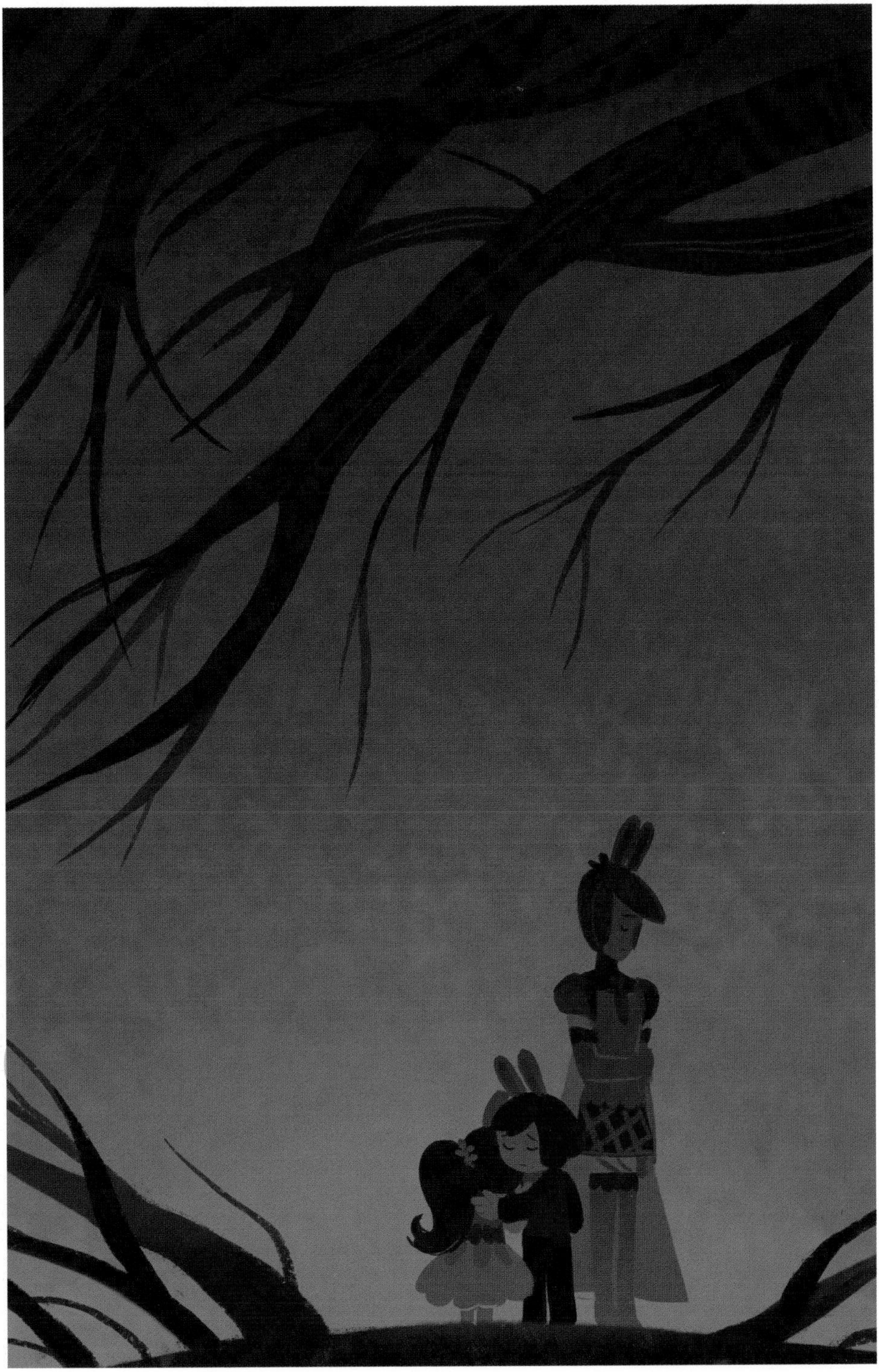

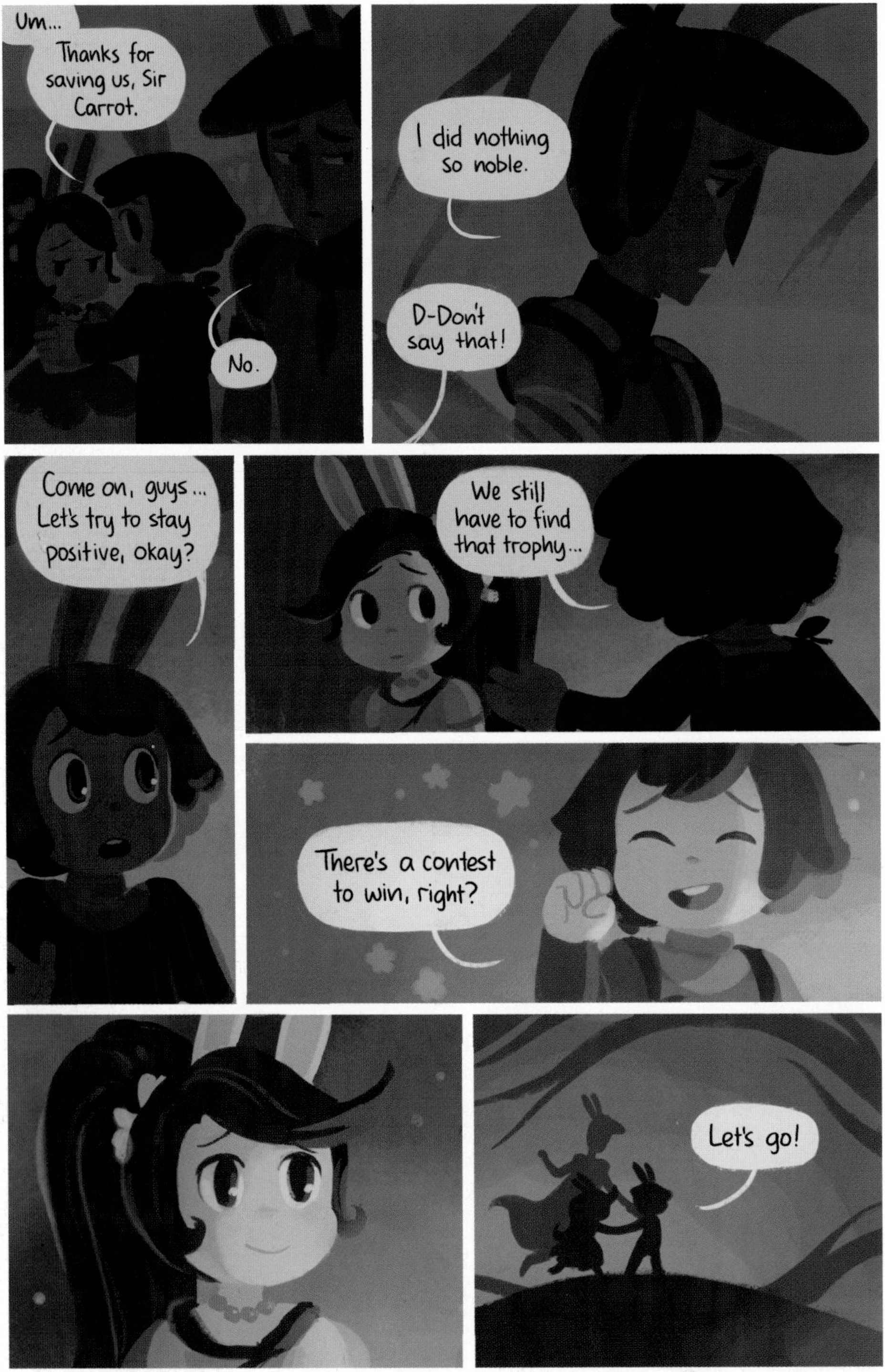
Um...
Thanks for saving us, Sir Carrot.
No.
I did nothing so noble.
D-Don't say that!
Come on, guys... Let's try to stay positive, okay?
We still have to find that trophy...
There's a contest to win, right?
Let's go!

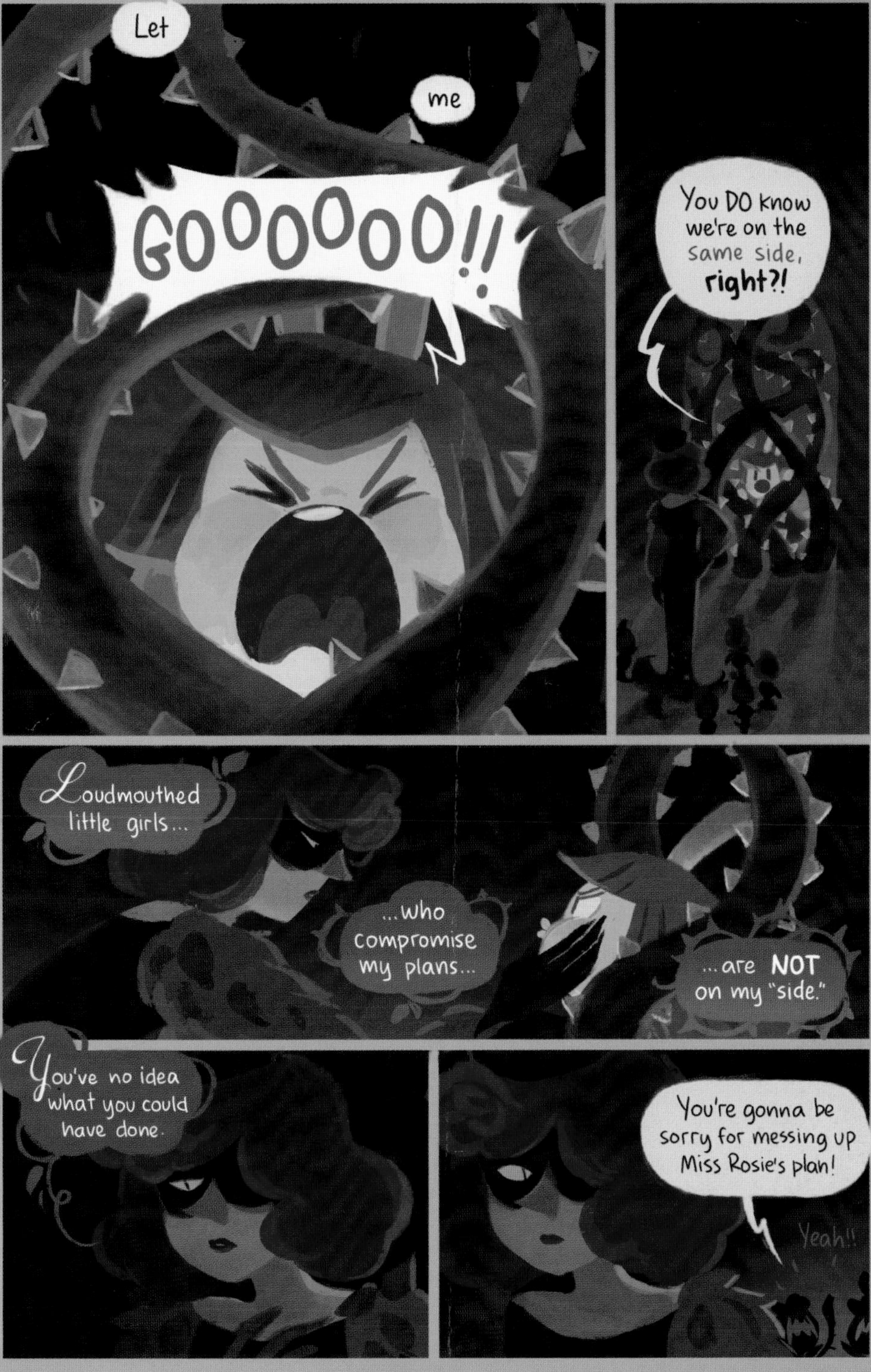
Let
me
GOOOOOO!!
You DO know we're on the same side, right?!
Loudmouthed little girls...
...who compromise my plans...
...are NOT on my "side."
You've no idea what you could have done.
You're gonna be sorry for messing up Miss Rosie's plan!
Yeah!!

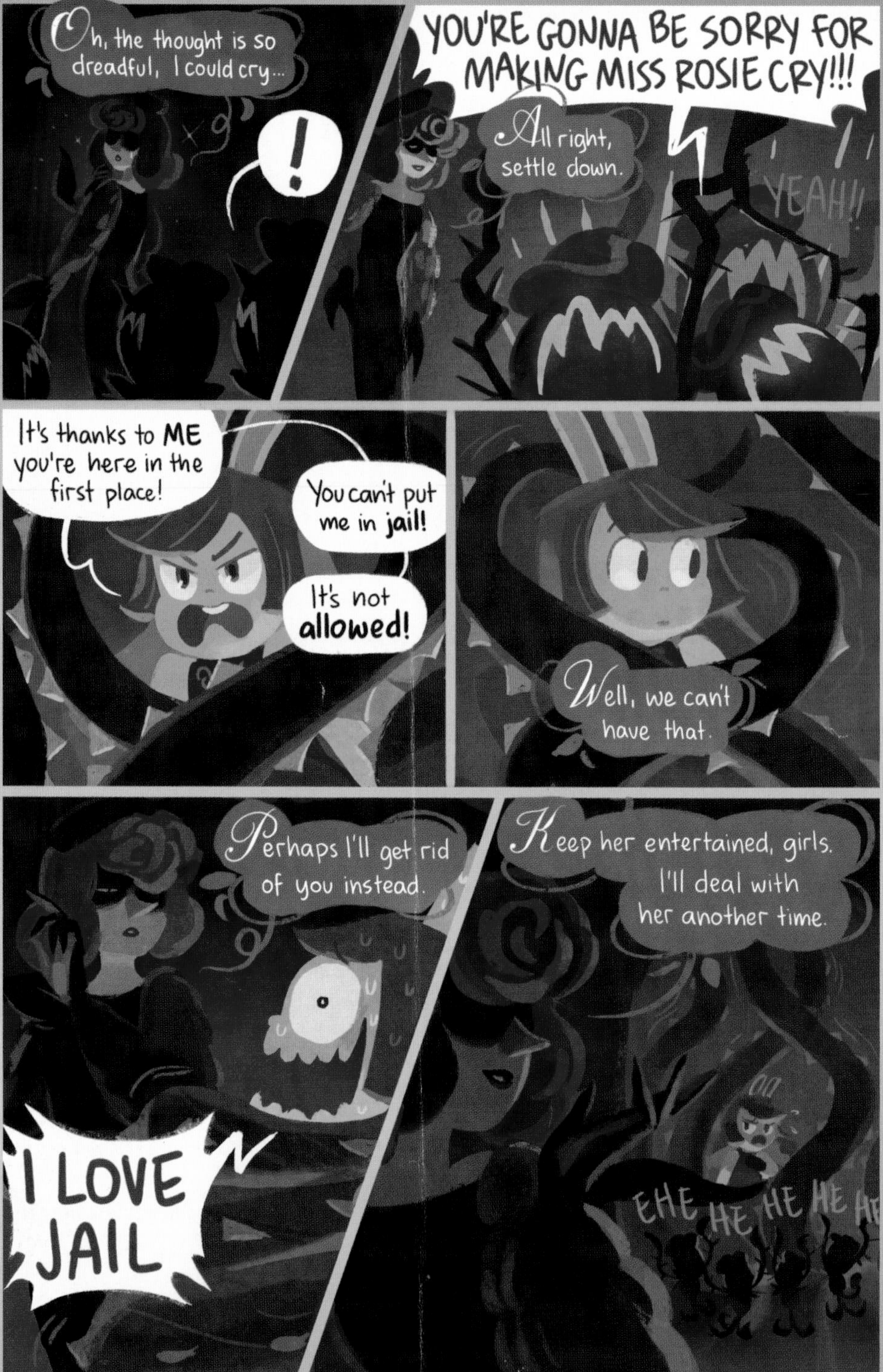
Oh, the thought is so dreadful, I could cry...
!
YOU'RE GONNA BE SORRY FOR MAKING MISS ROSIE CRY!!!
All right, settle down.
YEAH!!
It's thanks to **ME** you're here in the first place!
You can't put me in **jail**!
It's not **allowed**!
Well, we can't have that.
Perhaps I'll get rid of you instead.
I LOVE JAIL
Keep her entertained, girls. I'll deal with her another time.
EHE HE HE HE

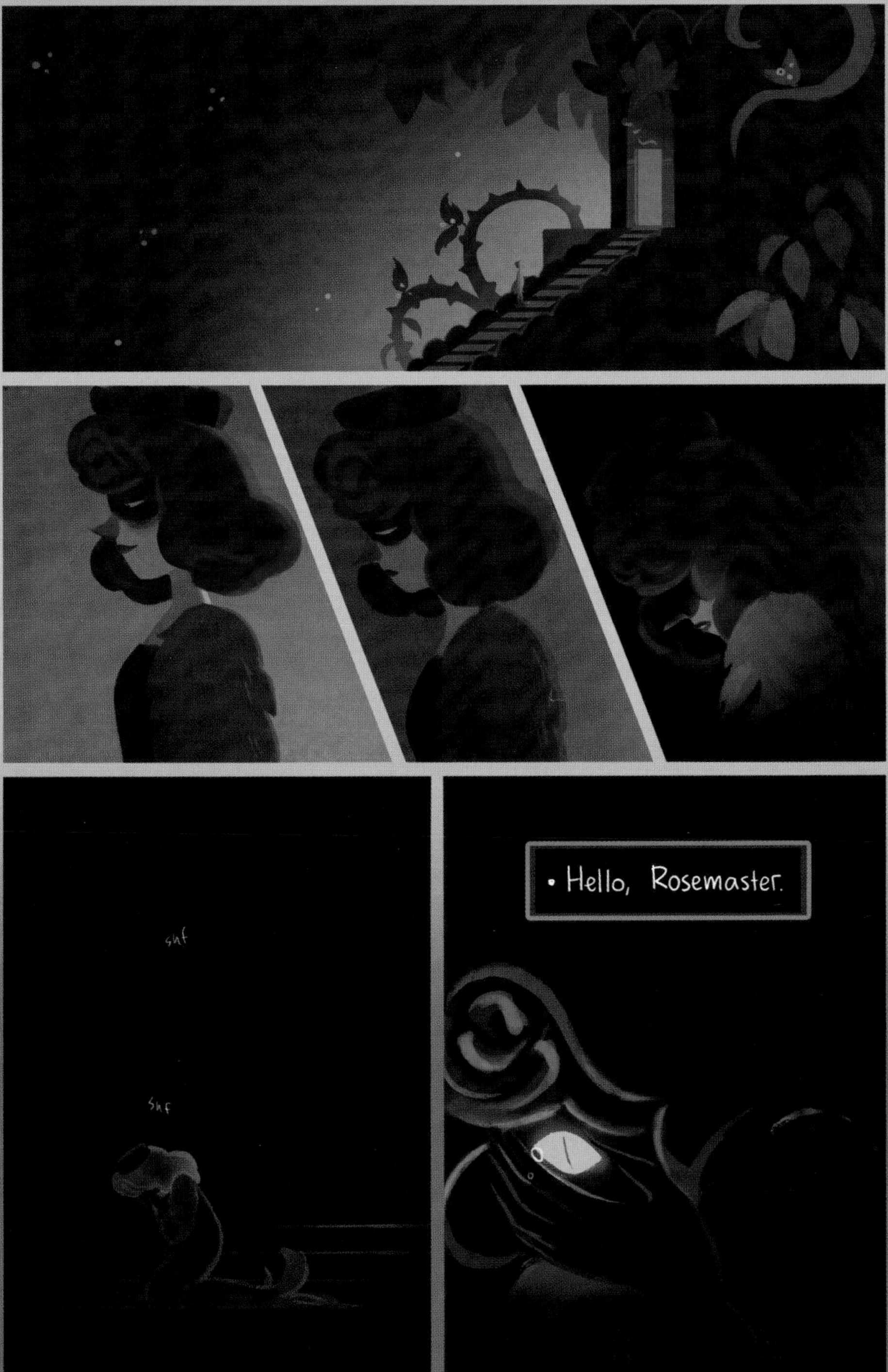

shf
shf
• Hello, Rosemaster.

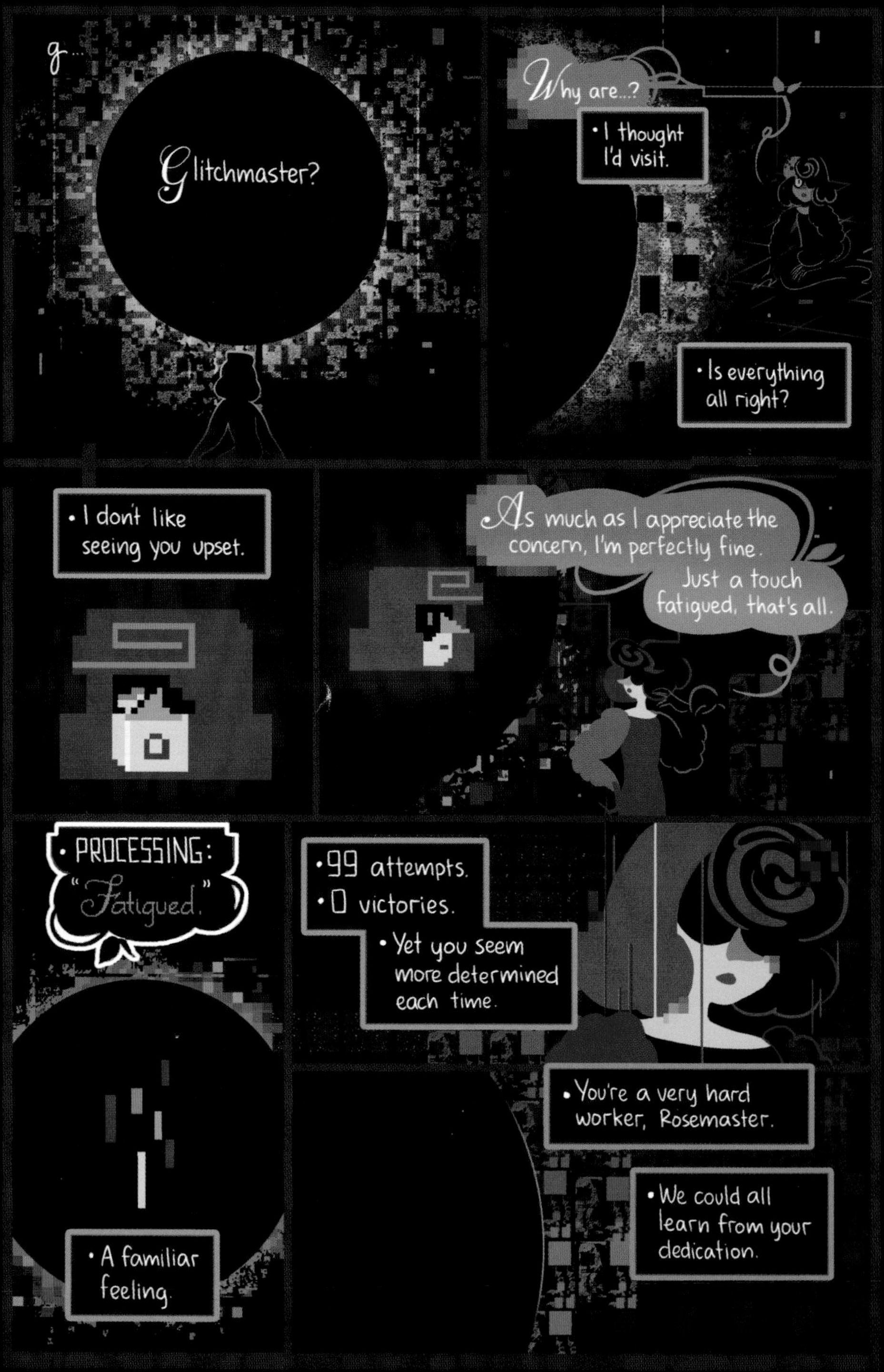
g...
Glitchmaster?
Why are...?
• I thought I'd visit.
• Is everything all right?
• I don't like seeing you upset.
As much as I appreciate the concern, I'm perfectly fine.
Just a touch fatigued, that's all.
• PROCESSING: "Fatigued."
• 99 attempts.
• 0 victories.
• Yet you seem more determined each time.
• A familiar feeling.
• You're a very hard worker, Rosemaster.
• We could all learn from your dedication.

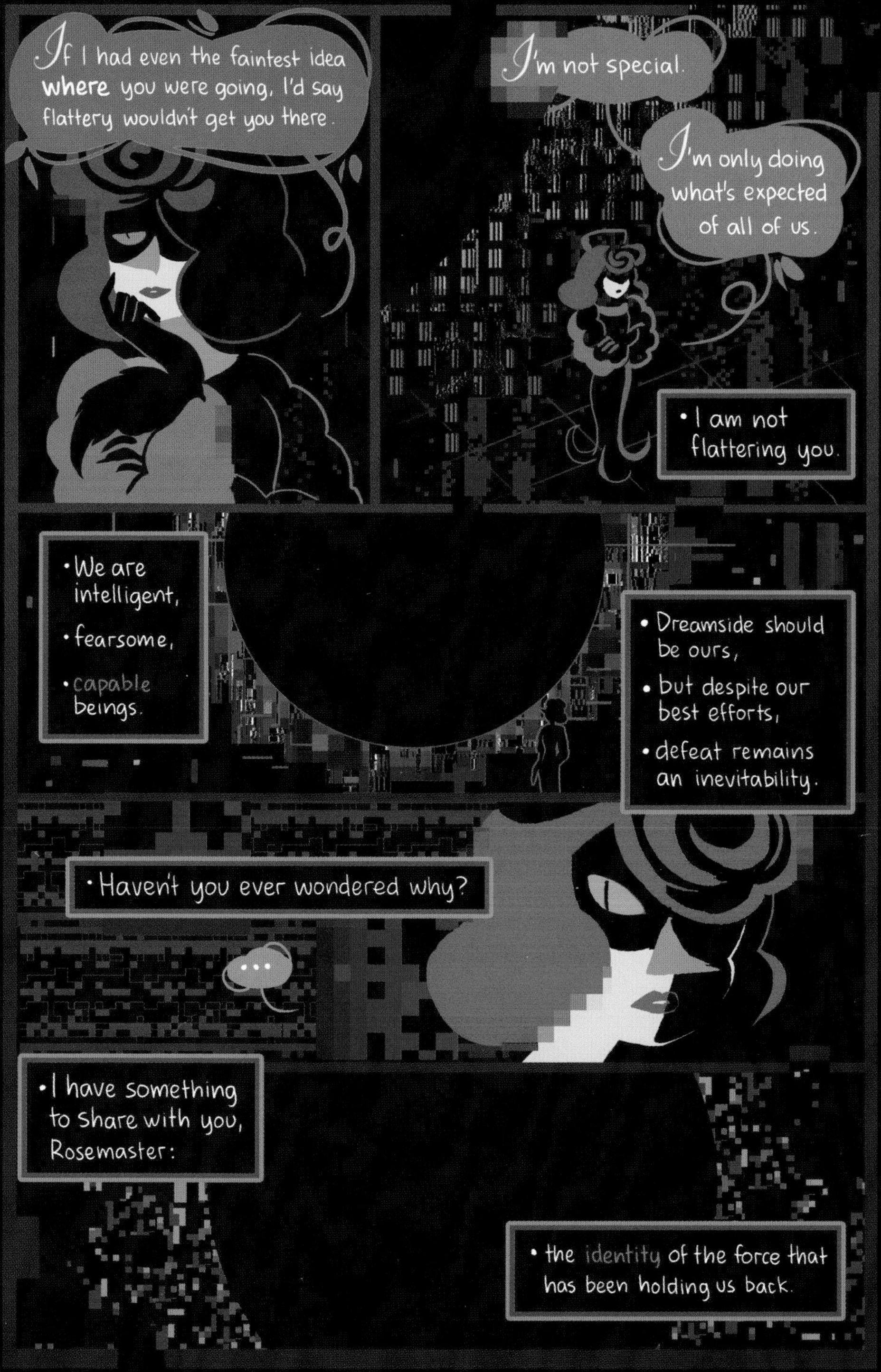
If I had even the faintest idea where you were going, I'd say flattery wouldn't get you there.
I'm not special.
I'm only doing what's expected of all of us.
• I am not flattering you.
• We are intelligent,
• fearsome,
• capable beings.
• Dreamside should be ours,
• but despite our best efforts,
• defeat remains an inevitability.
• Haven't you ever wondered why?
...
• I have something to share with you, Rosemaster:
• the identity of the force that has been holding us back.

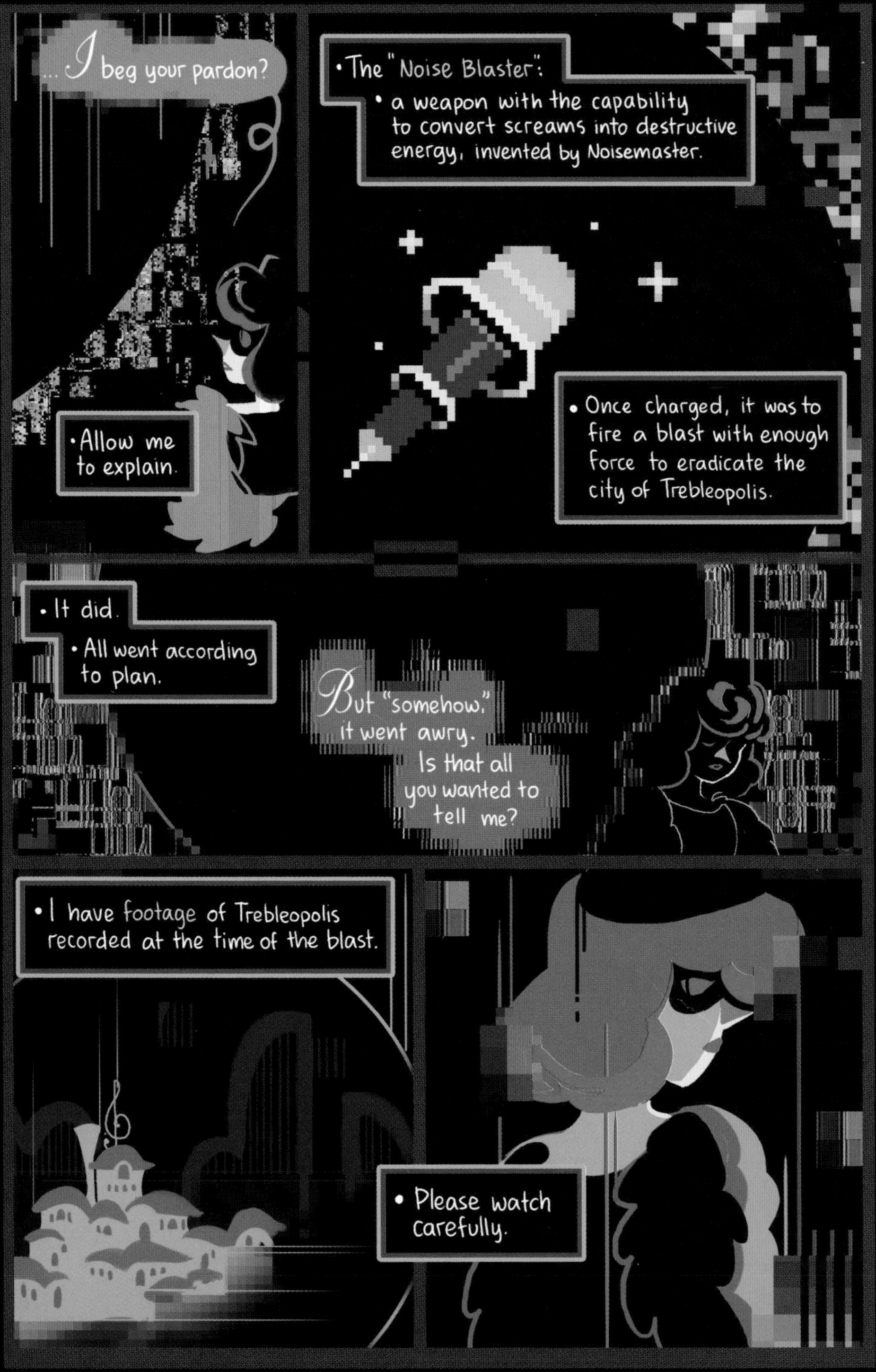

... I beg your pardon?
• Allow me to explain.
• The "Noise Blaster":
• a weapon with the capability to convert screams into destructive energy, invented by Noisemaster.
• Once charged, it was to fire a blast with enough force to eradicate the city of Trebleopolis.
• It did.
• All went according to plan.
But "somehow," it went awry.
Is that all you wanted to tell me?
• I have footage of Trebleopolis recorded at the time of the blast.
• Please watch carefully.

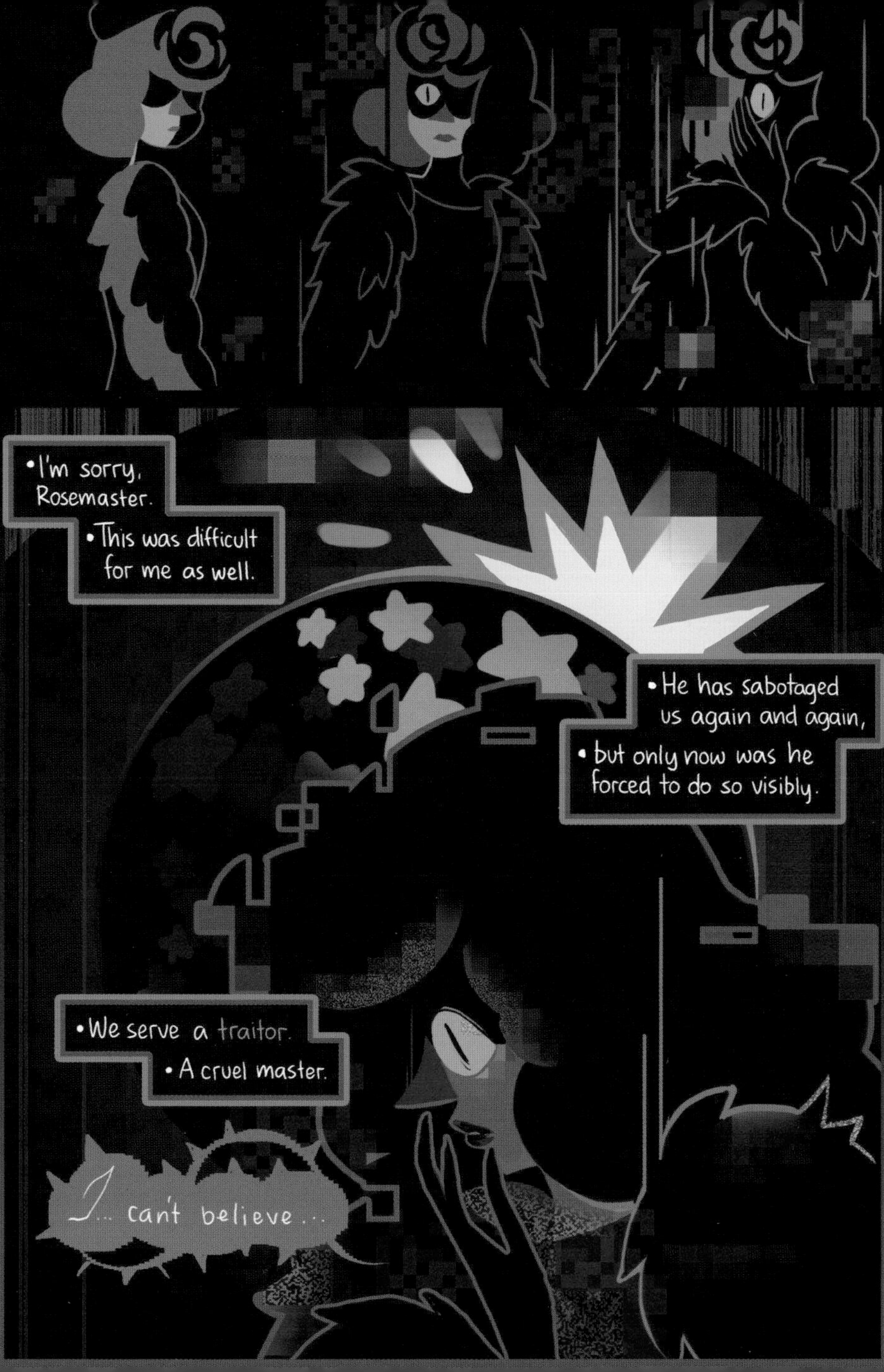

•I'm sorry, Rosemaster.
•This was difficult for me as well.
•He has sabotaged us again and again,
•but only now was he forced to do so visibly.
•We serve a traitor.
•A cruel master.
I... can't believe...

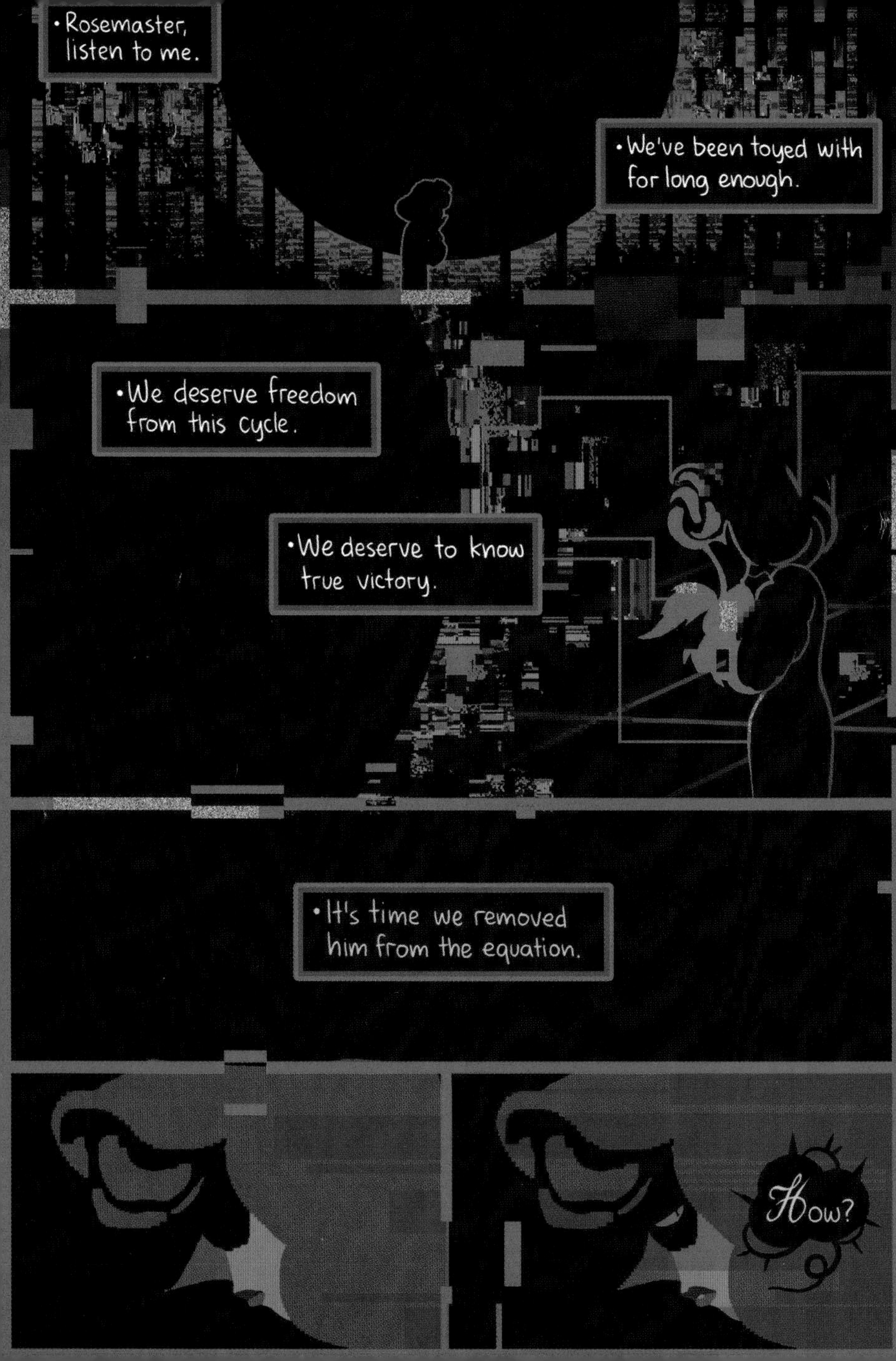
•Rosemaster, listen to me.
•We've been toyed with for long enough.
•We deserve freedom from this cycle.
•We deserve to know true victory.
•It's time we removed him from the equation.
How?

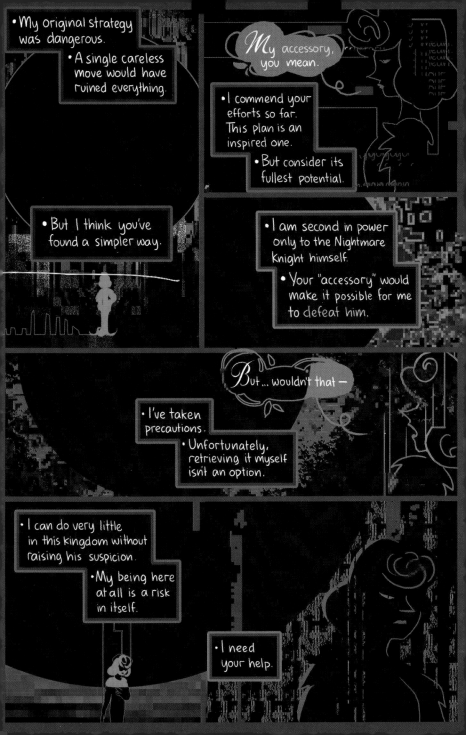

- My original strategy was dangerous.
  - A single careless move would have ruined everything.

My accessory, you mean.

- I commend your efforts so far. This plan is an inspired one.
  - But consider its fullest potential.

- But I think you've found a simpler way.

- I am second in power only to the Nightmare Knight himself.
  - Your "accessory" would make it possible for me to defeat him.

But... wouldn't that—

- I've taken precautions.
  - Unfortunately, retrieving it myself isn't an option.

- I can do very little in this kingdom without raising his suspicion.
  - My being here at all is a risk in itself.

- I need your help.

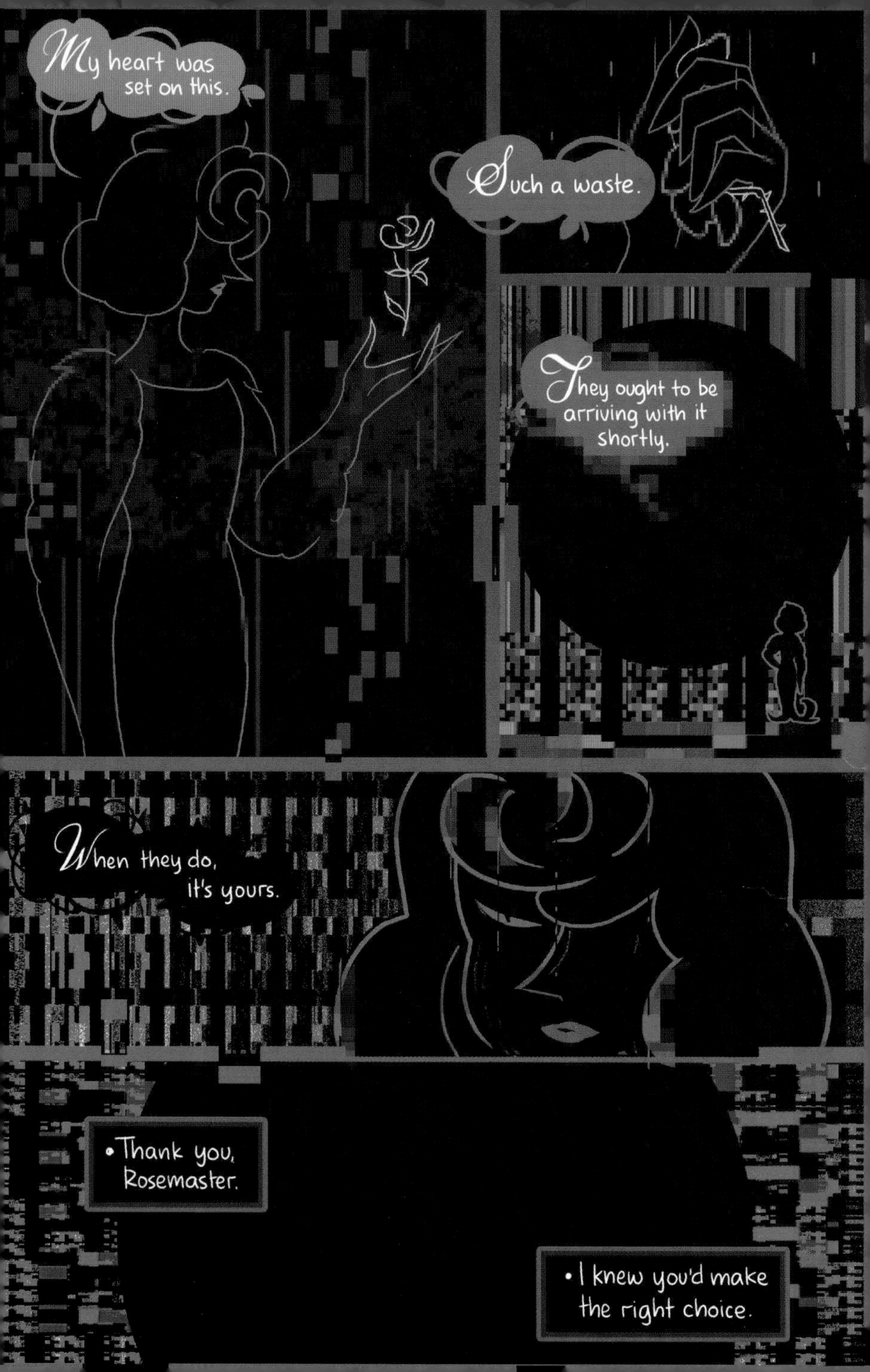
My heart was set on this.
Such a waste.
They ought to be arriving with it shortly.
When they do, it's yours.
•Thank you, Rosemaster.
•I knew you'd make the right choice.

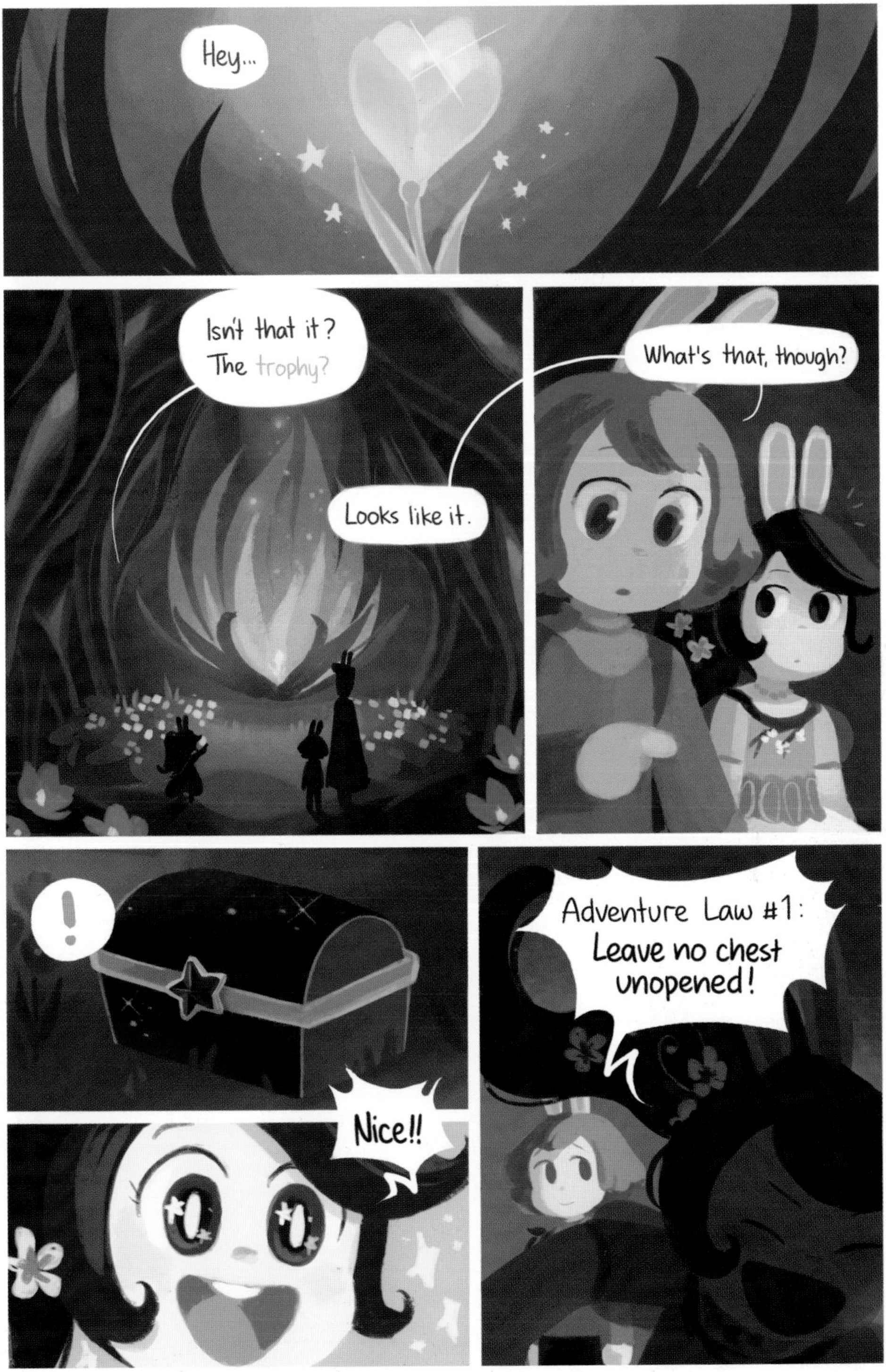
Hey...
Isn't that it? The trophy?
Looks like it.
What's that, though?
!
Nice!!
Adventure Law #1: Leave no chest unopened!

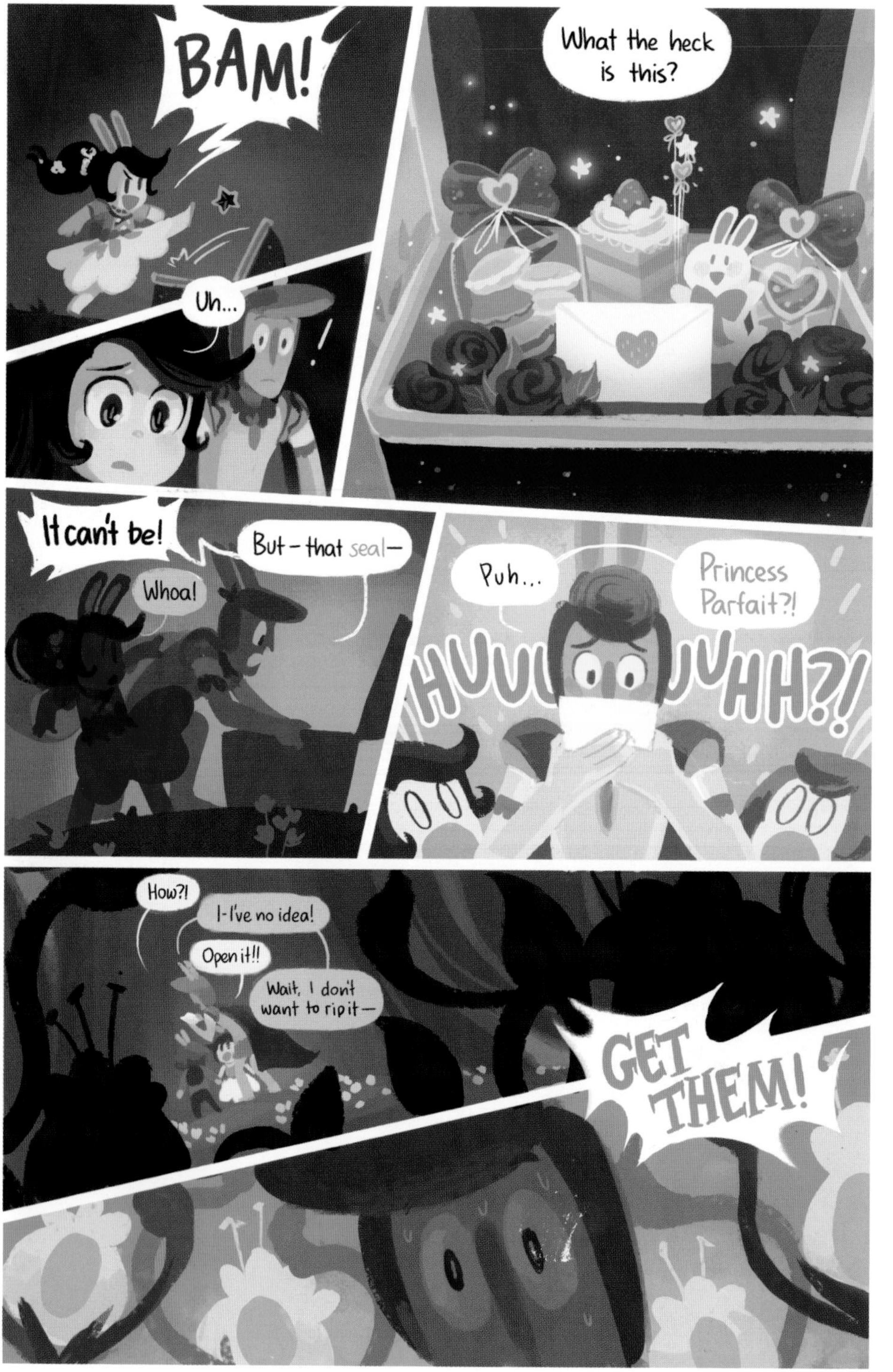
BAM!
What the heck is this?
Uh...
It can't be!
Whoa!
But—that seal—
Puh...
Princess Parfait?!
HUUUUUHH?!
How?!
I-I've no idea!
Open it!!
Wait, I don't want to rip it—
GET THEM!

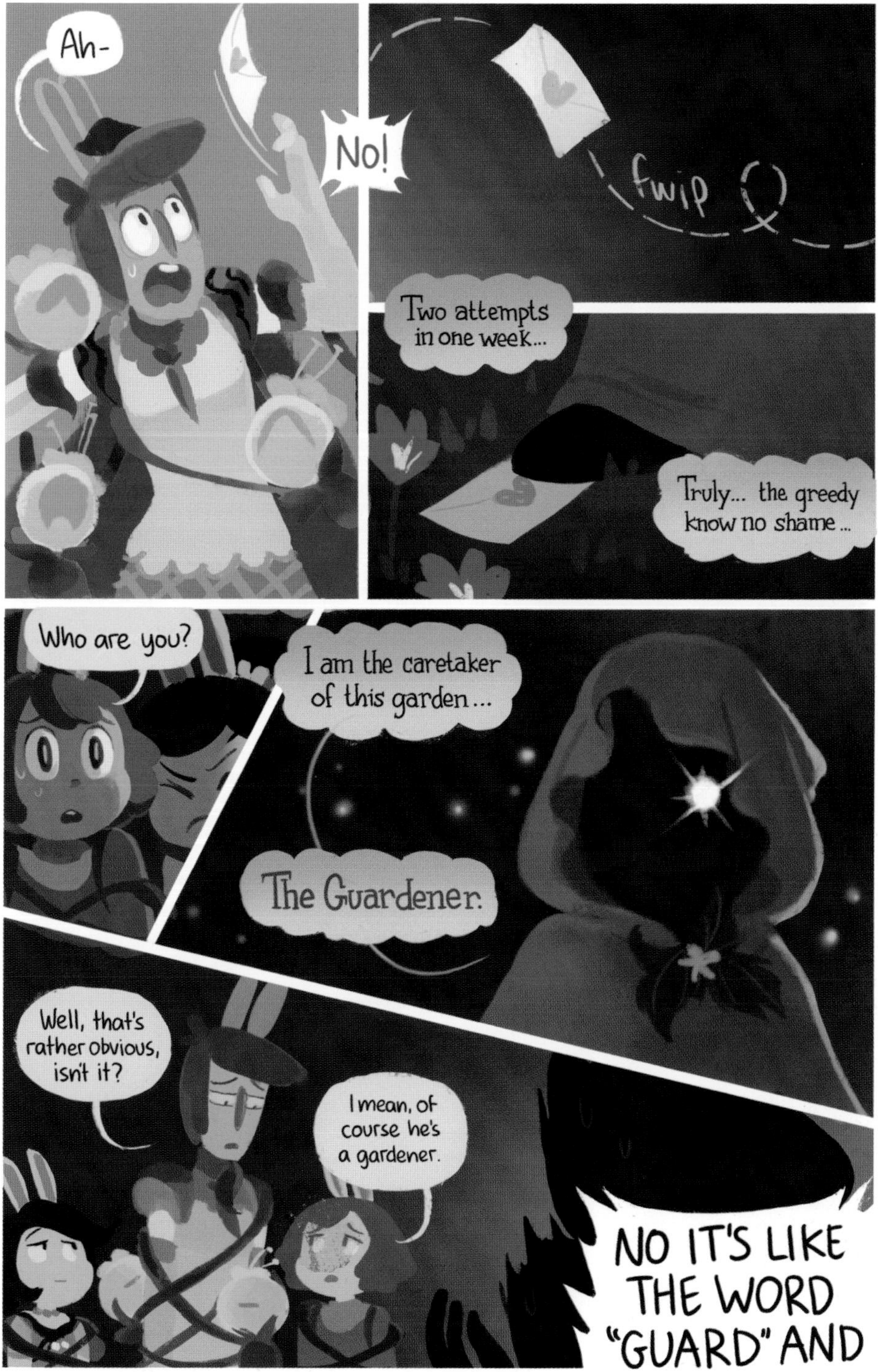

Ah-
No!
fwip
Two attempts in one week...
Truly... the greedy know no shame...
Who are you?
I am the caretaker of this garden...
The Guardener.
Well, that's rather obvious, isn't it?
I mean, of course he's a gardener.
NO IT'S LIKE THE WORD "GUARD" AND

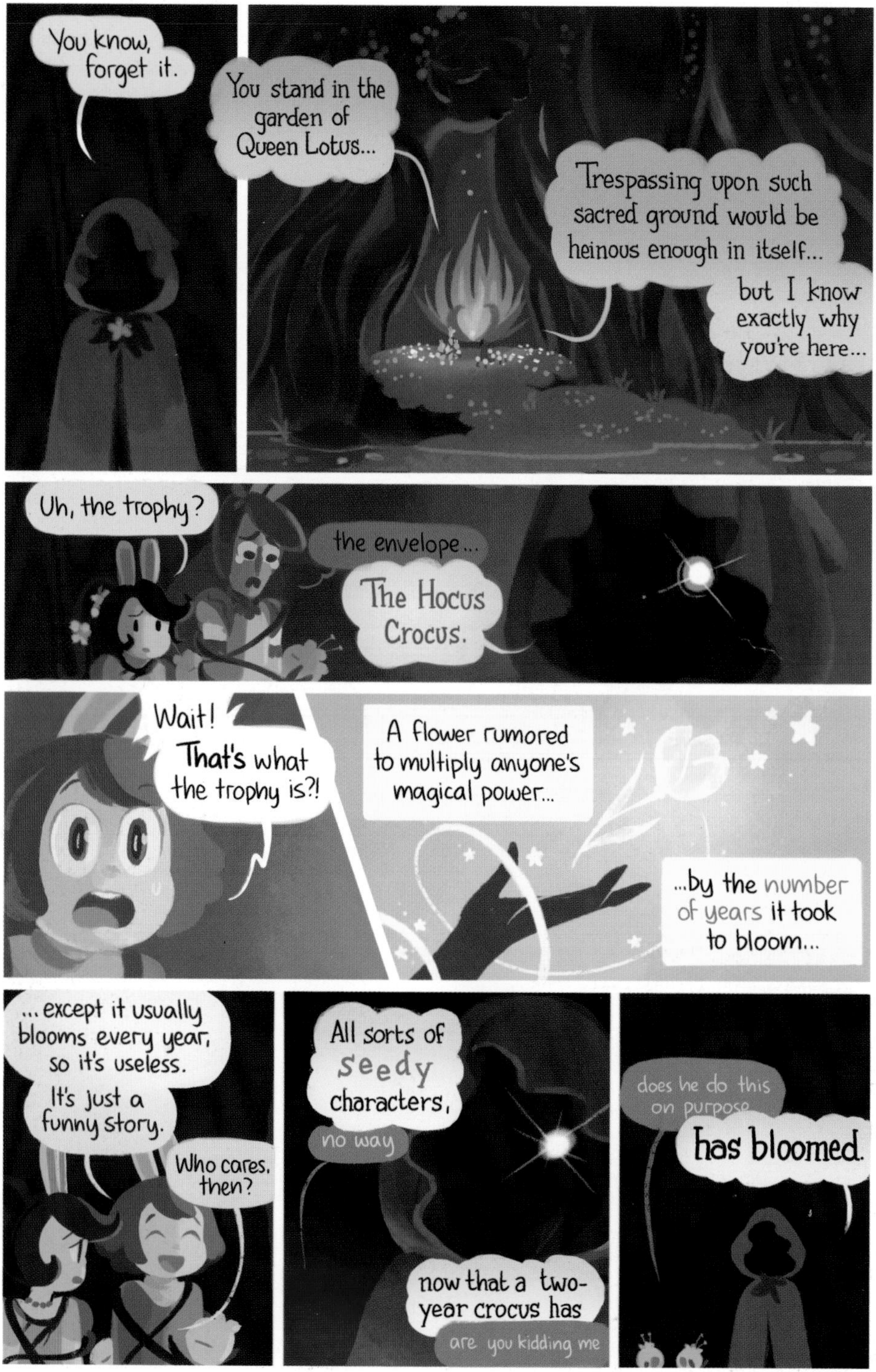

You know, forget it.
You stand in the garden of Queen Lotus...
Trespassing upon such sacred ground would be heinous enough in itself...
but I know exactly why you're here...
Uh, the trophy?
the envelope...
The Hocus Crocus.
Wait!
That's what the trophy is?!
A flower rumored to multiply anyone's magical power...
...by the number of years it took to bloom...
... except it usually blooms every year, so it's useless.
It's just a funny story.
Who cares, then?
All sorts of seedy characters,
no way
now that a two-year crocus has
are you kidding me
does he do this on purpose
has bloomed.

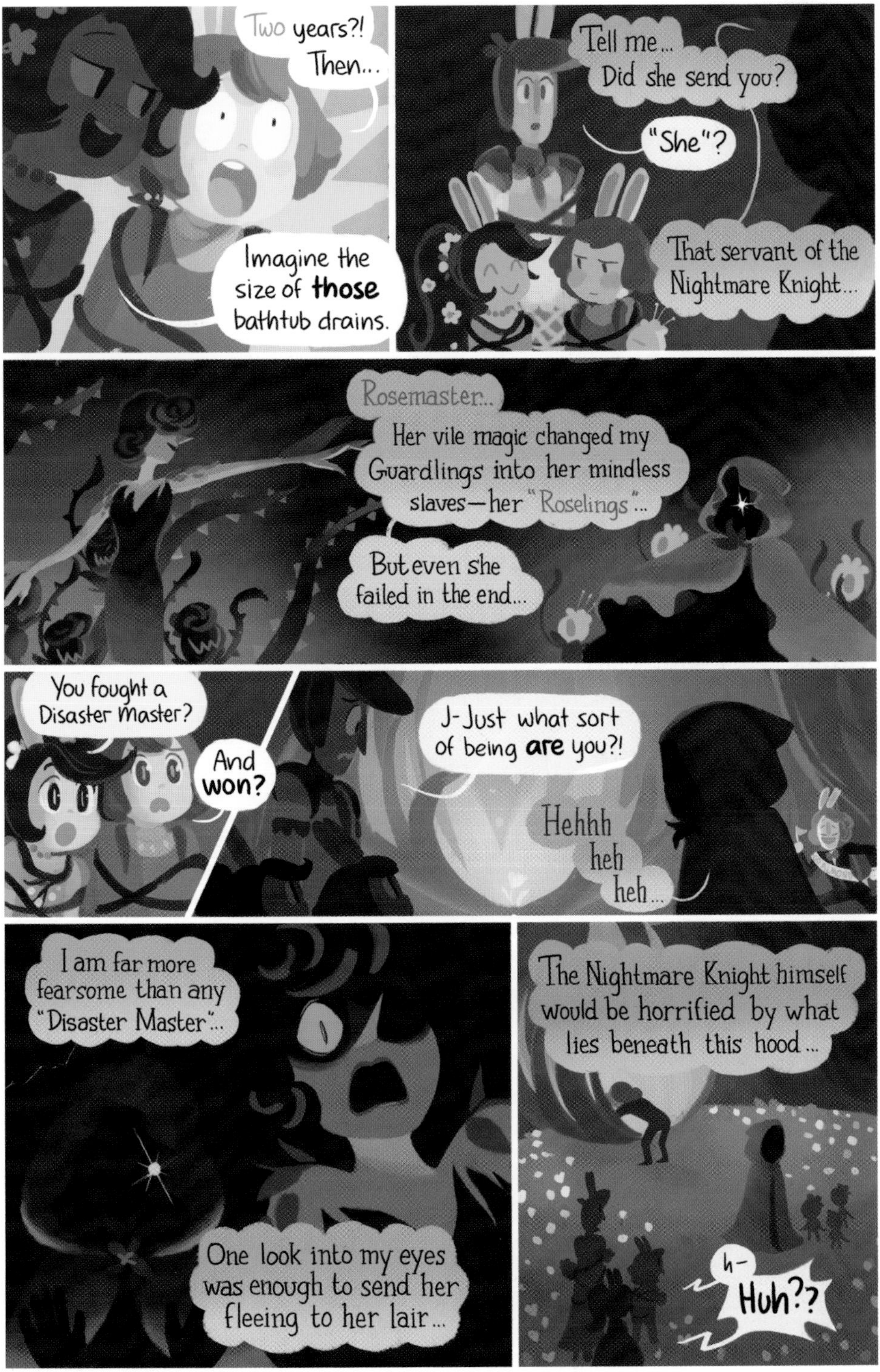
Two years?! Then...
Imagine the size of **those** bathtub drains.
Tell me... Did she send you?
"She"?
That servant of the Nightmare Knight...
Rosemaster...
Her vile magic changed my Guardlings into her mindless slaves—her "Roselings"...
But even she failed in the end...
You fought a Disaster Master?
And **won?**
J-Just what sort of being **are** you?!
Hehhh heh heh...
I am far more fearsome than any "Disaster Master"...
One look into my eyes was enough to send her fleeing to her lair...
The Nightmare Knight himself would be horrified by what lies beneath this hood...
h- Huh??

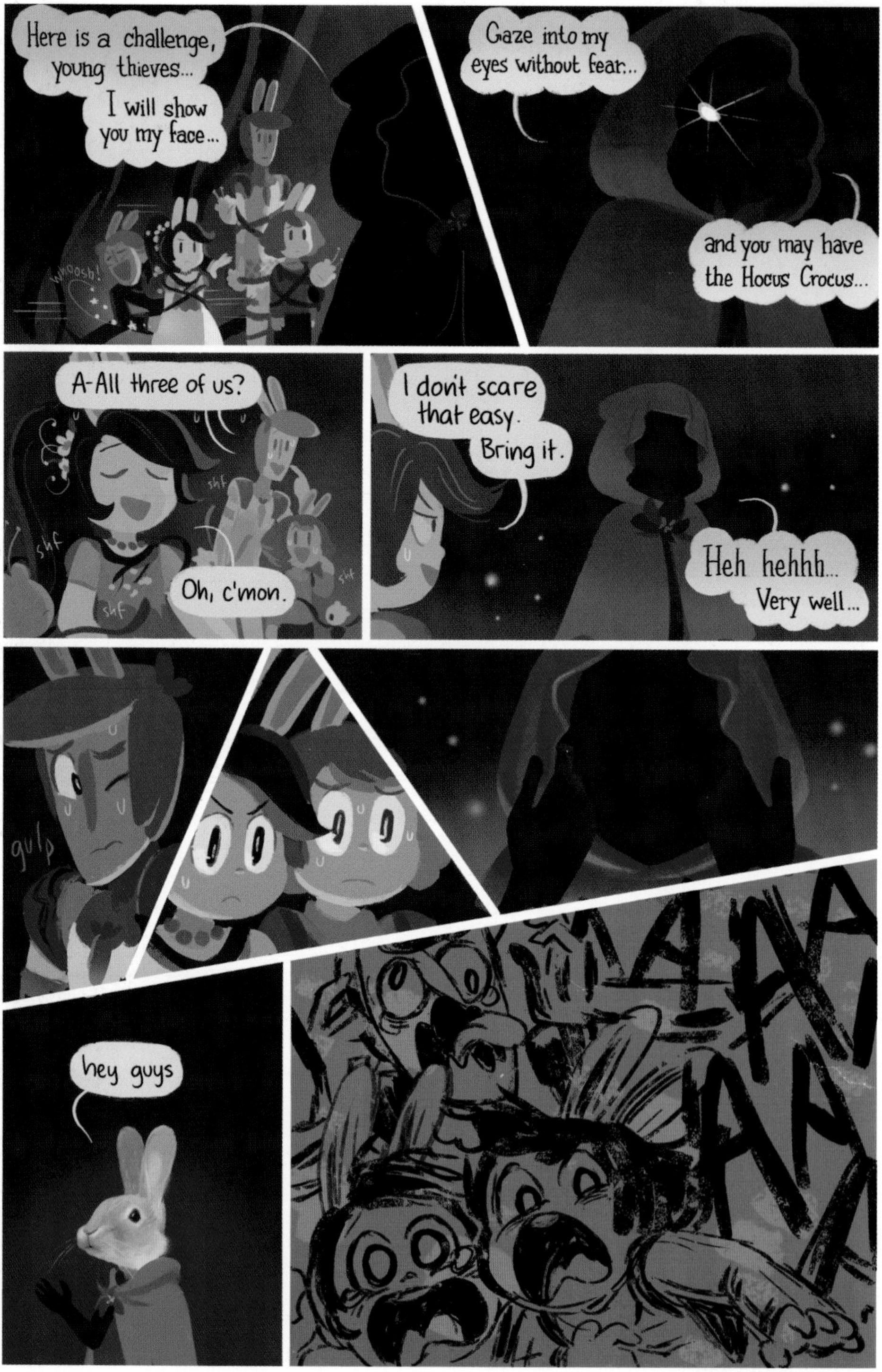
Here is a challenge, young thieves...
I will show you my face...
whoosh!
Gaze into my eyes without fear...
and you may have the Hocus Crocus...
A-All three of us?
shf
shf
shf
shf
Oh, c'mon.
I don't scare that easy. Bring it.
Heh hehhh... Very well...
gulp
hey guys

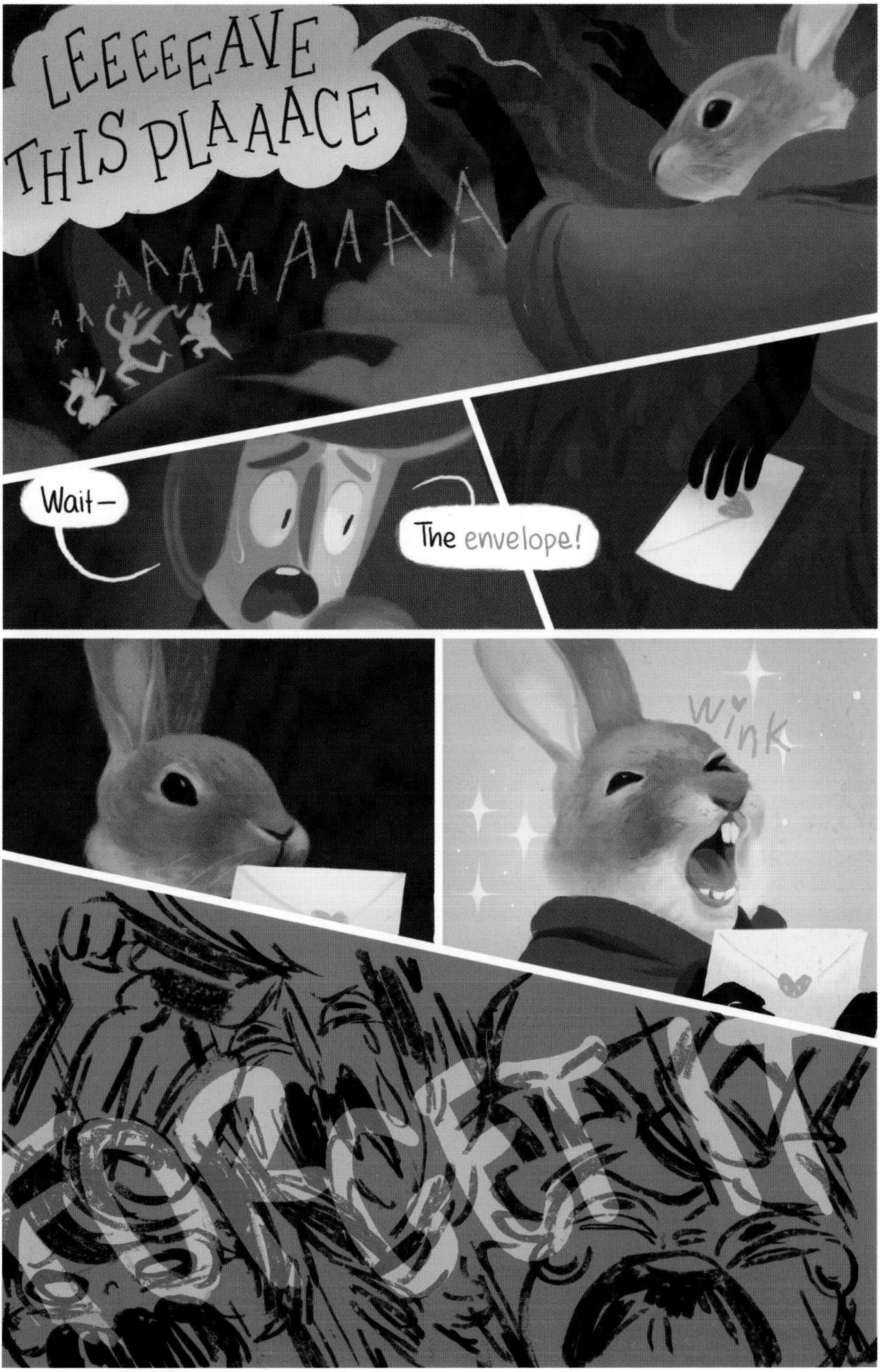
LEEEEEAVE THIS PLAAACE
AAAAAAAAAAA
Wait—
The envelope!
wink

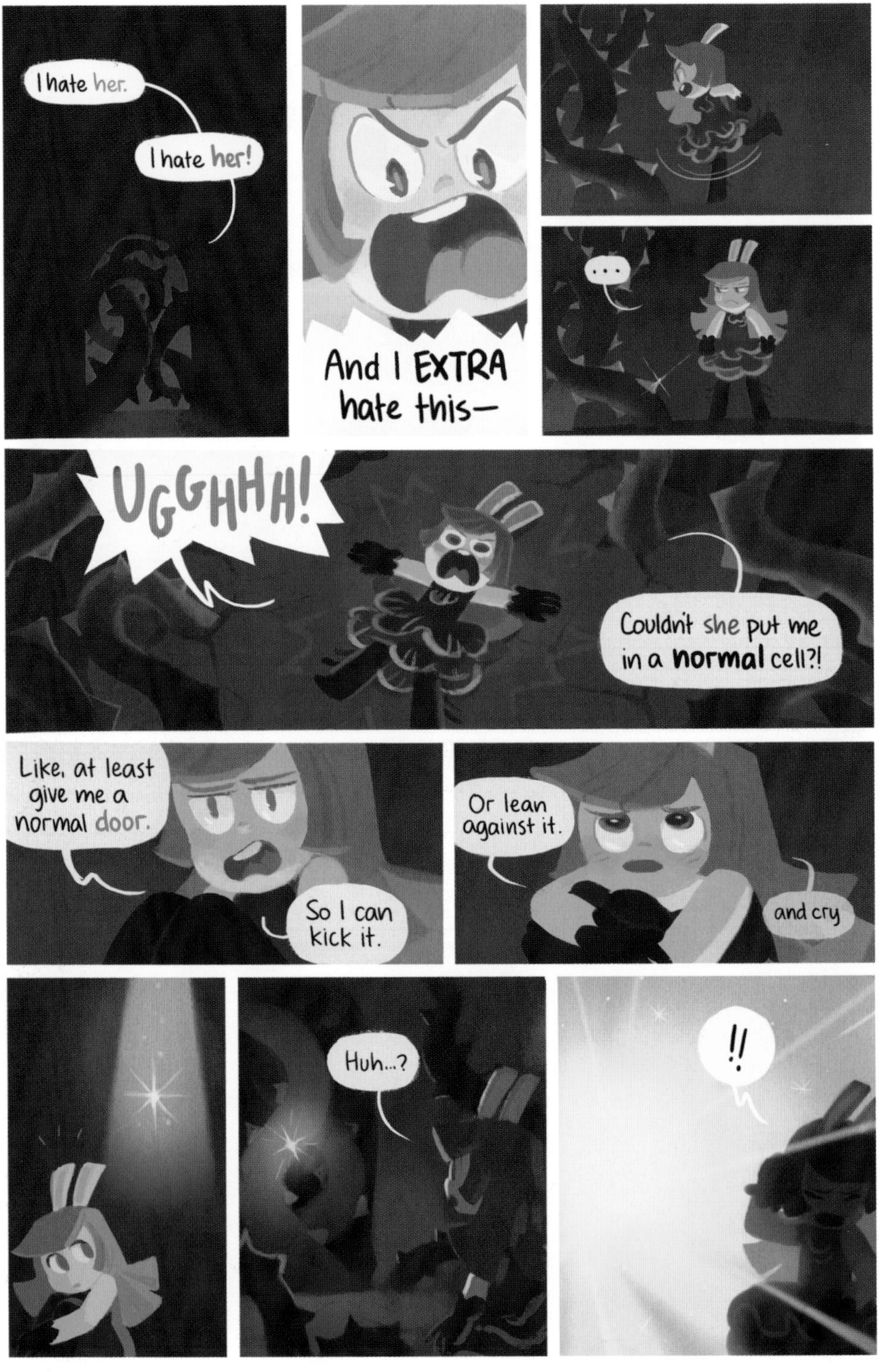
I hate her.
I hate her!
And I EXTRA hate this—
...
UGGHHA!
Couldn't she put me in a normal cell?!
Like, at least give me a normal door.
So I can kick it.
Or lean against it.
and cry
Huh...?
!!

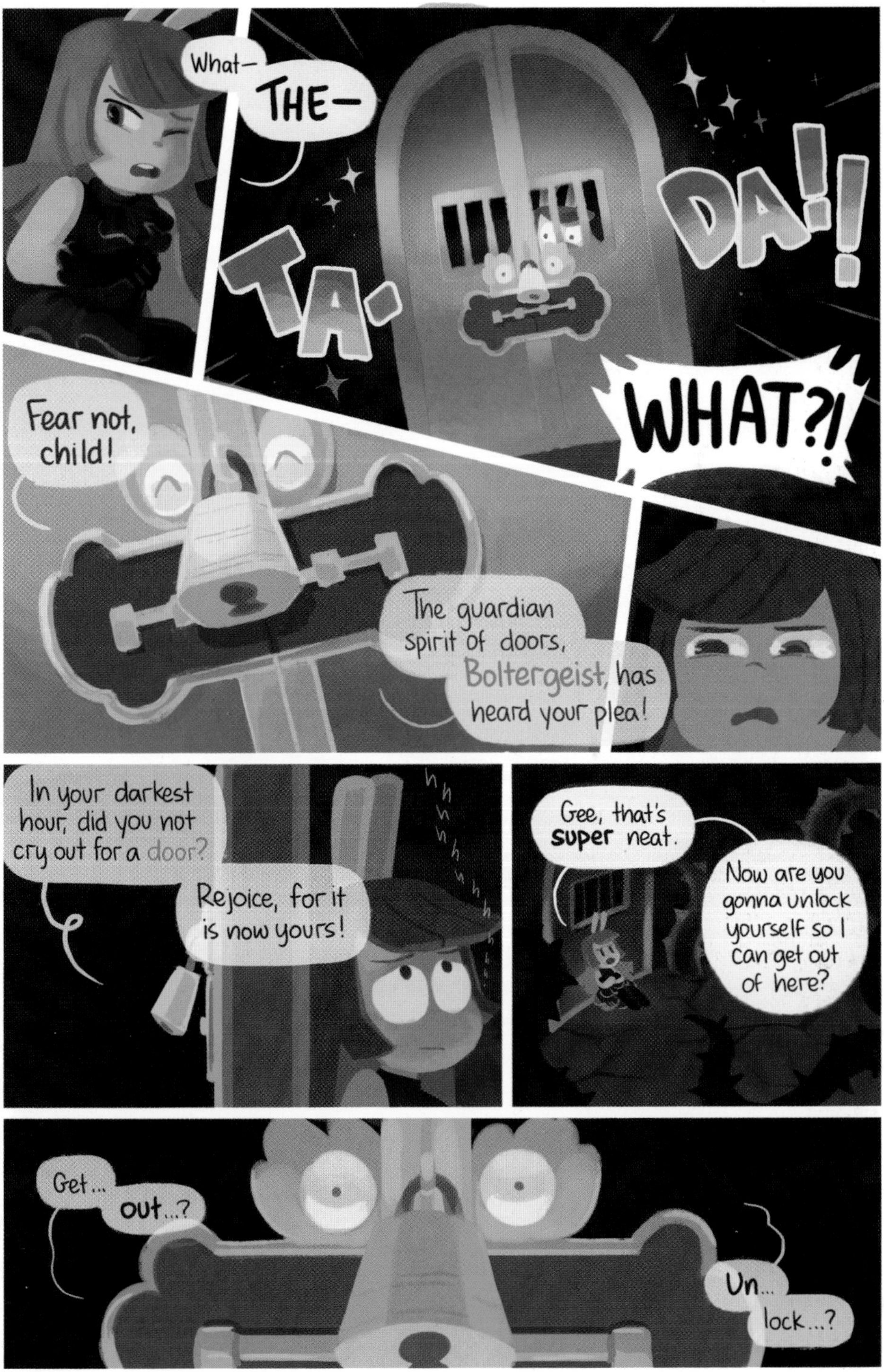
What-
THE-
TA-
DA!!
WHAT?!
Fear not, child!
The guardian spirit of doors, Boltergeist, has heard your plea!
In your darkest hour, did you not cry out for a door?
Rejoice, for it is now yours!
Gee, that's **super** neat.
Now are you gonna unlock yourself so I can get out of here?
Get... out...?
Un... lock...?

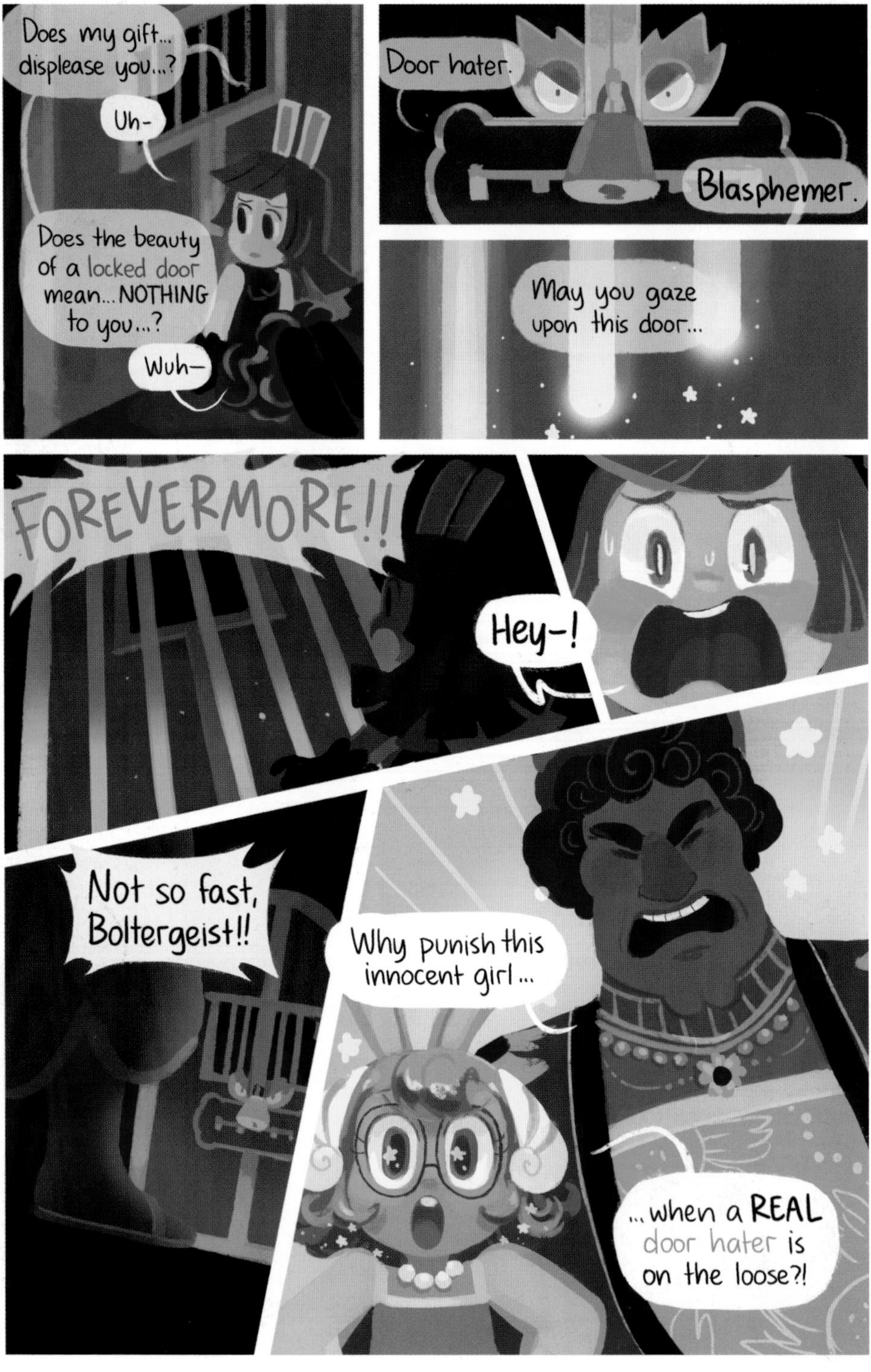

Does my gift... displease you...?
Uh-
Does the beauty of a locked door mean... NOTHING to you...?
Wuh-
Door hater.
Blasphemer.
May you gaze upon this door...
FOREVERMORE!!
Hey-!
Not so fast, Boltergeist!!
Why punish this innocent girl...
...when a REAL door hater is on the loose?!

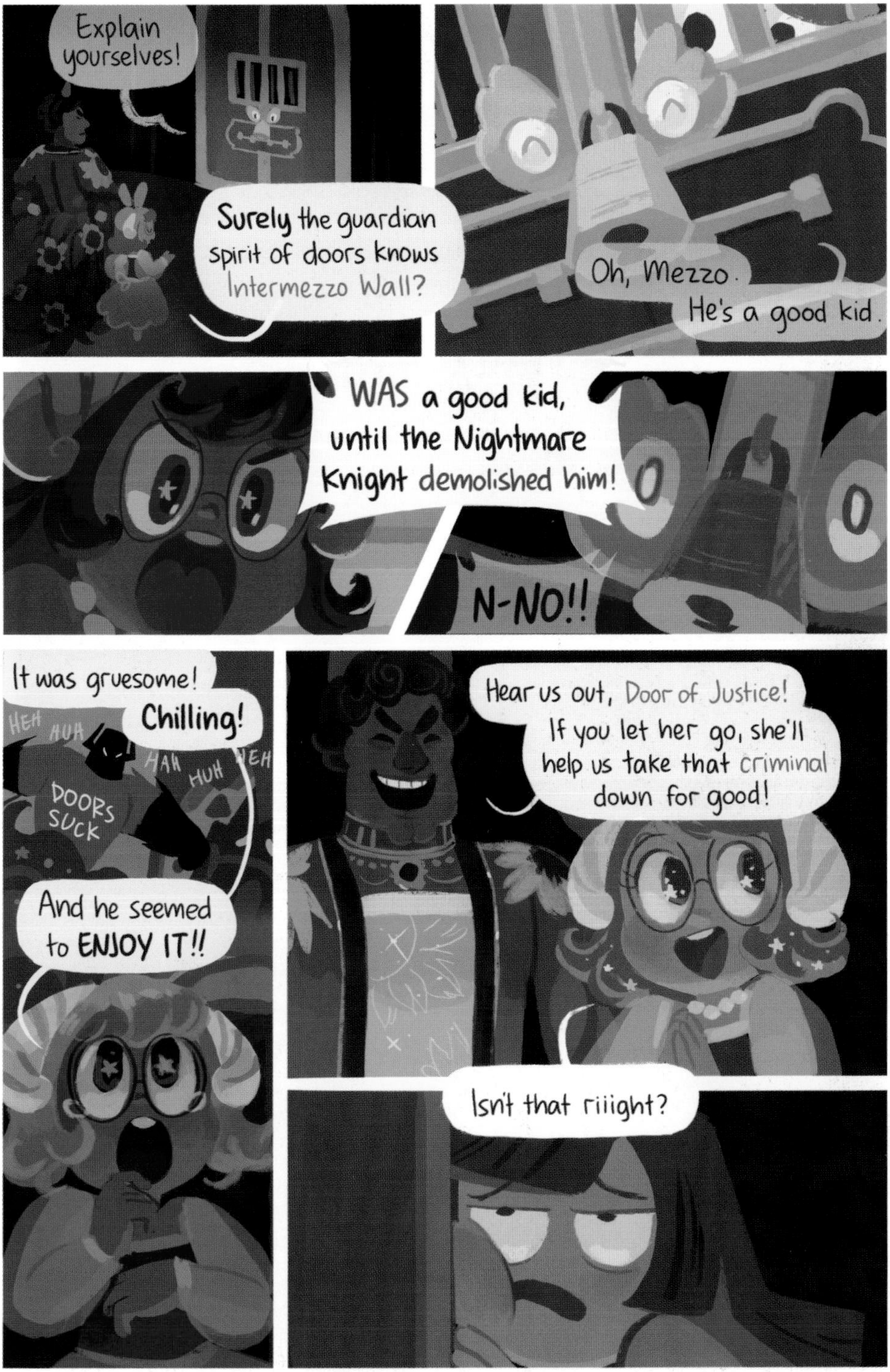
Explain yourselves!
Surely the guardian spirit of doors knows Intermezzo Wall?
Oh, Mezzo. He's a good kid.
WAS a good kid, until the Nightmare Knight demolished him!
N-NO!!
It was gruesome!
Chilling!
HEH HUH HAH HUH HEH
DOORS SUCK
And he seemed to ENJOY IT!!
Hear us out, Door of Justice! If you let her go, she'll help us take that criminal down for good!
Isn't that riiight?

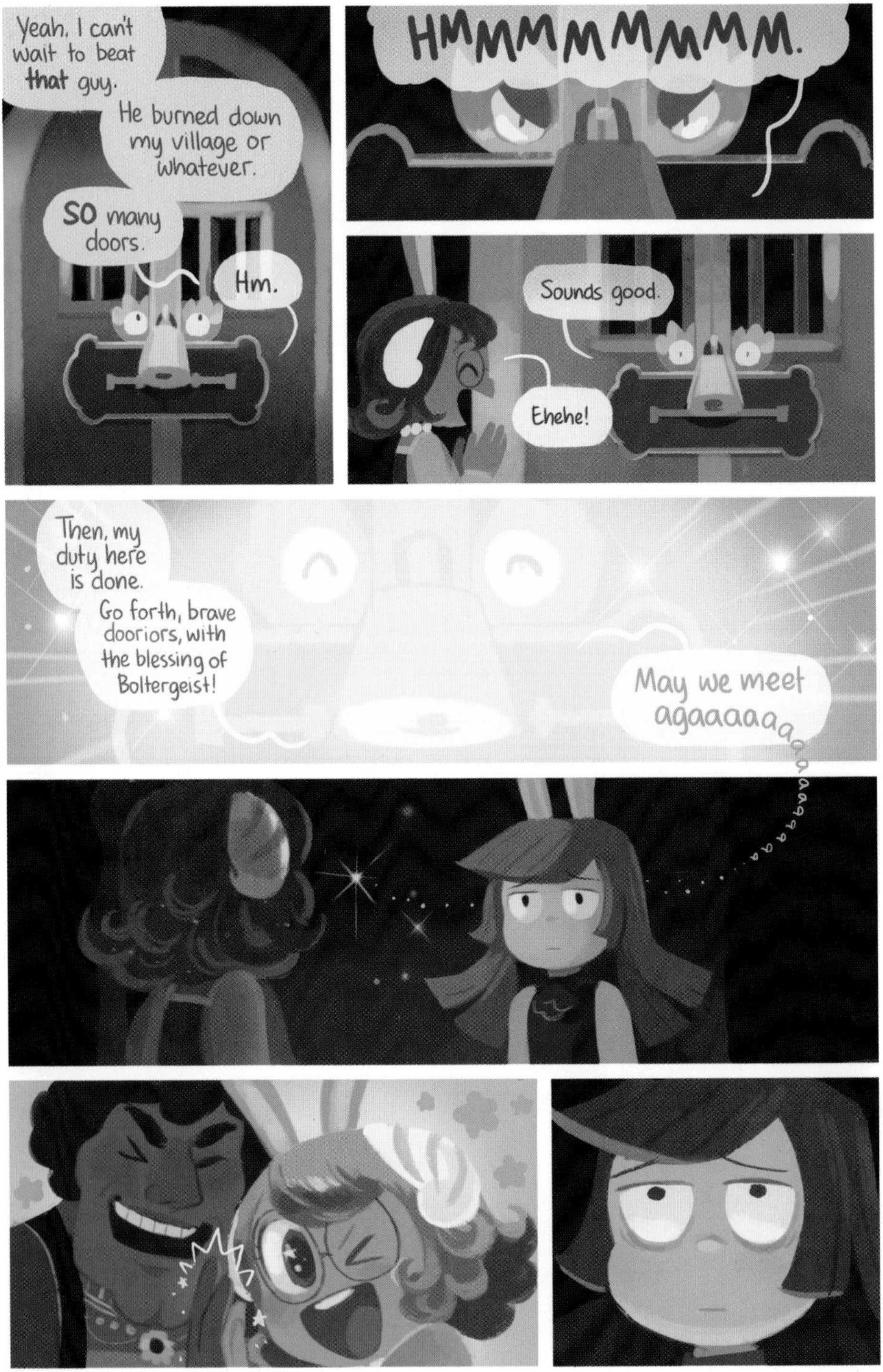

Yeah, I can't wait to beat **that** guy.
He burned down my village or whatever.
SO many doors.
Hm.
HMMMMMMMMM.
Sounds good.
Ehehe!
Then, my duty here is done.
Go forth, brave dooriors, with the blessing of Boltergeist!
May we meet agaaaaaaaaaaaaaaa

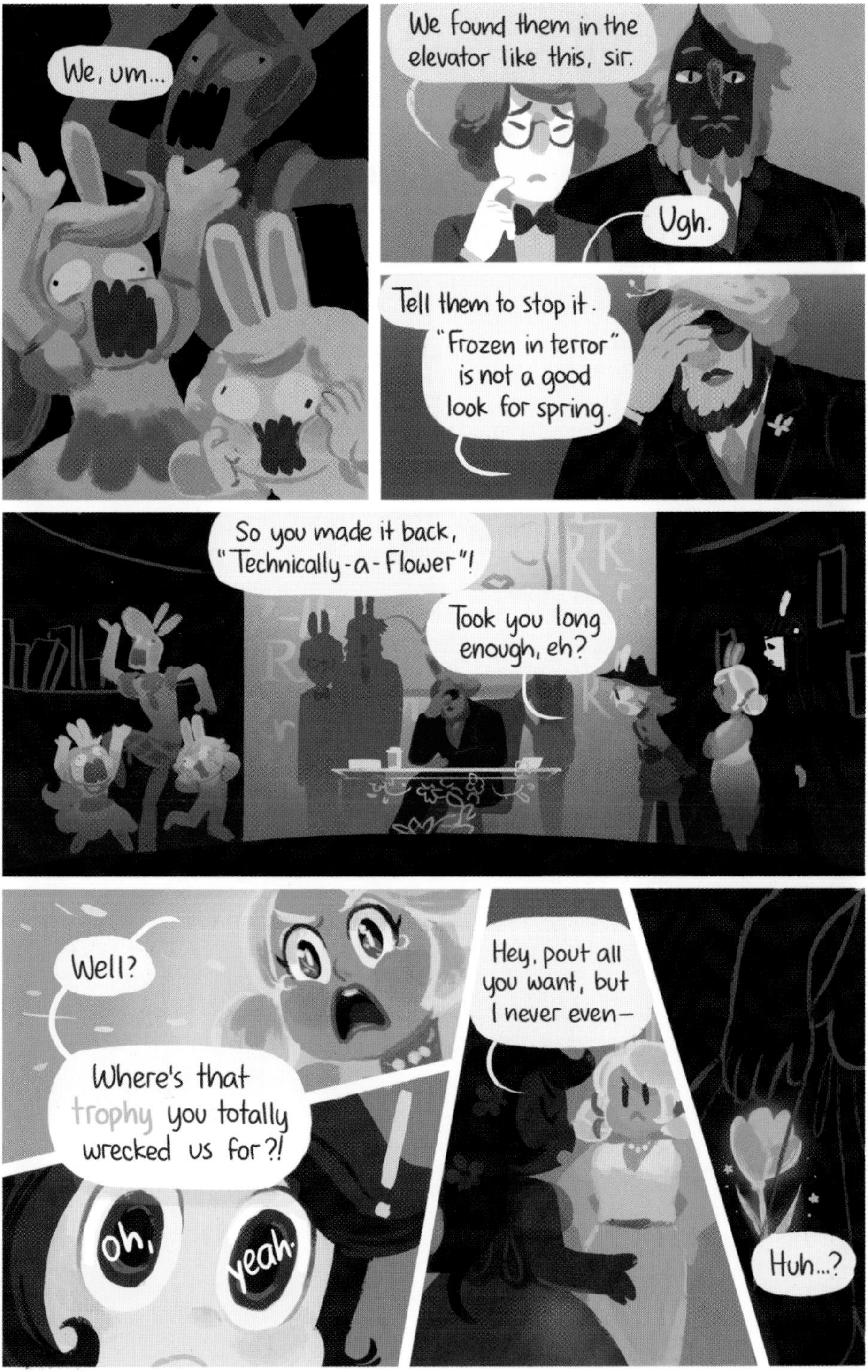
We, um...
We found them in the elevator like this, sir.
Ugh.
Tell them to stop it.
"Frozen in terror" is not a good look for spring.
So you made it back, "Technically-a-Flower"!
Took you long enough, eh?
Well?
Where's that trophy you totally wrecked us for?!
oh, yeah.
Hey, pout all you want, but I never even—
Huh...?

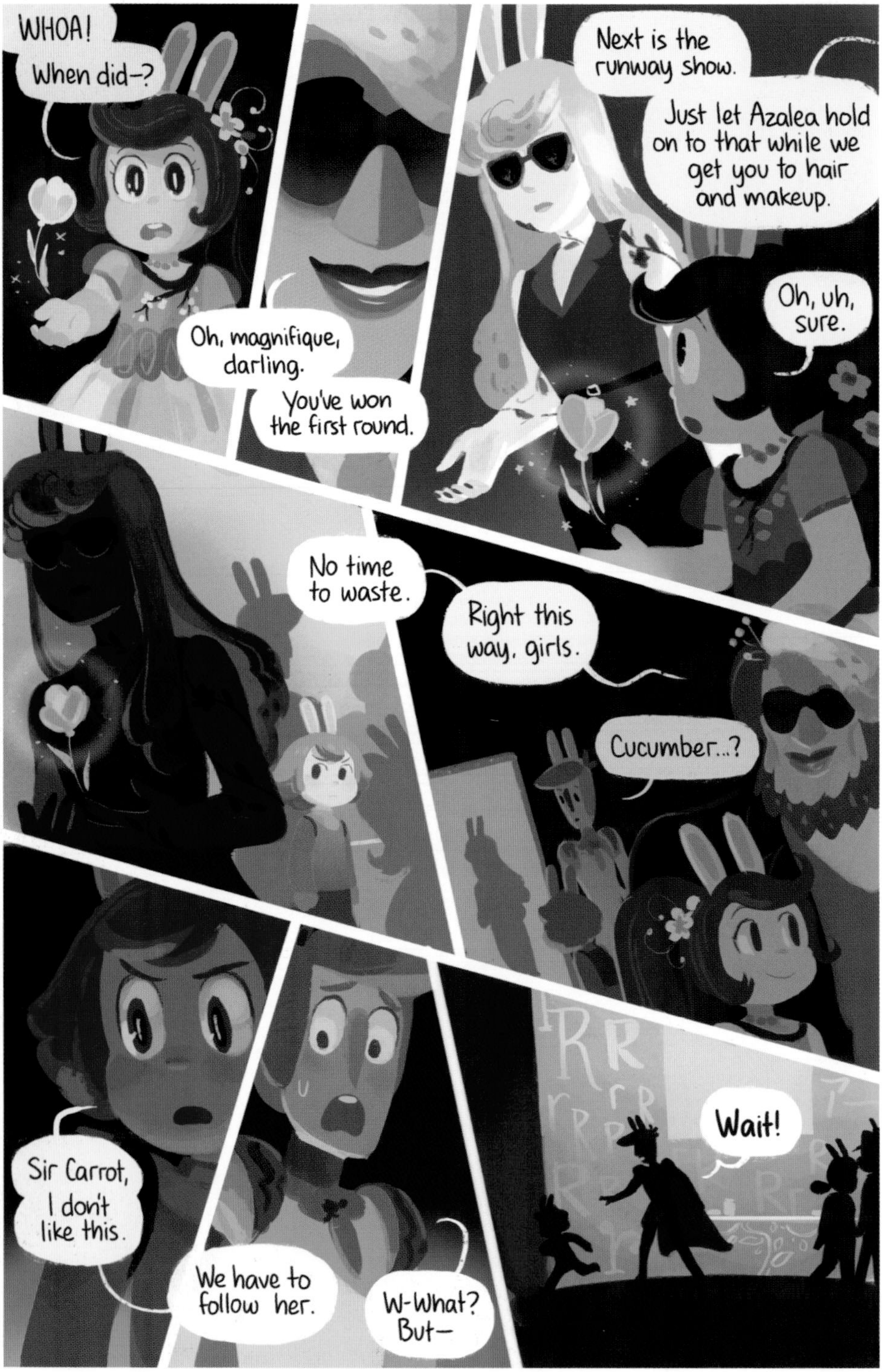
WHOA!
When did-?
Oh, magnifique, darling.
You've won the first round.
Next is the runway show.
Just let Azalea hold on to that while we get you to hair and makeup.
Oh, uh, sure.
No time to waste.
Right this way, girls.
Cucumber...?
Sir Carrot, I don't like this.
We have to follow her.
W-What? But-
Wait!

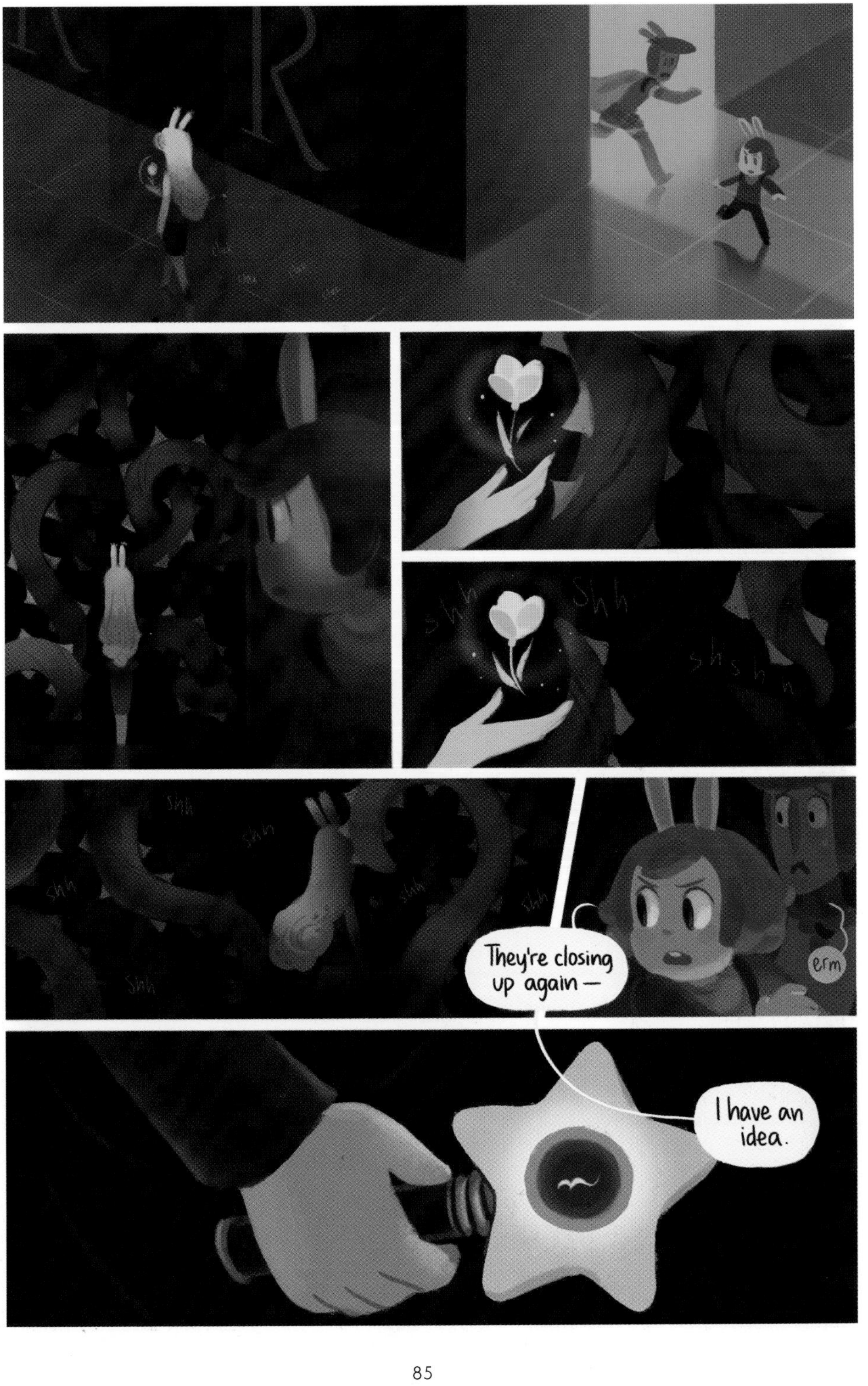
shh
shh
shshh
shh
shh
shh
shh
shh
They're closing up again—
erm
I have an idea.

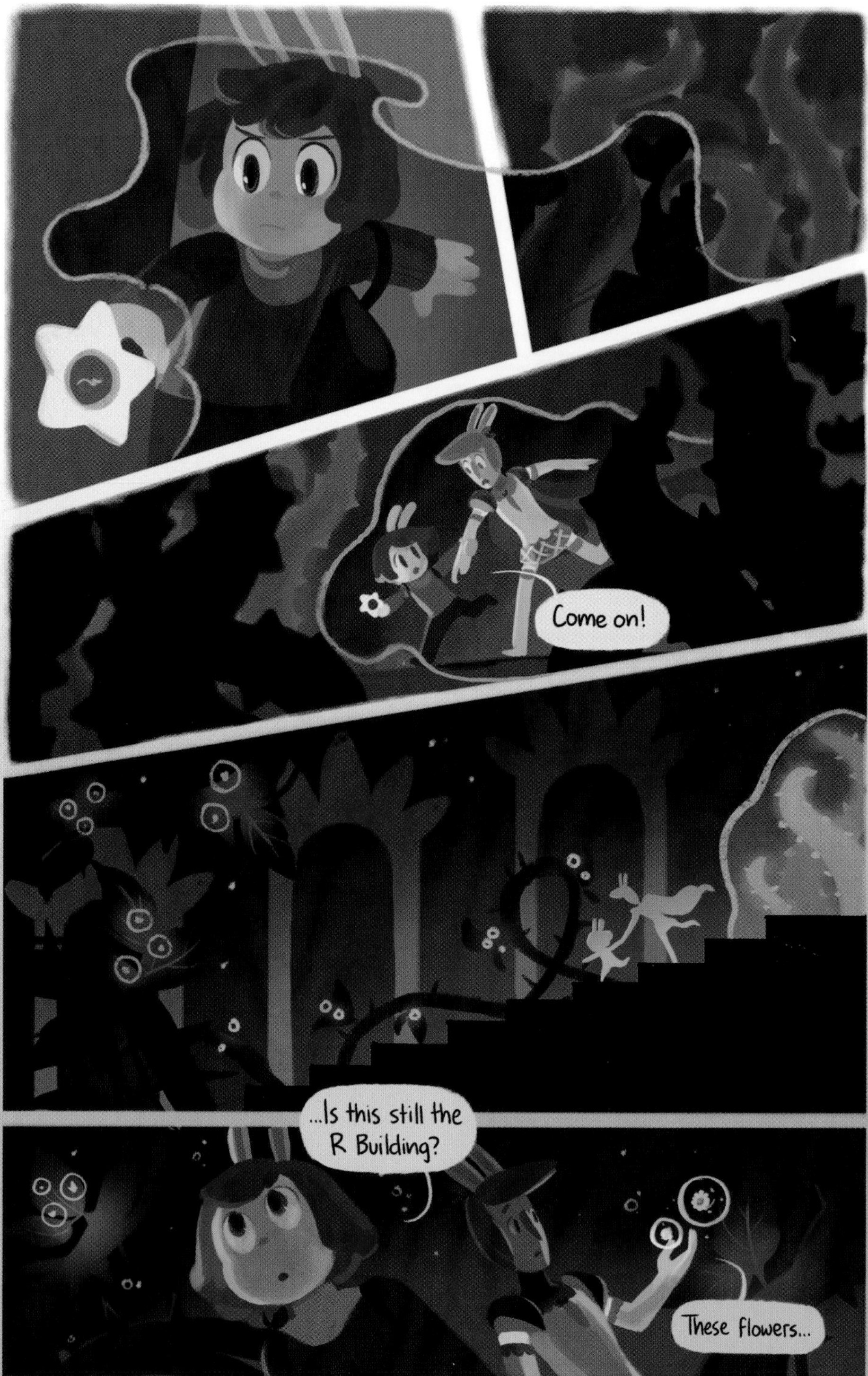
Come on!
...Is this still the R Building?
These flowers...

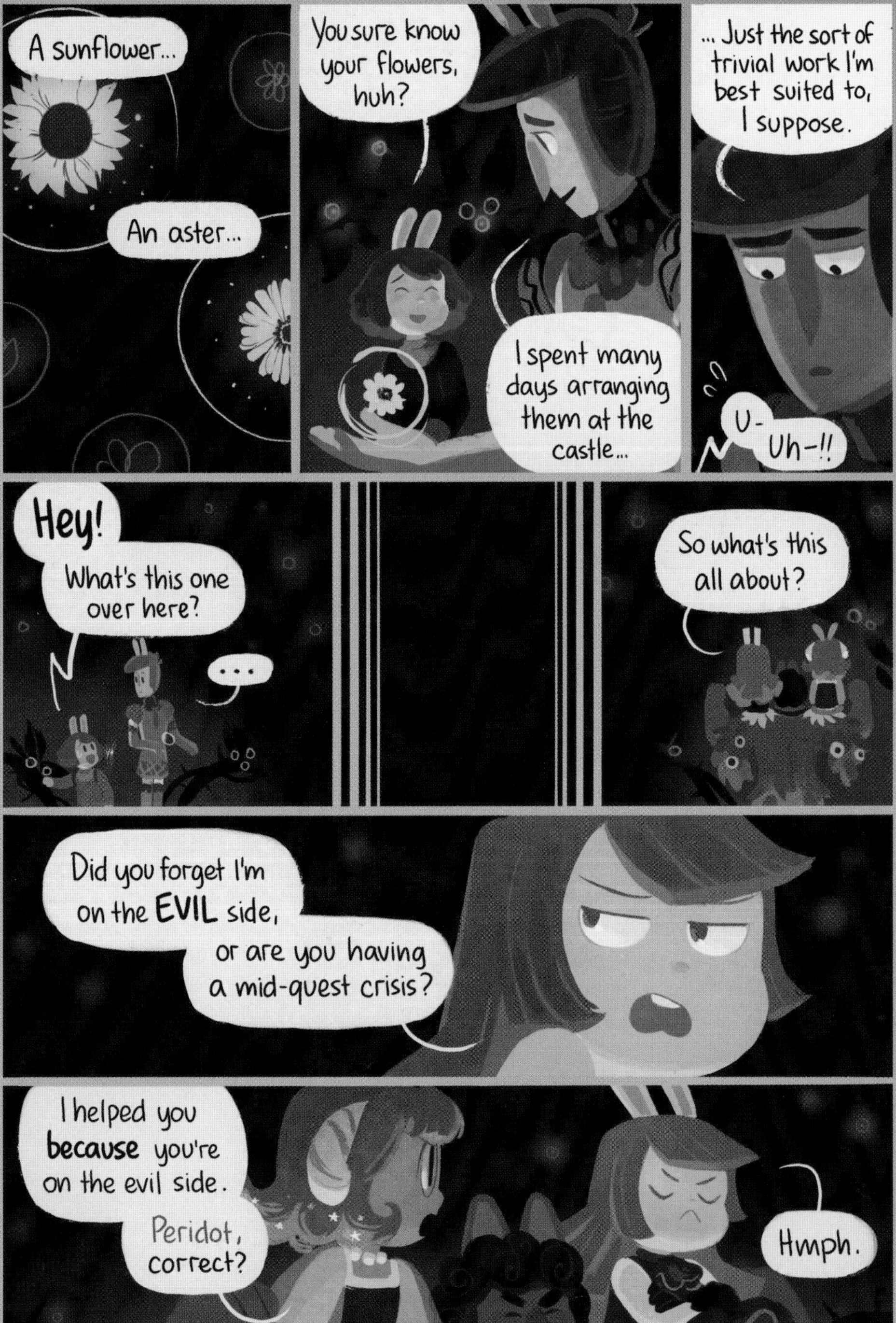
A sunflower...
An aster...
You sure know your flowers, huh?
I spent many days arranging them at the castle...
... Just the sort of trivial work I'm best suited to, I suppose.
U- Uh-!!
Hey!
What's this one over here?
...
So what's this all about?
Did you forget I'm on the EVIL side,
or are you having a mid-quest crisis?
I helped you because you're on the evil side.
Peridot, correct?
Hmph.

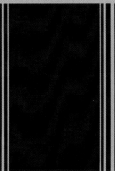

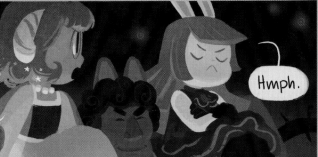

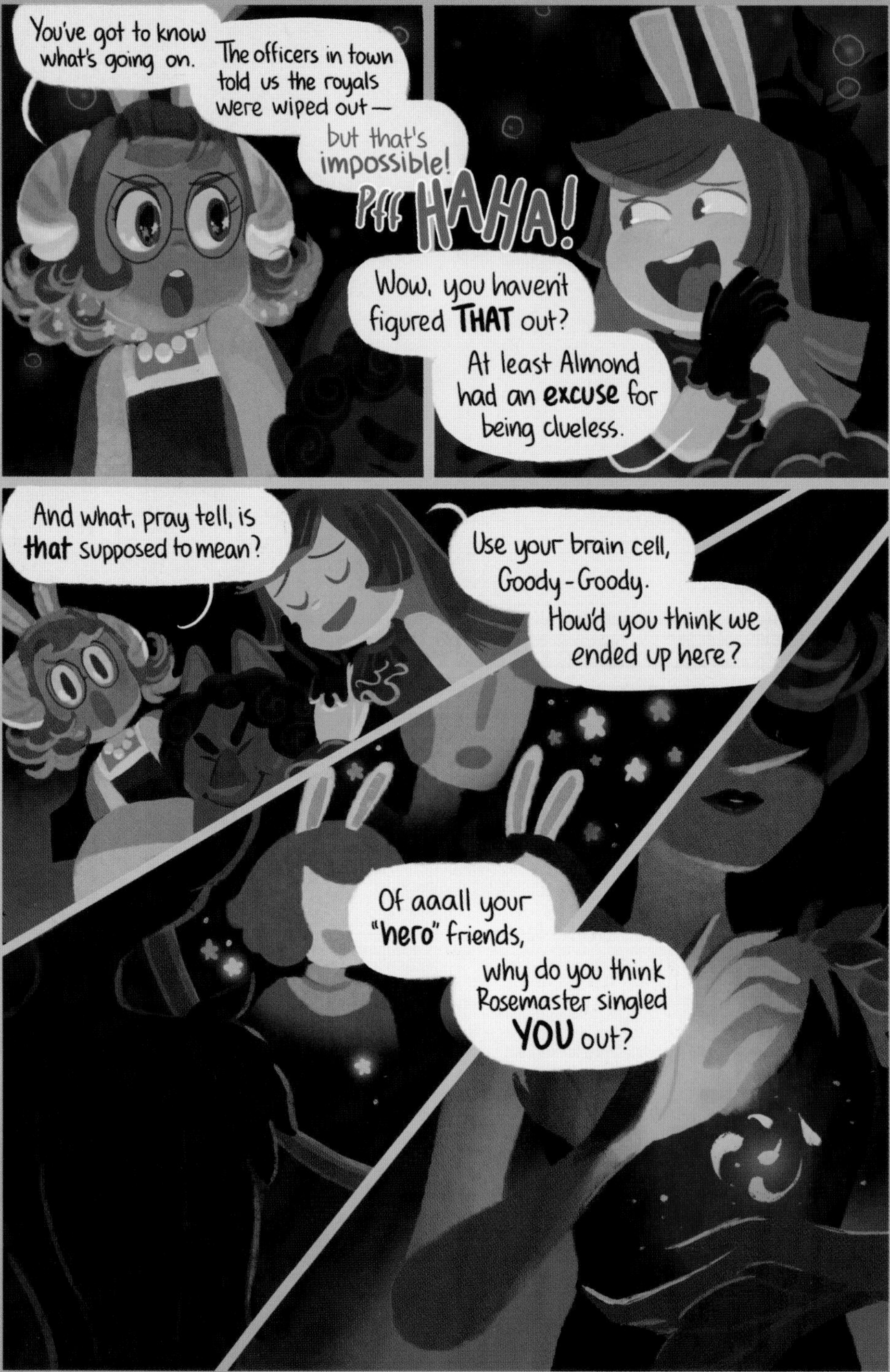
You've got to know what's going on.
The officers in town told us the royals were wiped out—
but that's impossible!
Pff HAHA!
Wow, you haven't figured THAT out?
At least Almond had an excuse for being clueless.
And what, pray tell, is that supposed to mean?
Use your brain cell, Goody-Goody.
How'd you think we ended up here?
Of aaall your "hero" friends,
why do you think Rosemaster singled YOU out?

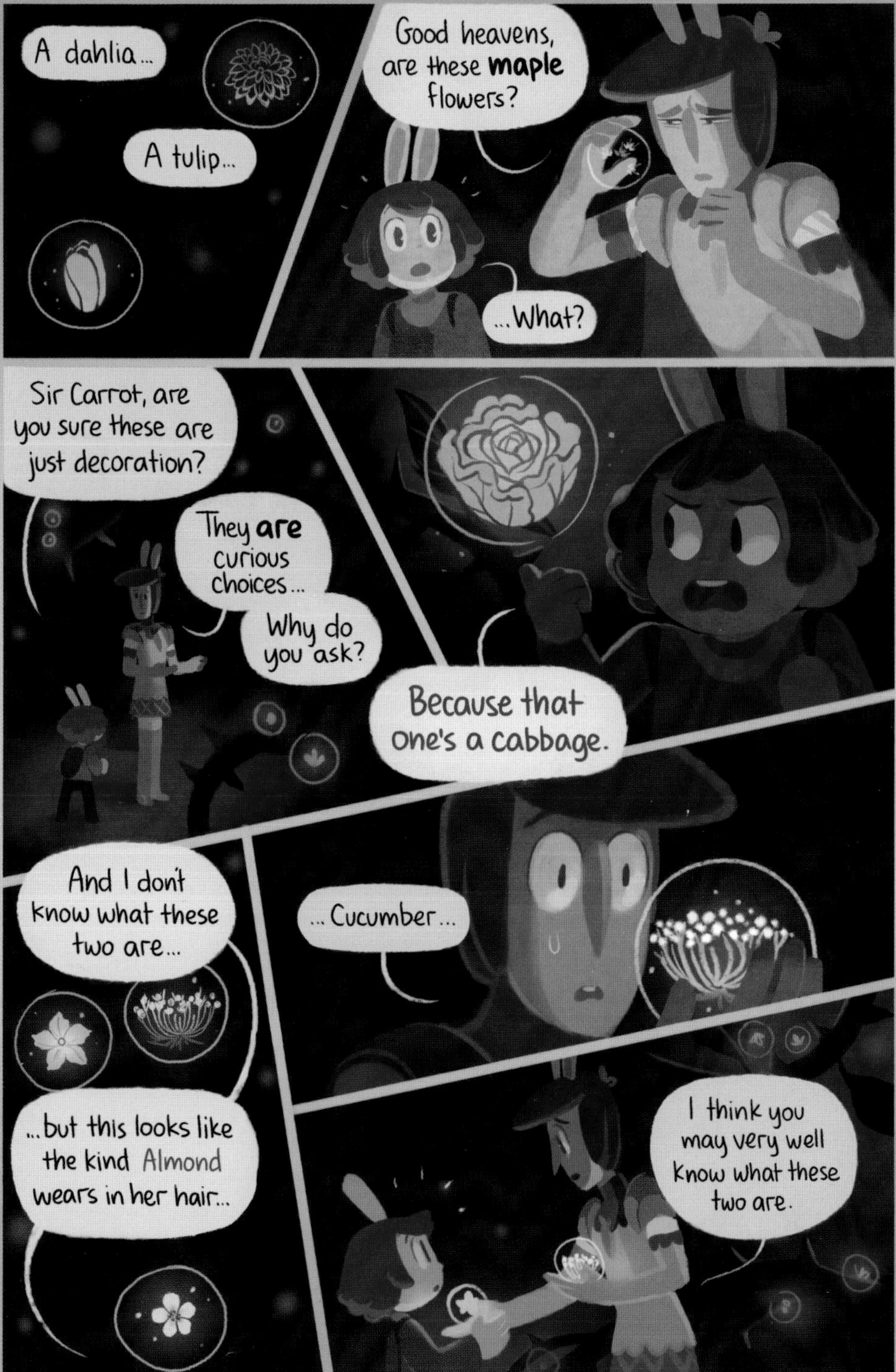

A dahlia...
A tulip...
Good heavens, are these **maple** flowers?
...What?
Sir Carrot, are you sure these are just decoration?
They **are** curious choices...
Why do you ask?
Because that one's a cabbage.
And I don't know what these two are...
...but this looks like the kind Almond wears in her hair...
...Cucumber...
I think you may very well know what these two are.

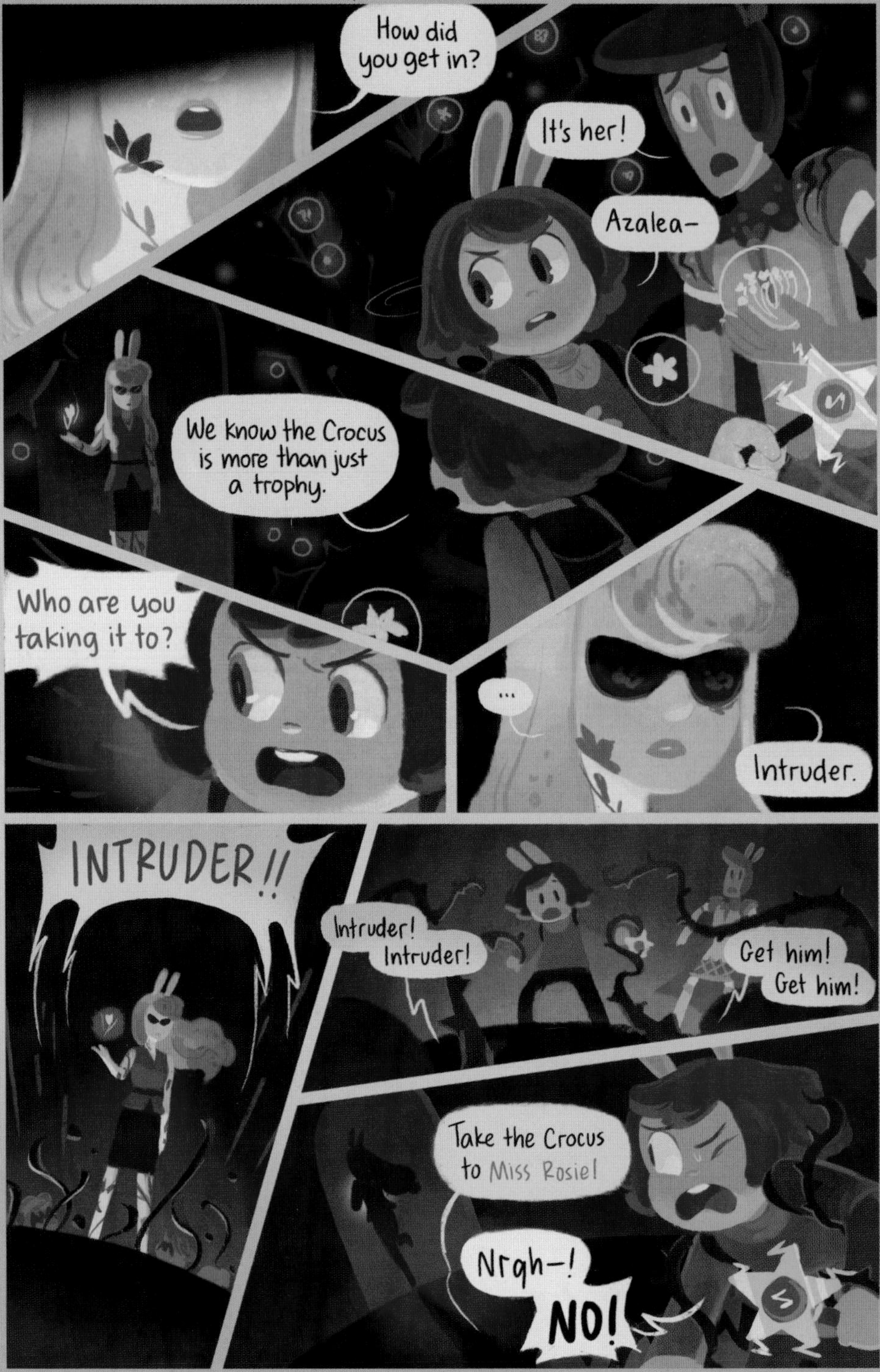
How did you get in?
It's her!
Azalea-
We know the Crocus is more than just a trophy.
Who are you taking it to?
...
Intruder.
INTRUDER!!
Intruder! Intruder!
Get him! Get him!
Take the Crocus to Miss Rosie!
Nrgh-!
NO!

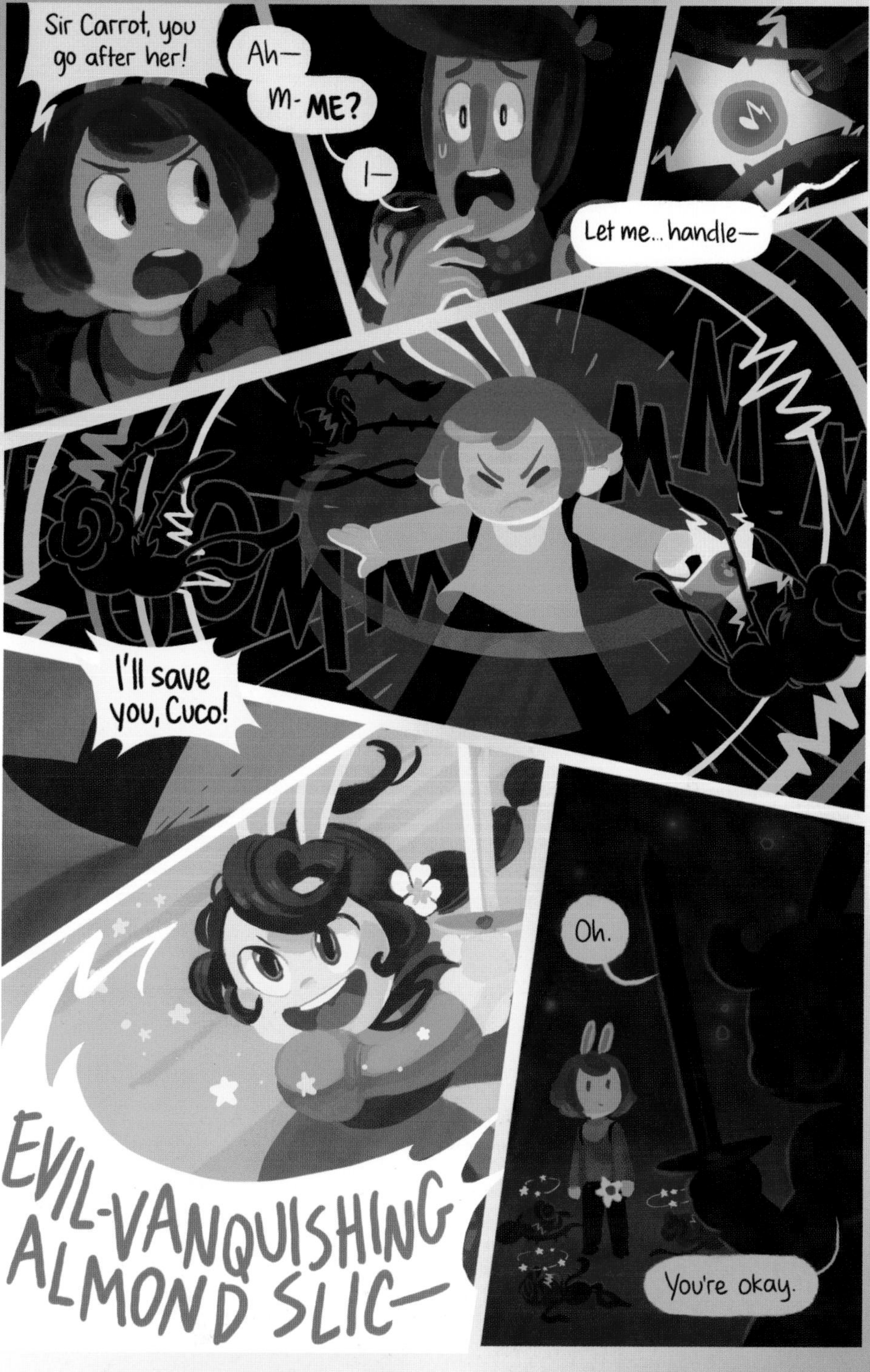

Sir Carrot, you go after her!
Ah— m- ME?
I—
Let me... handle—
I'll save you, Cuco!
EVIL-VANQUISHING ALMOND SLIC—
Oh.
You're okay.

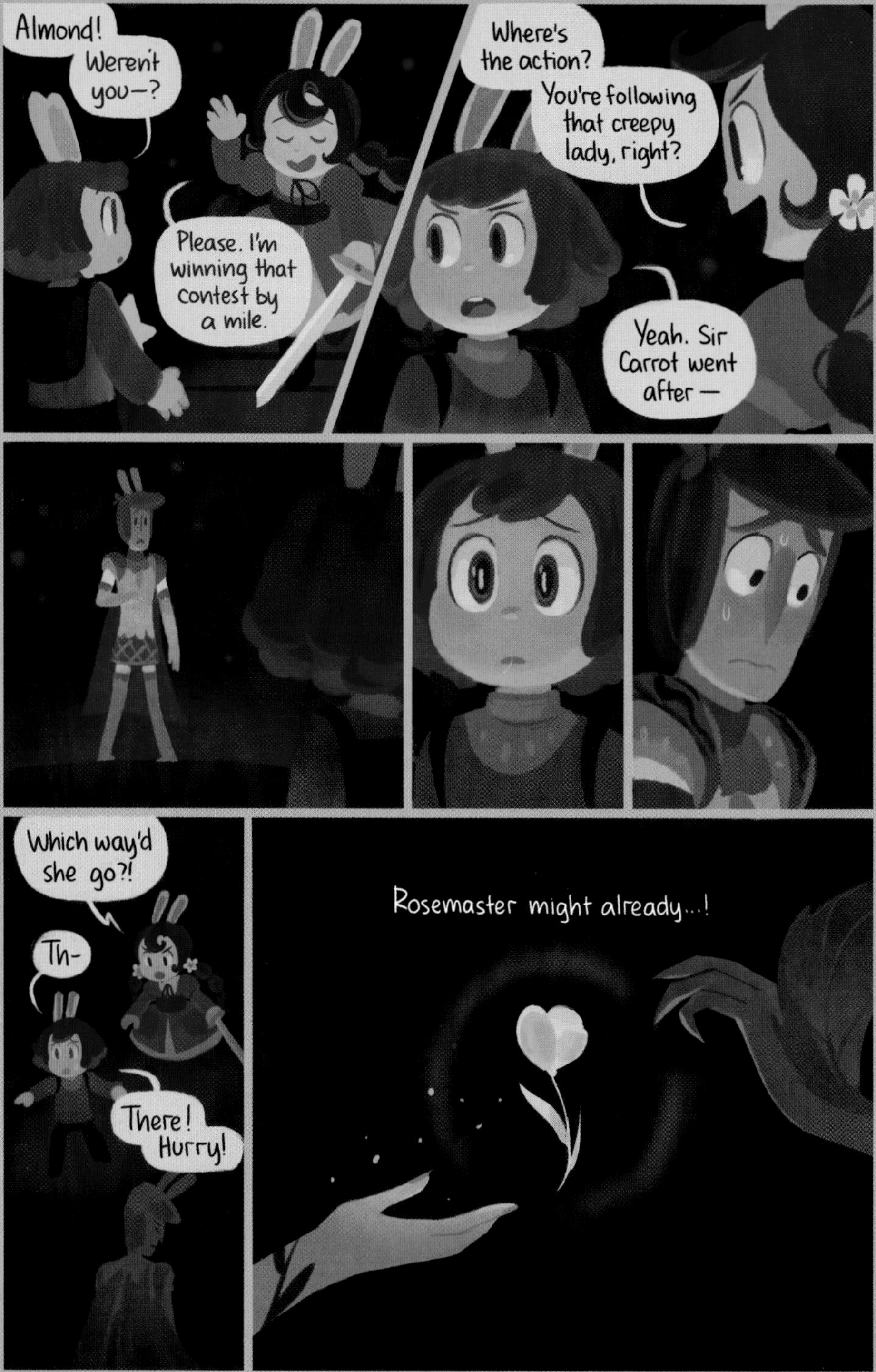

Almond! Weren't you—?
Please. I'm winning that contest by a mile.
Where's the action?
You're following that creepy lady, right?
Yeah. Sir Carrot went after—
Which way'd she go?!
Th-
There! Hurry!
Rosemaster might already...!

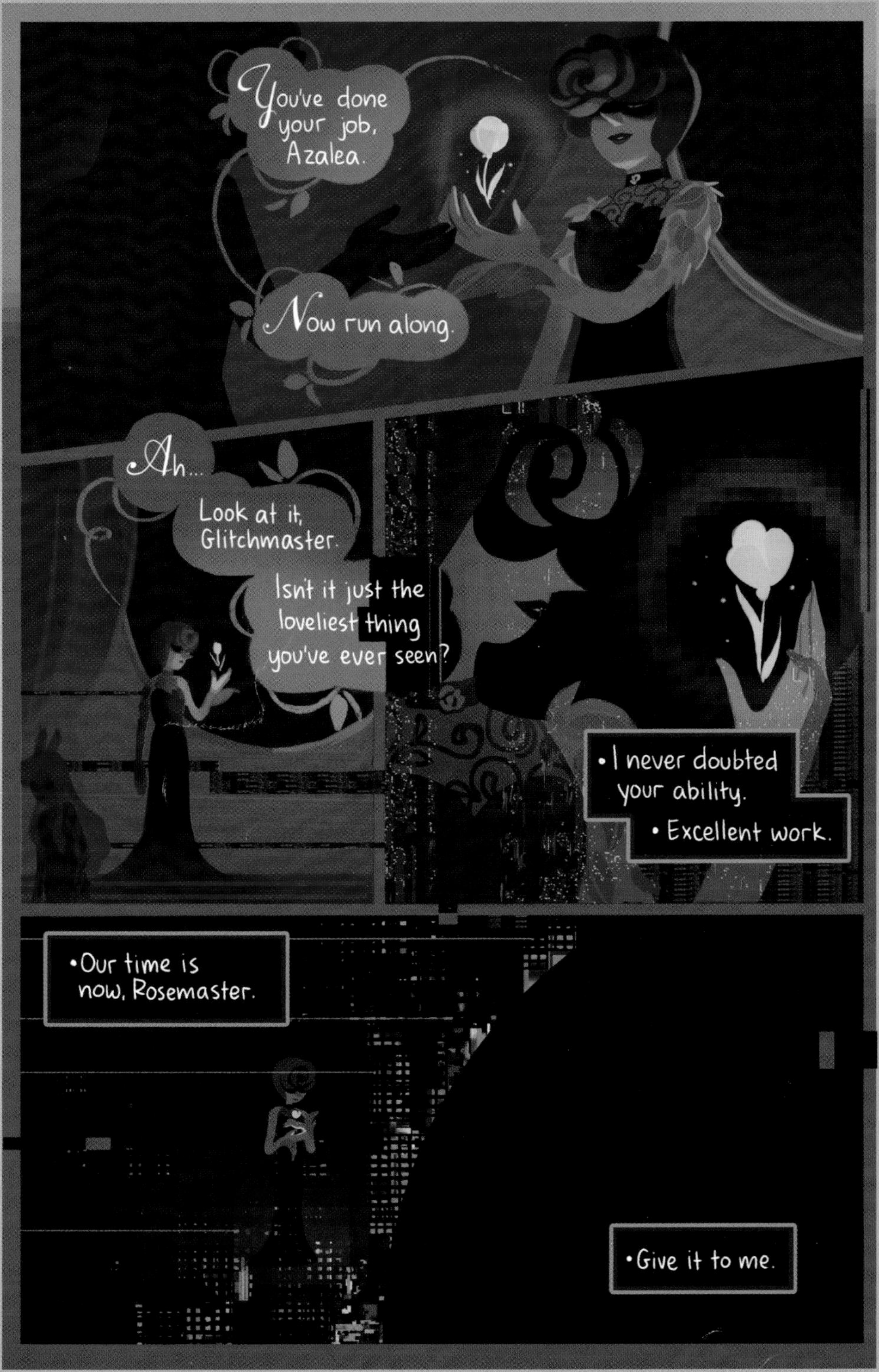
You've done your job, Azalea.
Now run along.
Ah...
Look at it, Glitchmaster.
Isn't it just the loveliest thing you've ever seen?
• I never doubted your ability.
• Excellent work.
• Our time is now, Rosemaster.
• Give it to me.

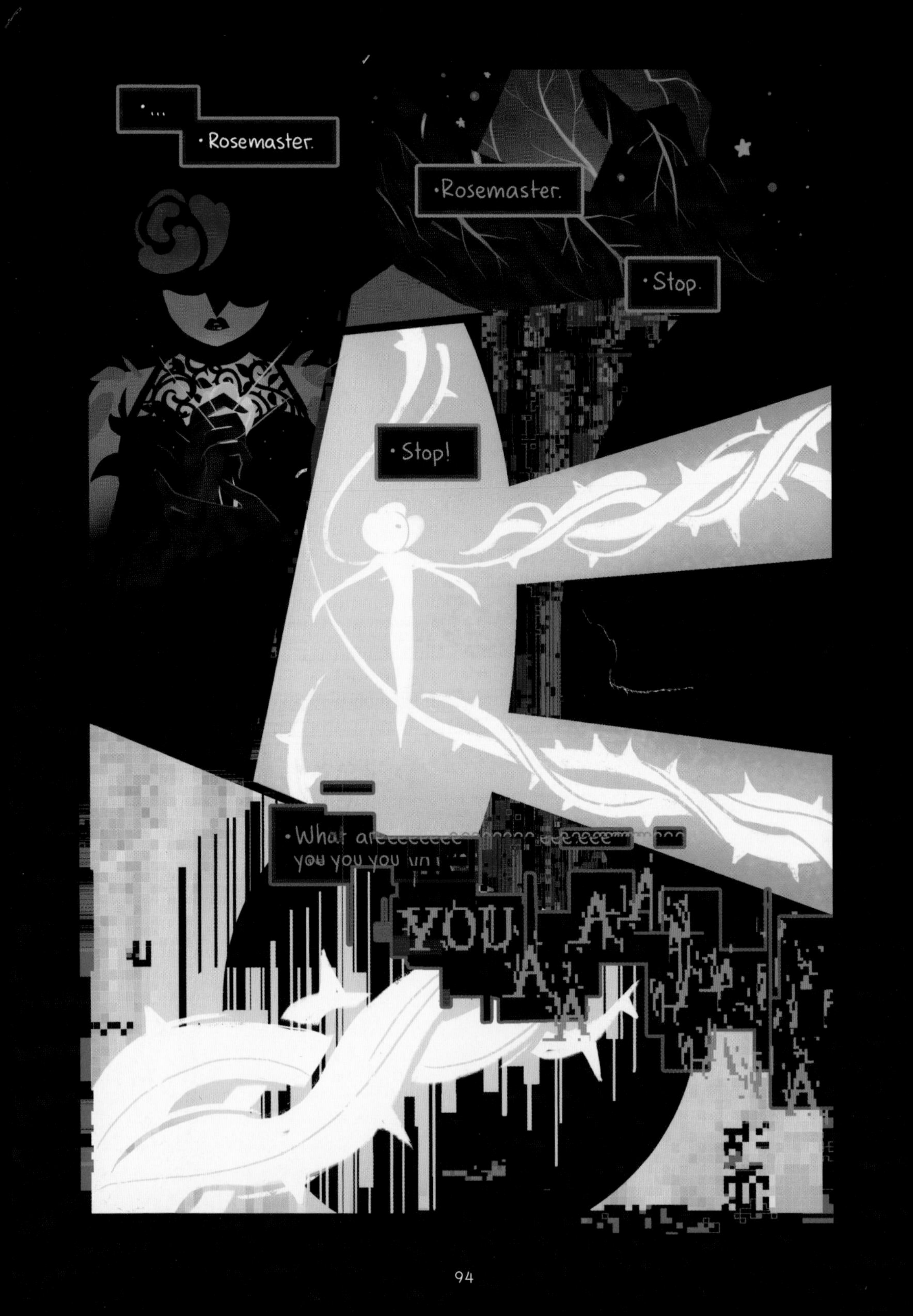
• ...
• Rosemaster.
• Rosemaster.
• Stop.
• Stop!
• What areeeeeeeee
you you you
YOU

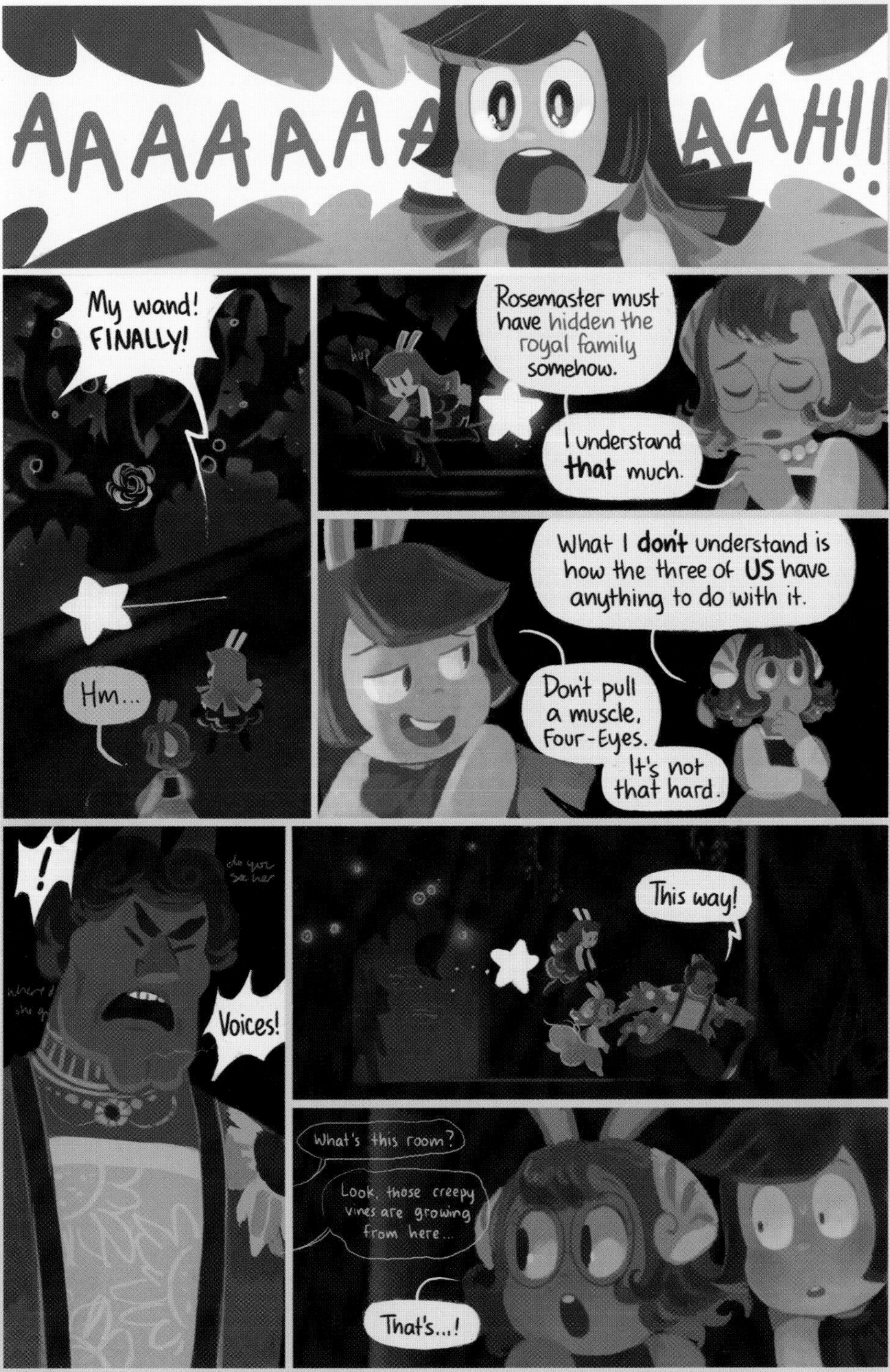
AAAAAAA AAH!!
My wand! FINALLY!
Rosemaster must have hidden the royal family somehow.
I understand that much.
Hm...
What I don't understand is how the three of US have anything to do with it.
Don't pull a muscle, Four-Eyes.
It's not that hard.
!
Voices!
This way!
What's this room?
Look, those creepy vines are growing from here...
That's...!

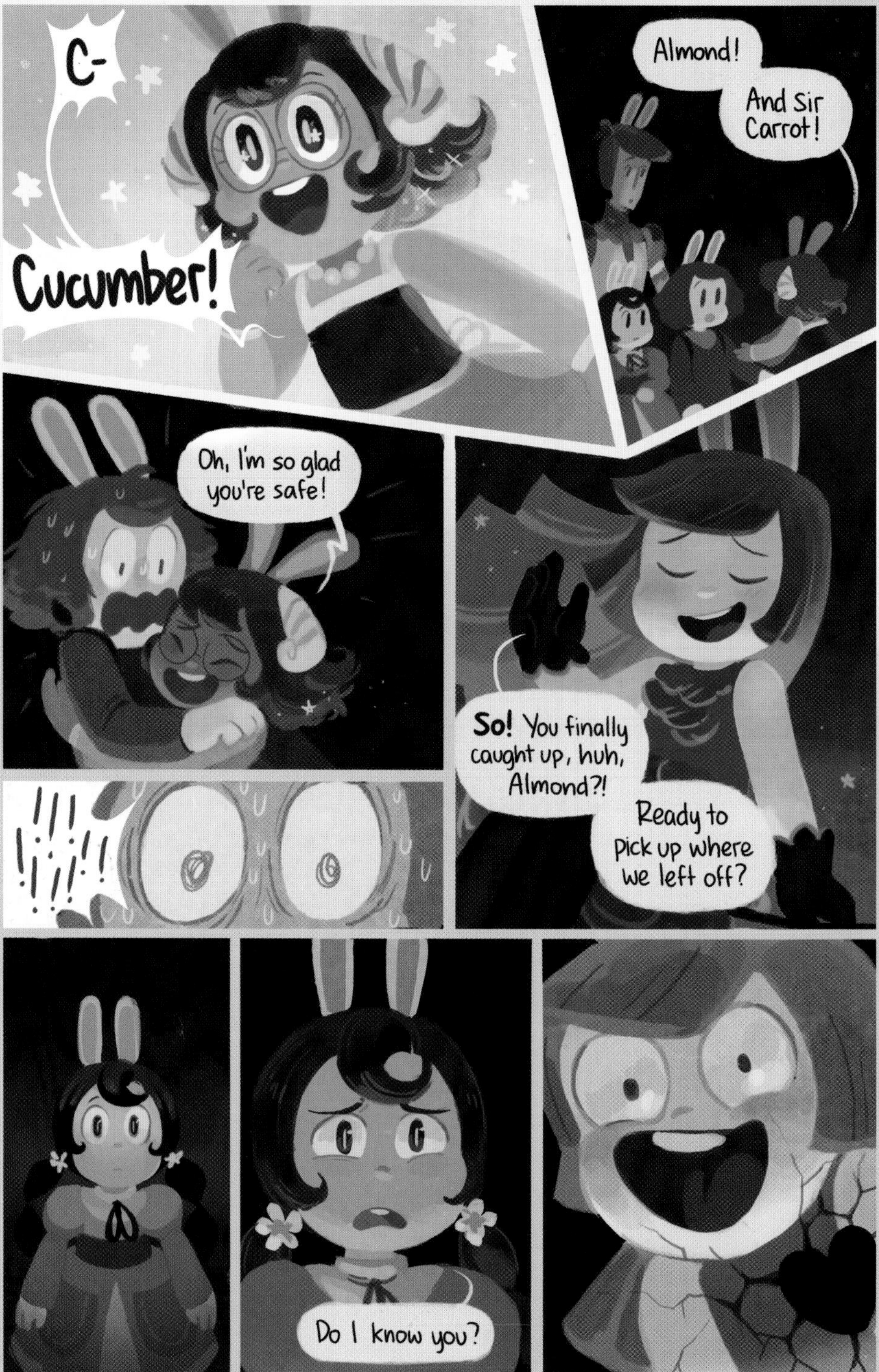
C-
Cucumber!
Almond!
And Sir Carrot!
Oh, I'm so glad you're safe!
So! You finally caught up, huh, Almond?!
Ready to pick up where we left off?
!!!
!!!!!
Do I know you?

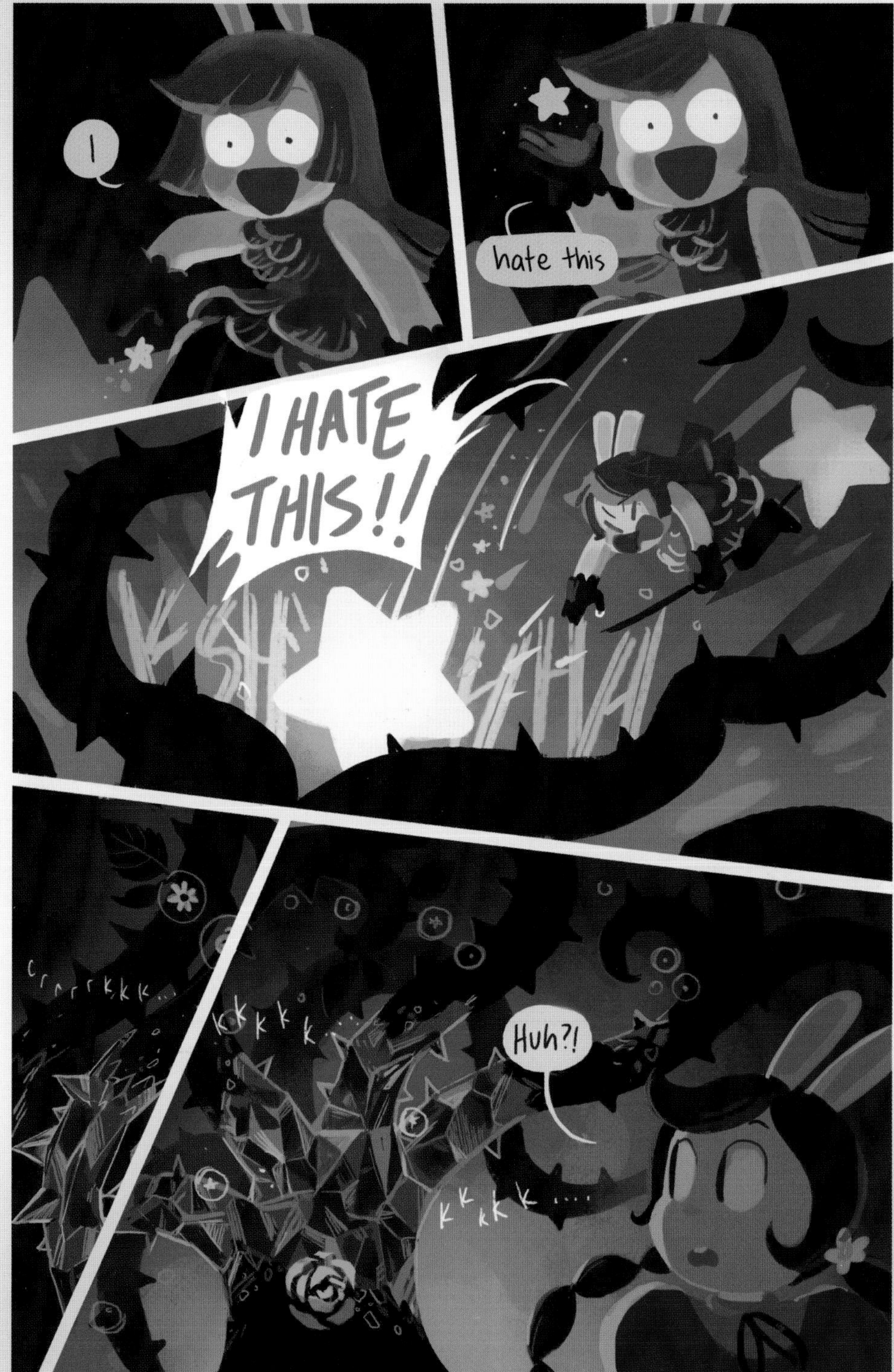
I
hate this
I HATE THIS!!
Crrrrkkk...
kkkkk...
Huh?!
kkkkk....

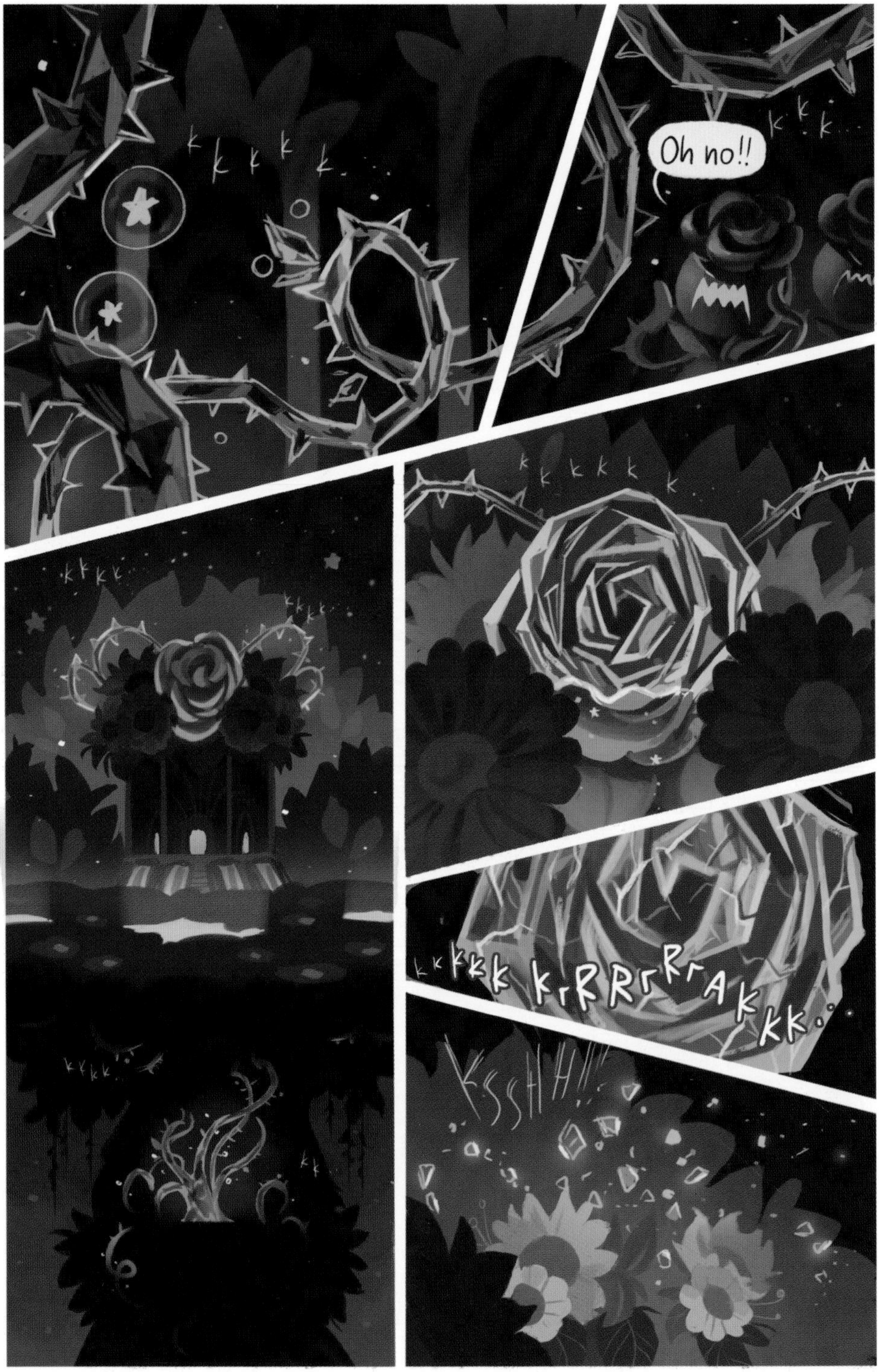
K K K K K . .
K K K . .
Oh no!!
K K K K K K . .
K K K K . .
K K K K . .
K K K K . .
K K
K K K K K K K R R R R R A K K K . .
KSSHH!!!

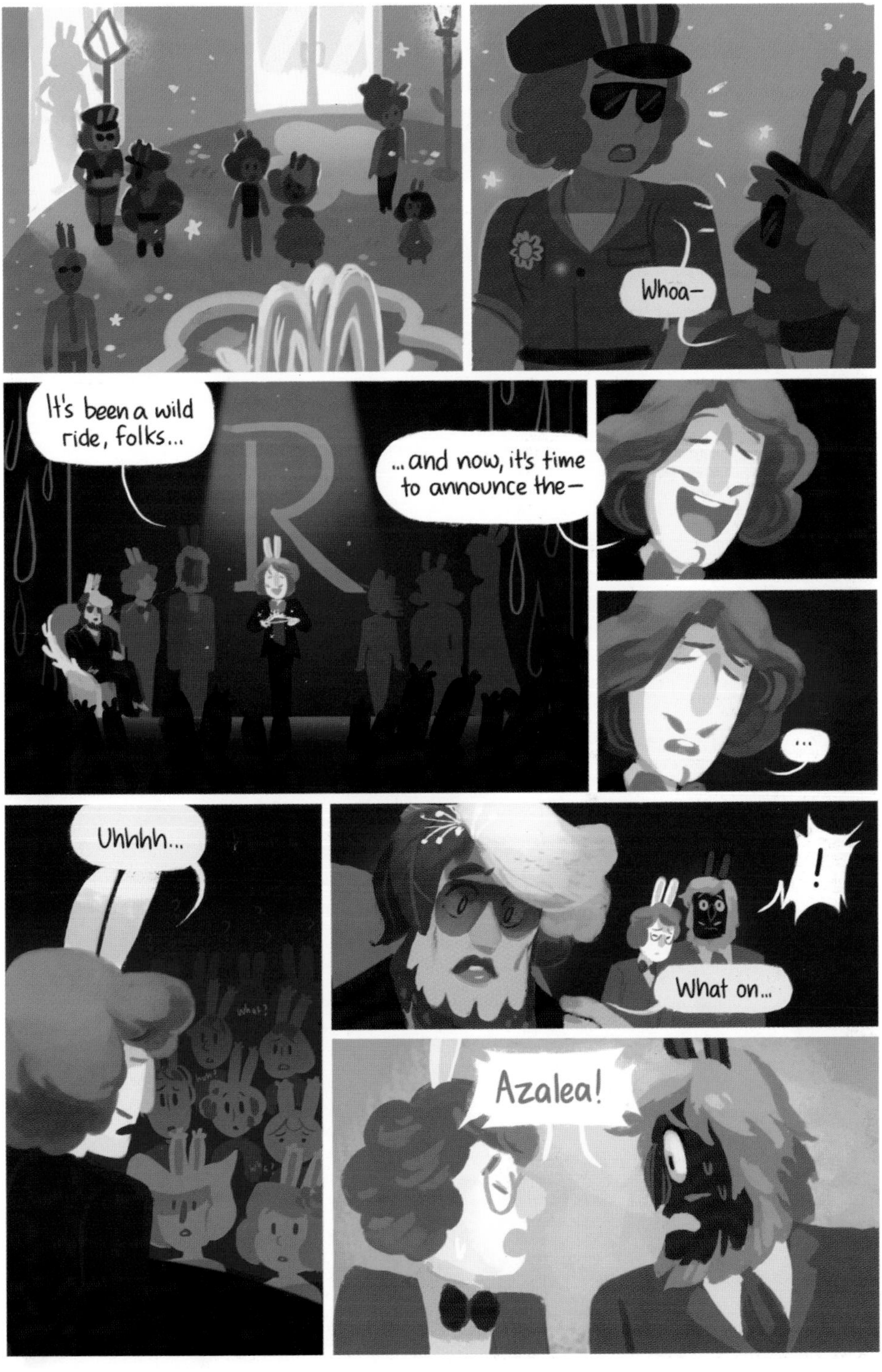
Whoa-
It's been a wild ride, folks...
...and now, it's time to announce the-
...
Uhhhh...
!
What on...
Azalea!

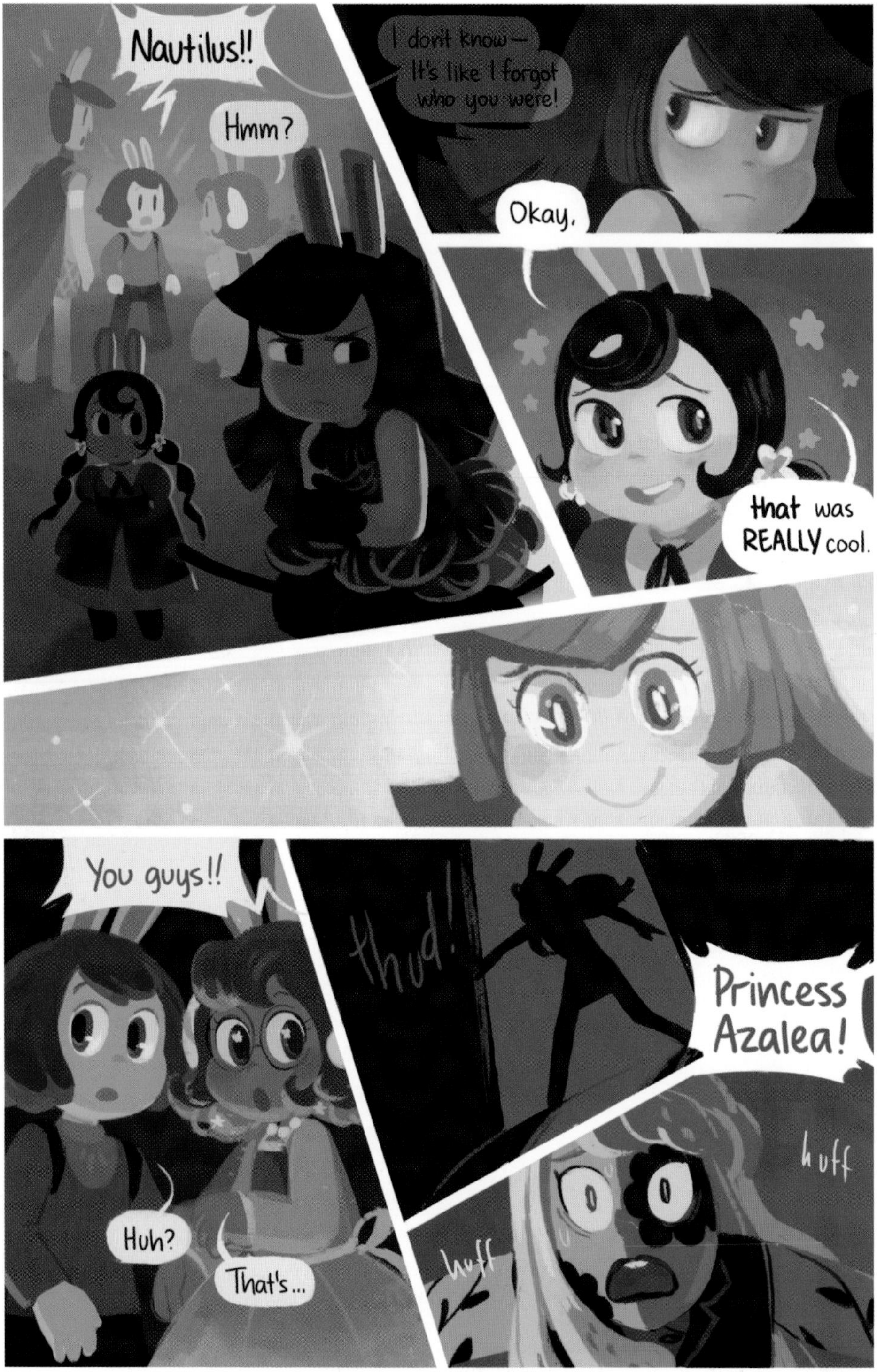
Nautilus!!
Hmm?
I don't know—
It's like I forgot
who you were!
Okay.
that was
REALLY cool.
You guys!!
Huh?
That's...
thud!
Princess
Azalea!
huff
huff

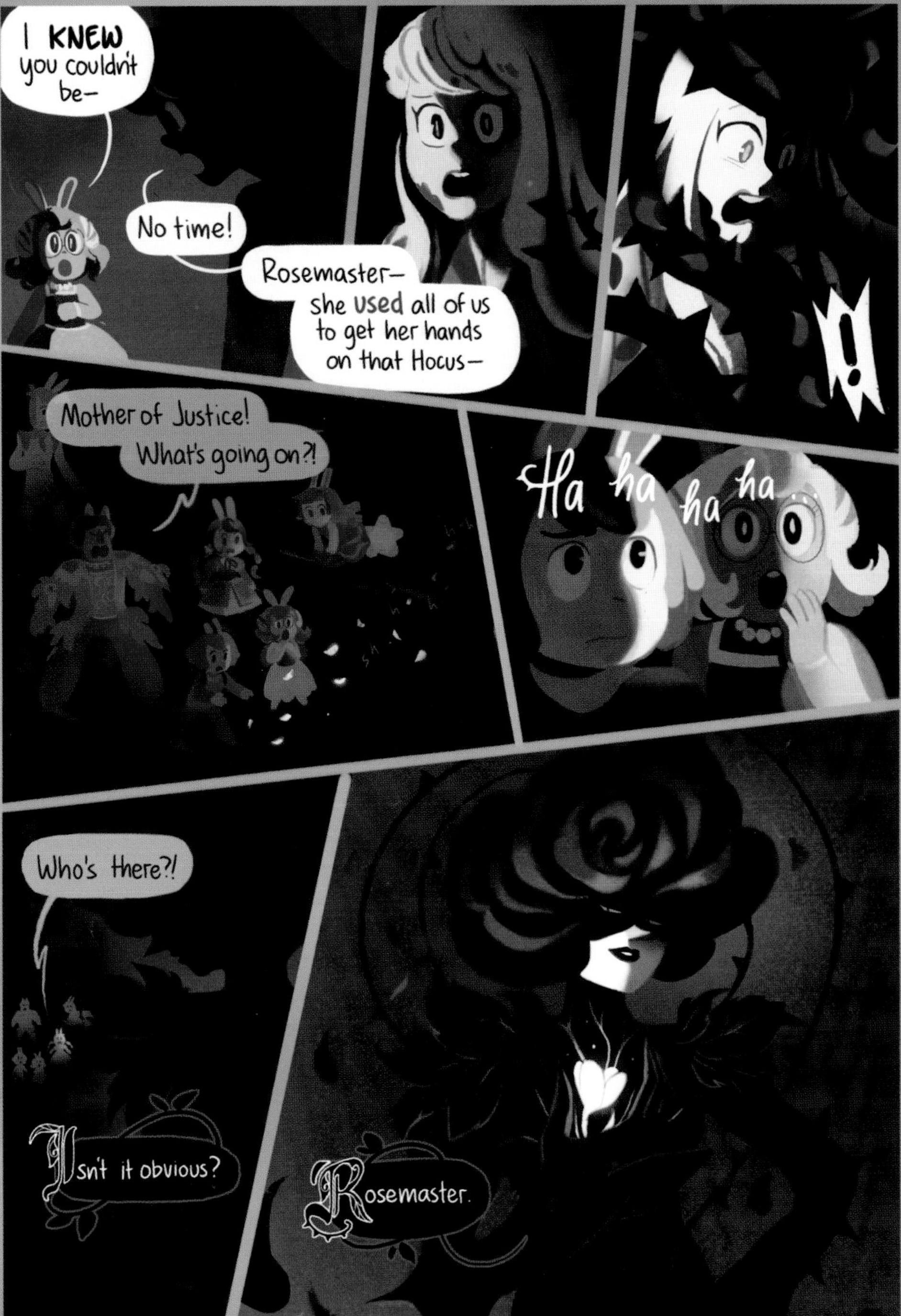
I KNEW you couldn't be–
No time!
Rosemaster– she used all of us to get her hands on that Hocus–
!
Mother of Justice! What's going on?!
Ha ha ha ha
Who's there?!
Isn't it obvious?
Rosemaster.

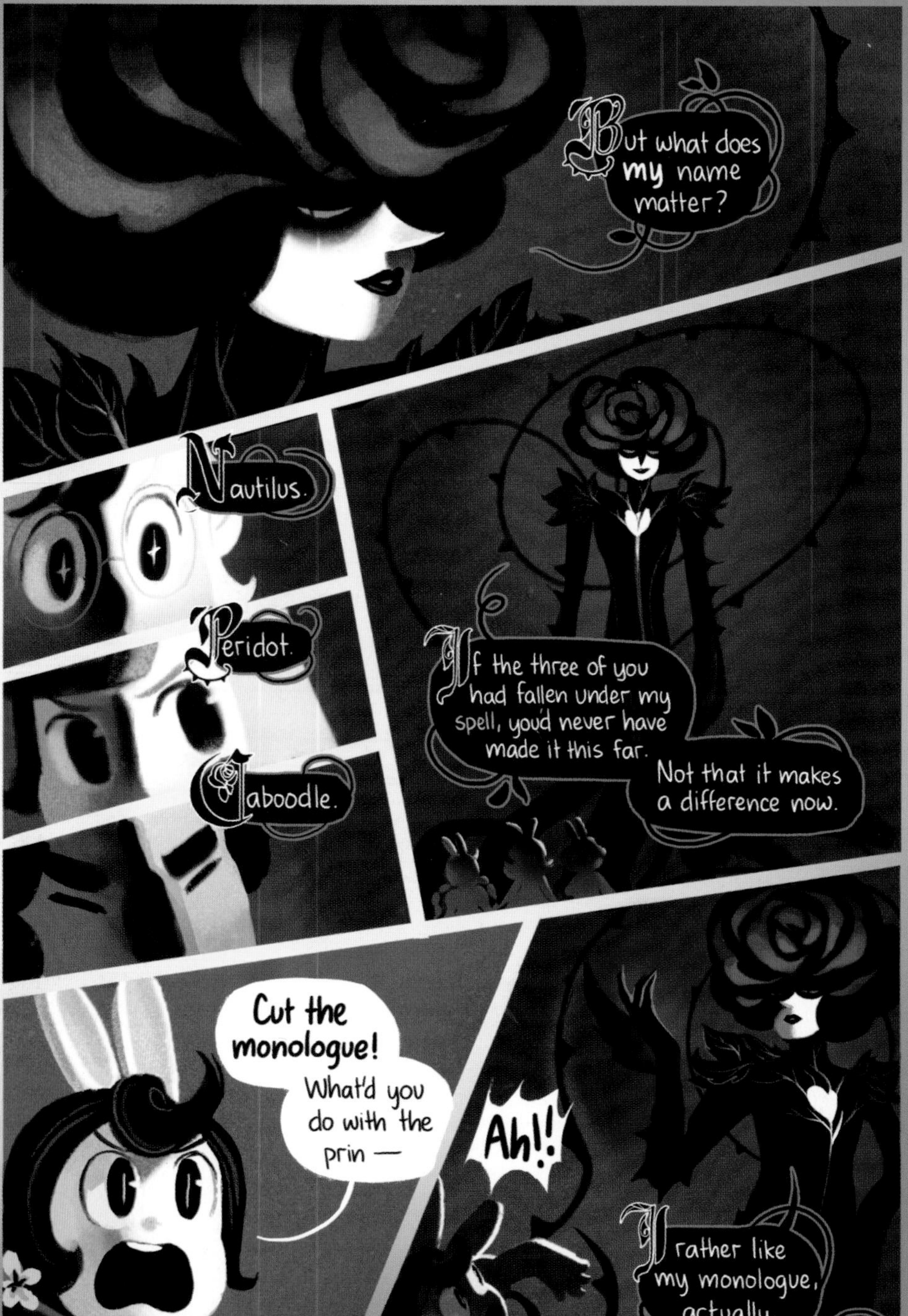

But what does **my** name matter?
Nautilus.
Peridot.
Caboodle.
If the three of you had fallen under my spell, you'd never have made it this far.
Not that it makes a difference now.
Cut the monologue!
What'd you do with the prin —
Ah!!
I rather like my monologue, actually.
No need to be rude.

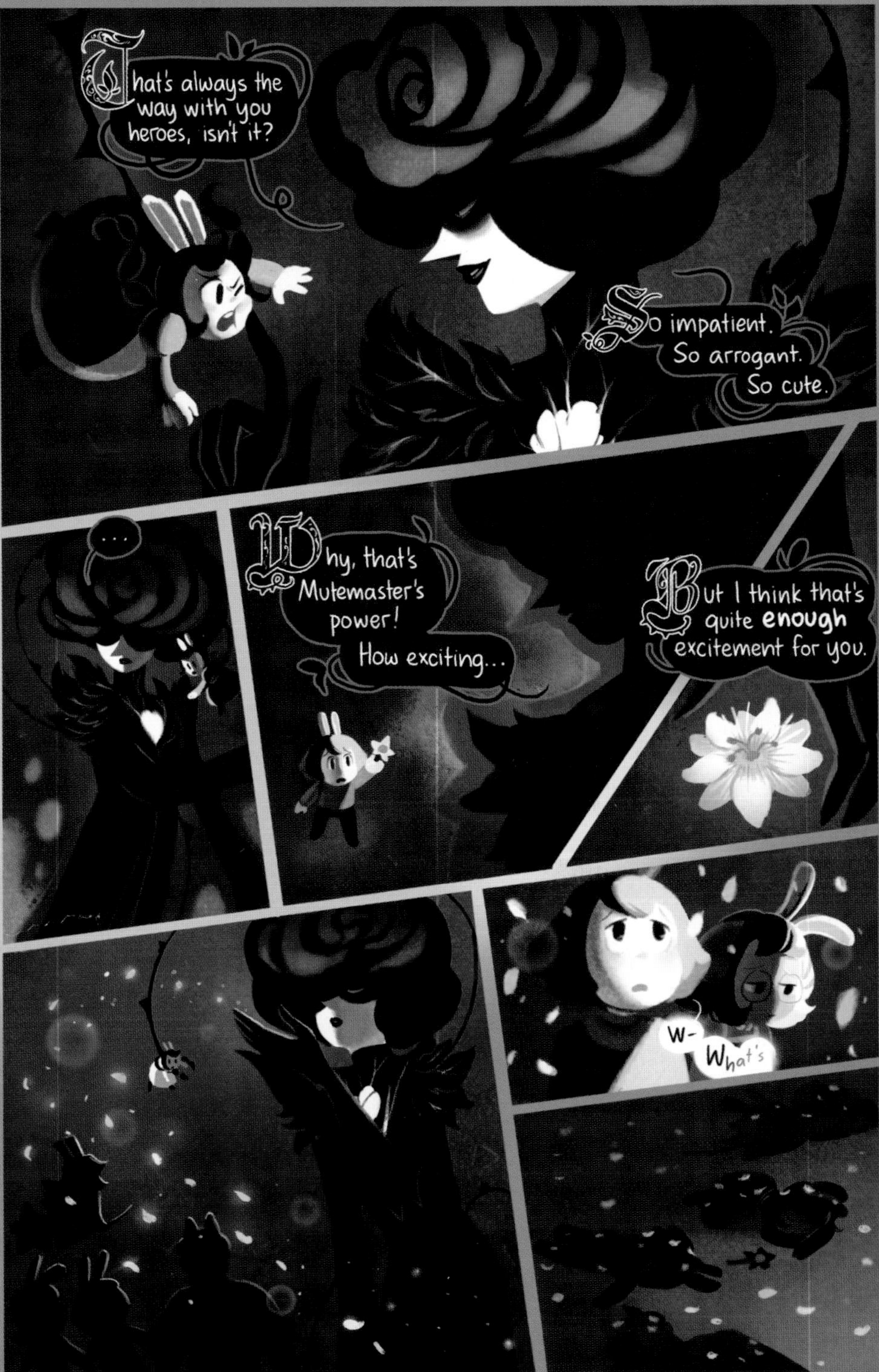
That's always the way with you heroes, isn't it?
So impatient. So arrogant. So cute.
...
Why, that's Mutemaster's power! How exciting...
But I think that's quite **enough** excitement for you.
W-
What's

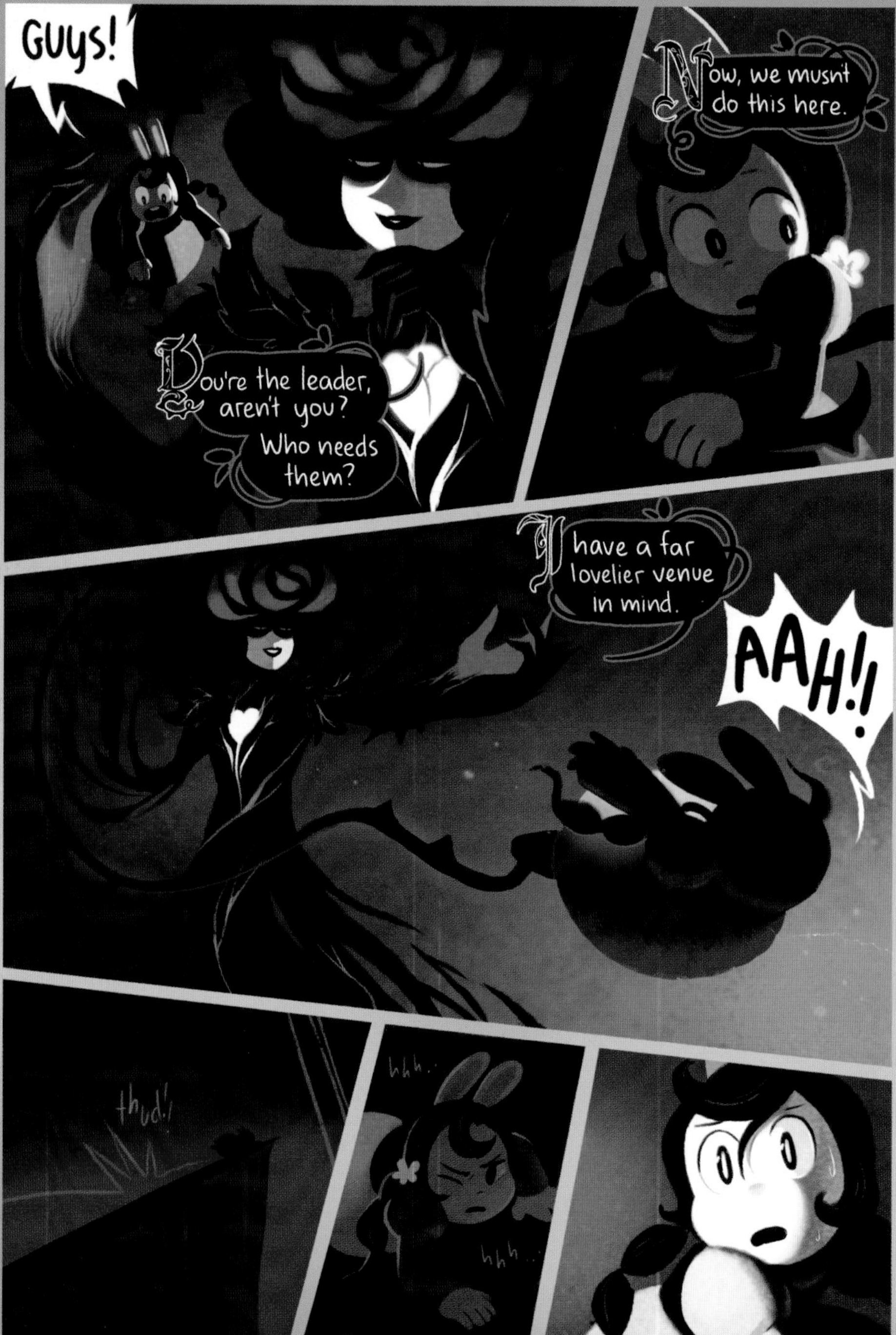
GUYS!
You're the leader, aren't you?
Who needs them?
Now, we musn't do this here.
I have a far lovelier venue in mind.
AAH!!
thud!
hhh..
hhh..

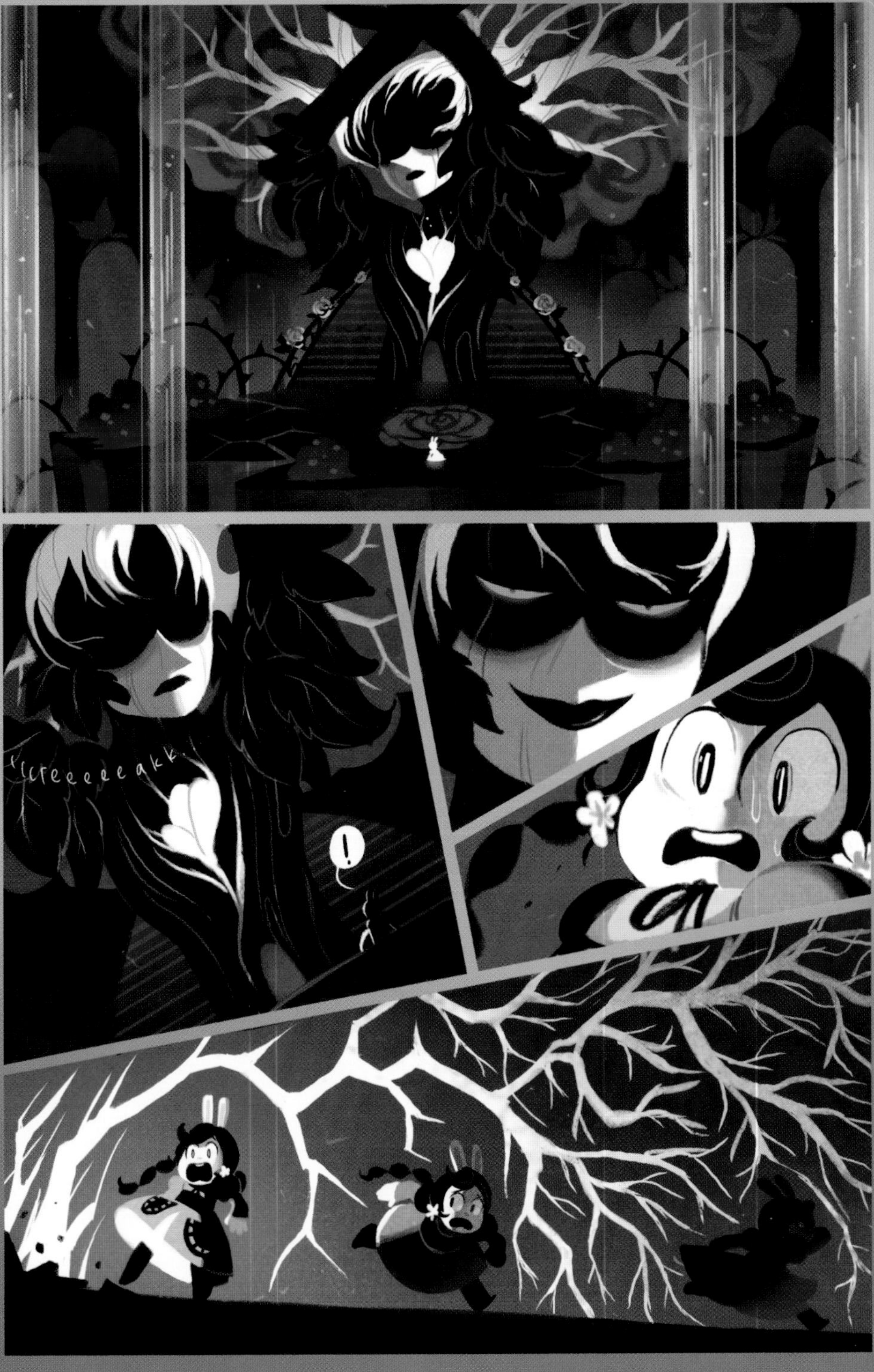
creeeeeakk
!

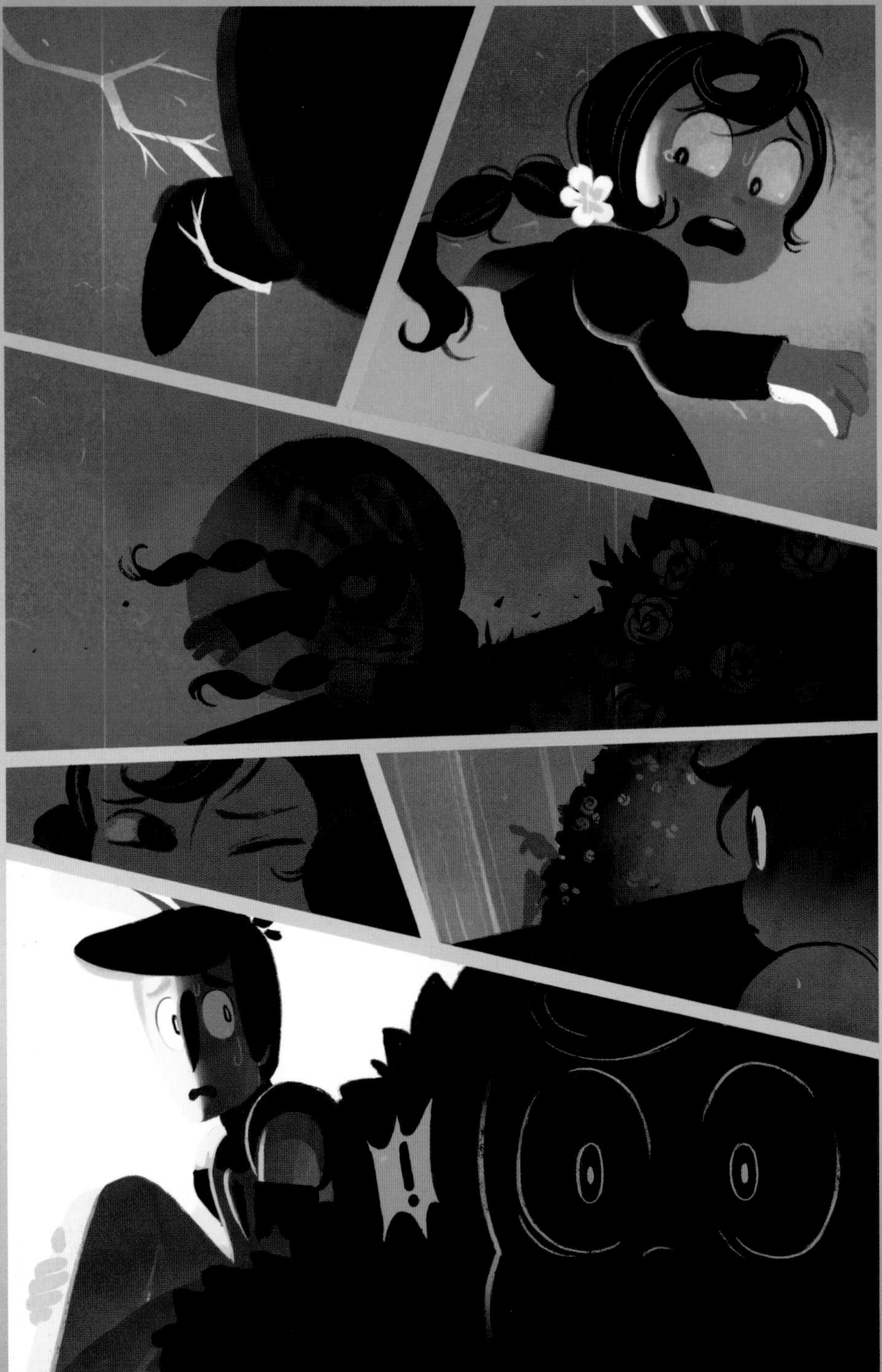
!

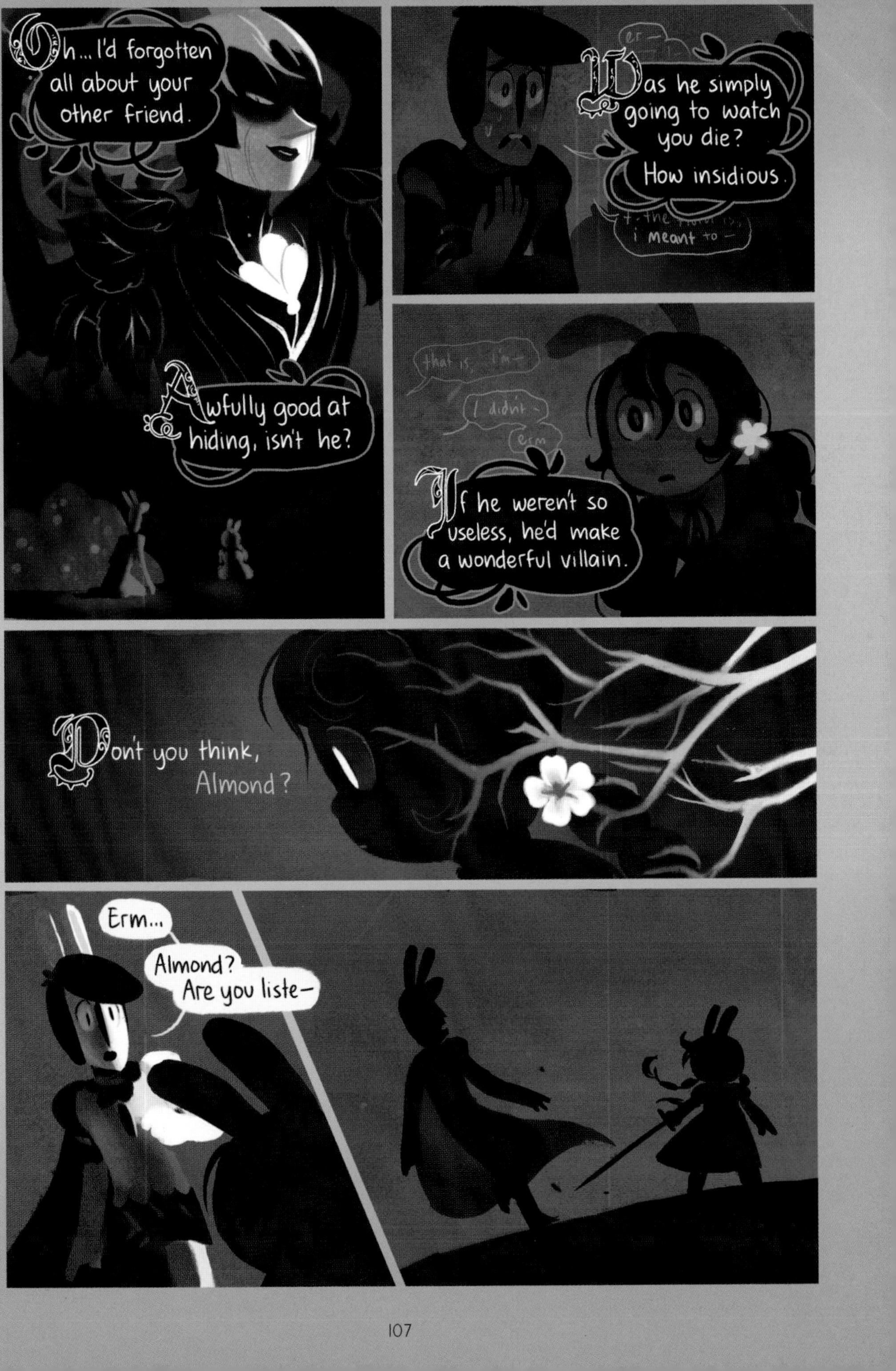

Oh... I'd forgotten all about your other friend.
er—
Was he simply going to watch you die?
How insidious.
i meant to—
Awfully good at hiding, isn't he?
that is, I'm—
I didn't
erm
If he weren't so useless, he'd make a wonderful villain.
Don't you think, Almond?
Erm...
Almond? Are you liste—

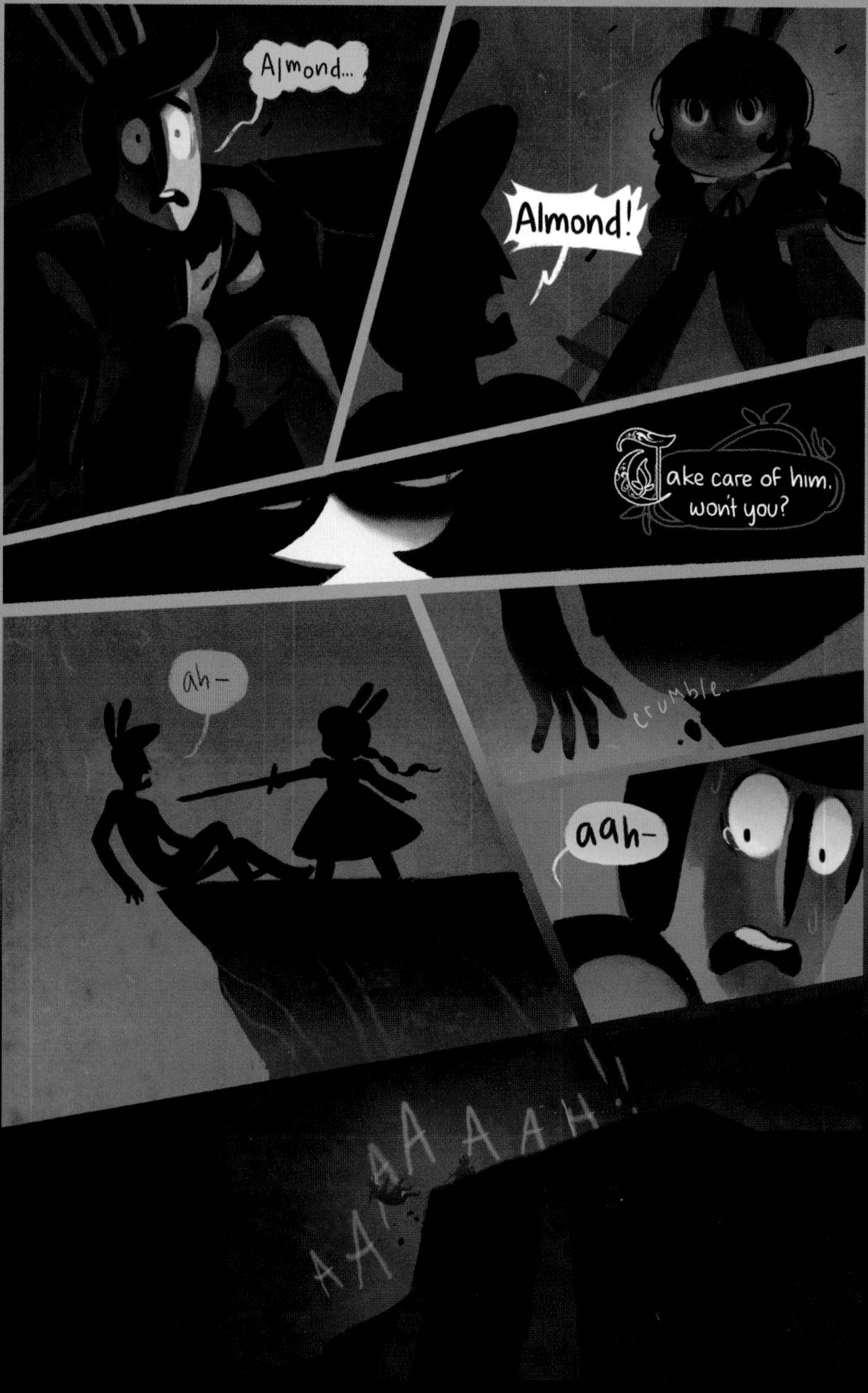
Almond...
Almond!
Take care of him, won't you?
ah-
crumble.
aah-
AAAAAAAH!!

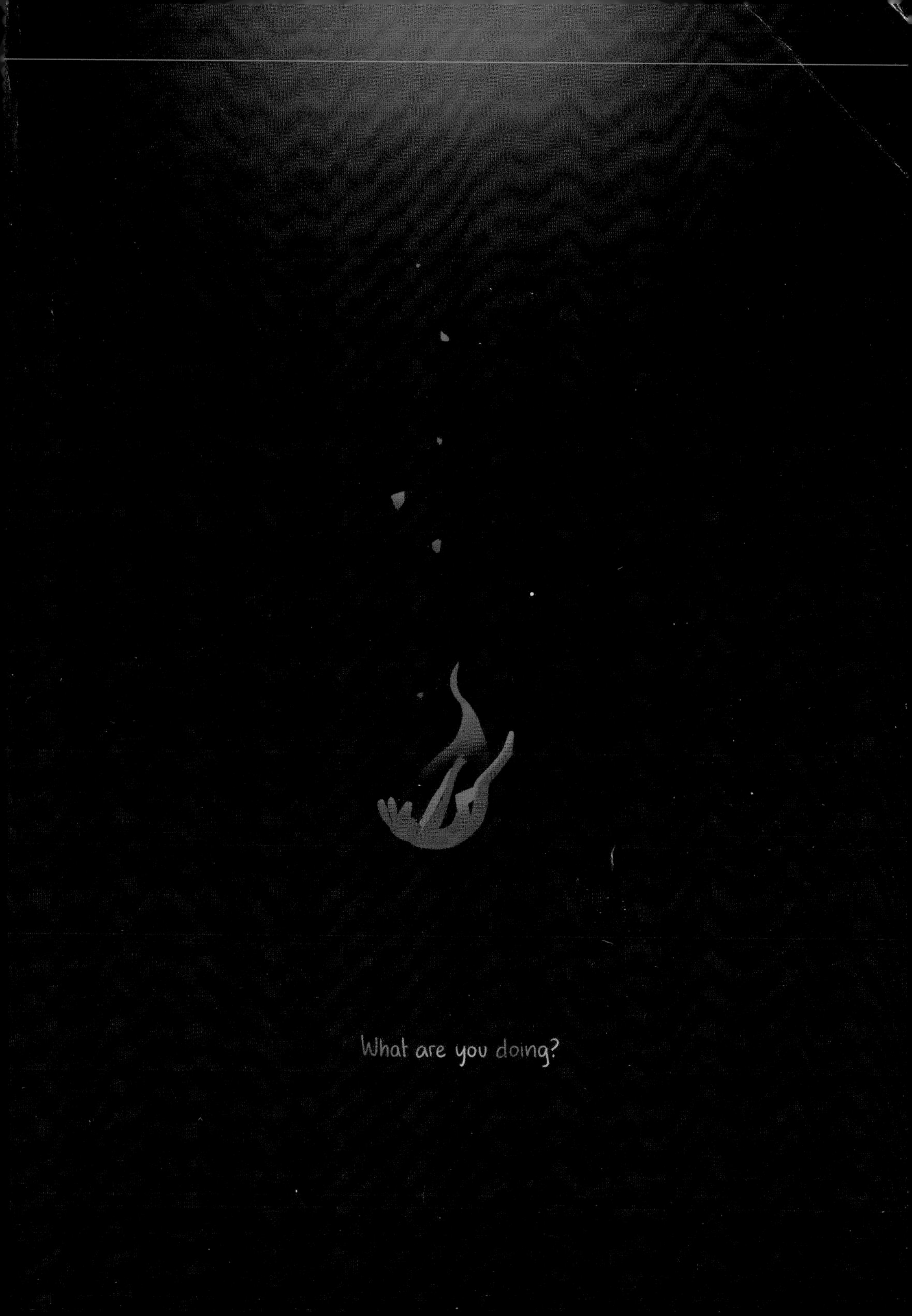
What are you doing?

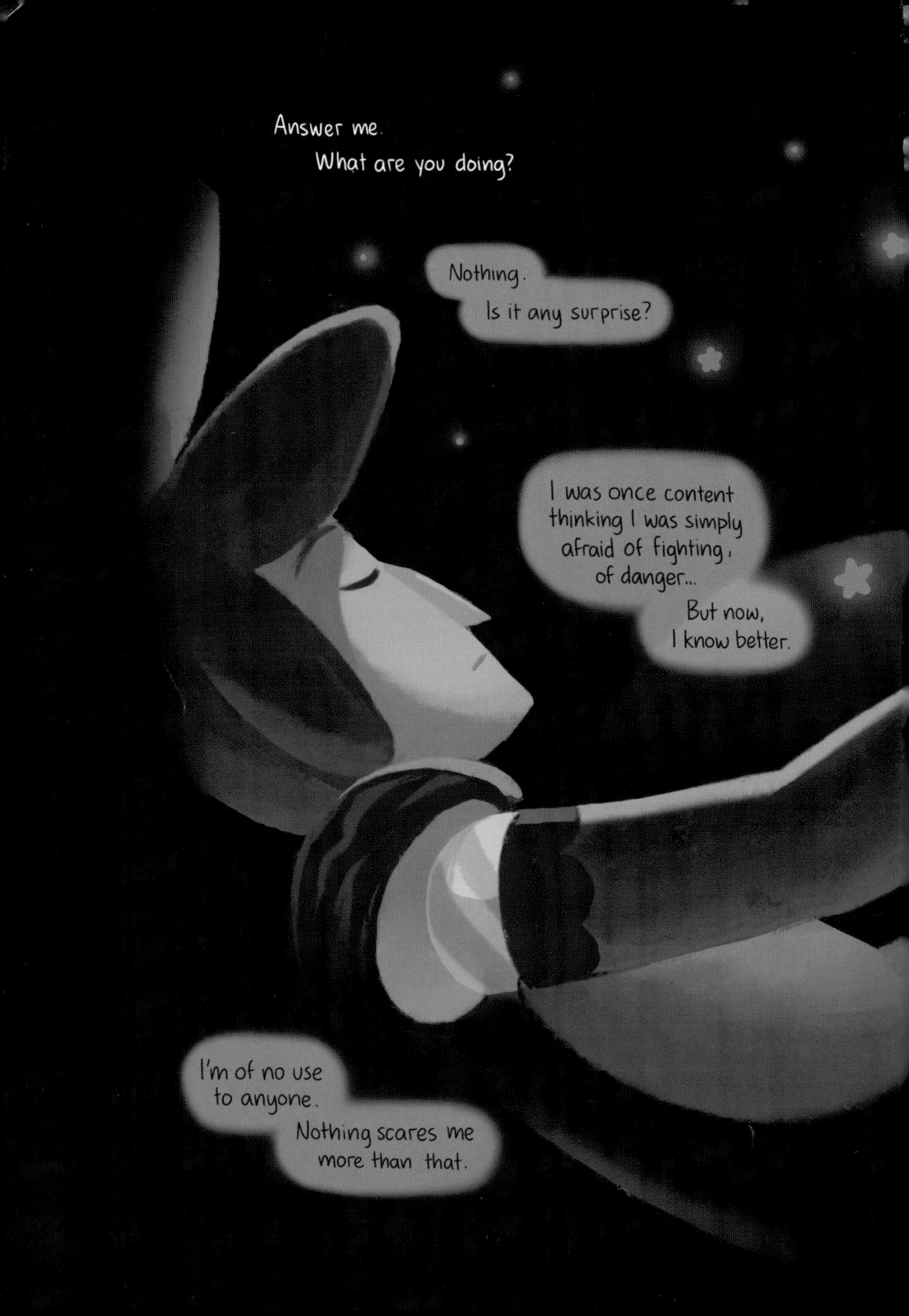
Answer me.
What are you doing?
Nothing.
Is it any surprise?
I was once content thinking I was simply afraid of fighting, of danger...
But now, I know better.
I'm of no use to anyone.
Nothing scares me more than that.

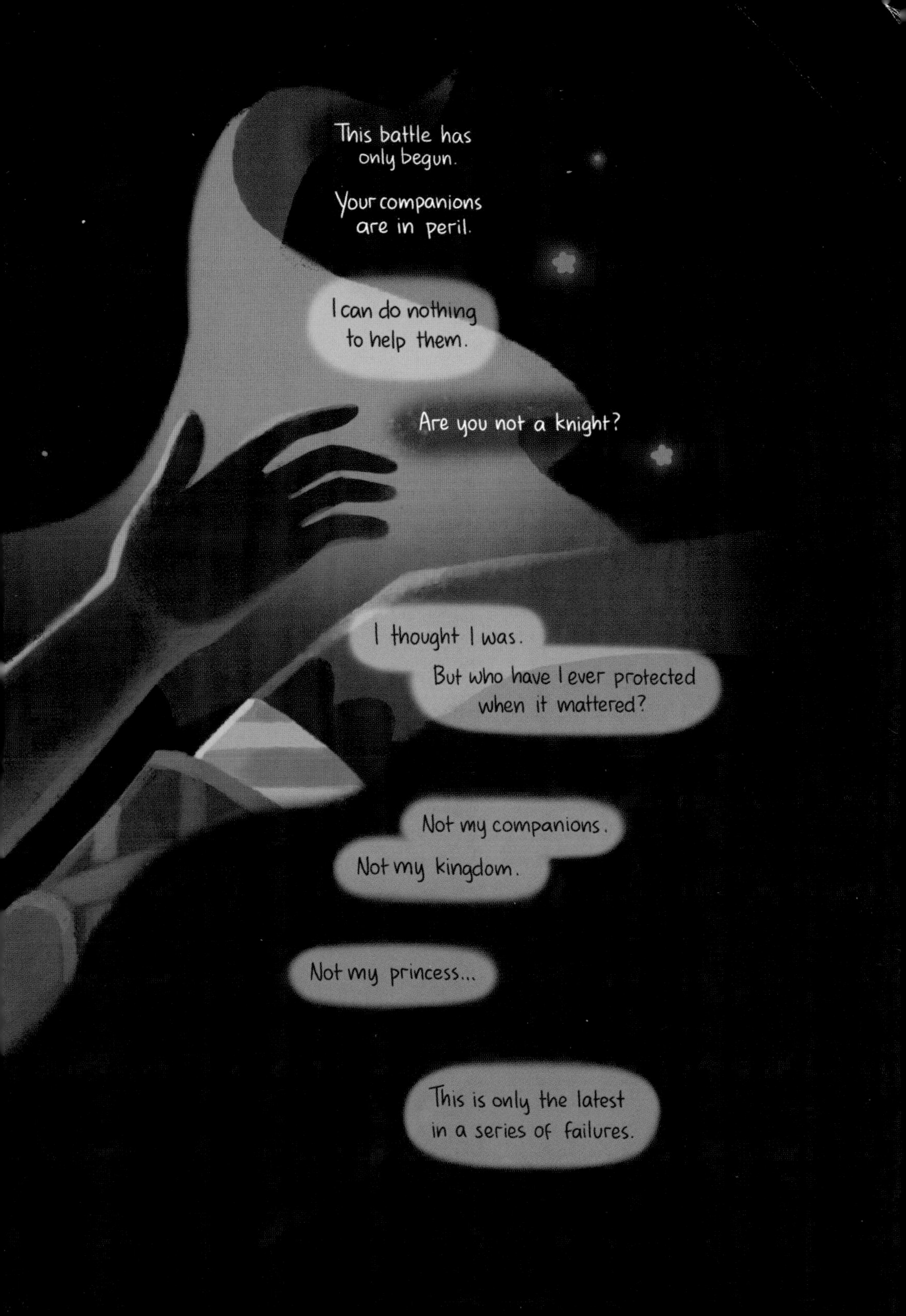
This battle has only begun.
Your companions are in peril.
I can do nothing to help them.
Are you not a knight?
I thought I was.
But who have I ever protected when it mattered?
Not my companions.
Not my kingdom.
Not my princess...
This is only the latest in a series of failures.

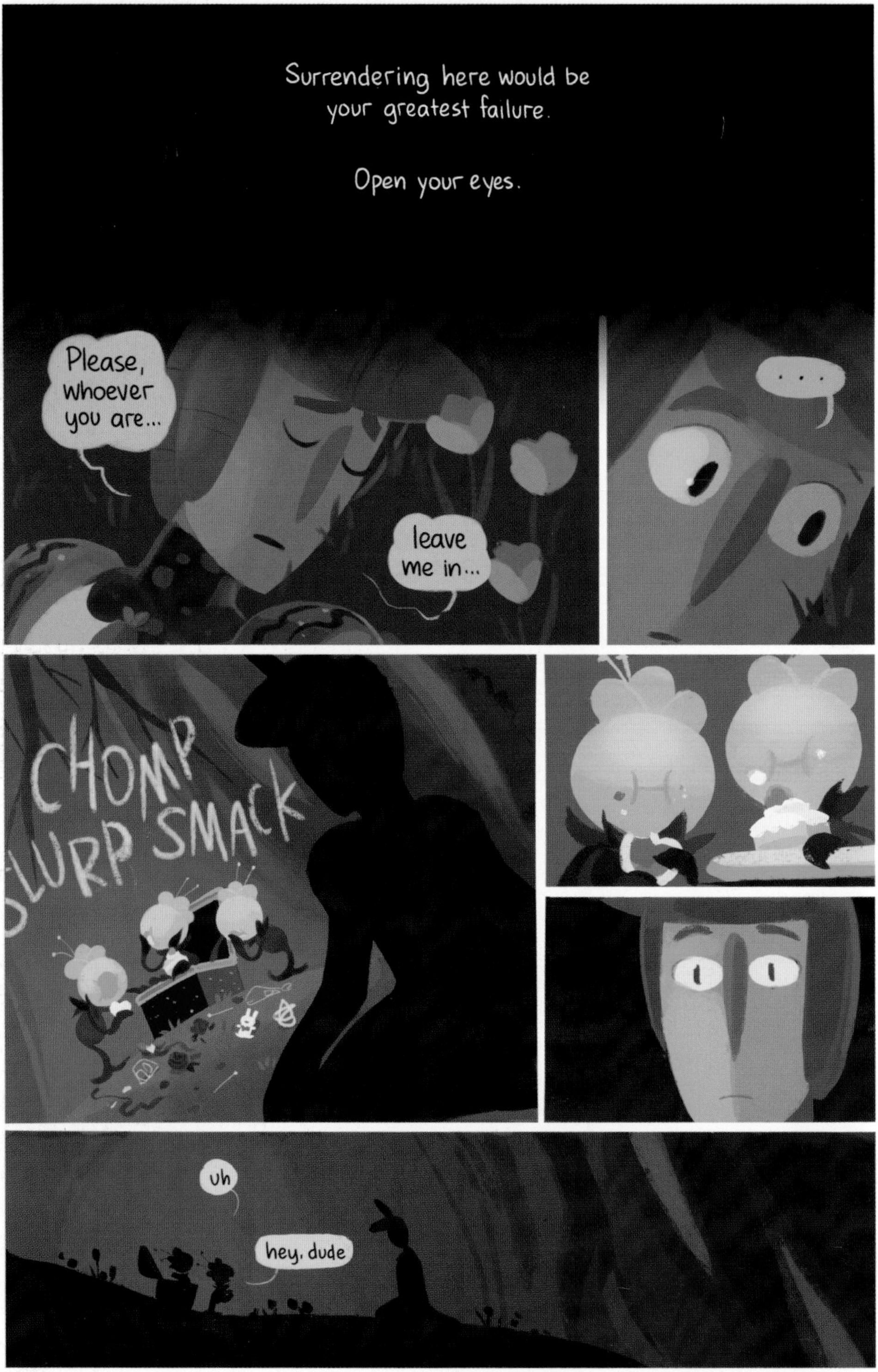
Surrendering here would be your greatest failure.
Open your eyes.
Please, whoever you are...
leave me in...
...
CHOMP
SLURP SMACK
uh
hey, dude

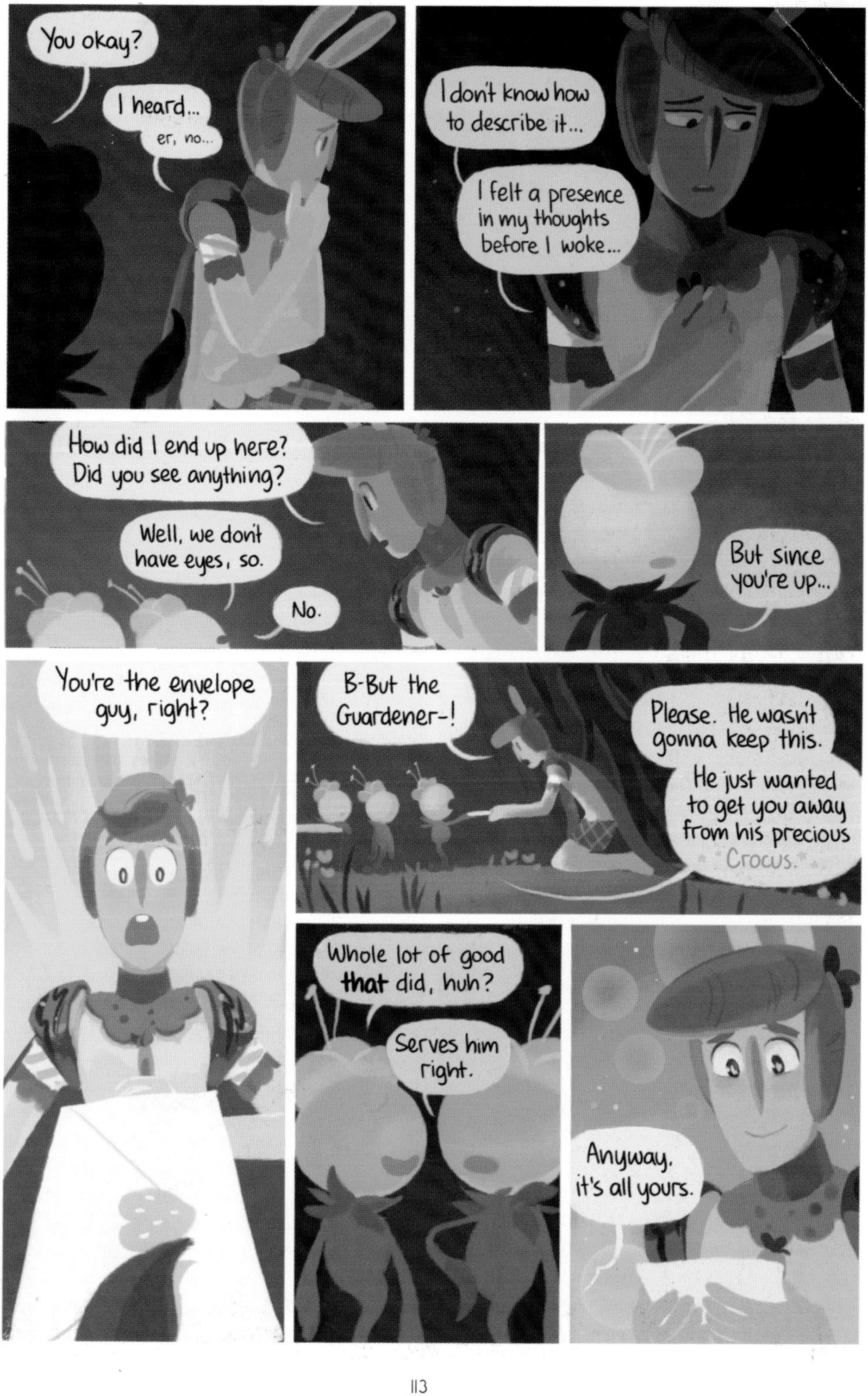
You okay?
I heard...
er, no...
I don't know how to describe it...
I felt a presence in my thoughts before I woke...
How did I end up here? Did you see anything?
Well, we don't have eyes, so.
No.
But since you're up...
You're the envelope guy, right?
B-But the Guardener-!
Please. He wasn't gonna keep this.
He just wanted to get you away from his precious Crocus.
Whole lot of good **that** did, huh?
Serves him right.
Anyway, it's all yours.

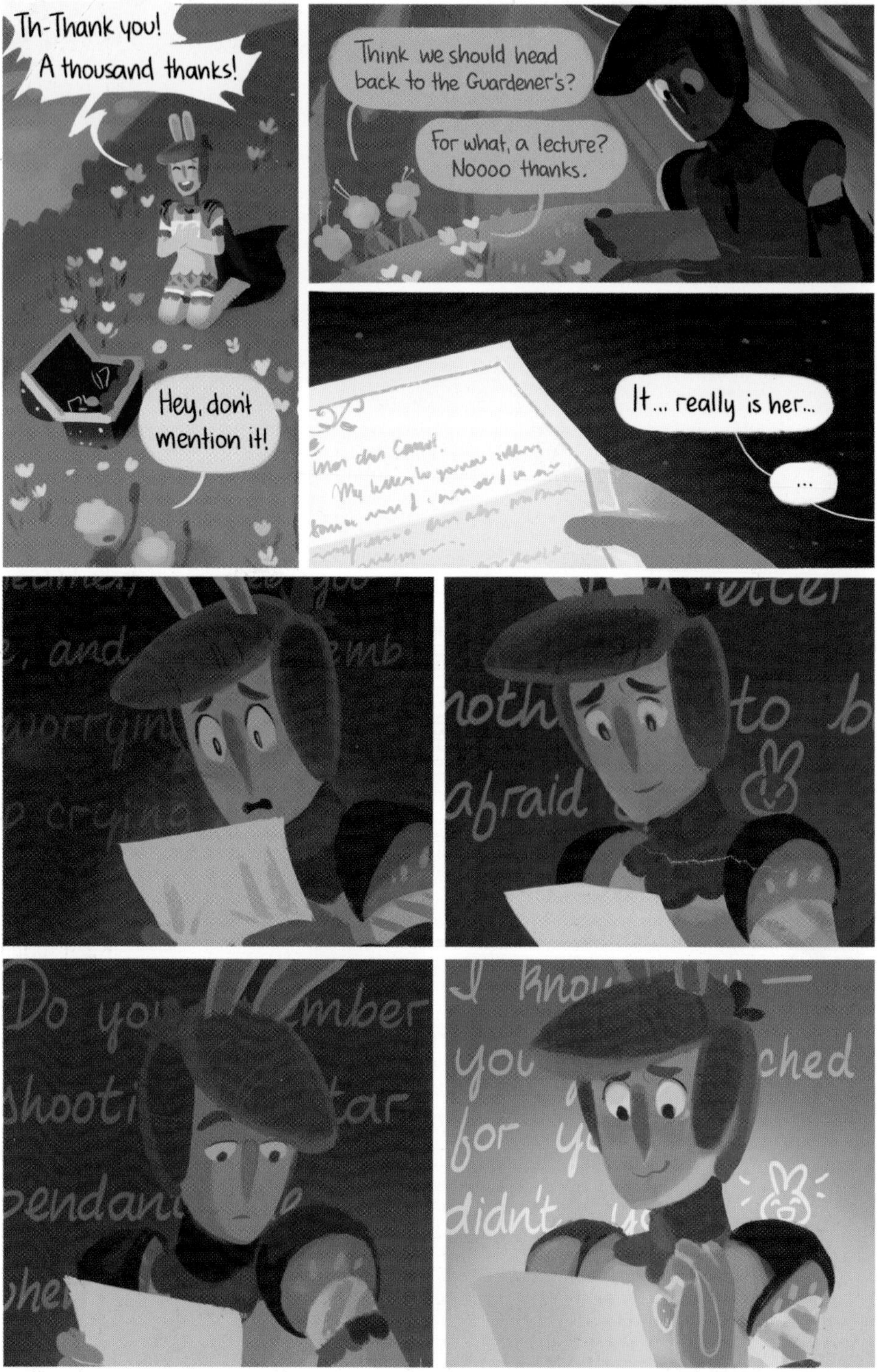
Th-Thank you! A thousand thanks!
Hey, don't mention it!
Think we should head back to the Guardener's?
For what, a lecture? Noooo thanks.
It... really is her...
...

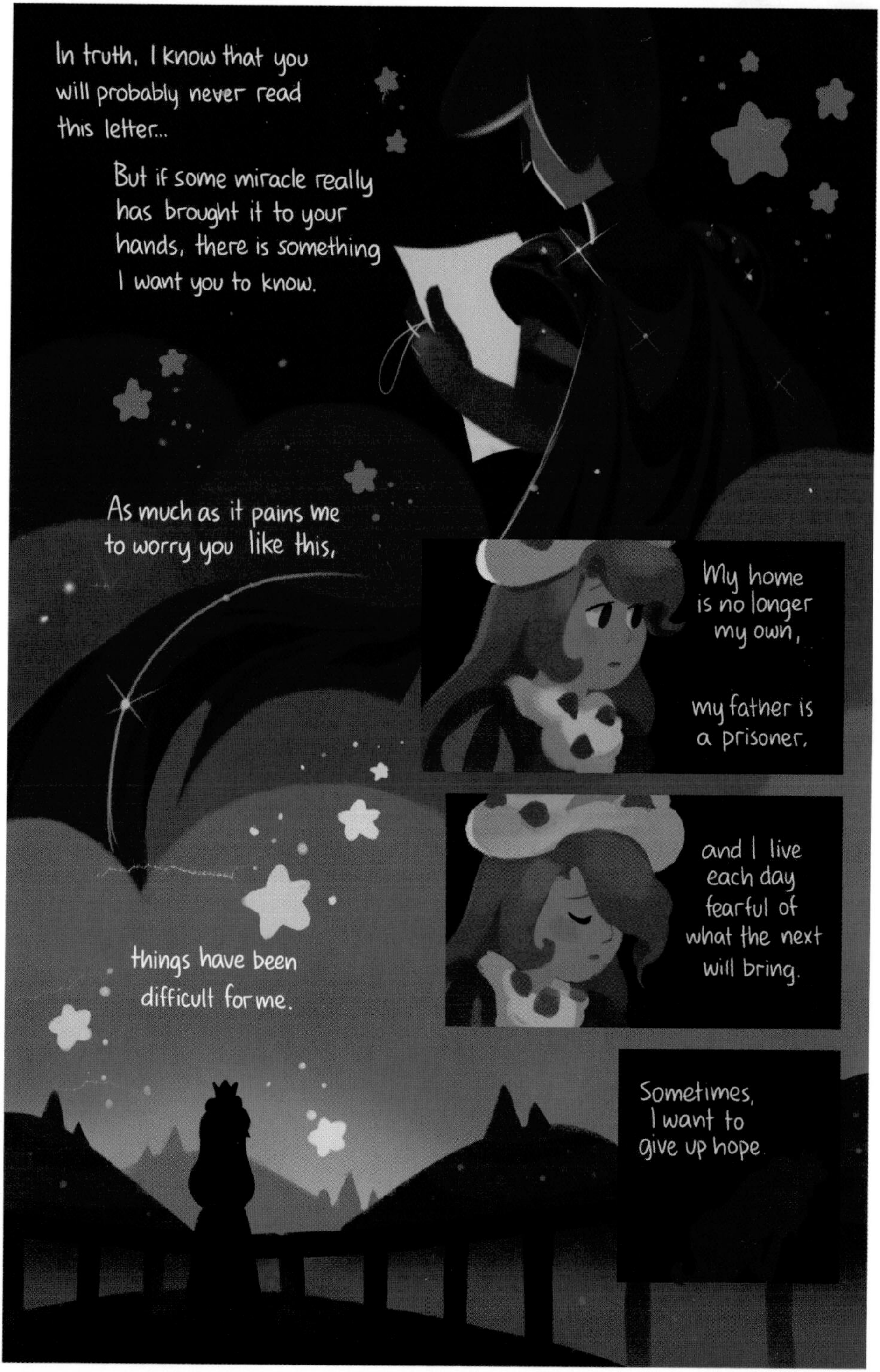
In truth, I know that you will probably never read this letter...
But if some miracle really has brought it to your hands, there is something I want you to know.
As much as it pains me to worry you like this,
My home is no longer my own,
my father is a prisoner,
and I live each day fearful of what the next will bring.
things have been difficult for me.
Sometimes, I want to give up hope.

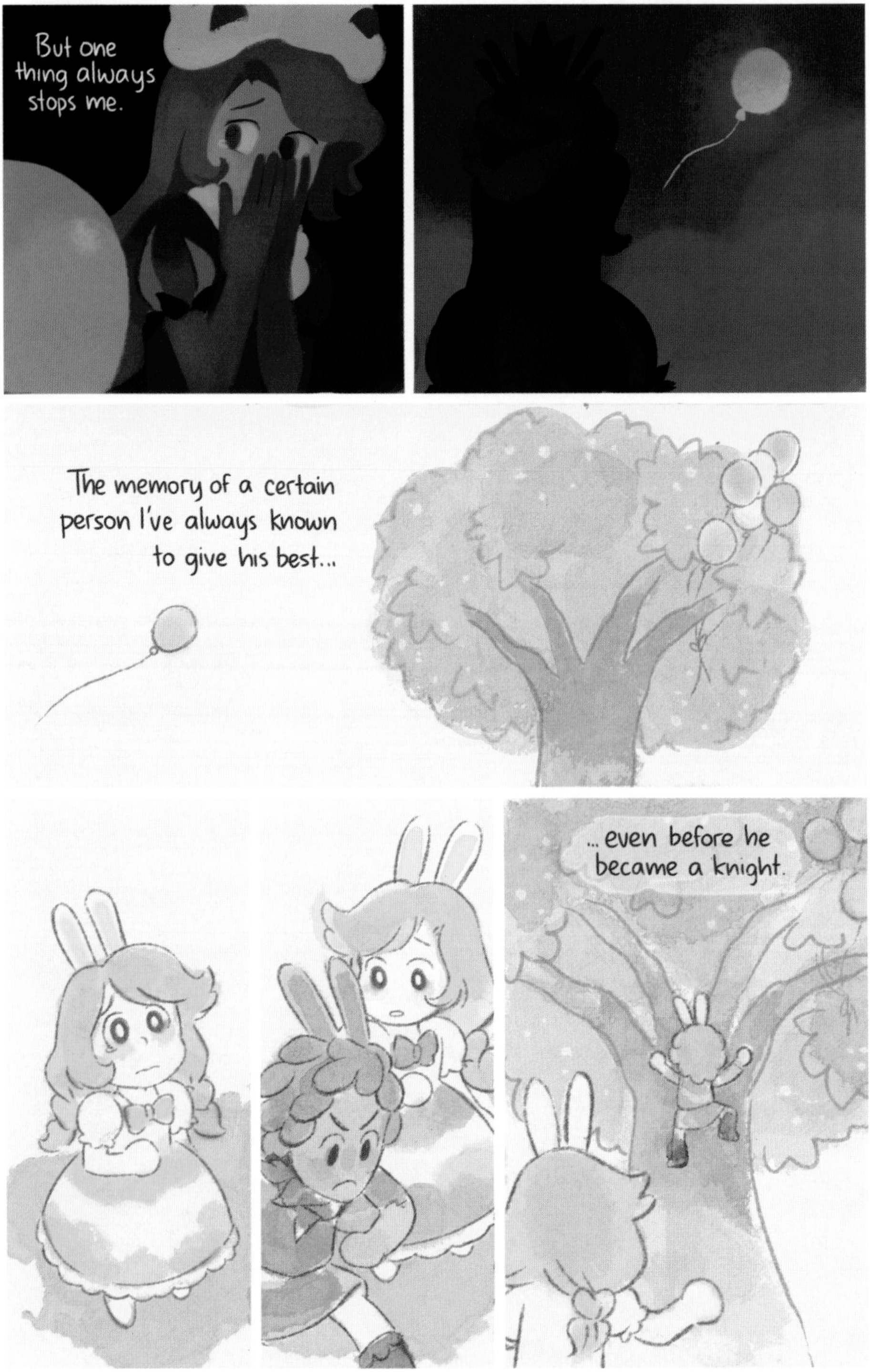
But one thing always stops me.
The memory of a certain person I've always known to give his best...
...even before he became a knight.

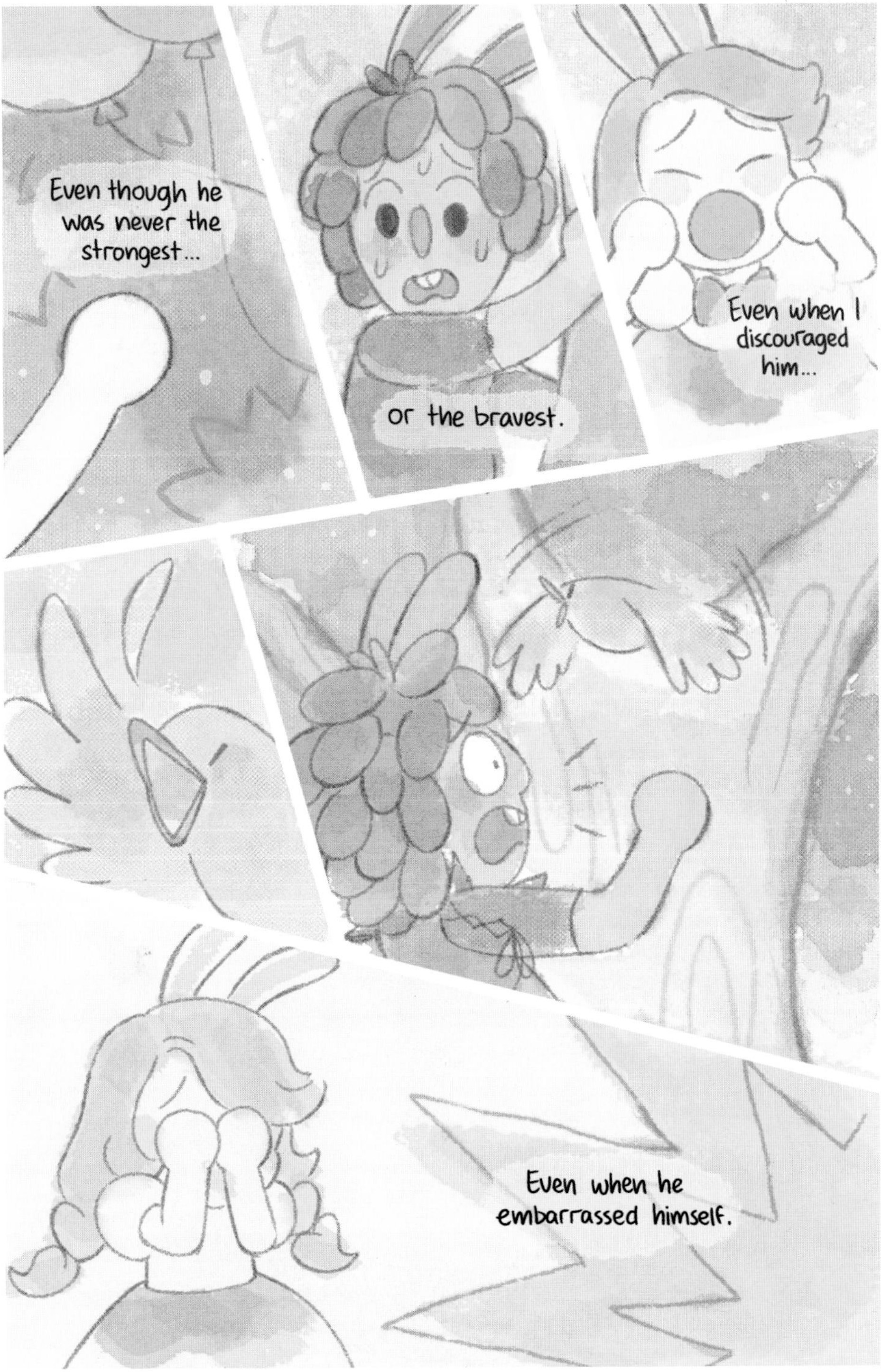
Even though he was never the strongest...
or the bravest.
Even when I discouraged him...
Even when he embarrassed himself.

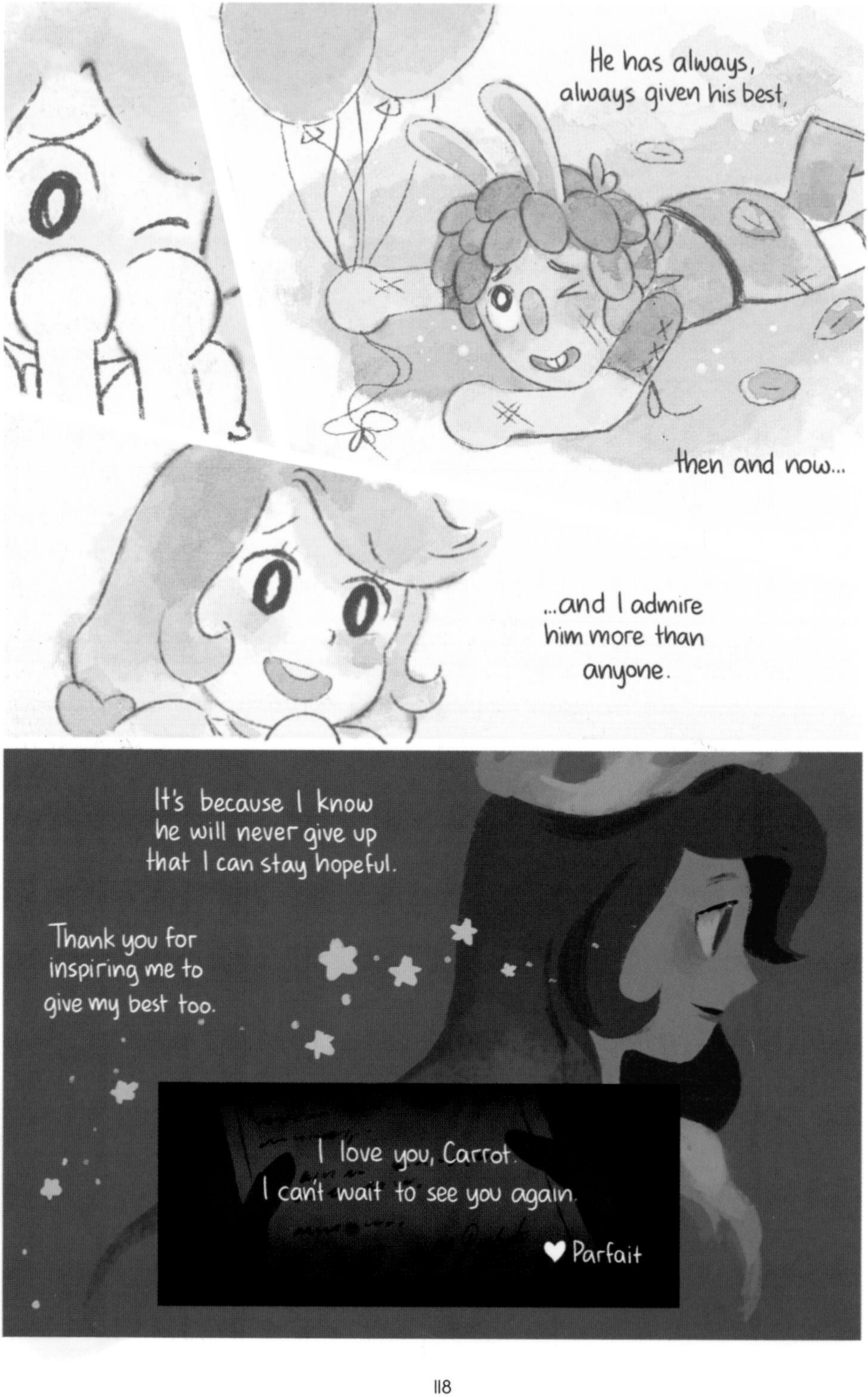
He has always, always given his best,
then and now...
...and I admire him more than anyone.
It's because I know he will never give up that I can stay hopeful.
Thank you for inspiring me to give my best too.
I love you, Carrot.
I can't wait to see you again.
♥ Parfait

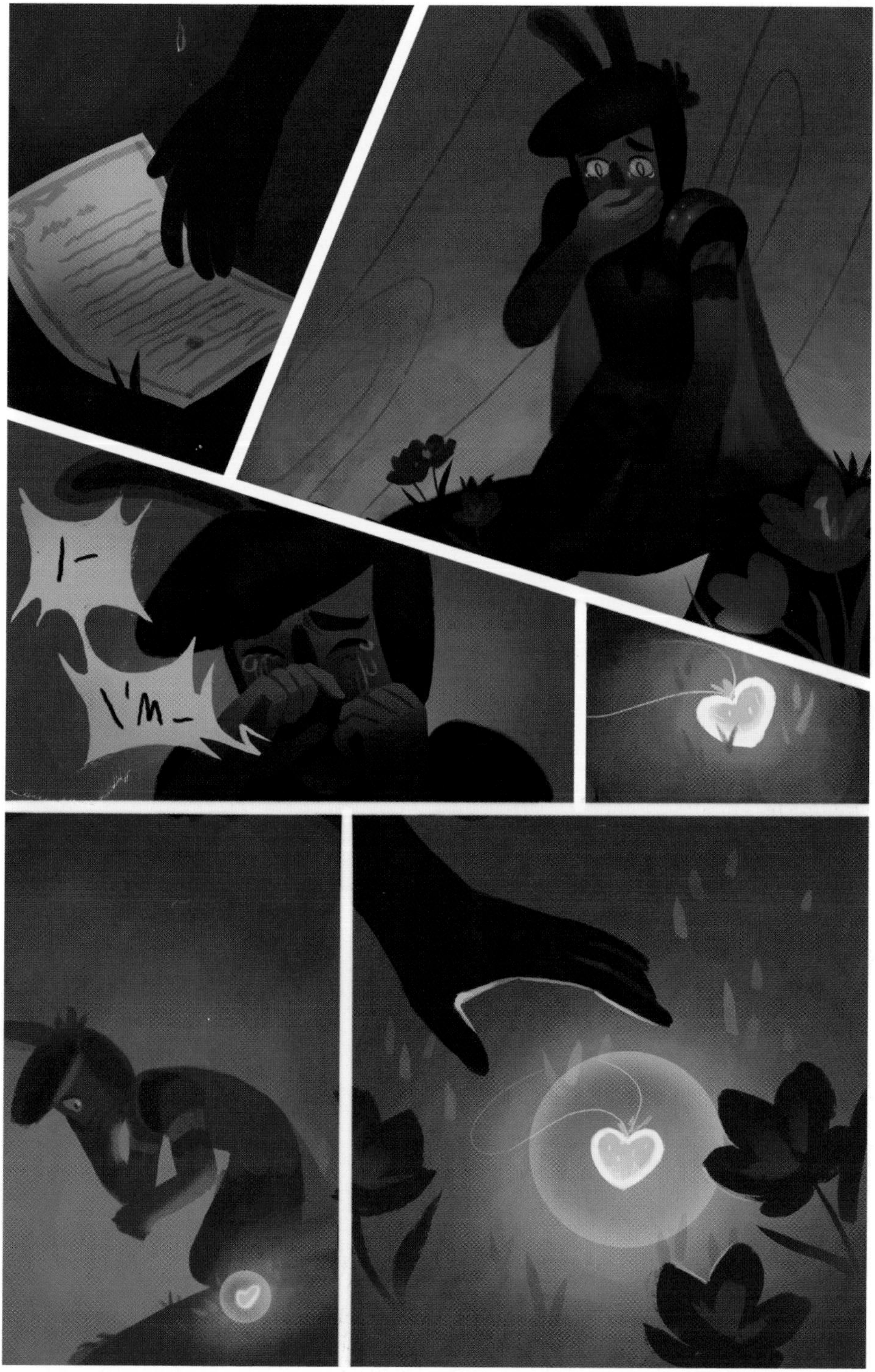
I-
I'm_

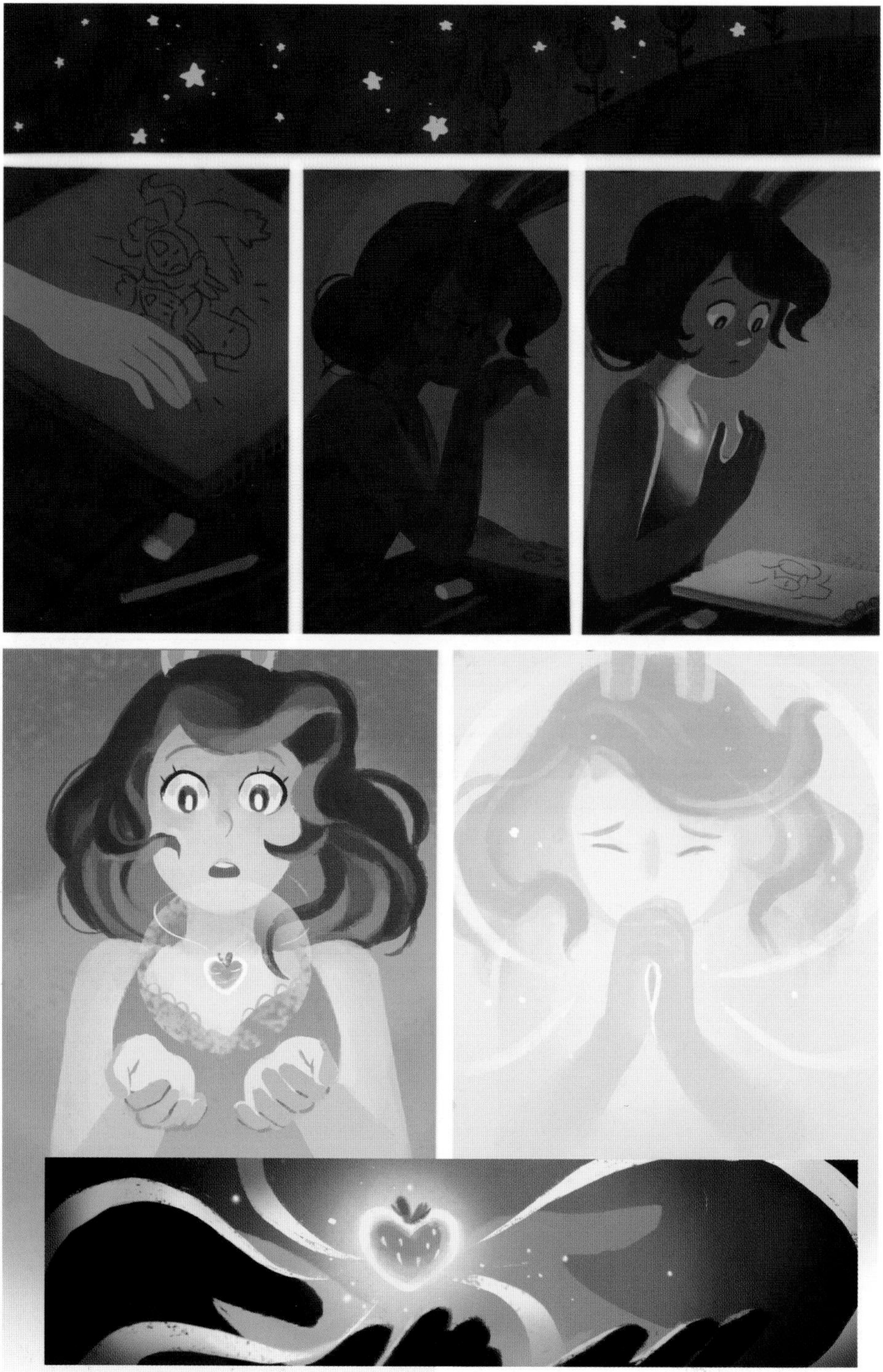

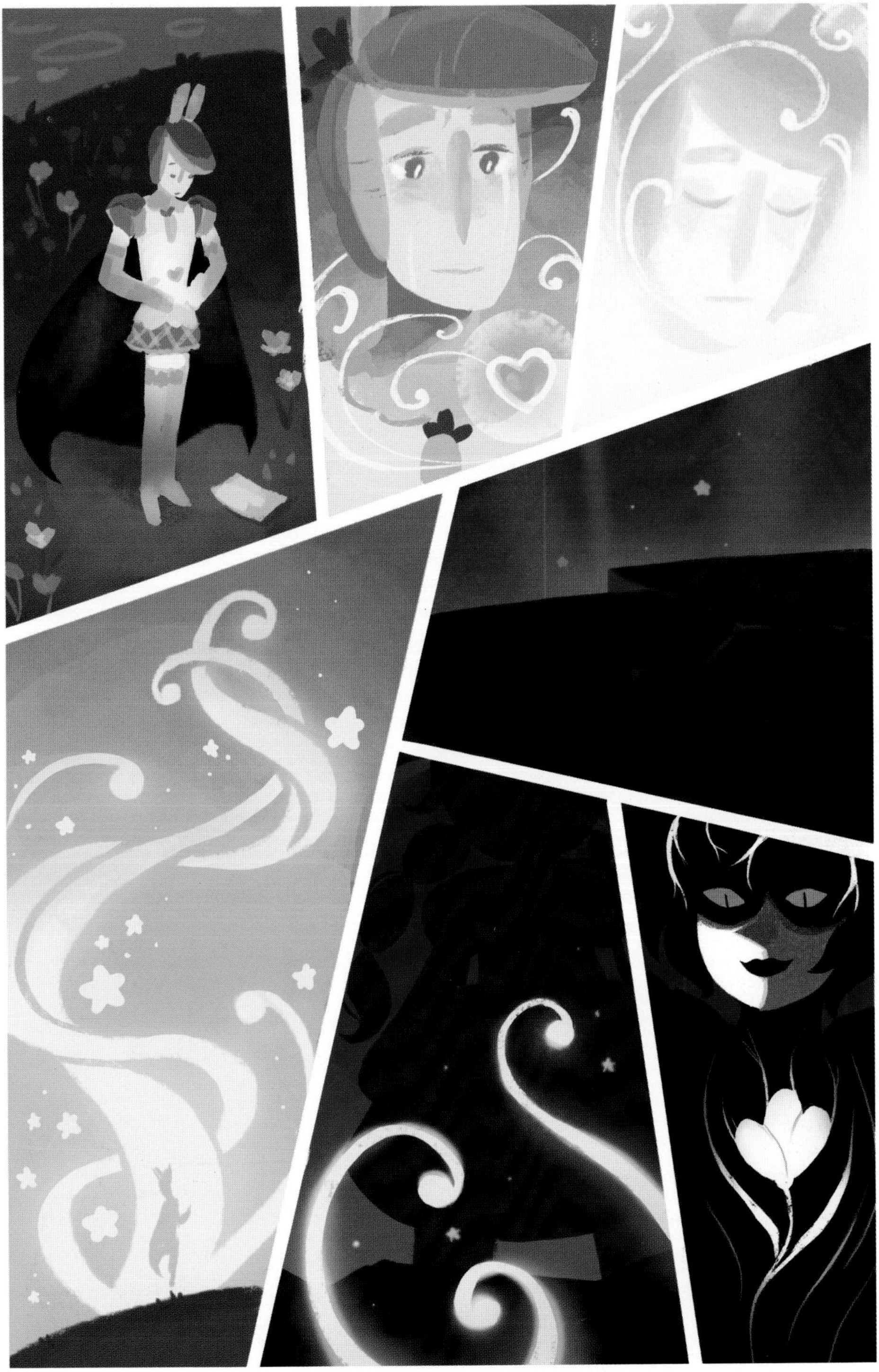

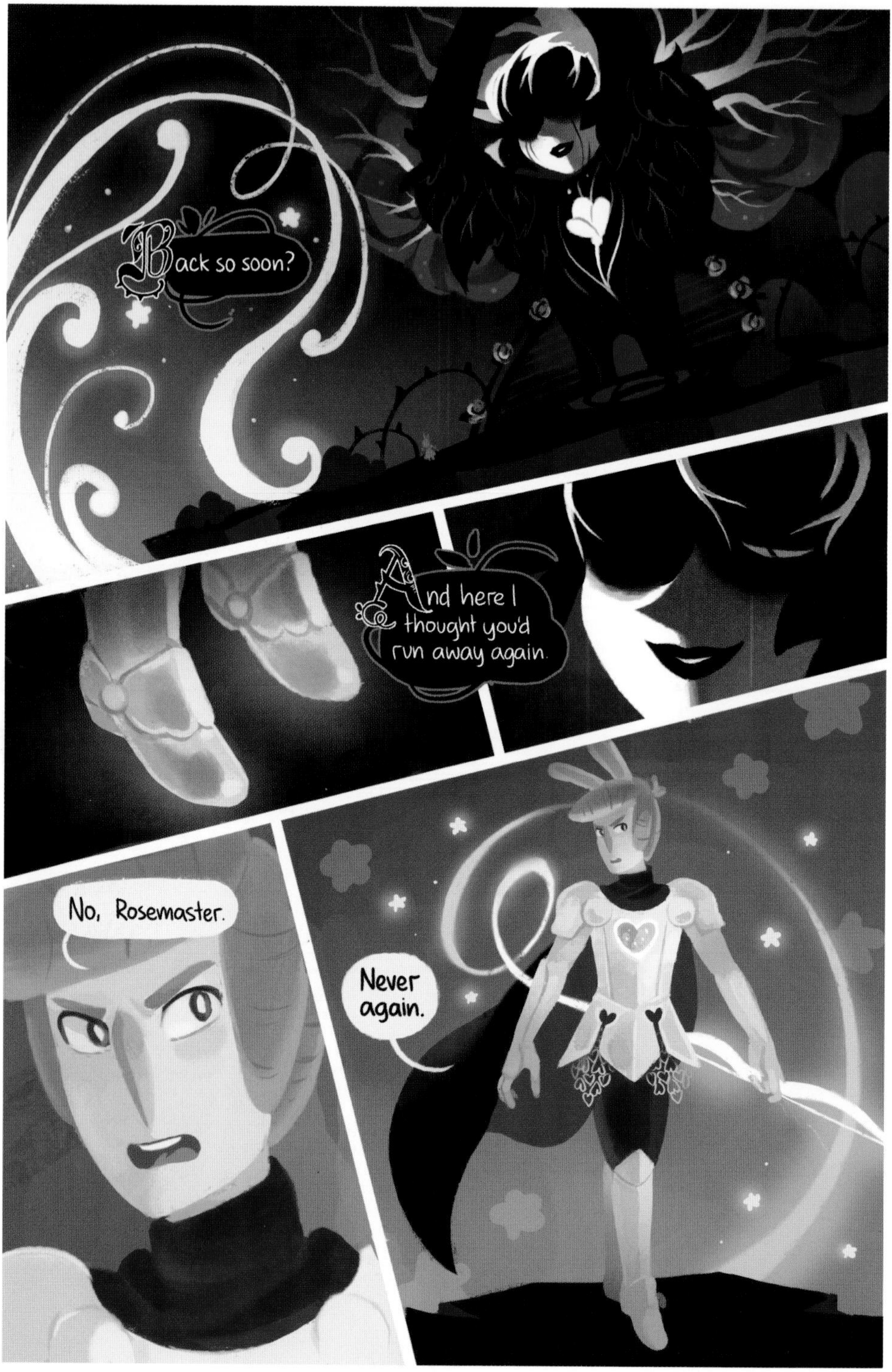

Back so soon?
And here I thought you'd run away again.
No, Rosemaster.
Never again.

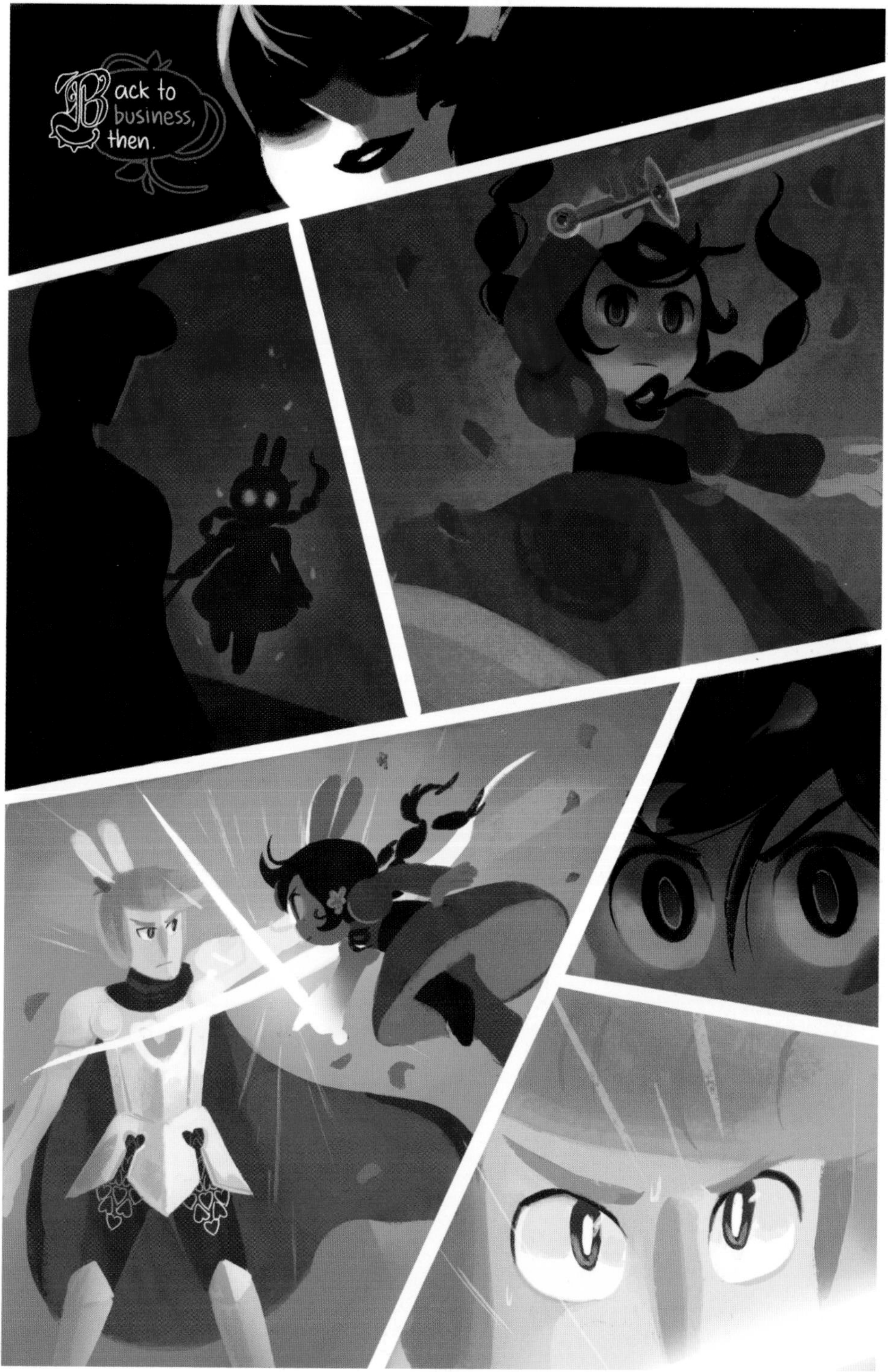
Back to business, then.

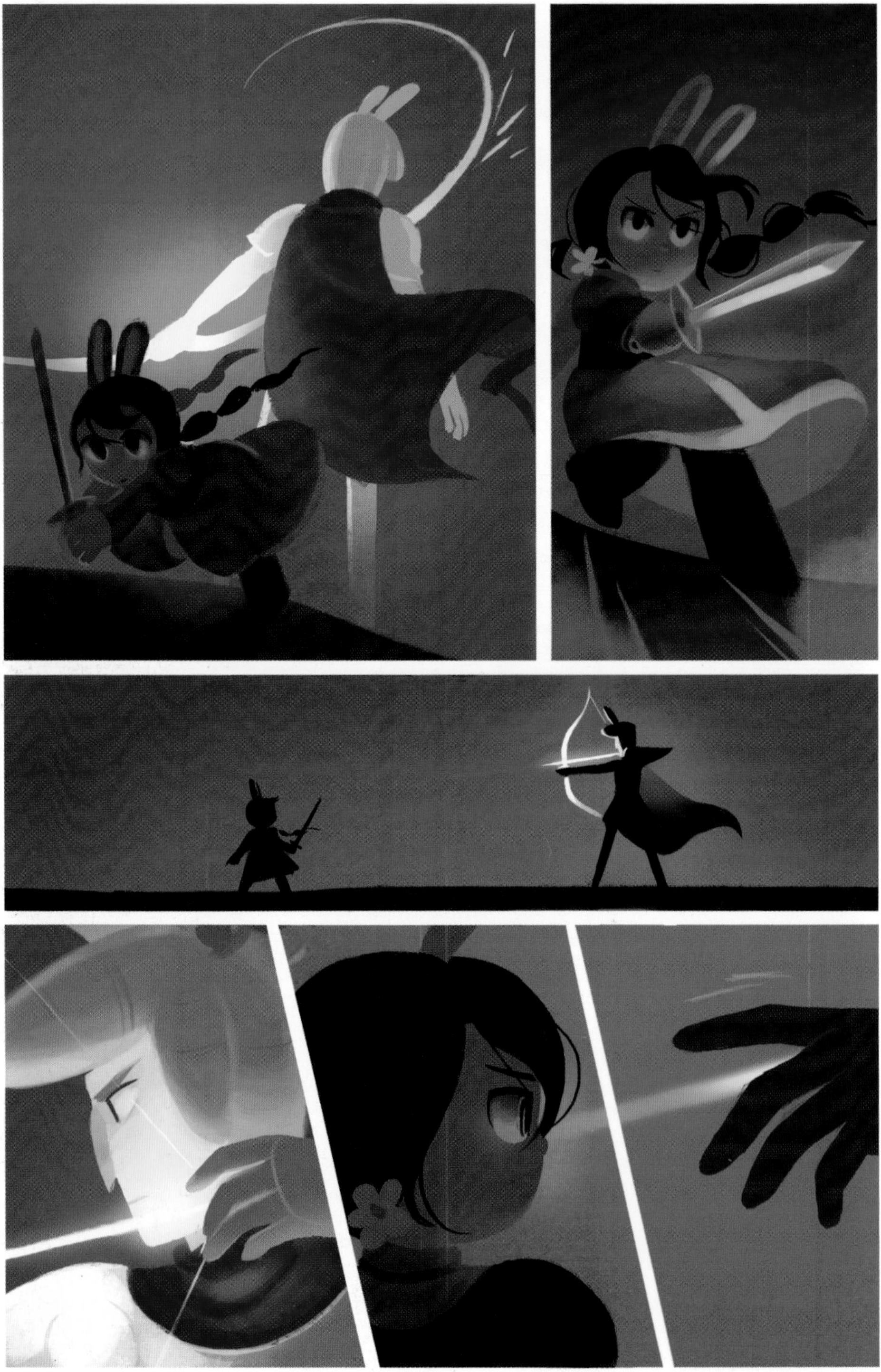

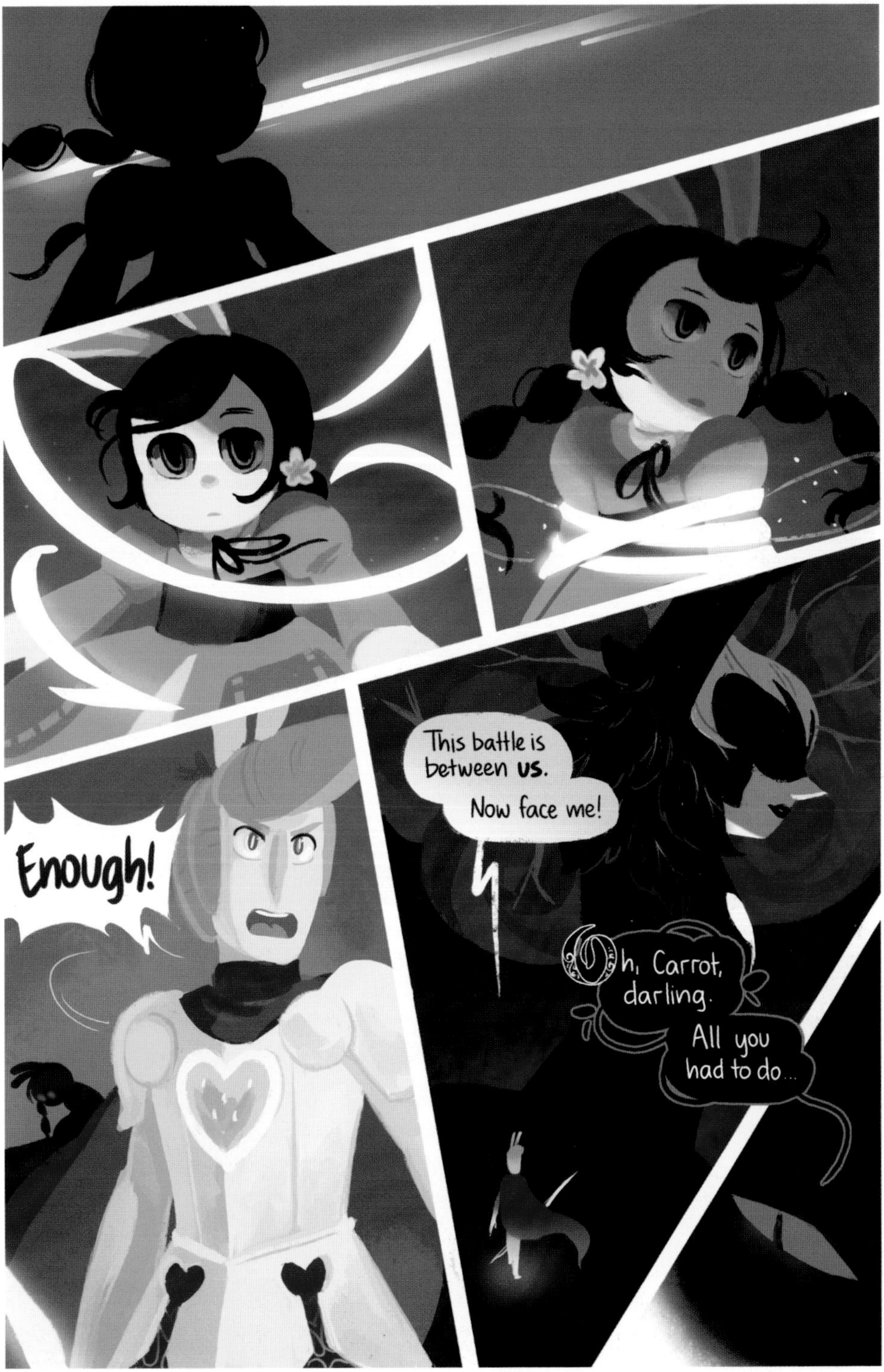
Enough!
This battle is between **us**.
Now face me!
Oh, Carrot, darling.
All you had to do...

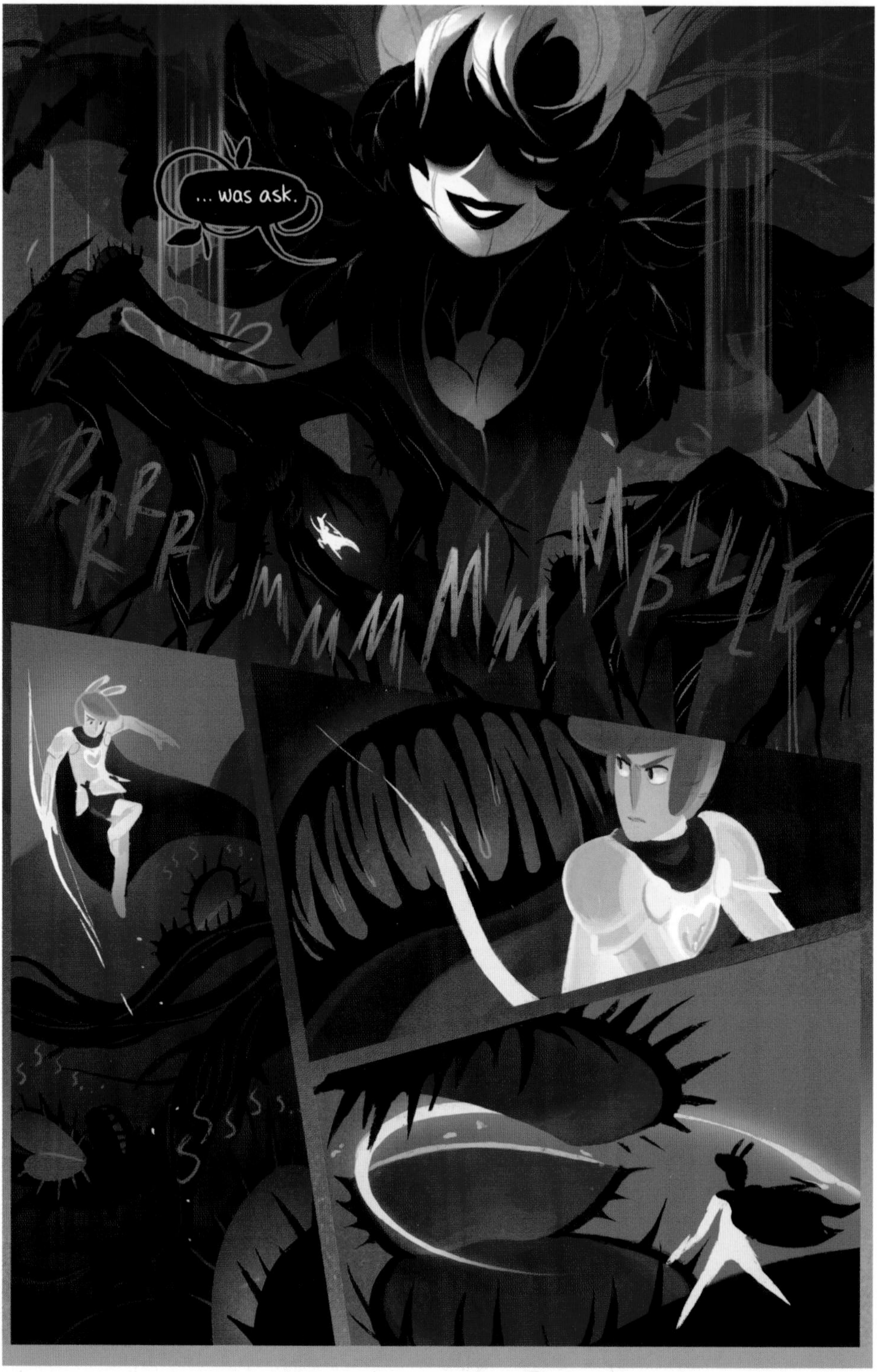
... was ask.
RRRRUMMMMMMBLLE

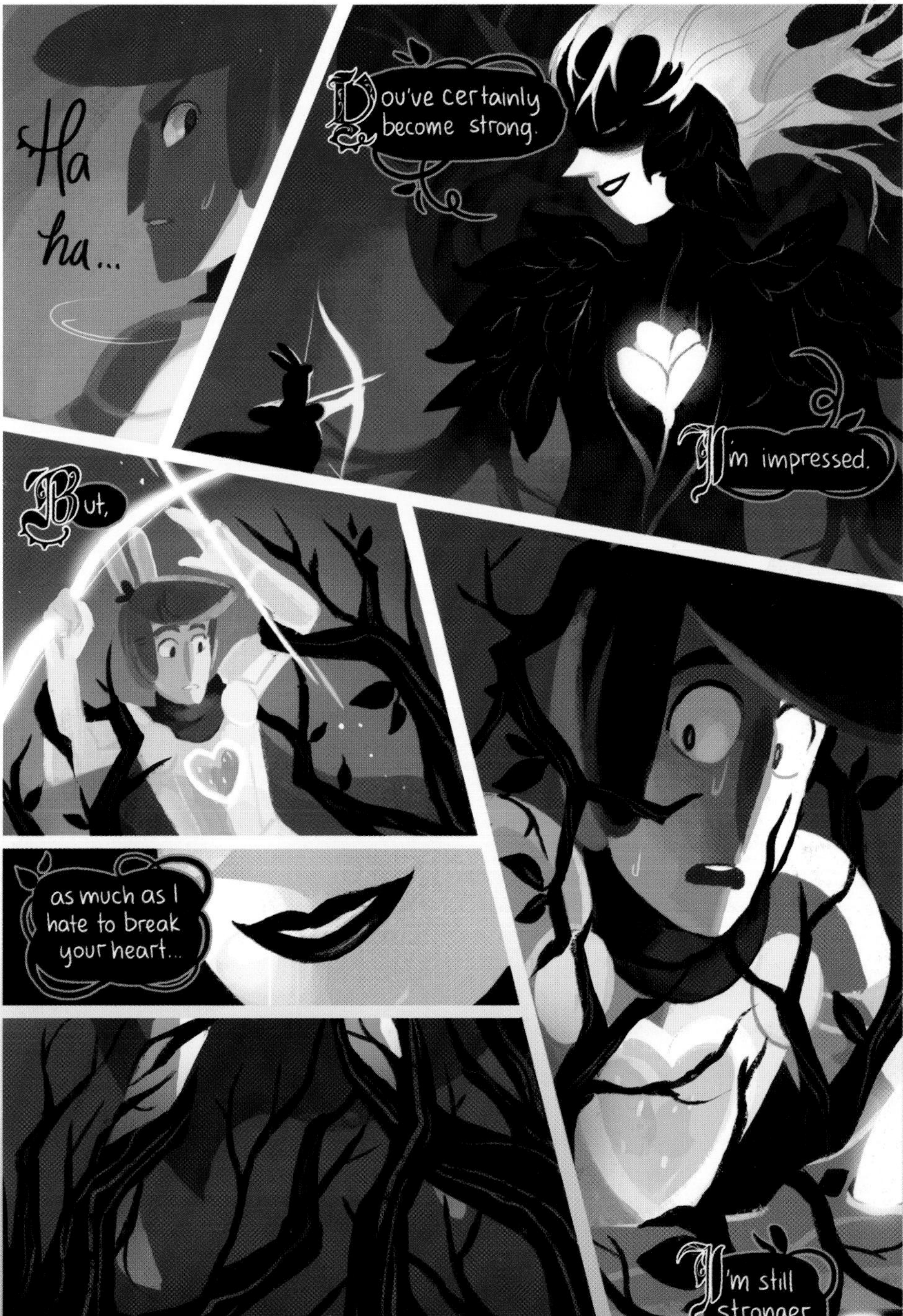
Ha ha...
You've certainly become strong.
I'm impressed.
But,
as much as I hate to break your heart...
I'm still stronger.

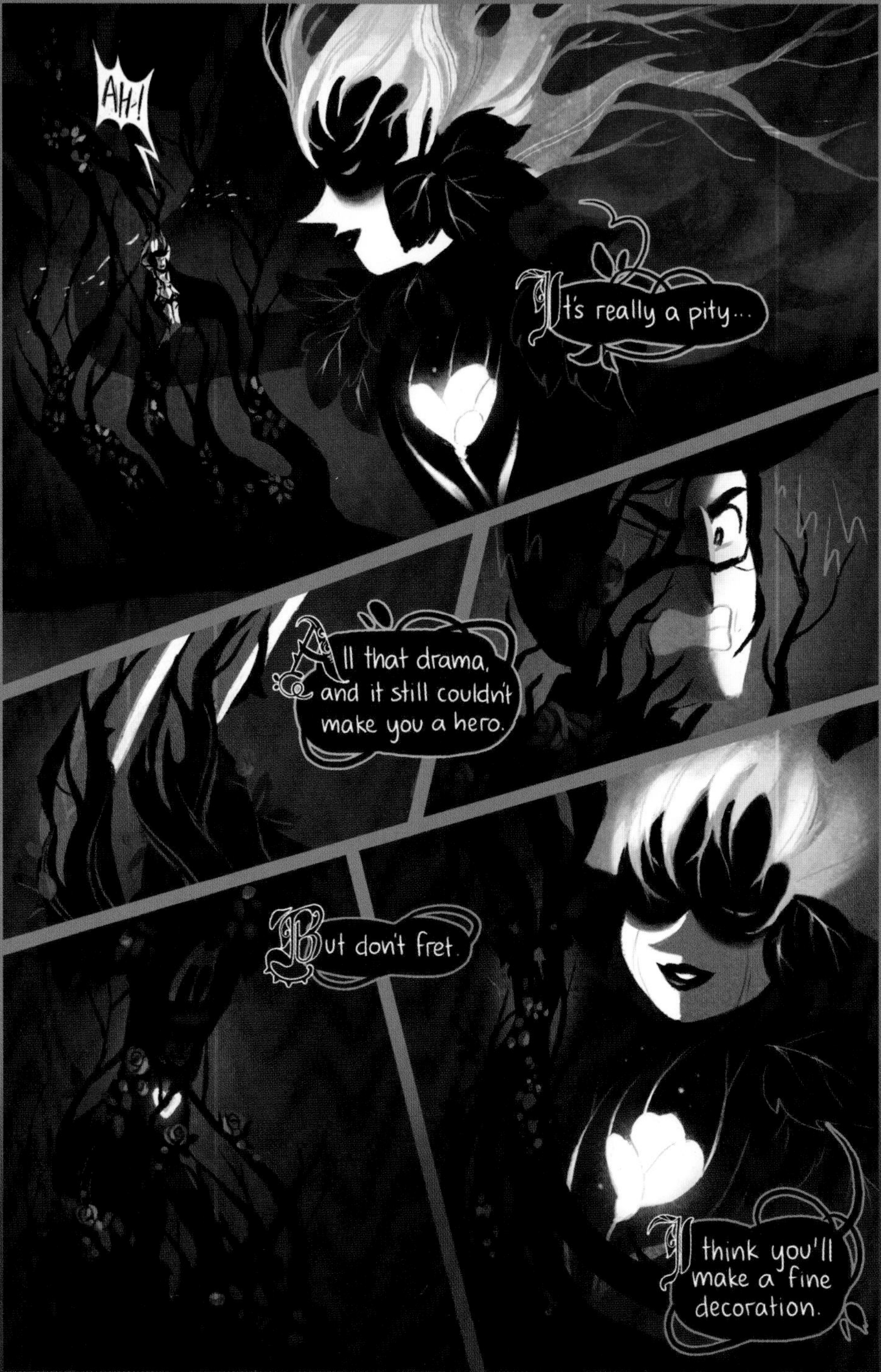
AH-!
It's really a pity...
All that drama, and it still couldn't make you a hero.
But don't fret.
I think you'll make a fine decoration.

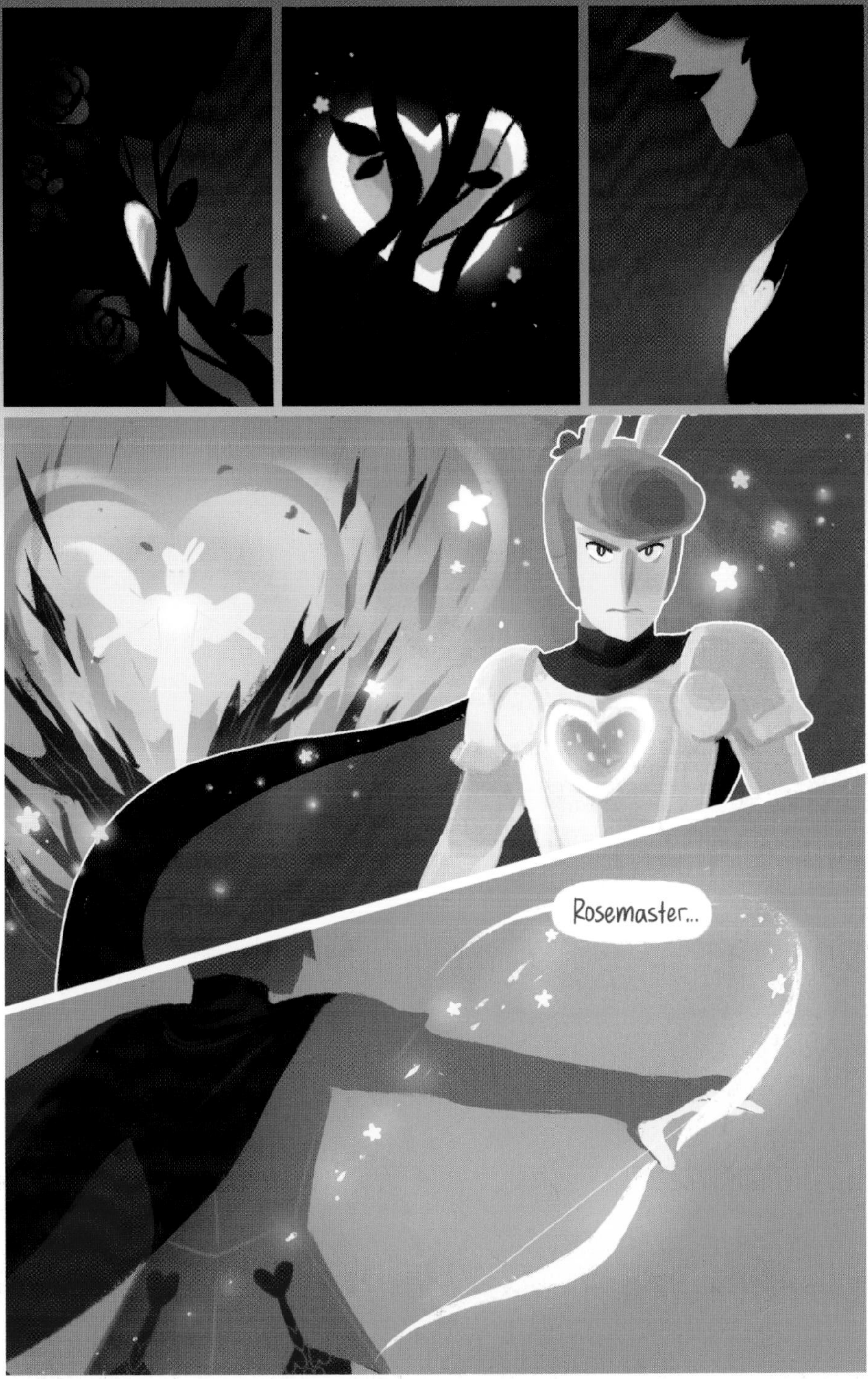
Rosemaster...

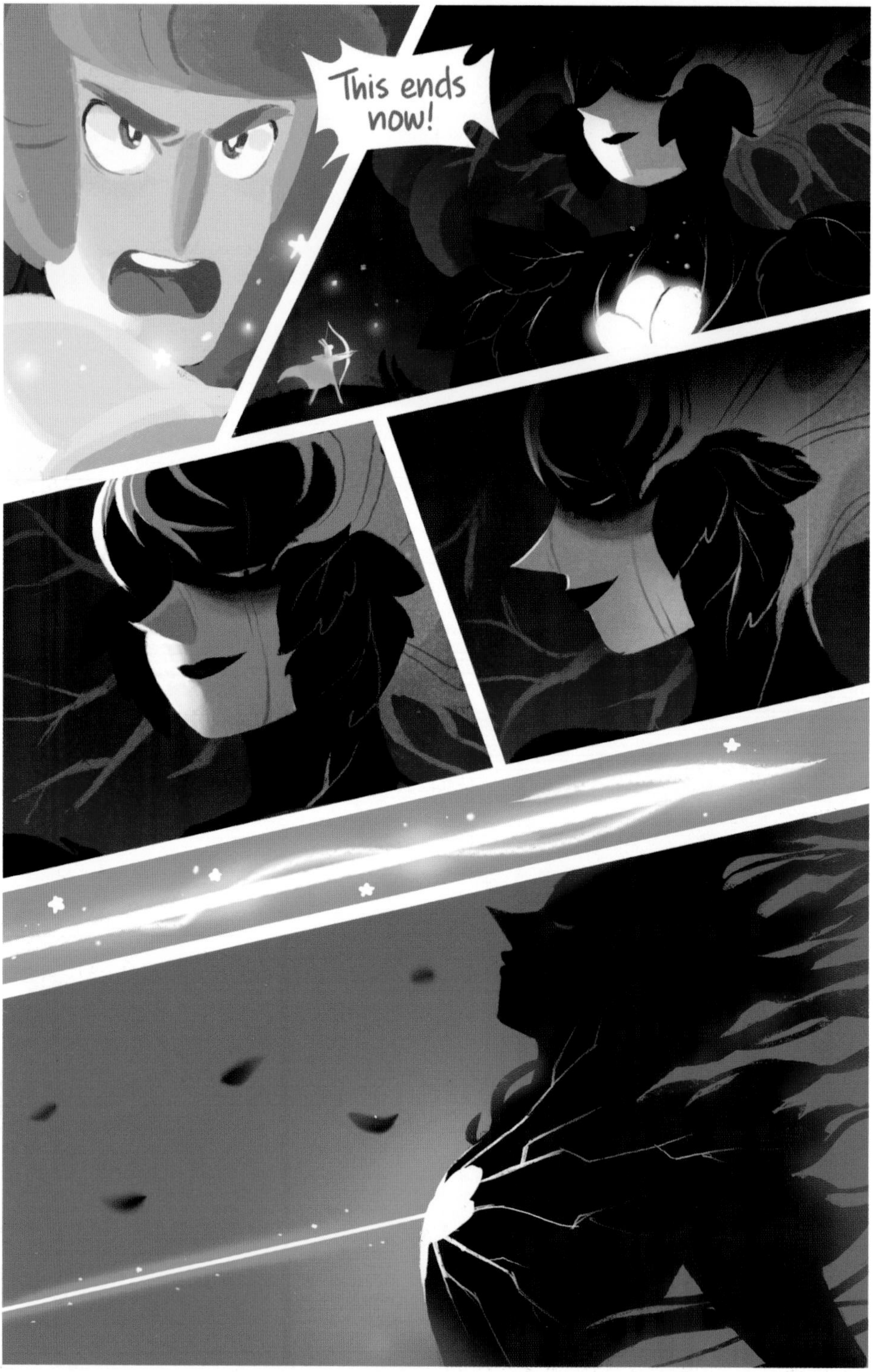
This ends now!

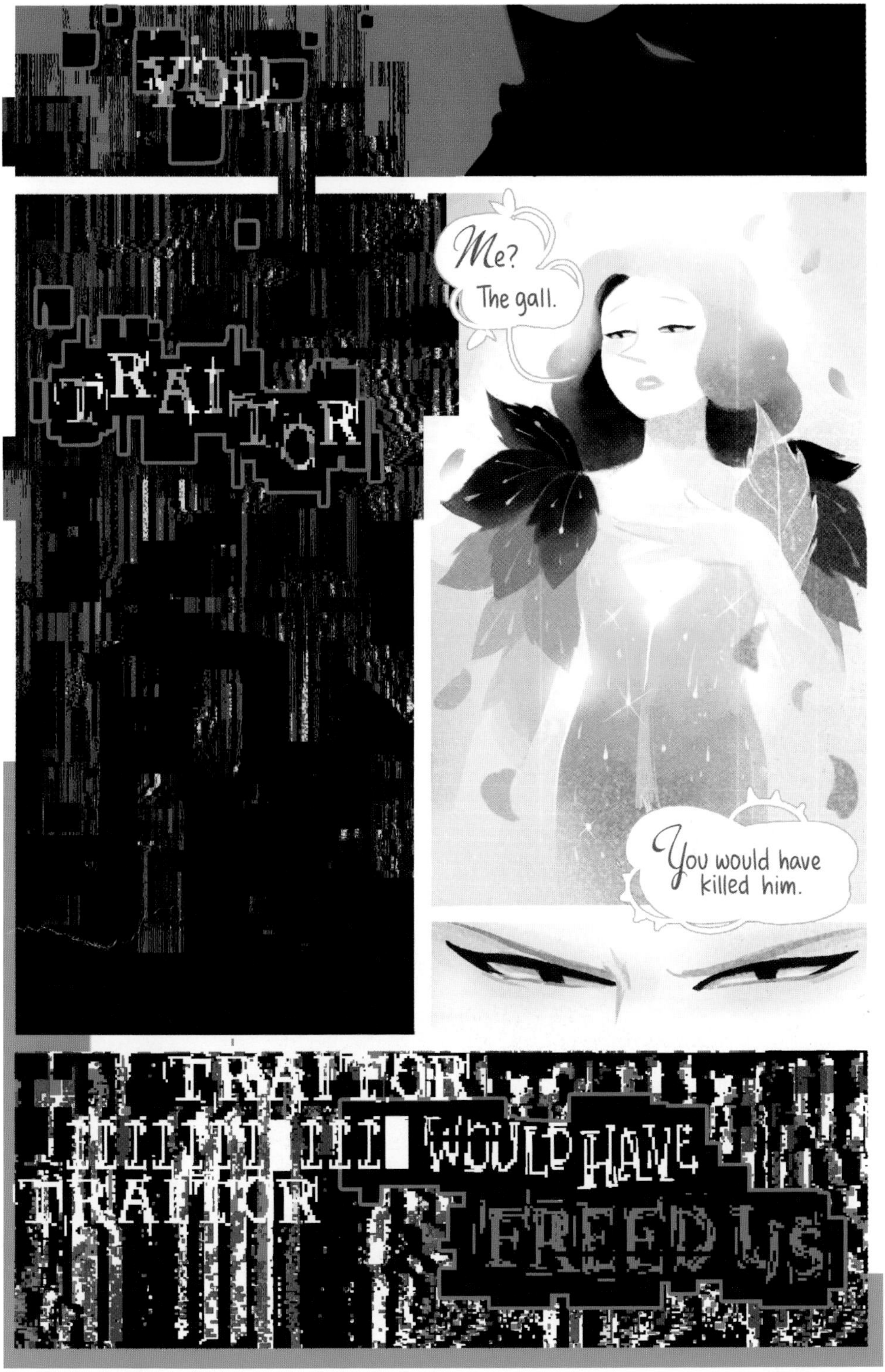
YOU
TRAITOR
Me? The gall.
You would have killed him.
TRAITOR
TRAITOR
WOULD HAVE FREED US

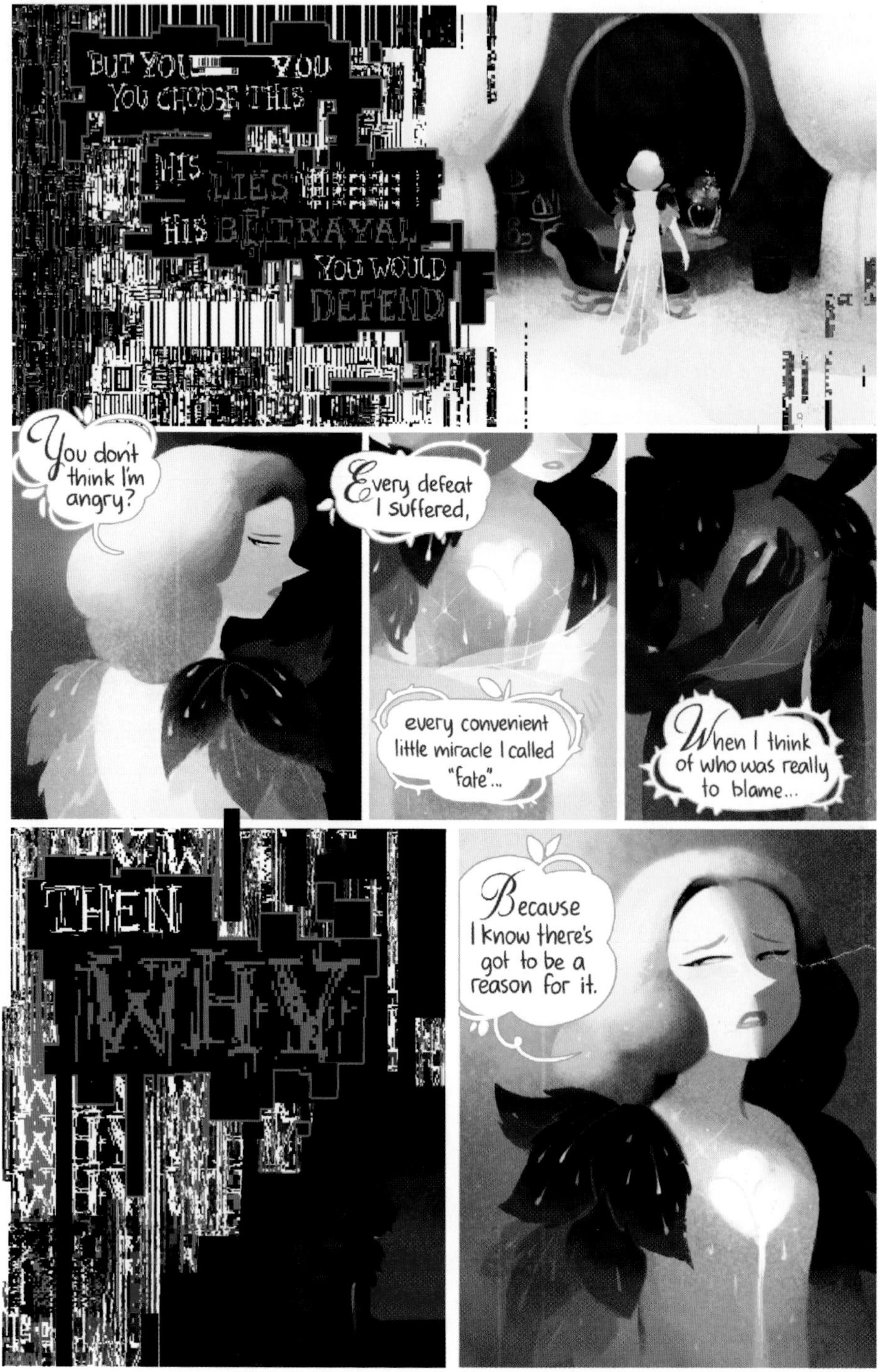

BUT YOU— YOU
YOU CHOOSE THIS
HIS LIES
HIS BETRAYAL
YOU WOULD DEFEND
You don't think I'm angry?
Every defeat I suffered,
every convenient little miracle I called "fate"...
When I think of who was really to blame...
THEN WHY
Because I know there's got to be a reason for it.

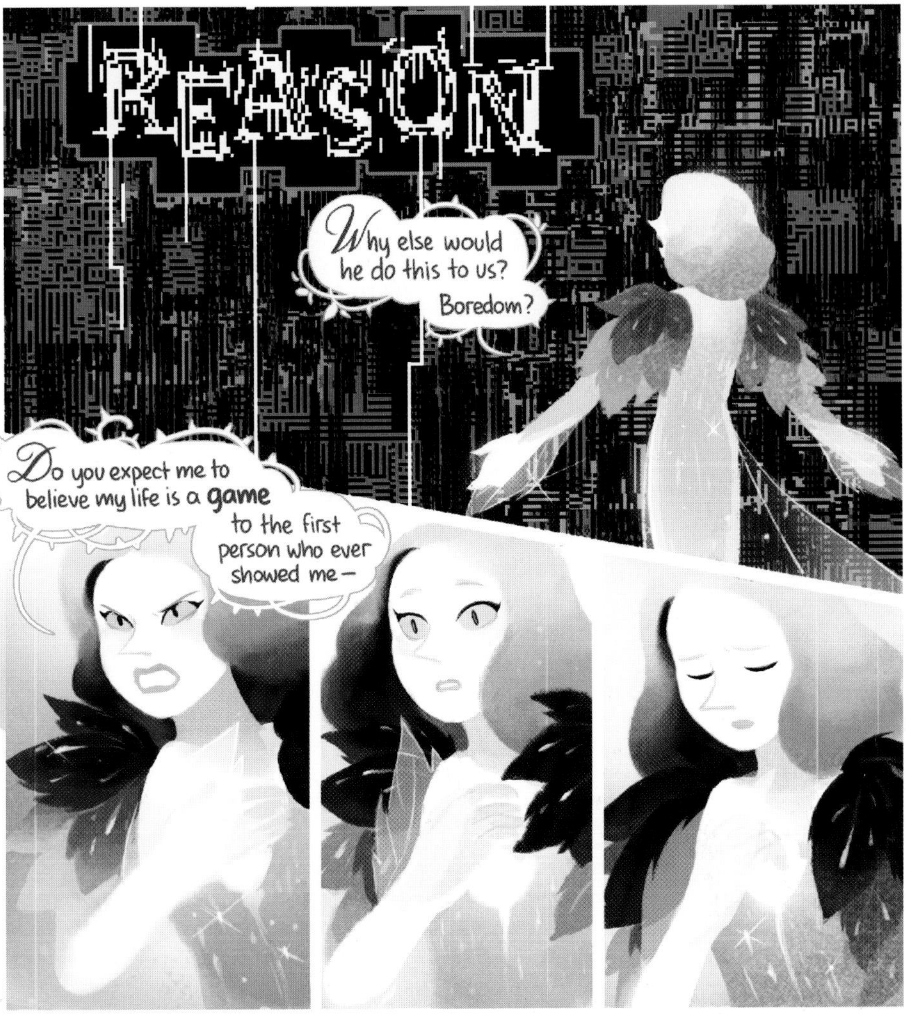
REASON
Why else would he do this to us? Boredom?
Do you expect me to believe my life is a **game**
to the first person who ever showed me—

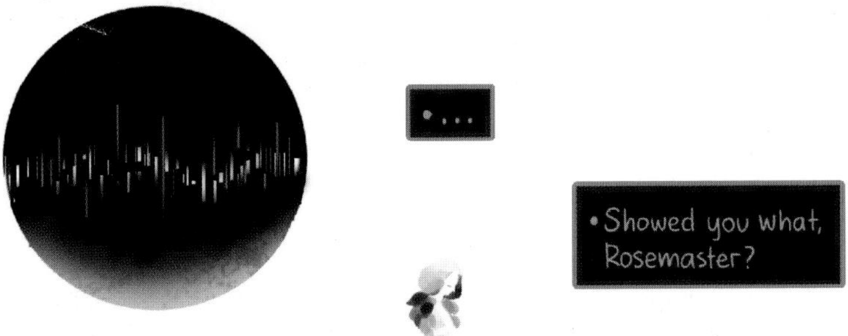
•...
•Showed you what, Rosemaster?

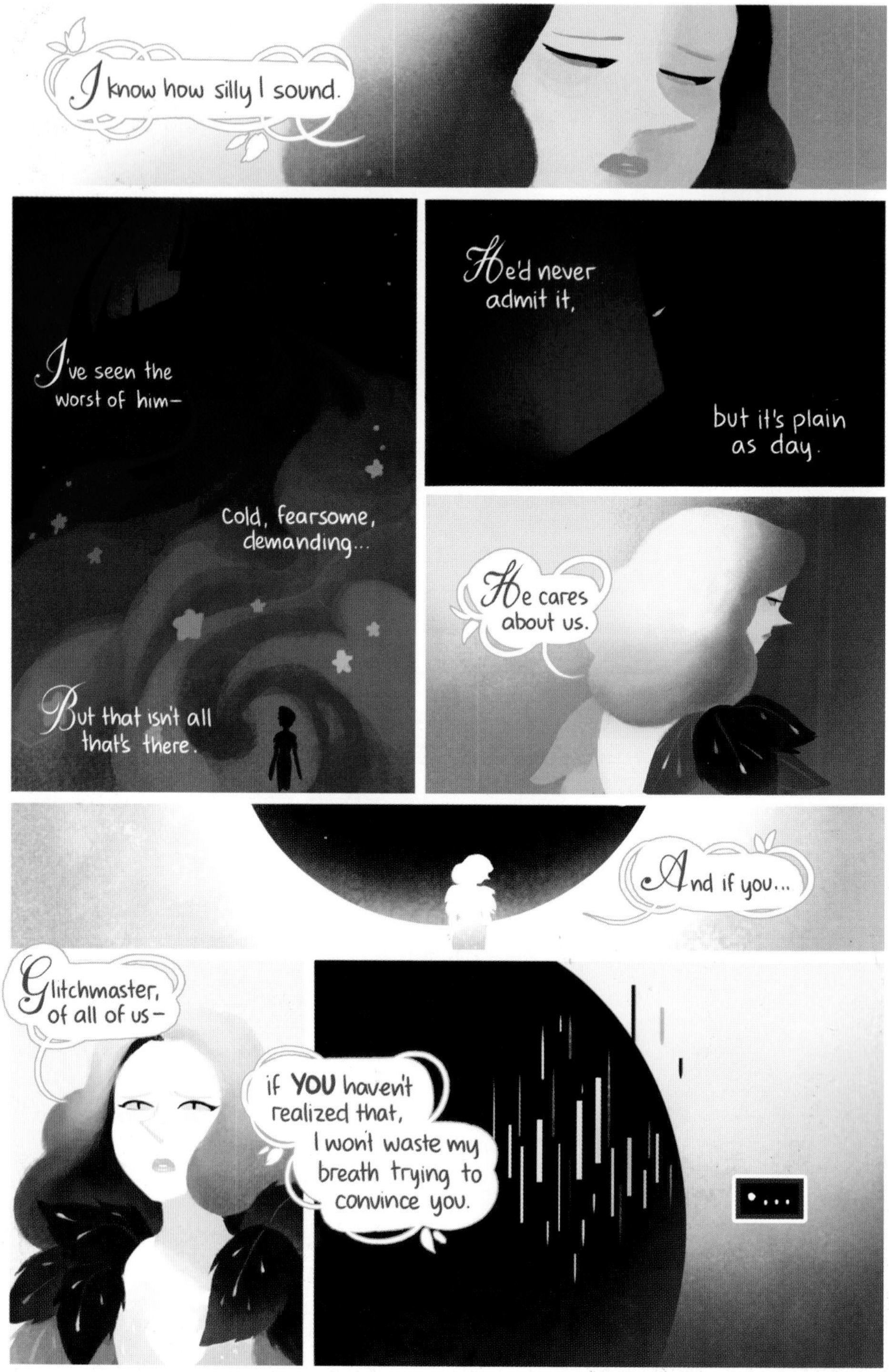
I know how silly I sound.
I've seen the worst of him—
Cold, fearsome, demanding...
But that isn't all that's there.
He'd never admit it,
but it's plain as day.
He cares about us.
And if you...
Glitchmaster, of all of us—
if YOU haven't realized that, I won't waste my breath trying to convince you.
•...

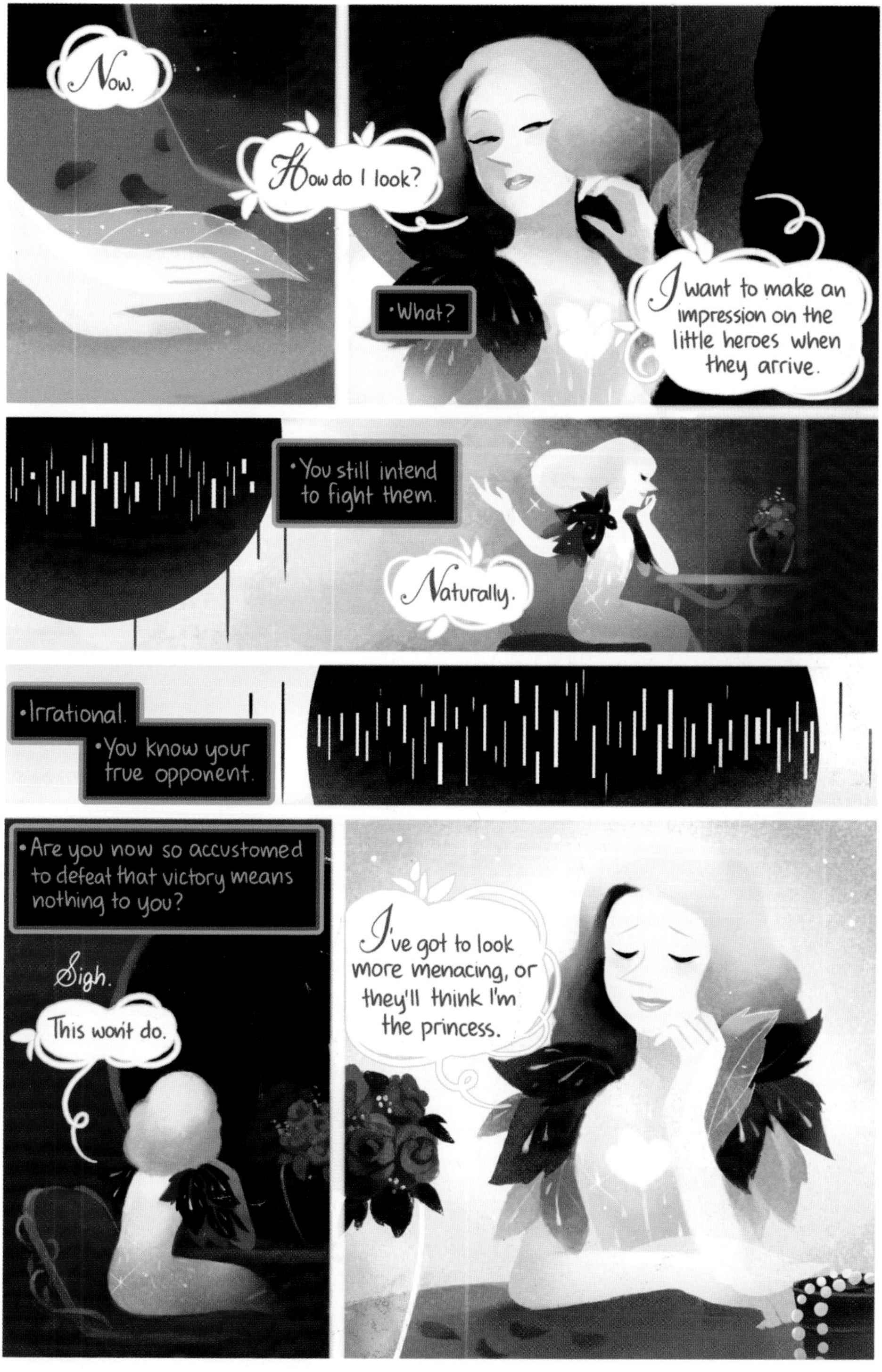
Now.
How do I look?
•What?
I want to make an impression on the little heroes when they arrive.
•You still intend to fight them.
Naturally.
•Irrational.
•You know your true opponent.
•Are you now so accustomed to defeat that victory means nothing to you?
Sigh.
This won't do.
I've got to look more menacing, or they'll think I'm the princess.

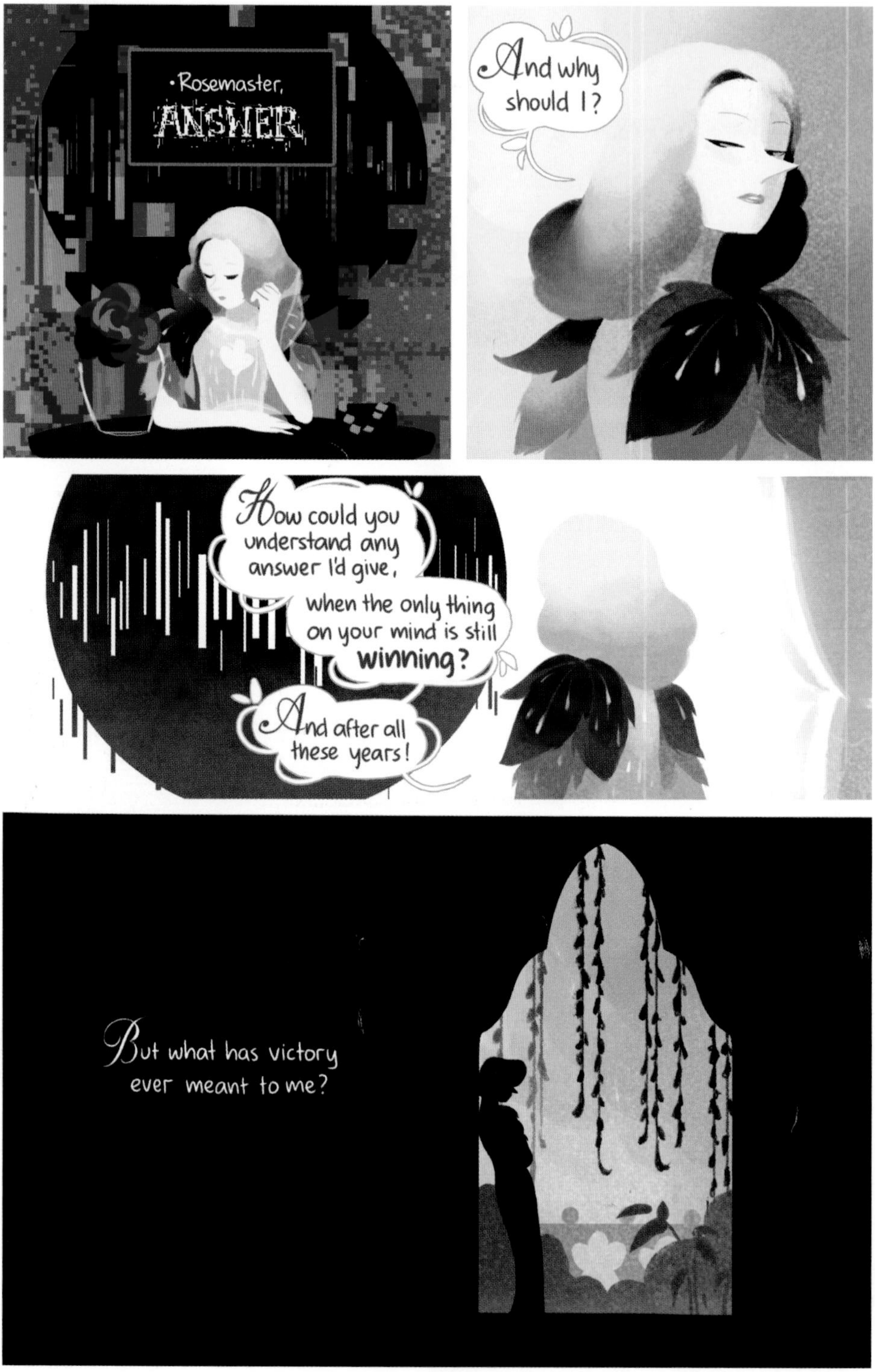

• Rosemaster,
ANSWER
And why should I?
How could you understand any answer I'd give,
when the only thing on your mind is still winning?
And after all these years!
But what has victory ever meant to me?

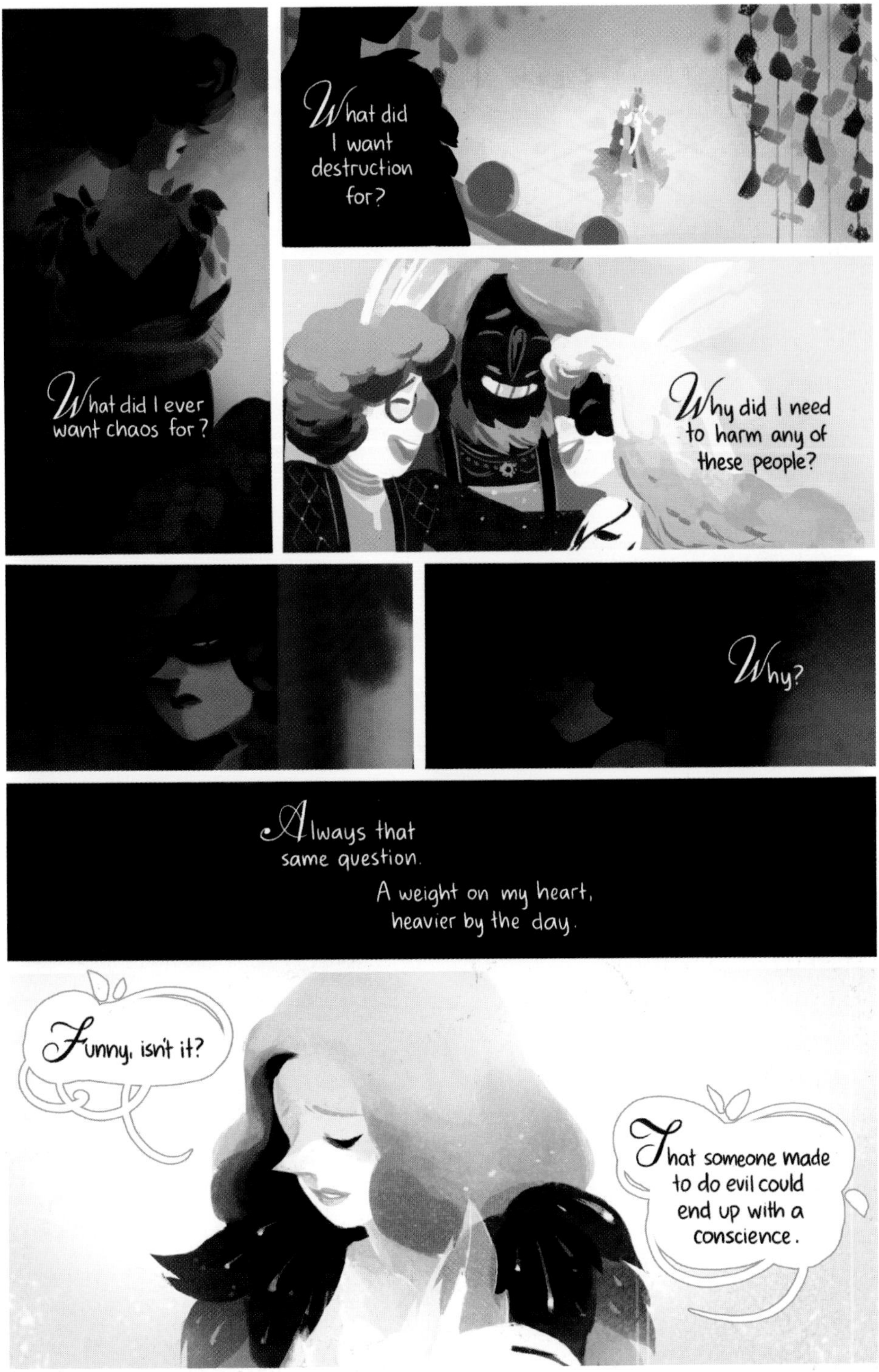
What did I ever want chaos for?
What did I want destruction for?
Why did I need to harm any of these people?
Why?
Always that same question.
A weight on my heart, heavier by the day.
Funny, isn't it?
That someone made to do evil could end up with a conscience.

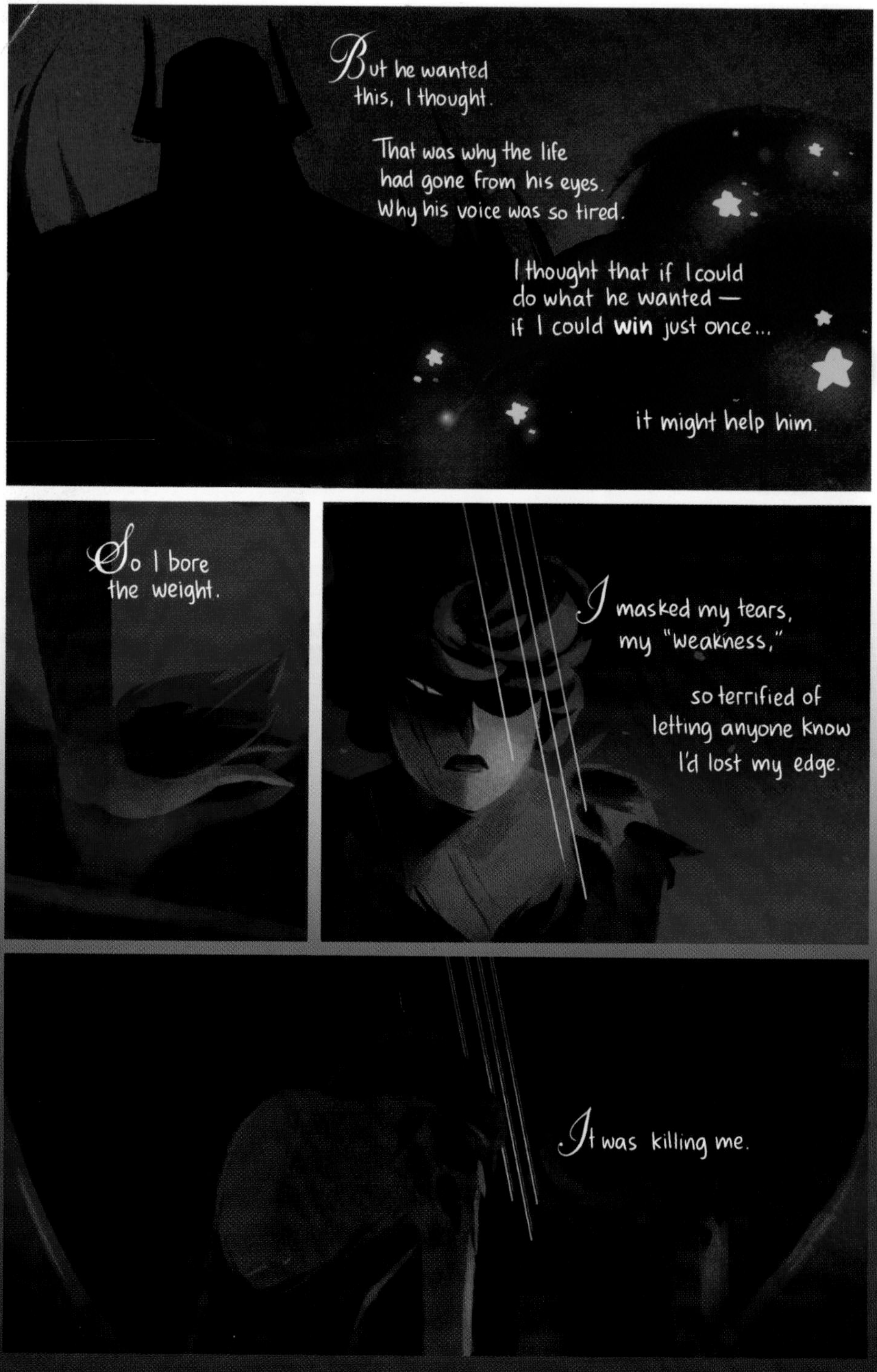
But he wanted this, I thought.
That was why the life had gone from his eyes. Why his voice was so tired.
I thought that if I could do what he wanted — if I could **win** just once...
it might help him.
So I bore the weight.
I masked my tears, my "weakness,"
so terrified of letting anyone know I'd lost my edge.
It was killing me.

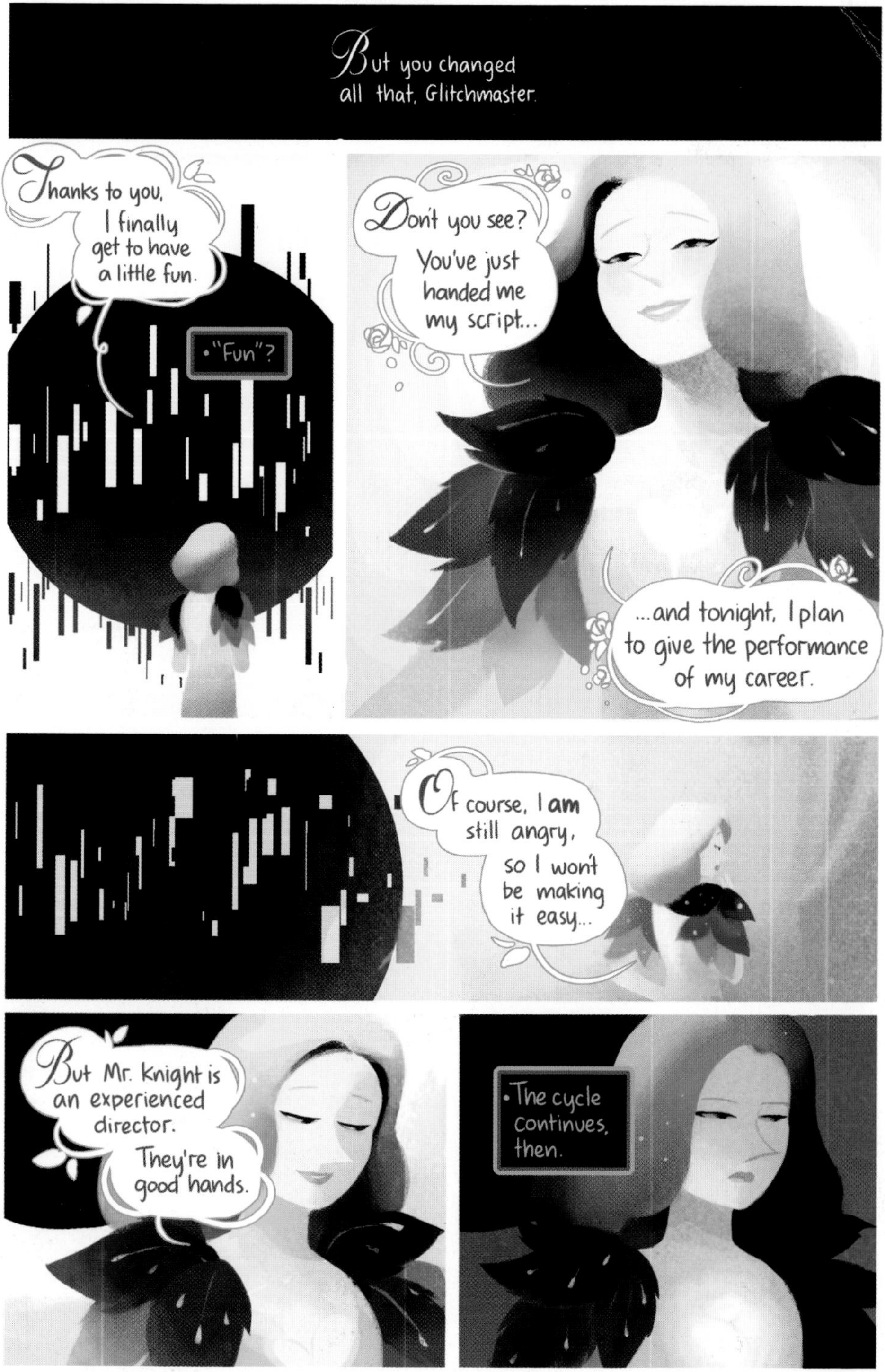
But you changed all that, Glitchmaster.
Thanks to you, I finally get to have a little fun.
•"Fun"?
Don't you see? You've just handed me my script...
...and tonight, I plan to give the performance of my career.
Of course, I **am** still angry, so I won't be making it easy...
But Mr. Knight is an experienced director. They're in good hands.
•The cycle continues, then.

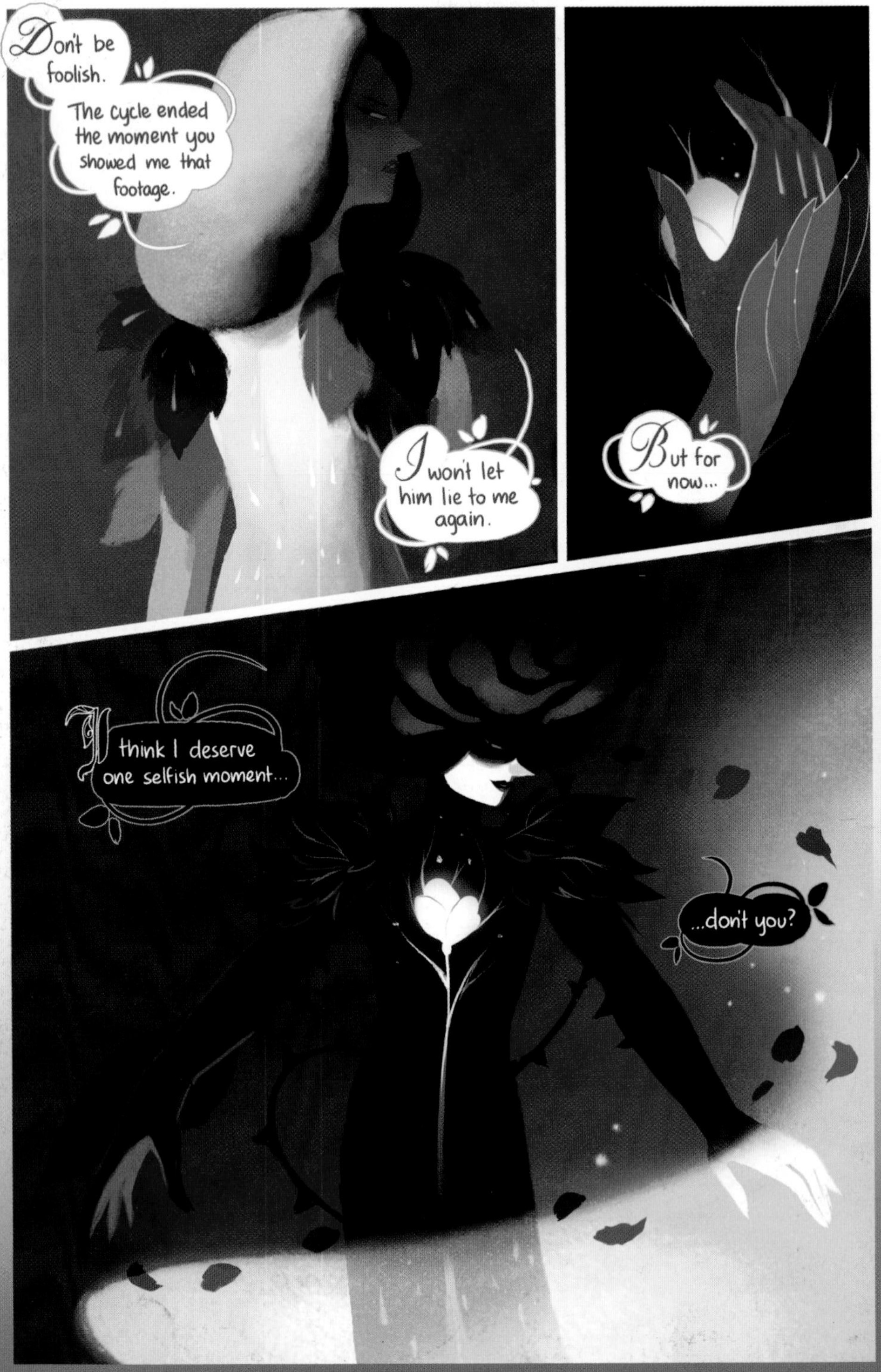
Don't be foolish.
The cycle ended the moment you showed me that footage.
I won't let him lie to me again.
But for now...
I think I deserve one selfish moment...
...don't you?

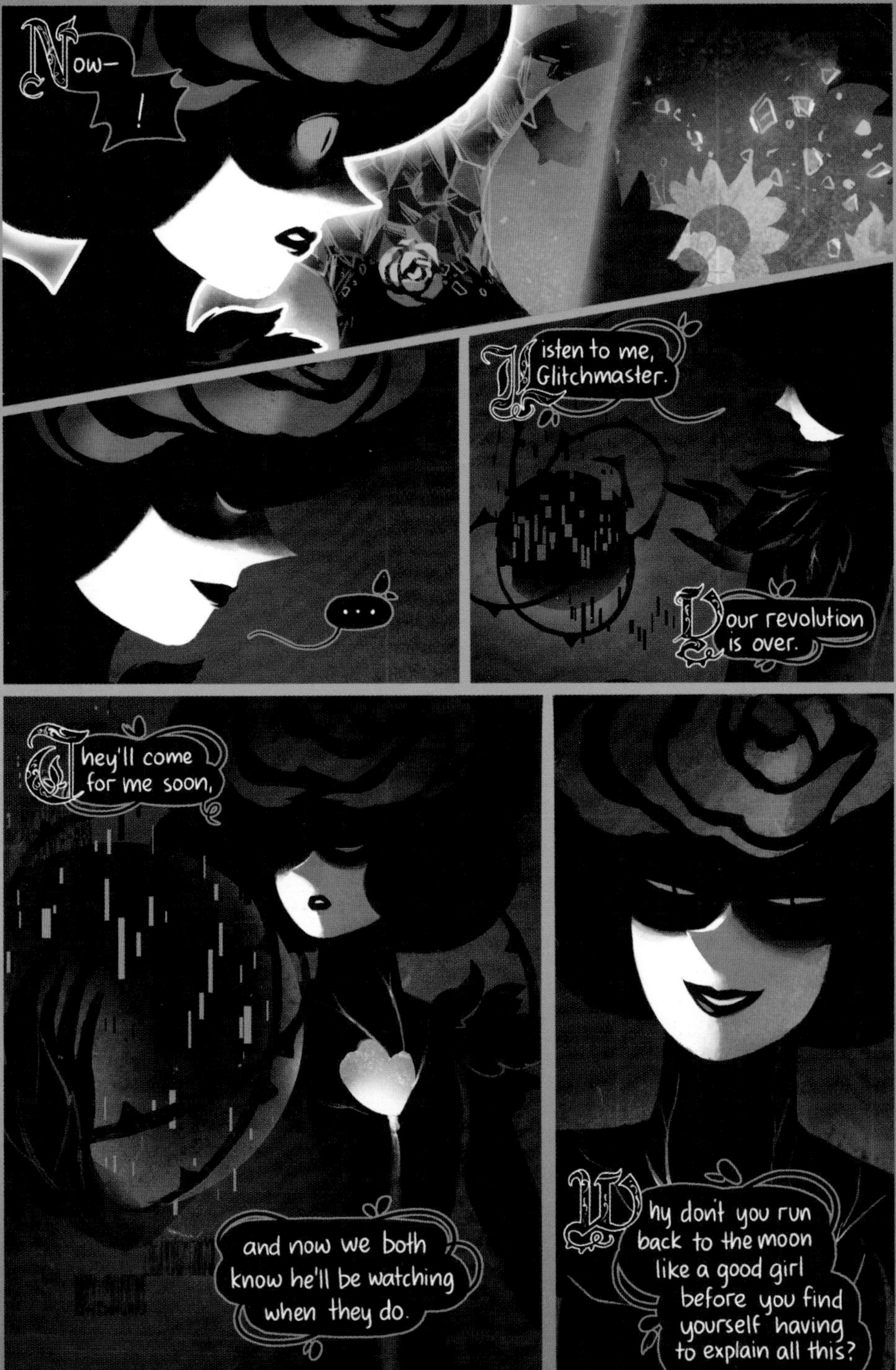
Now-
!
...
Listen to me, Glitchmaster.
Your revolution is over.
They'll come for me soon,
and now we both know he'll be watching when they do.
Why dont you run back to the moon like a good girl before you find yourself having to explain all this?

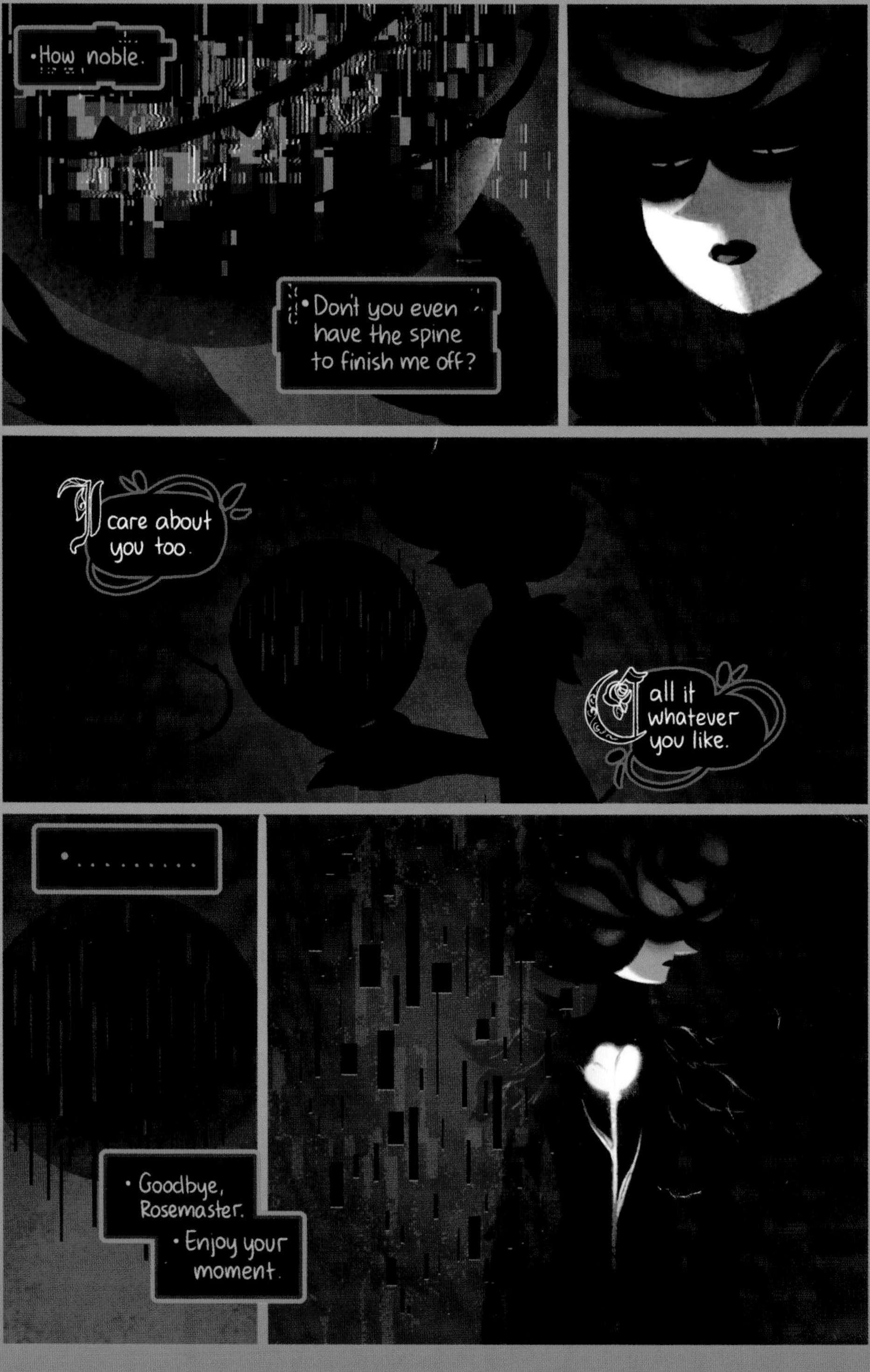
• How noble.
• Don't you even have the spine to finish me off?
I care about you too.
Call it whatever you like.
• . . . .
• Goodbye, Rosemaster.
• Enjoy your moment.

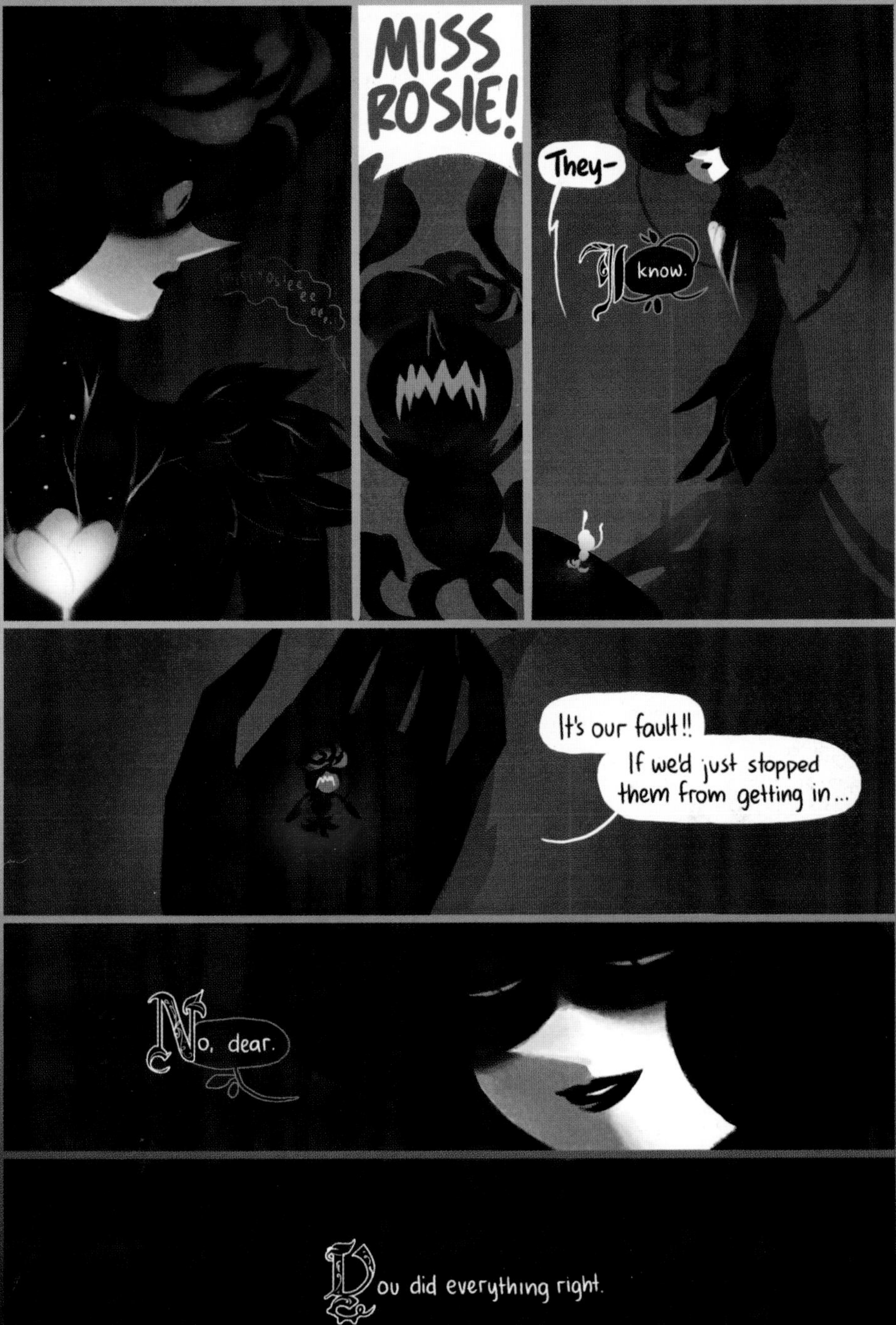
MISS ROSIE!
They-
I know.
It's our fault!! If we'd just stopped them from getting in...
No, dear.
You did everything right.

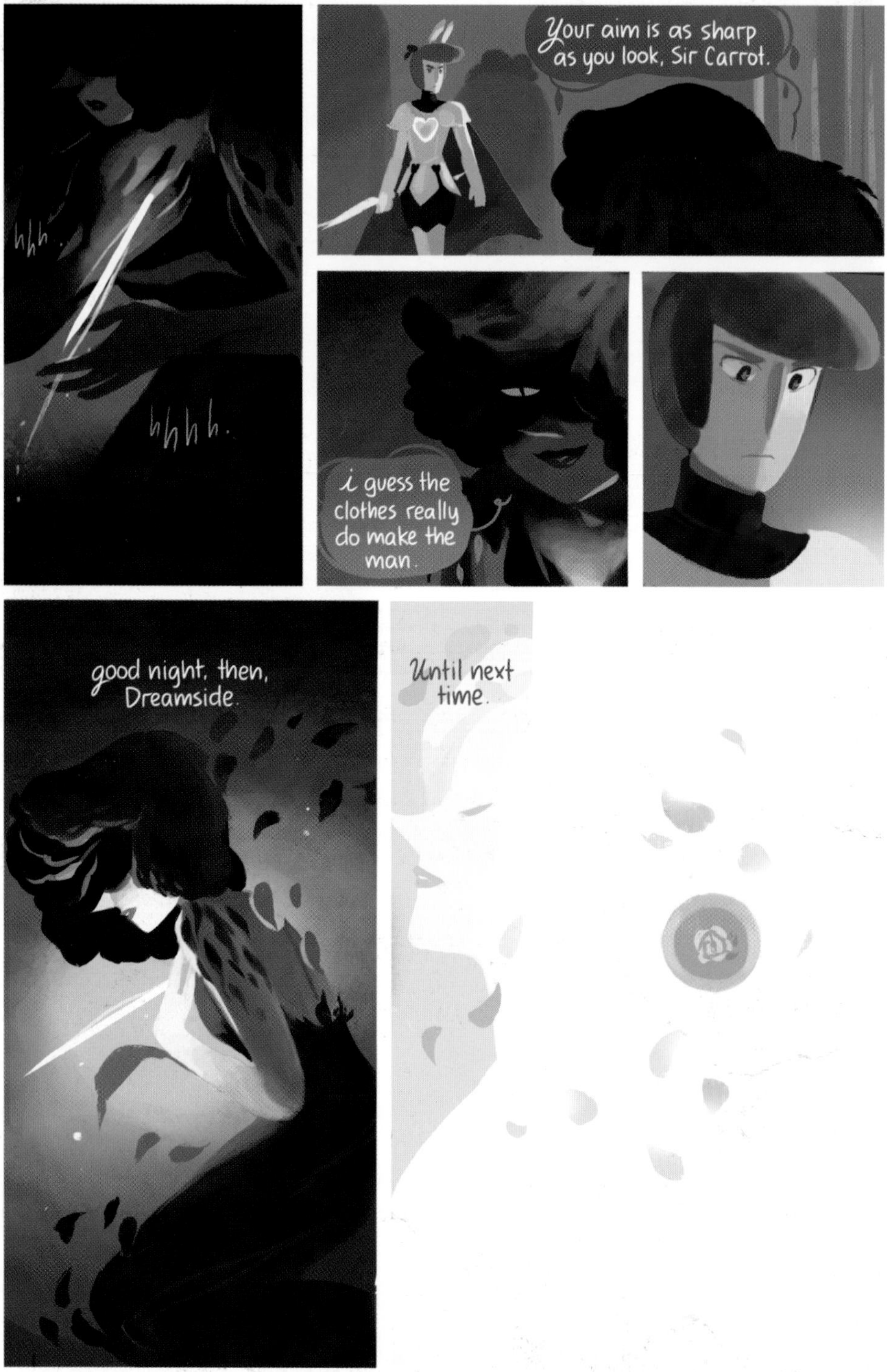
hhh.
hhhh.
Your aim is as sharp as you look, Sir Carrot.
i guess the clothes really do make the man.
good night, then, Dreamside.
Until next time.

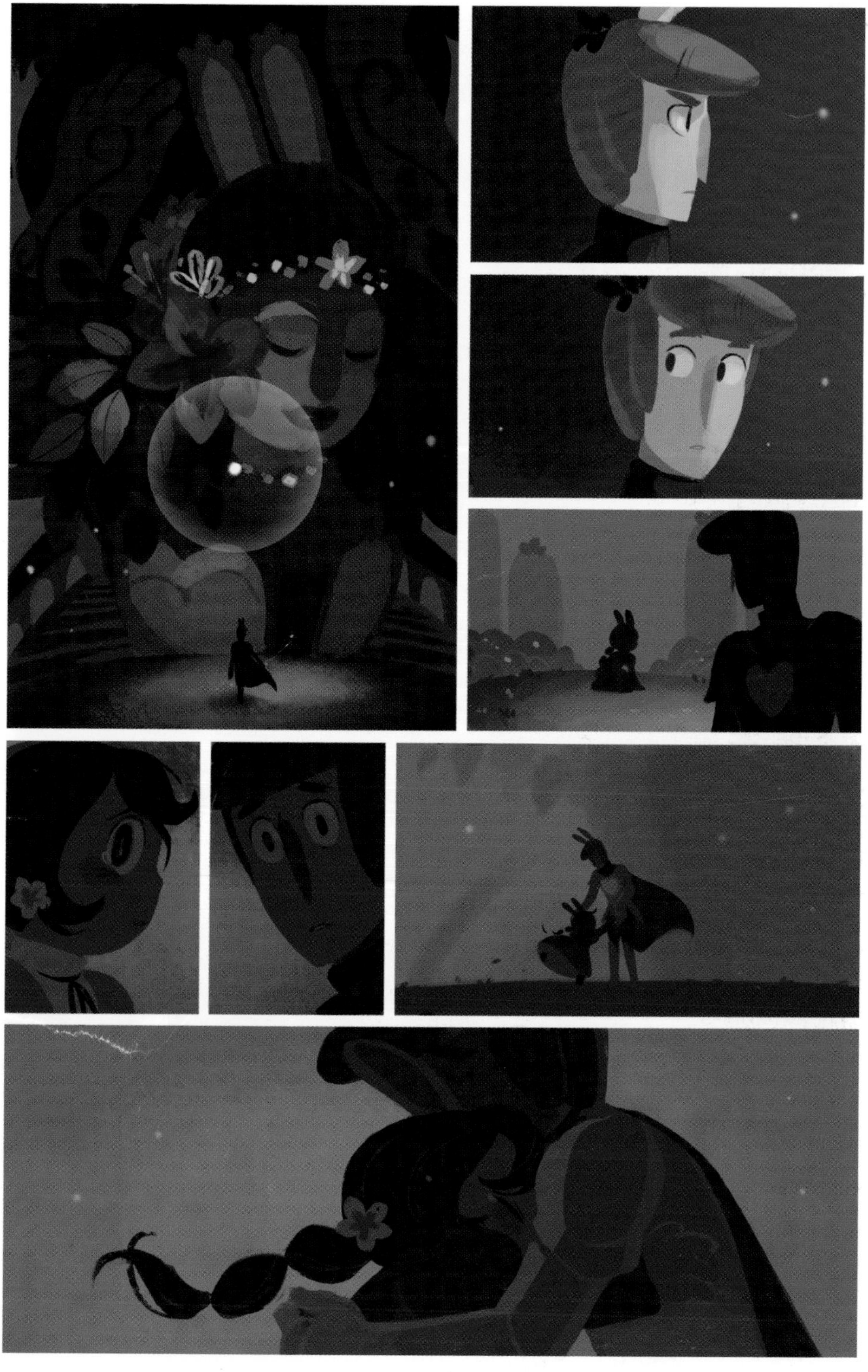

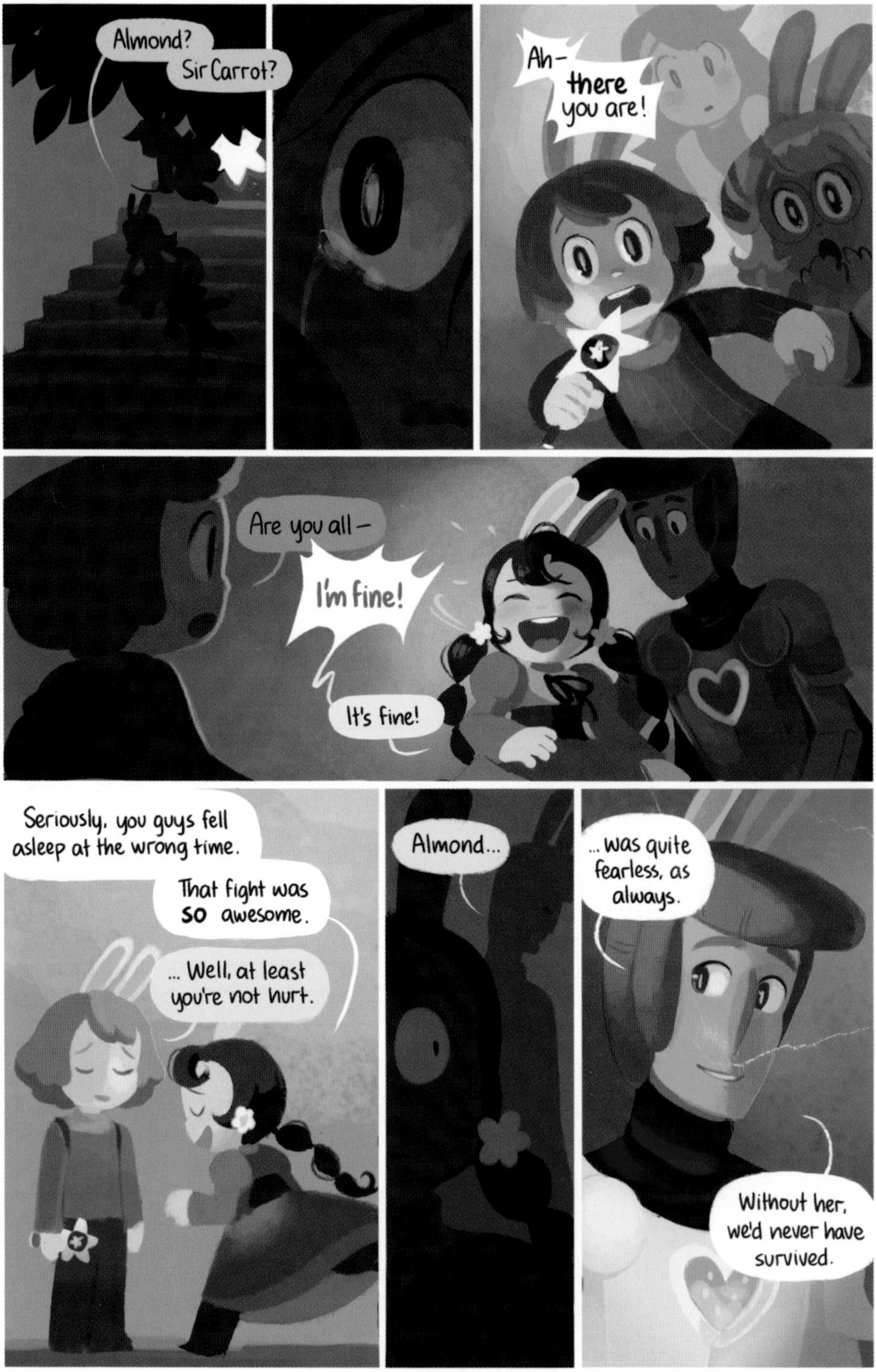
Almond?
Sir Carrot?
Ah– there you are!
Are you all–
I'm fine!
It's fine!
Seriously, you guys fell asleep at the wrong time.
That fight was SO awesome.
... Well, at least you're not hurt.
Almond...
...was quite fearless, as always.
Without her, we'd never have survived.

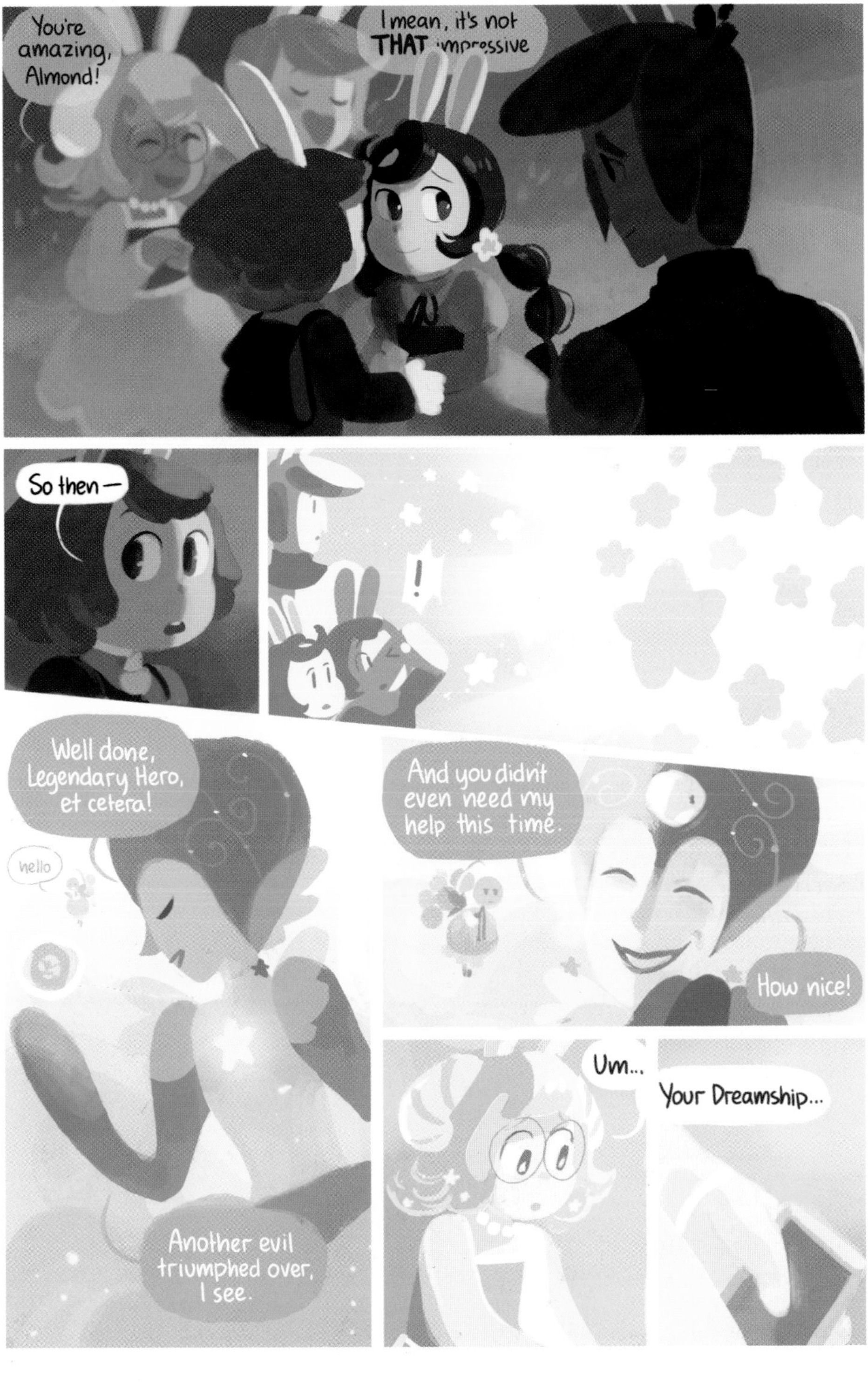

You're amazing, Almond!
I mean, it's not THAT impressive
So then—
!
Well done, Legendary Hero, et cetera!
hello
Another evil triumphed over, I see.
And you didn't even need my help this time.
How nice!
Um...
Your Dreamship...

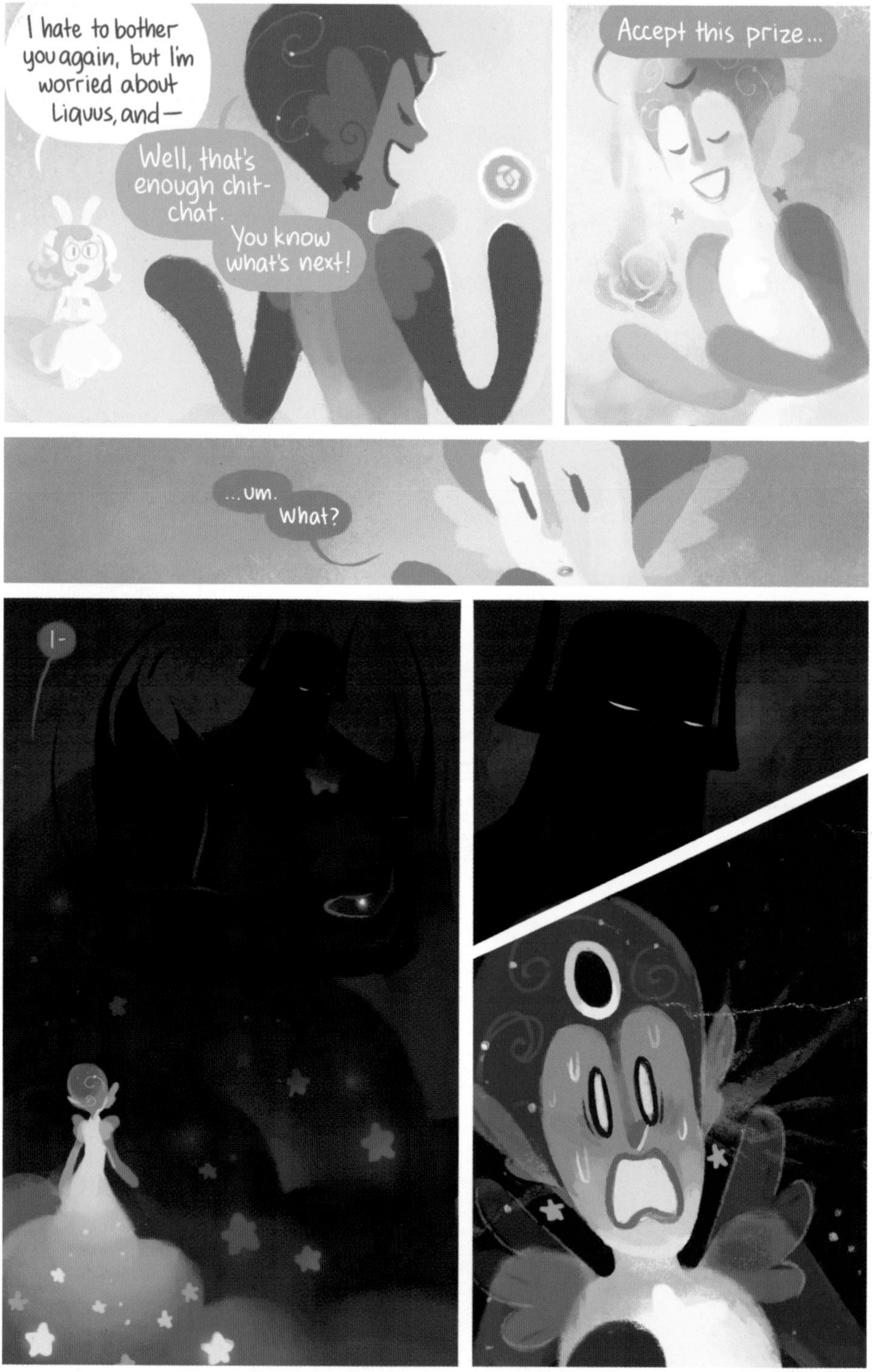
I hate to bother you again, but I'm worried about Liquus, and—
Well, that's enough chit-chat.
You know what's next!
Accept this prize...
...um.
What?
I-

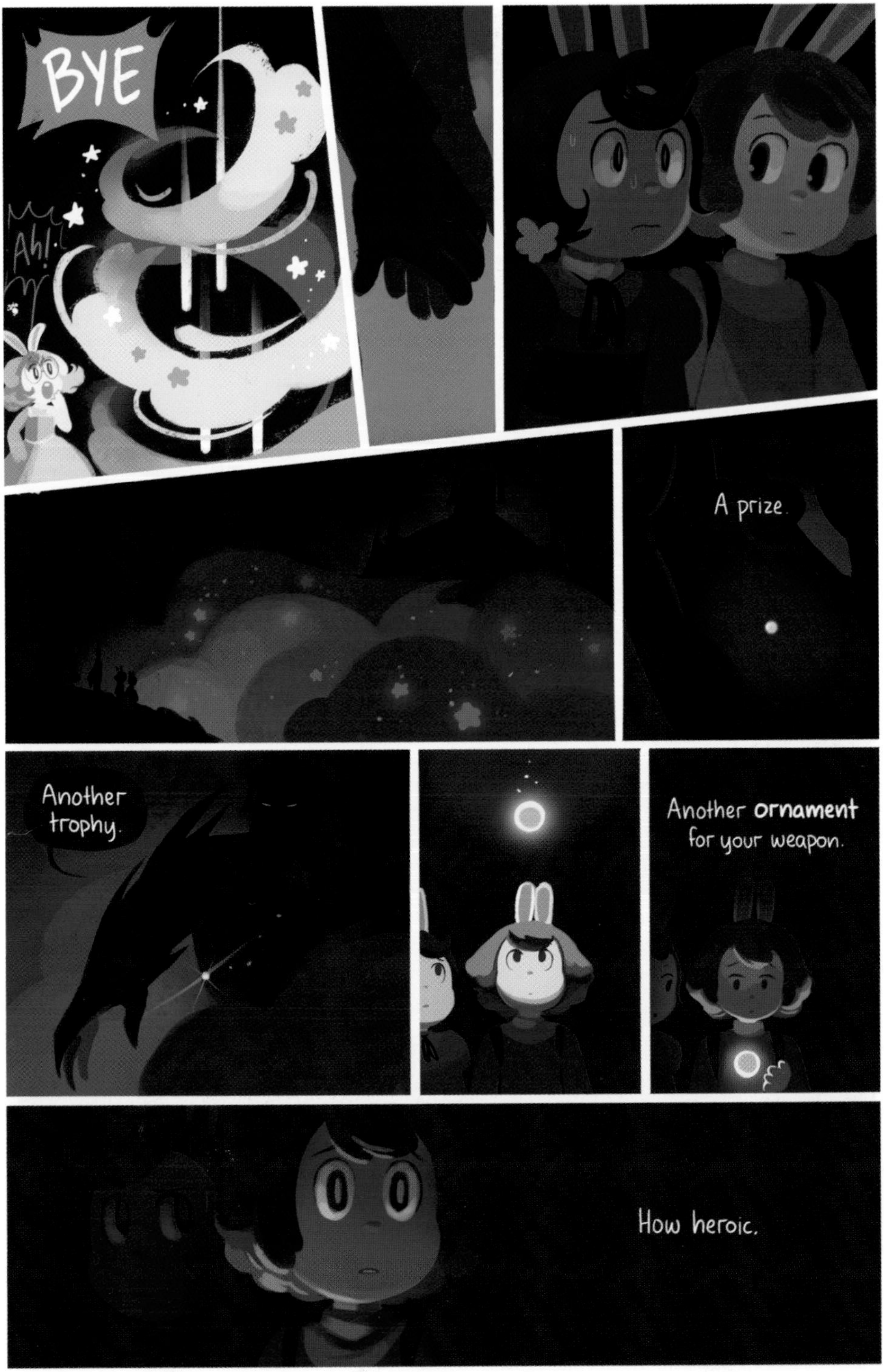
BYE
Ah!
A prize.
Another trophy.
Another **ornament** for your weapon.
How heroic.

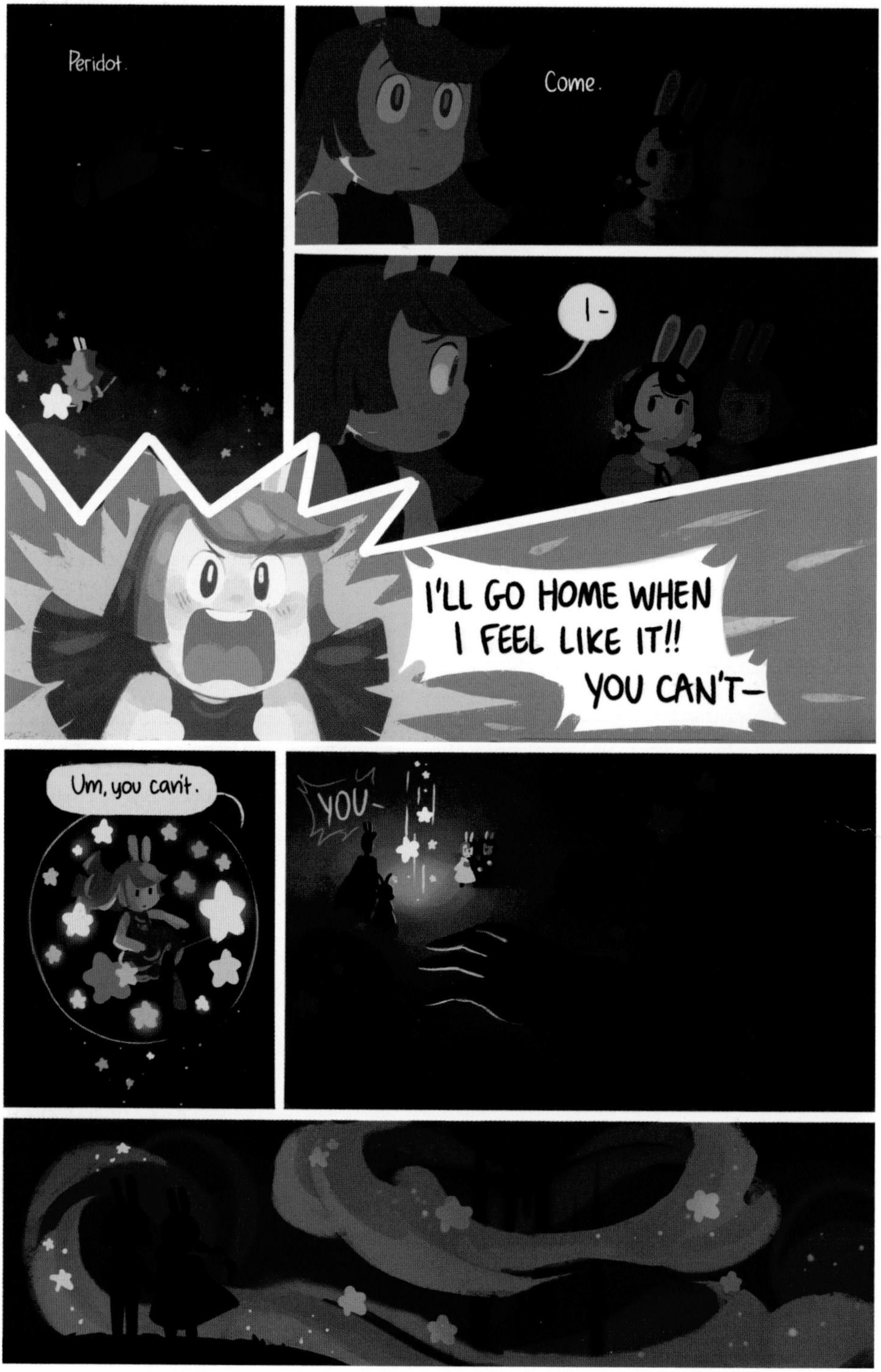
Peridot.
Come.
I-
I'LL GO HOME WHEN I FEEL LIKE IT!! YOU CAN'T-
Um, you can't.
YOU-

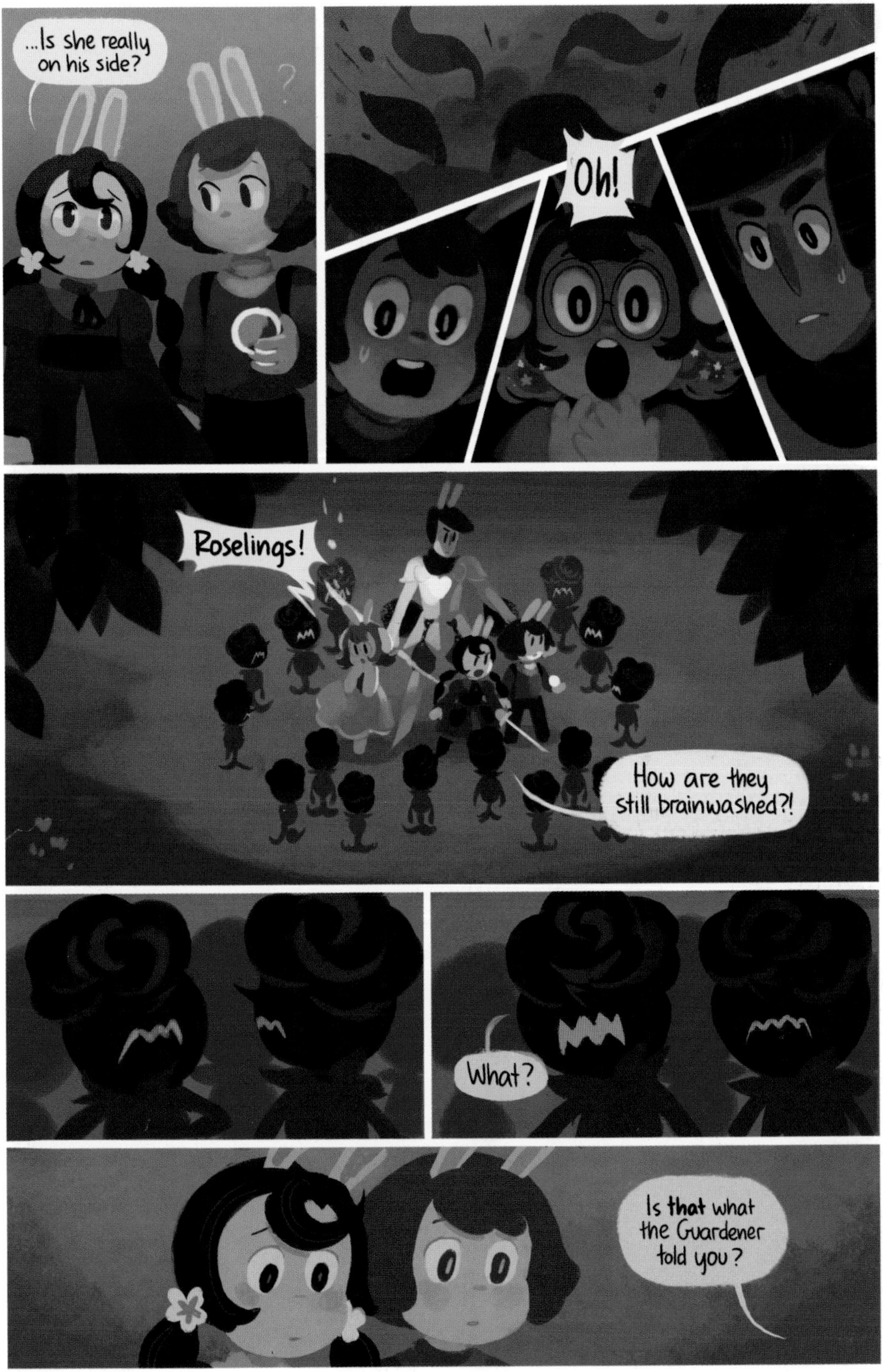
...Is she really on his side?
?
Oh!
Roselings!
How are they still brainwashed?!
What?
Is **that** what the Guardener told you?

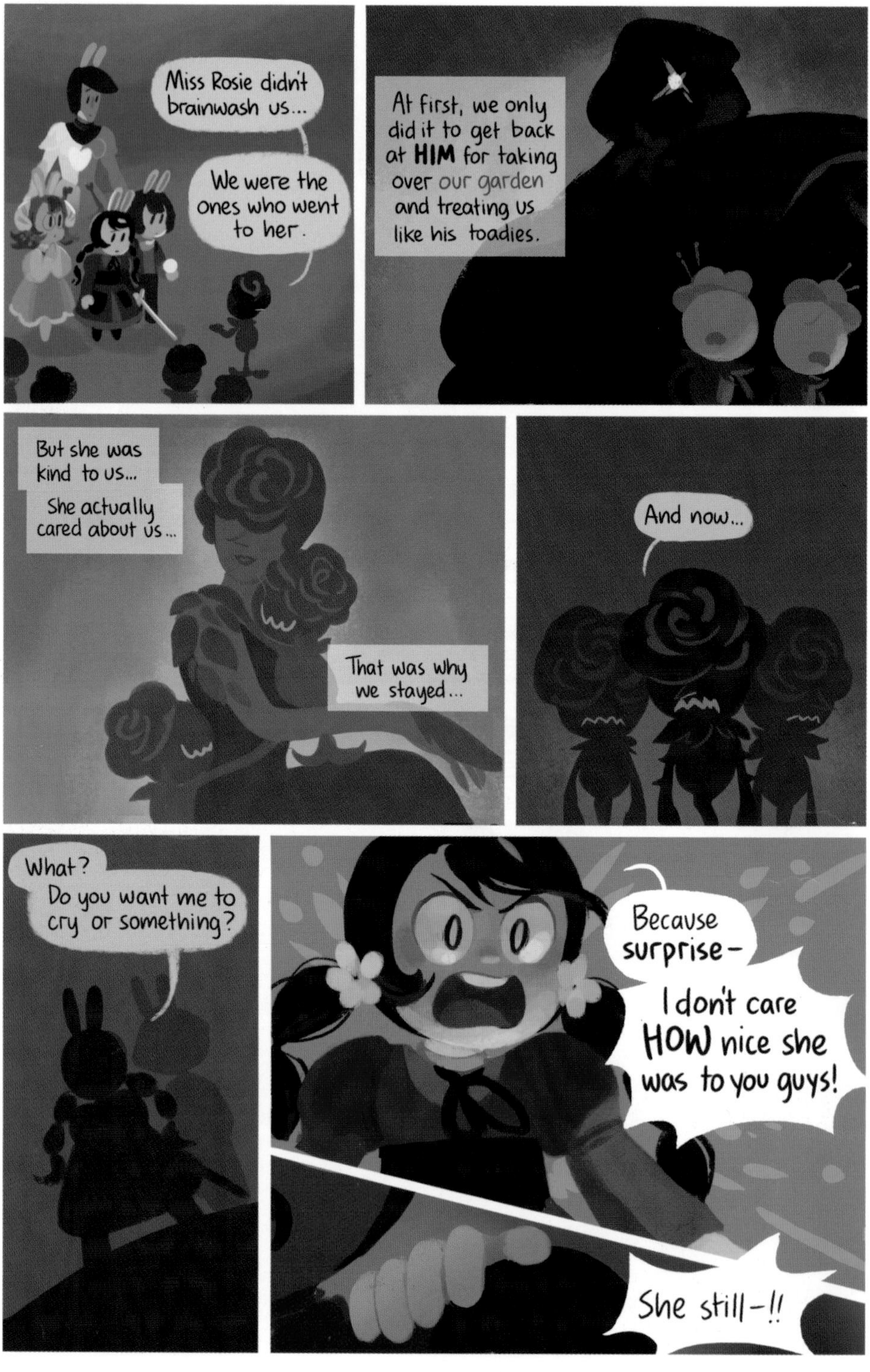

Miss Rosie didn't brainwash us...
We were the ones who went to her.
At first, we only did it to get back at HIM for taking over our garden and treating us like his toadies.
But she was kind to us...
She actually cared about us...
That was why we stayed...
And now...
What? Do you want me to cry or something?
Because surprise–
I don't care HOW nice she was to you guys!
She still–!!

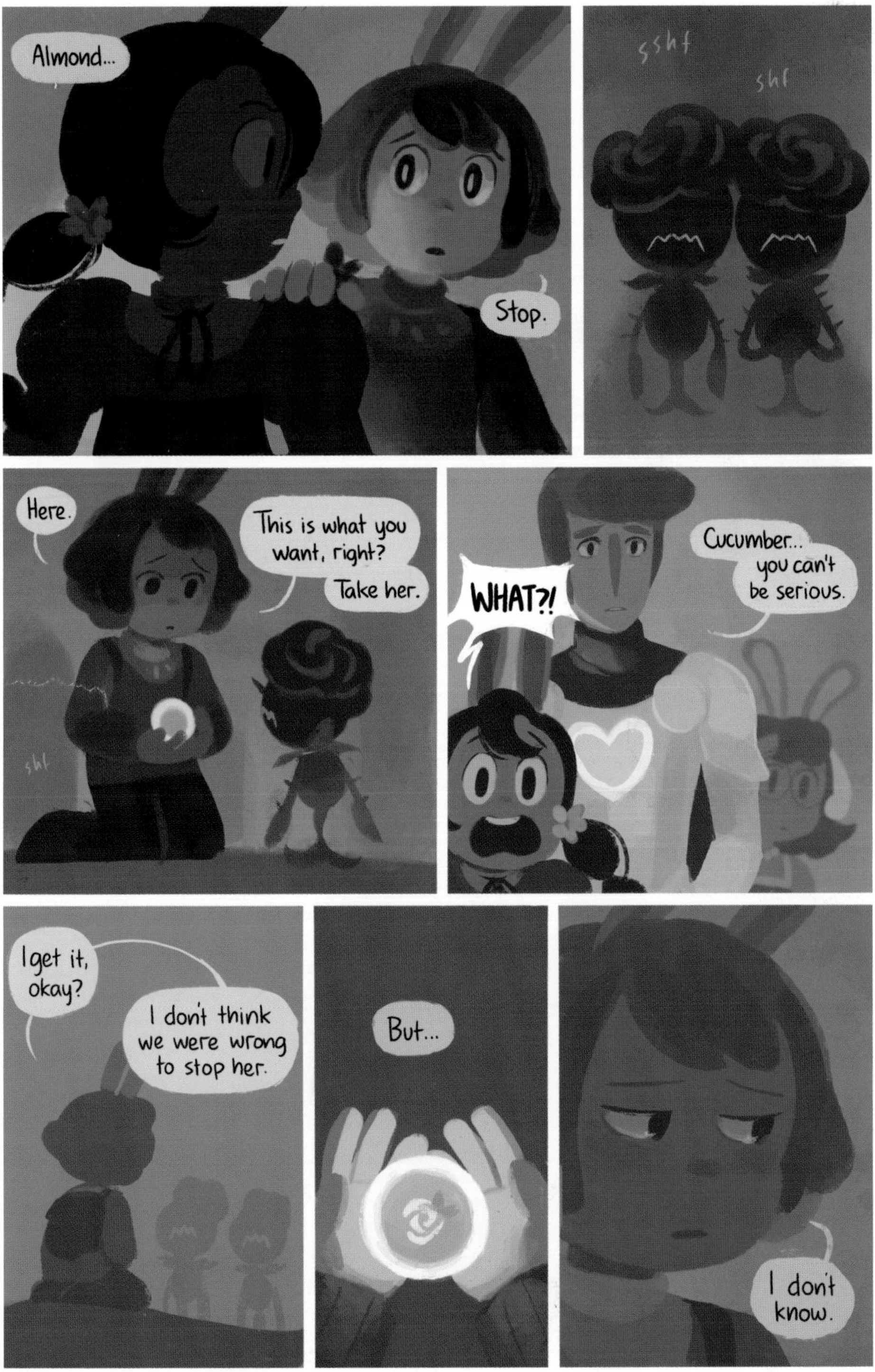
Almond...
Stop.
sshf
shf
Here.
This is what you want, right?
Take her.
shf
WHAT?!
Cucumber... you can't be serious.
I get it, okay?
I don't think we were wrong to stop her.
But...
I don't know.

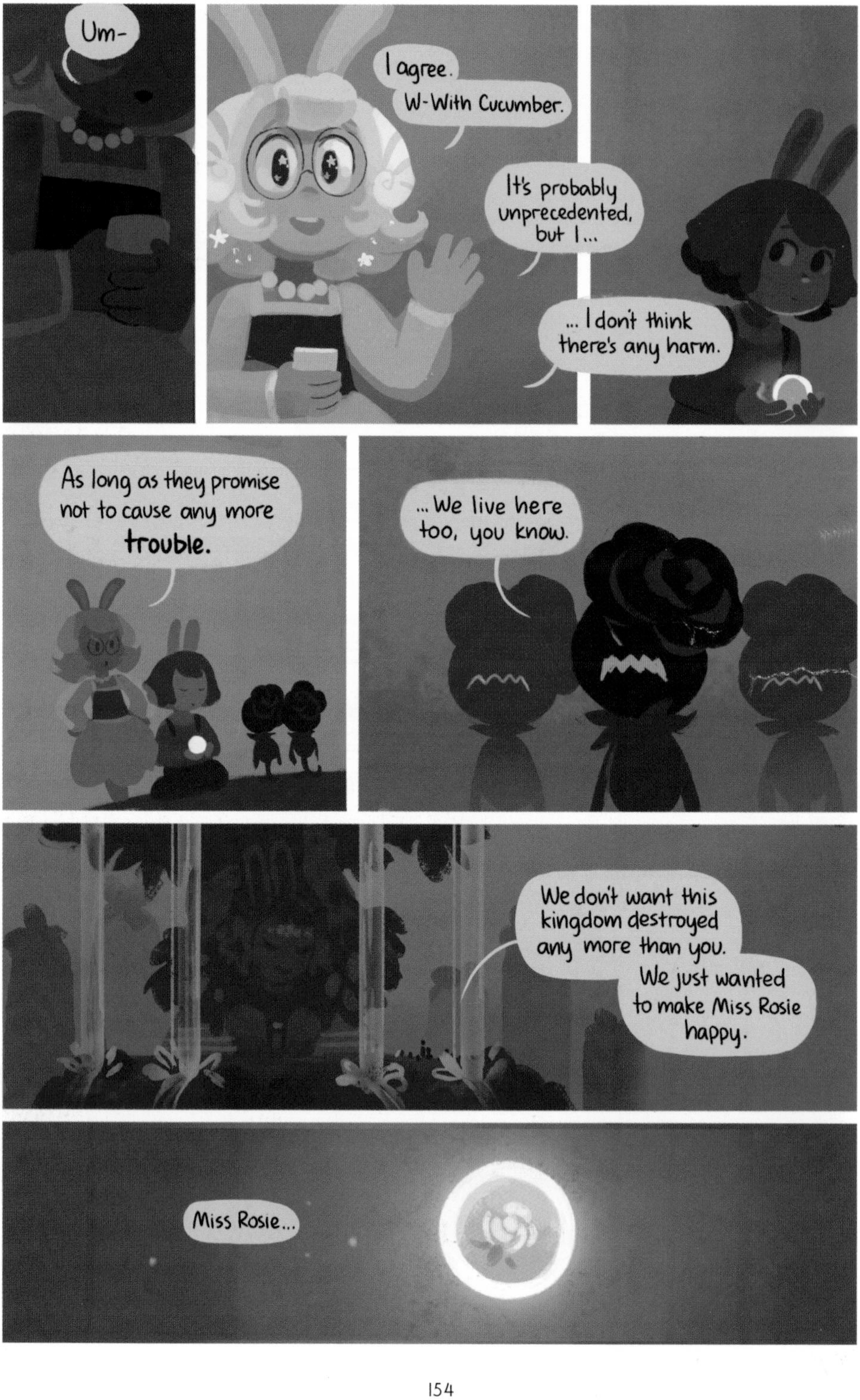
Um-
I agree.
W-With Cucumber.
It's probably unprecedented, but I...
... I don't think there's any harm.
As long as they promise not to cause any more trouble.
... We live here too, you know.
We don't want this kingdom destroyed any more than you.
We just wanted to make Miss Rosie happy.
Miss Rosie...

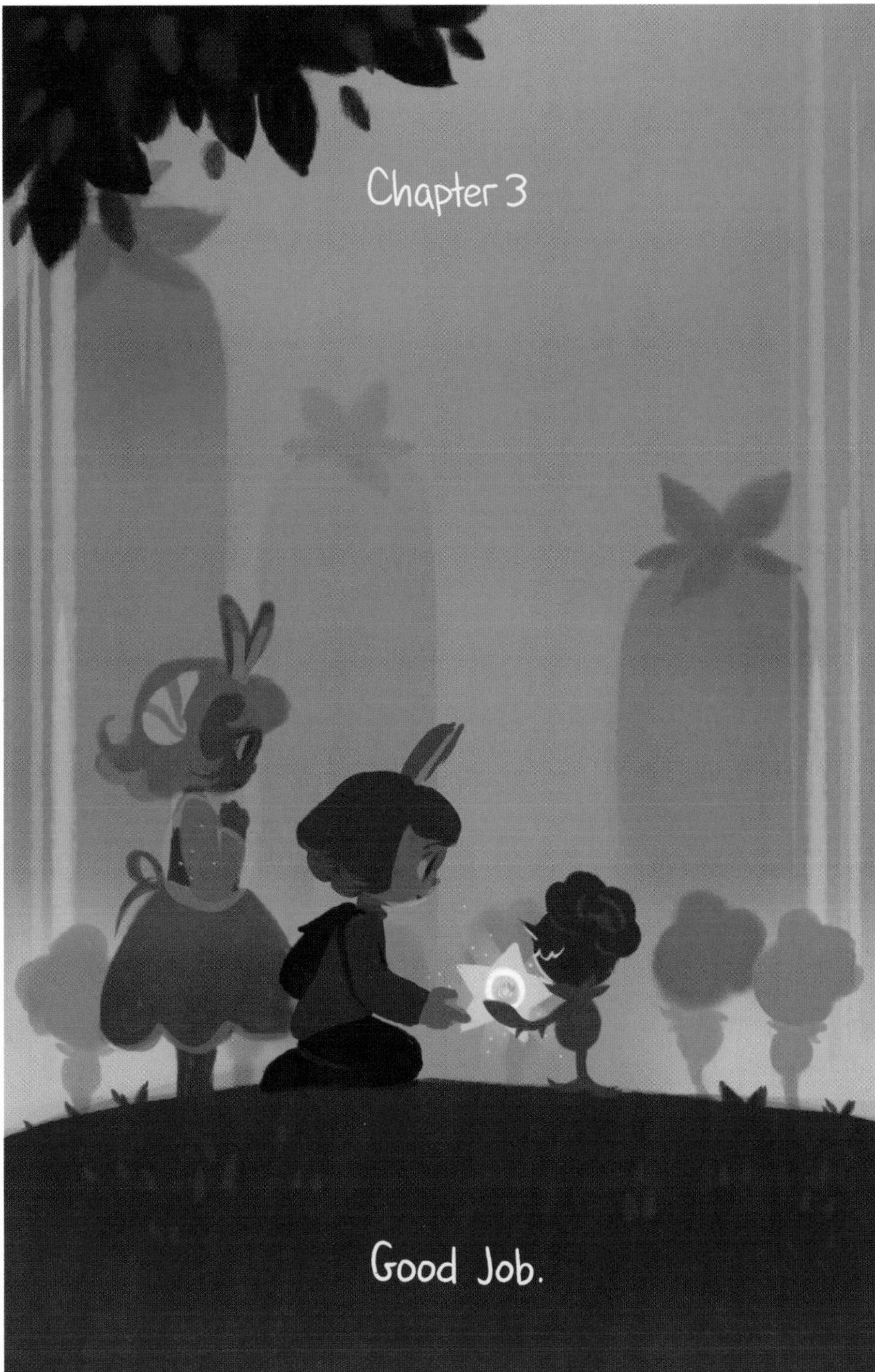
Chapter 3
Good Job.

Miss Rosie ...

Miss Rosie.

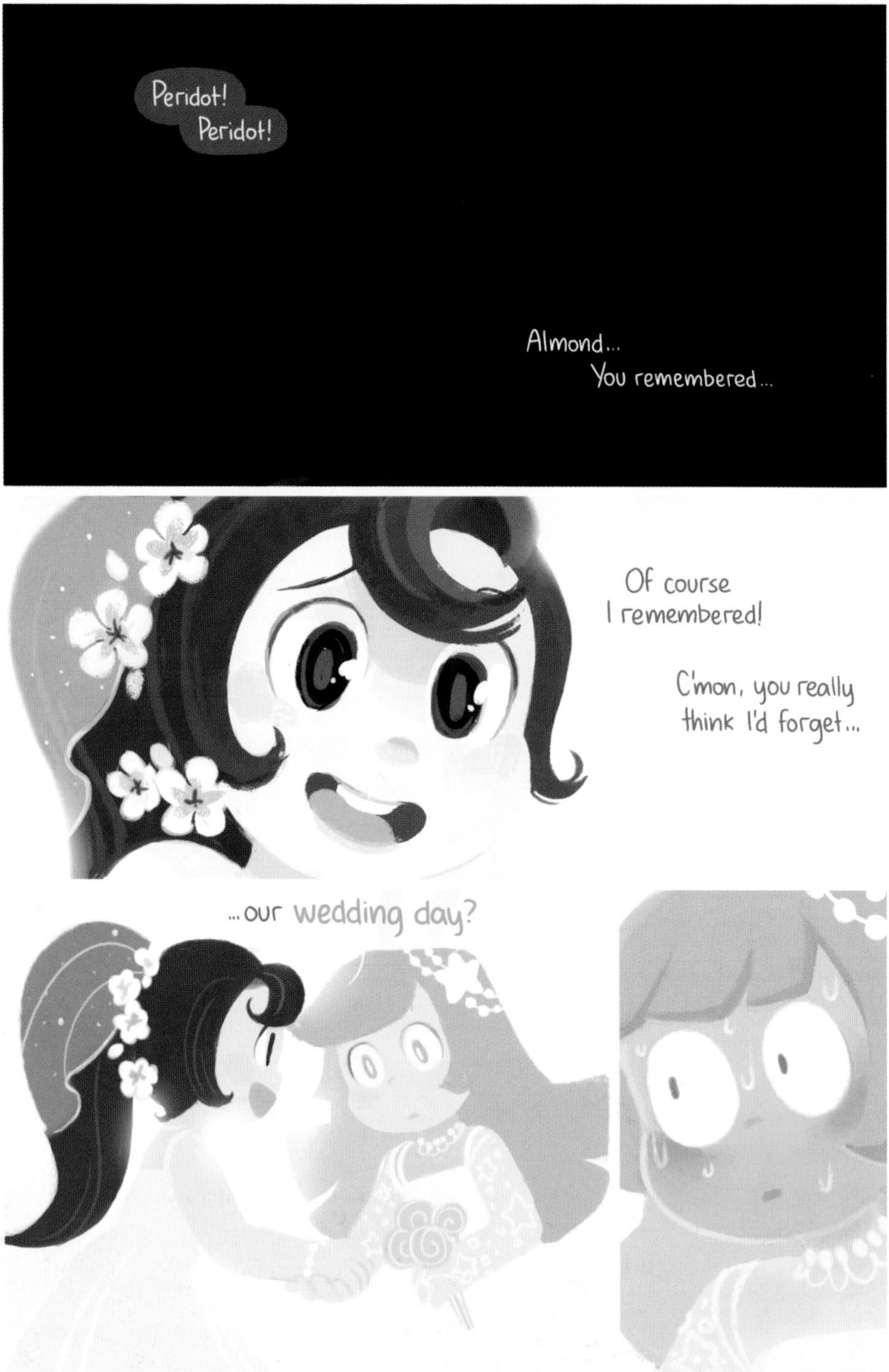
Peridot!
Peridot!
Almond...
You remembered...
Of course I remembered!
C'mon, you really think I'd forget...
...our wedding day?

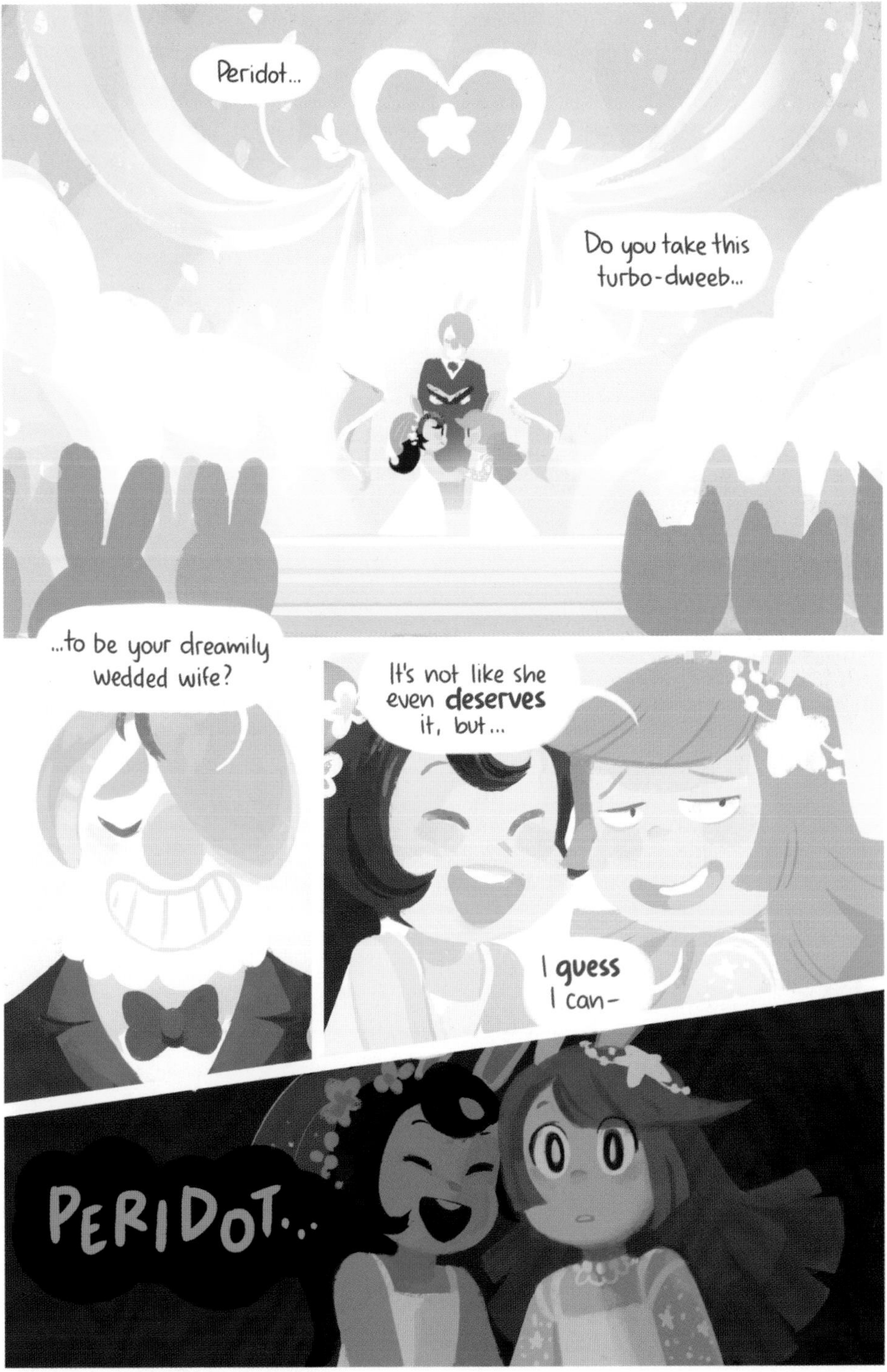
Peridot...
Do you take this turbo-dweeb...
...to be your dreamily wedded wife?
It's not like she even **deserves** it, but...
I **guess** I can-
PERIDOT...

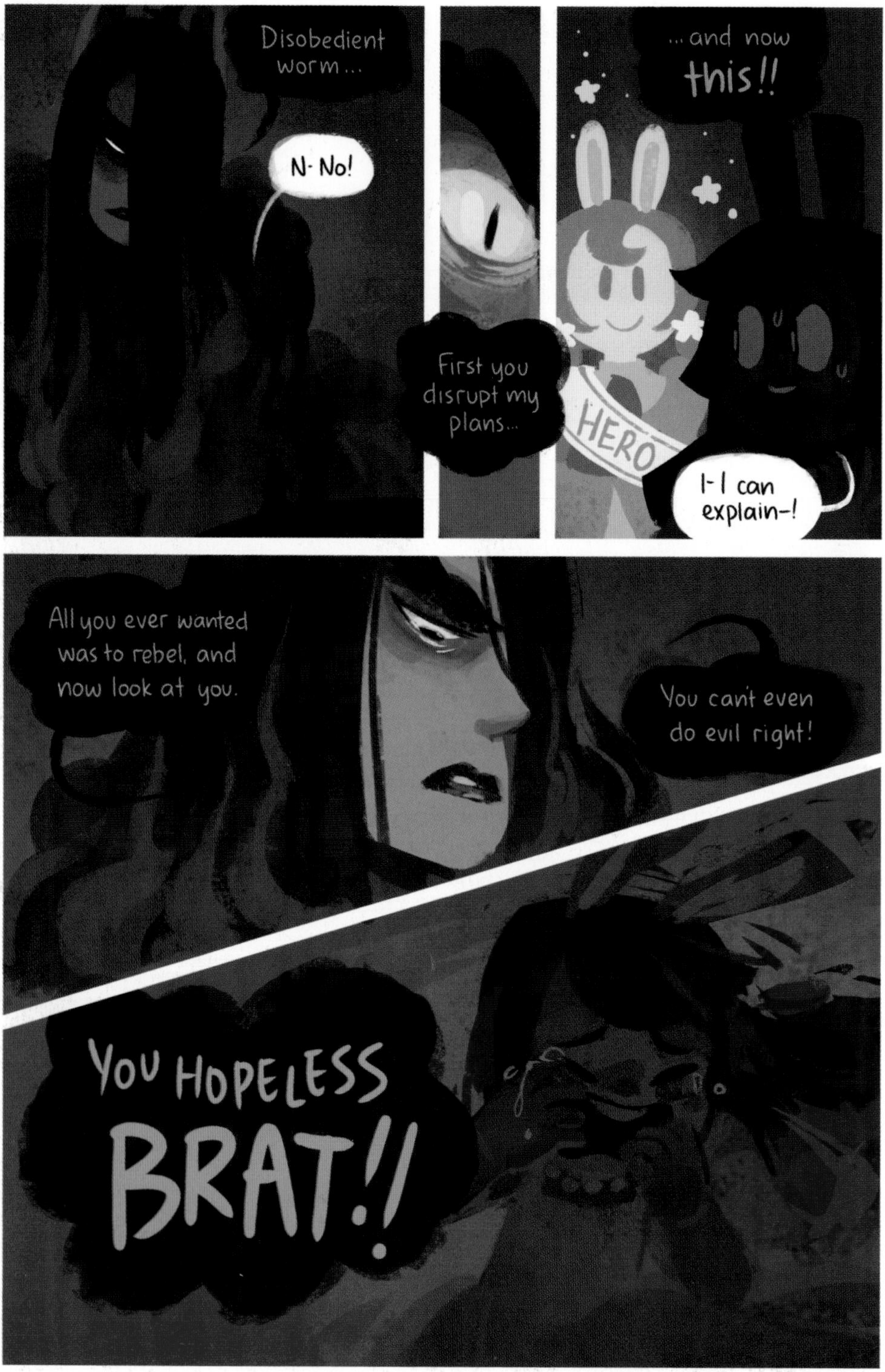
Disobedient worm...
N-No!
First you disrupt my plans...
...and now this!!
HERO
I-I can explain-!
All you ever wanted was to rebel, and now look at you.
You can't even do evil right!
YOU HOPELESS BRAT!!

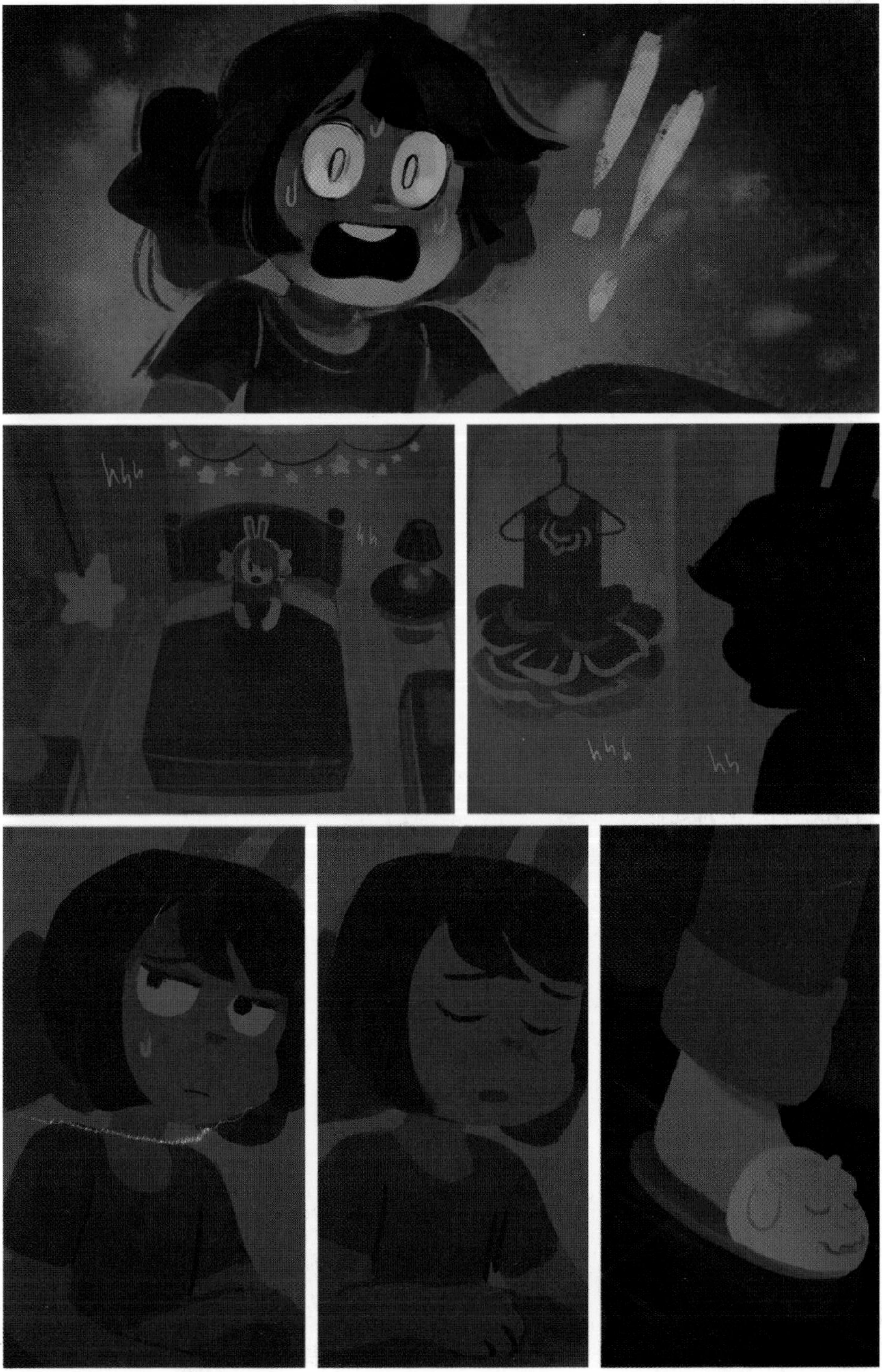
!!
hhh
hh
hhh
hh

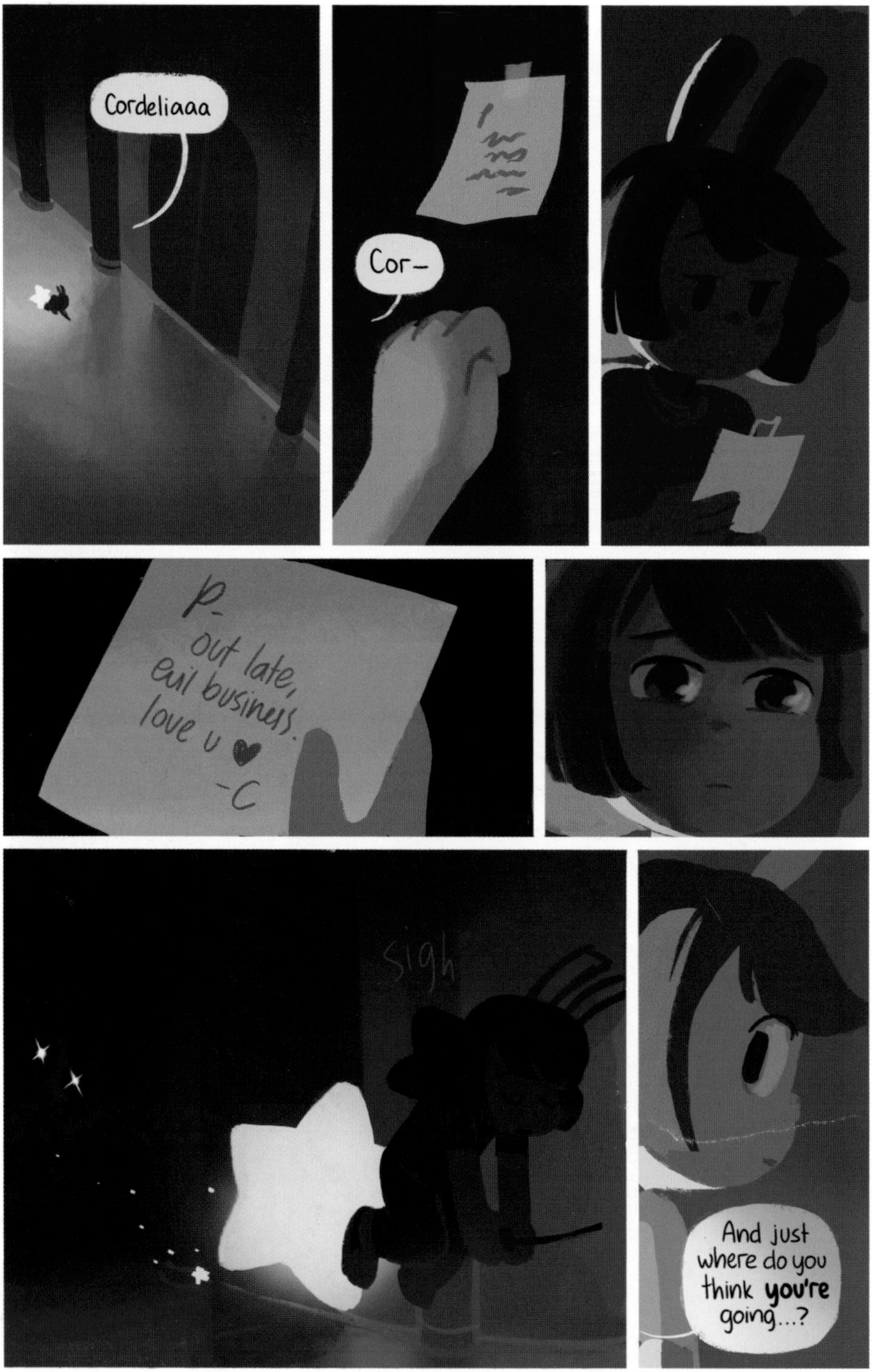
Cordeliaaa
Cor—
P-
out late,
evil business.
love u ♥
-C
sigh
And just where do you think **you're** going...?

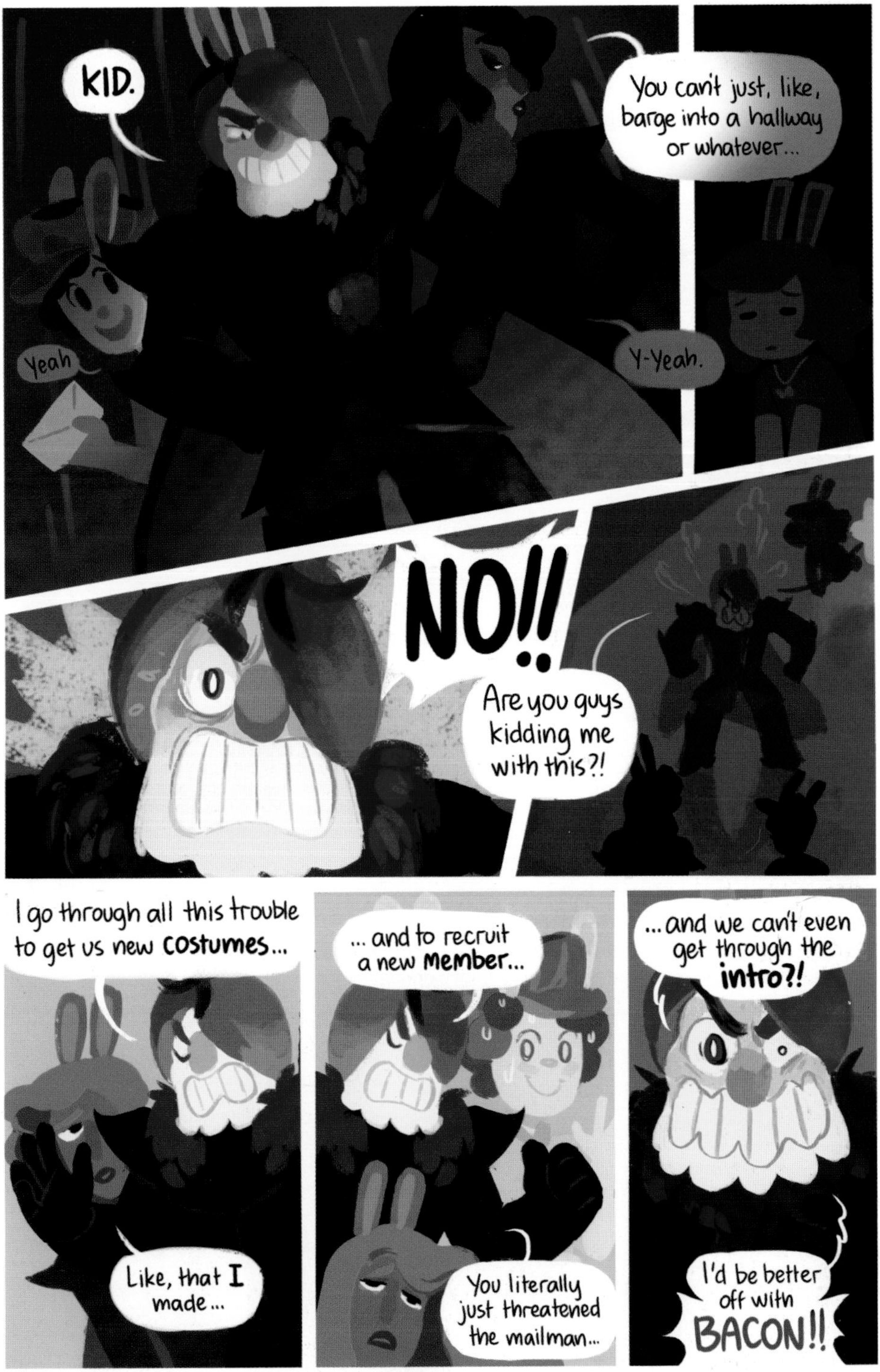
KID.
You can't just, like, barge into a hallway or whatever...
Yeah
Y-Yeah.
NO!!
Are you guys kidding me with this?!
I go through all this trouble to get us new **costumes**...
Like, that **I** made...
... and to recruit a new **member**...
You literally just threatened the mailman...
... and we can't even get through the **intro?!**
I'd be better off with BACON!!

N-NOT

I mean, heh, why would a manly piece of cake like ME need somebody like THAT around ever, am I right or am I right

I don't know why I even bother pretending to be a ditz, it's not like you actually listen to a word that comes out of my mouth

HEY, WAIT!!

We have to practice our routine!

Practice on somebody who caaaaares

What a bunch of freaks...

shf

shf

shf

?

shf

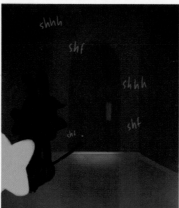

shhh

shf

shhh

shf

shf

shf

shf

shf

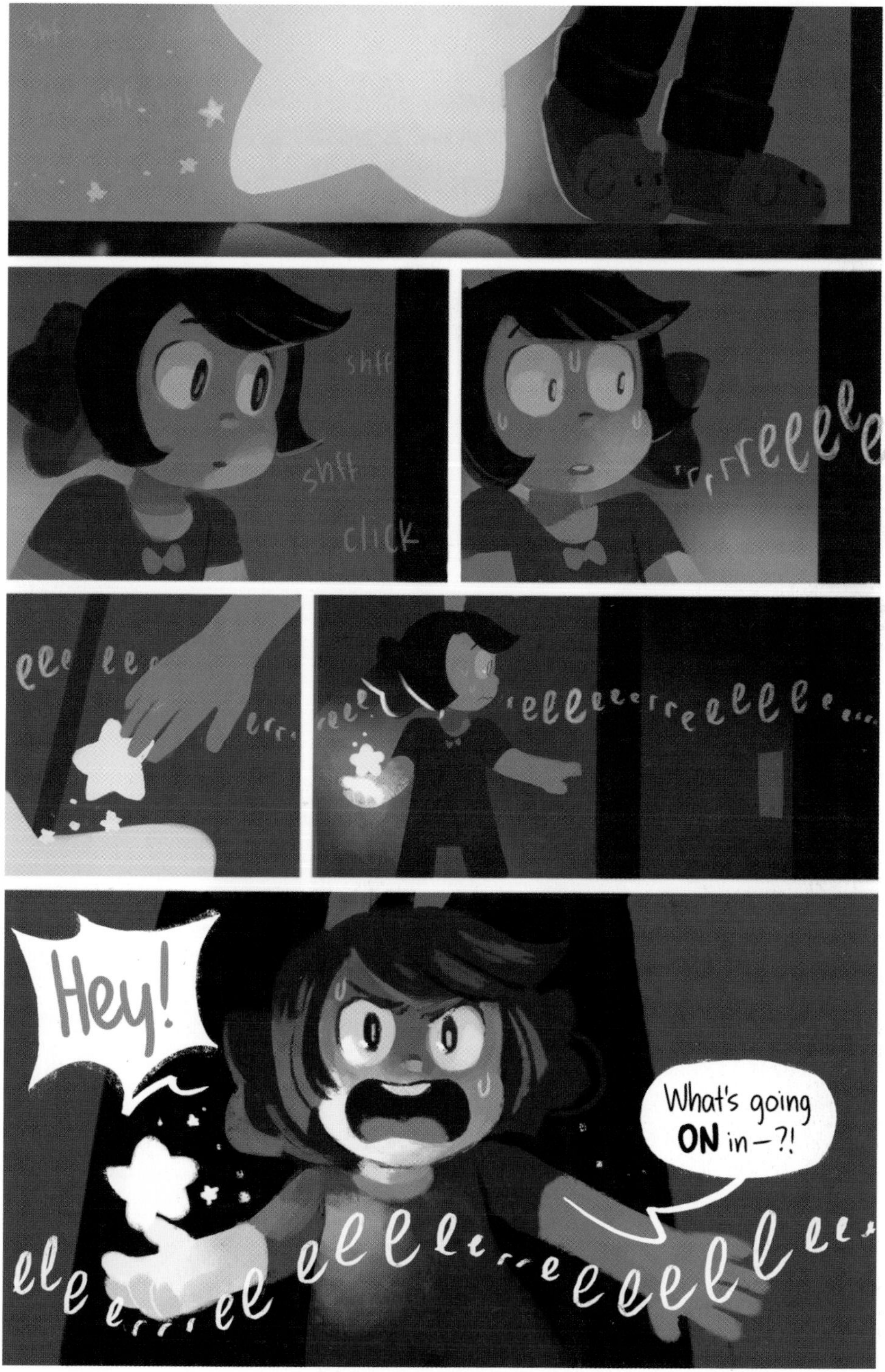
shff
shff
shff
shff
click
rrreeeee
eee eee
eee...
reeeeeeeeereeeeee...
Hey!
What's going ON in–?!
eeeeerrrreeeeereeeeeeeeeeee...

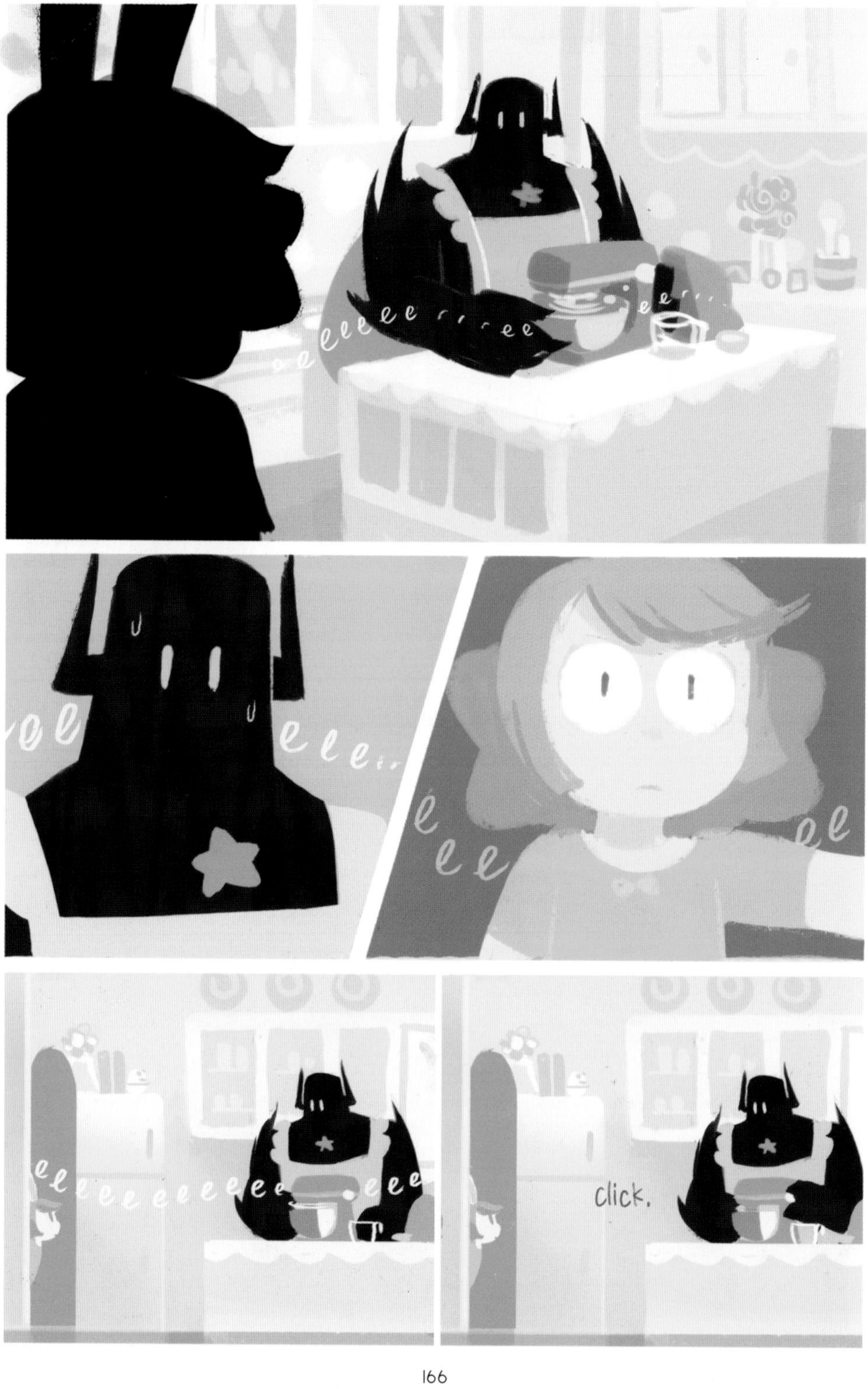
click.

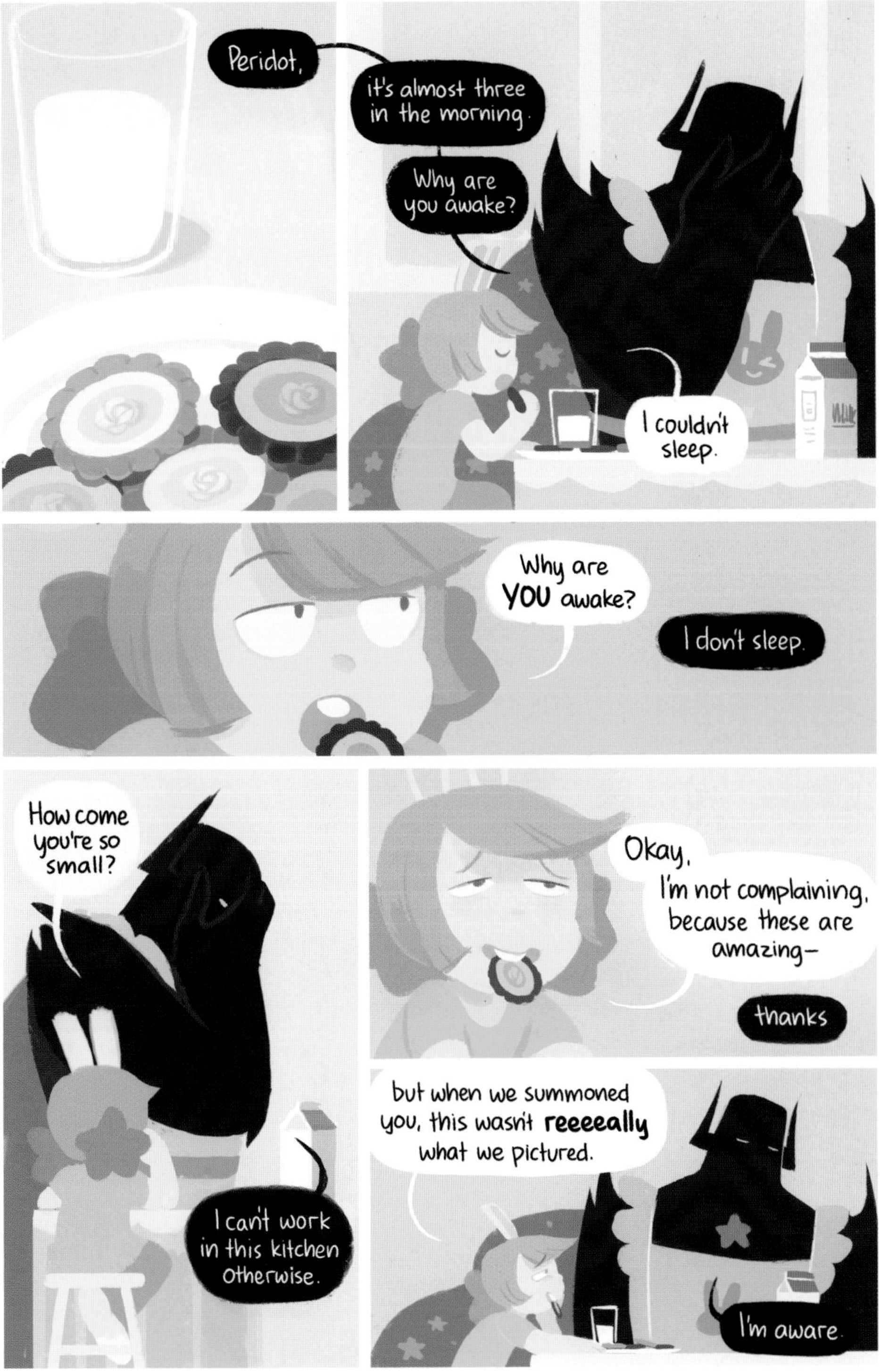
Peridot,
it's almost three in the morning.
Why are you awake?
I couldn't sleep.
Why are YOU awake?
I don't sleep.
How come you're so small?
I can't work in this kitchen otherwise.
Okay,
I'm not complaining, because these are amazing—
thanks
but when we summoned you, this wasn't **reeeeally** what we pictured.
I'm aware.

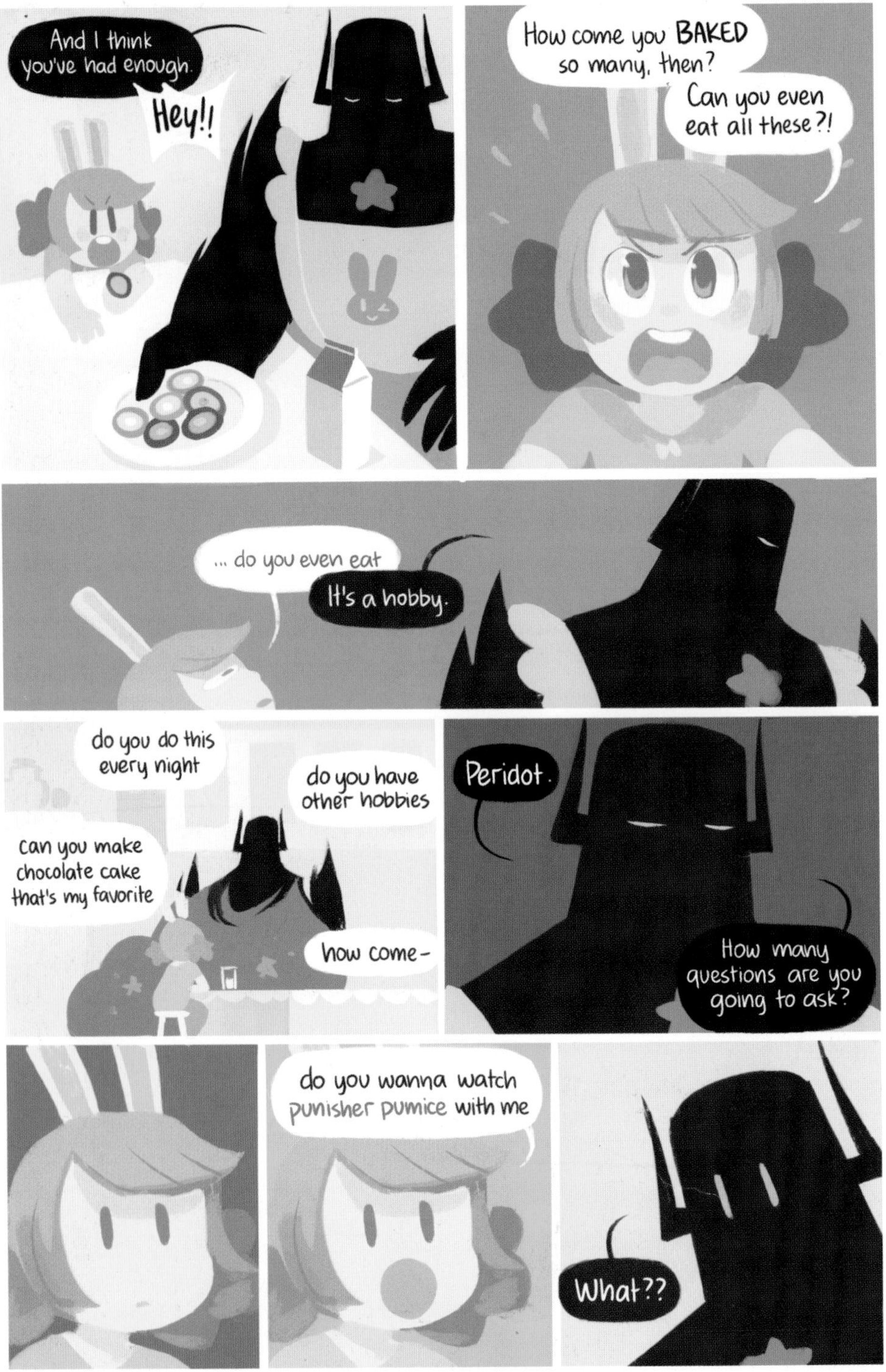
And I think you've had enough.
Hey!!
How come you BAKED so many, then?
Can you even eat all these?!
... do you even eat
It's a hobby.
do you do this every night
can you make chocolate cake that's my favorite
do you have other hobbies
how come-
Peridot.
How many questions are you going to ask?
do you wanna watch punisher pumice with me
What??

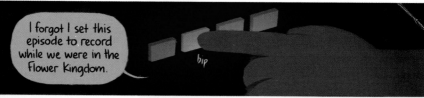

I forgot I set this episode to record while we were in the Flower Kingdom.

bip

♪ Make wayyyy for my heart ♪

♪ it's coming throoough ♪

Punisher Pumice

I never expected you to be interested in something like this.

♪ I know my passion can set the whole, world ♪ (ooh!) ♪

♪ I feel a sparkle of love within meeee ♪

♪ (there's a magic inside) ♪

♪ no matter what evil rises, there's a power ♪

Yeah, well,

I didn't think you'd be into sugar cookies, so what's your point?

They were shortbread.

♪ I'll neeever fall, I'll giiive it my all ♪

♪ I'm a pillar of love, stand tall ♪

shhhhh whatever it's starting

♪ I'm sending my heaaart, straight to yooooou ♪

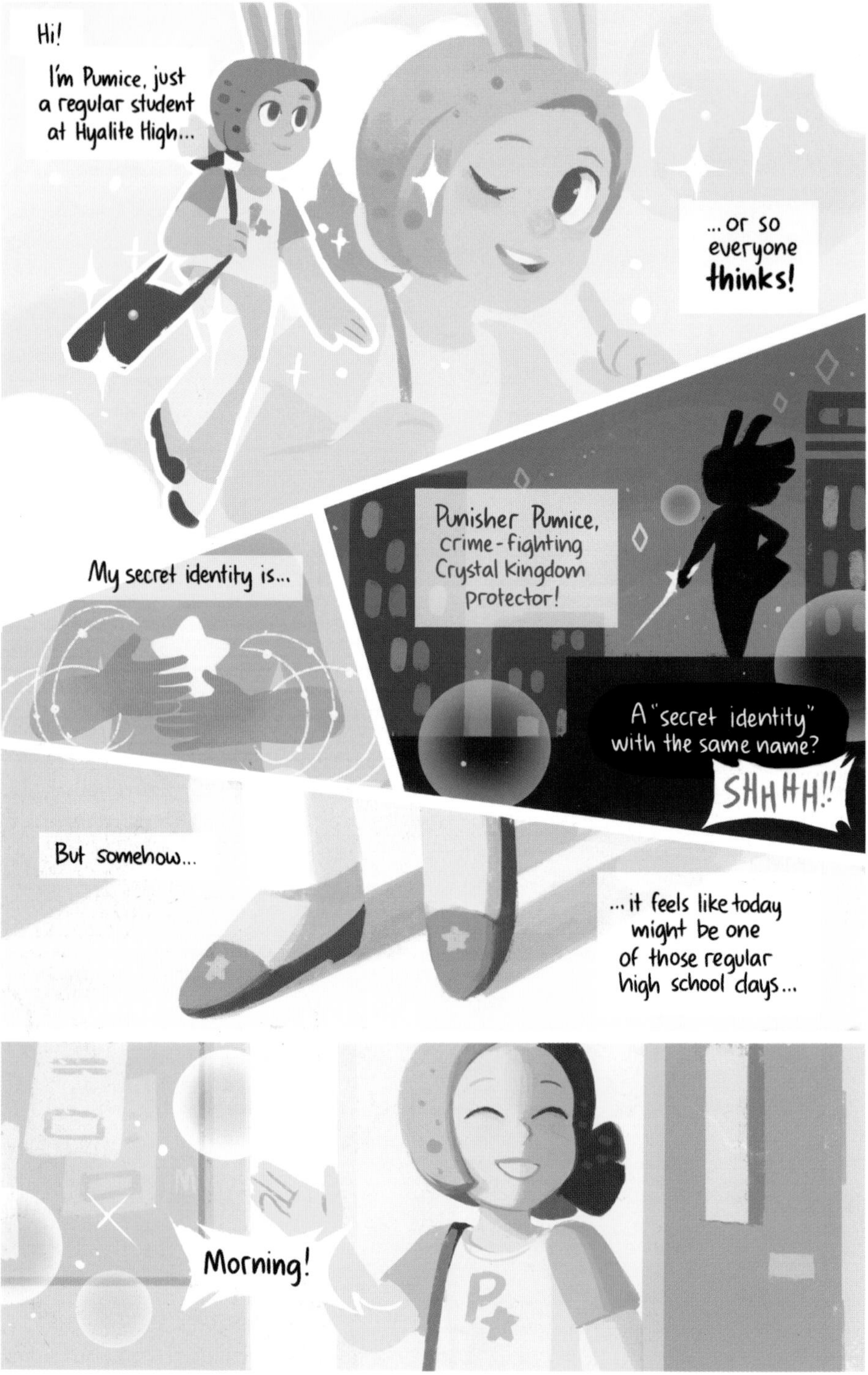
Hi!
I'm Pumice, just a regular student at Hyalite High...
...or so everyone **thinks!**
My secret identity is...
Punisher Pumice, crime-fighting Crystal Kingdom protector!
A "secret identity" with the same name?
SHHHH!!
But somehow...
...it feels like today might be one of those regular high school days...
Morning!

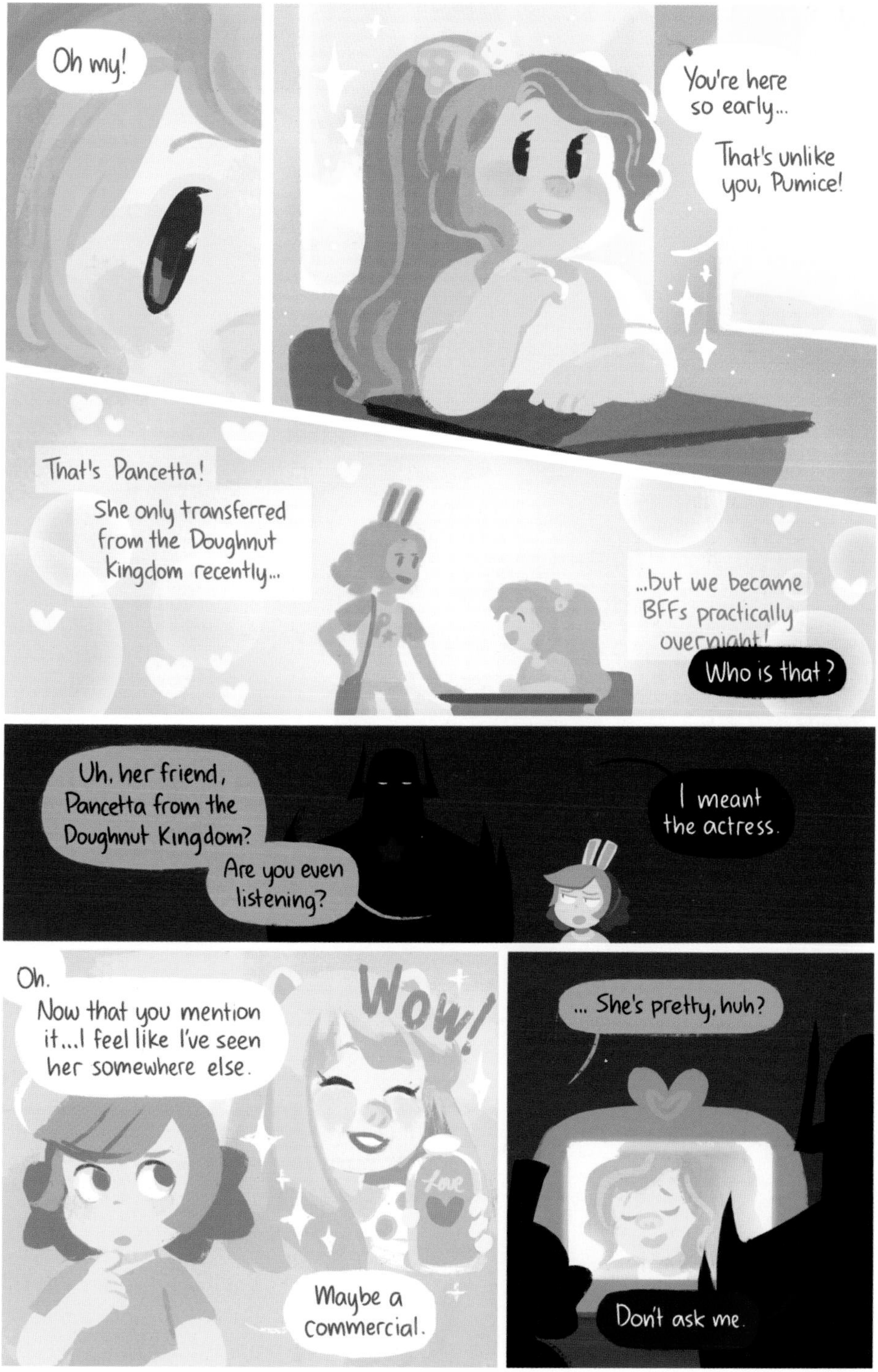
Oh my!
You're here so early...
That's unlike you, Pumice!
That's Pancetta!
She only transferred from the Doughnut Kingdom recently...
...but we became BFFs practically overnight!
Who is that?
Uh, her friend, Pancetta from the Doughnut Kingdom?
Are you even listening?
I meant the actress.
Oh.
Now that you mention it...I feel like I've seen her somewhere else.
WOW!
Maybe a commercial.
... She's pretty, huh?
Don't ask me.

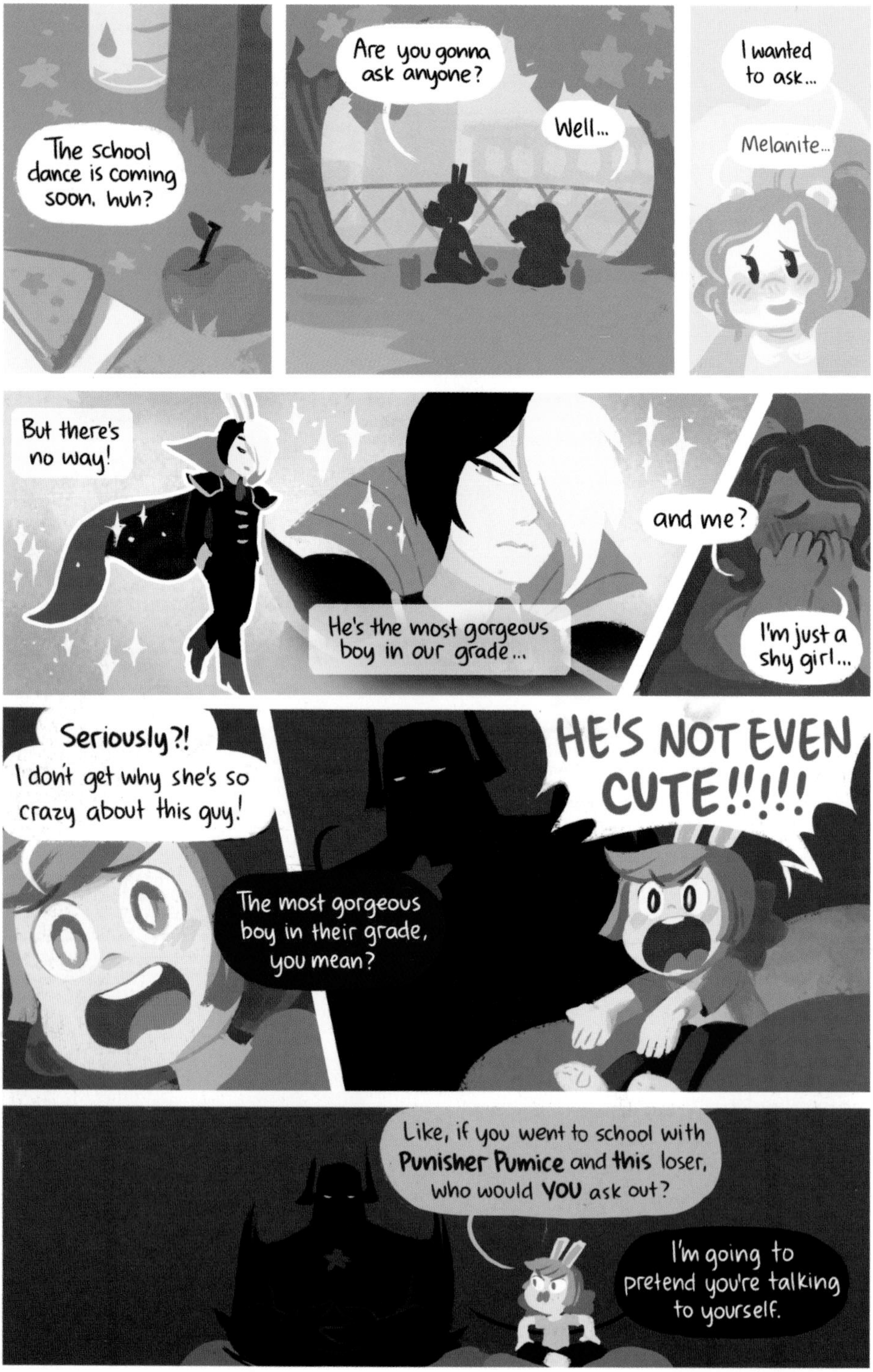
The school dance is coming soon, huh?
Are you gonna ask anyone?
Well...
I wanted to ask...
Melanite...
But there's no way!
He's the most gorgeous boy in our grade...
and me?
I'm just a shy girl...
Seriously?! I don't get why she's so crazy about this guy!
The most gorgeous boy in their grade, you mean?
HE'S NOT EVEN CUTE!!!!!
Like, if you went to school with **Punisher Pumice** and **this** loser, who would **YOU** ask out?
I'm going to pretend you're talking to yourself.

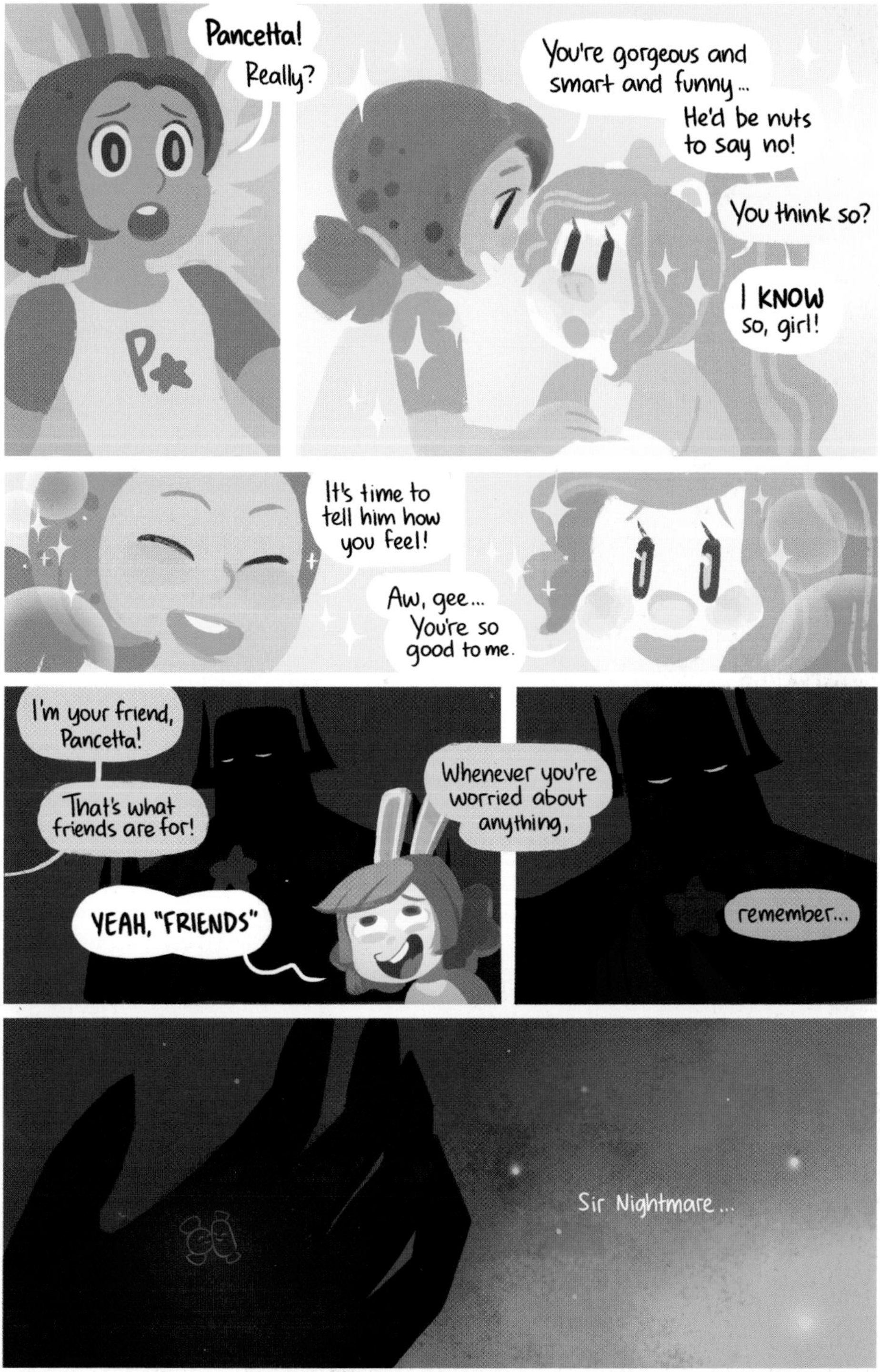

Pancetta!
Really?
You're gorgeous and smart and funny...
He'd be nuts to say no!
You think so?
I KNOW so, girl!
It's time to tell him how you feel!
Aw, gee... You're so good to me.
I'm your friend, Pancetta!
That's what friends are for!
YEAH, "FRIENDS"
Whenever you're worried about anything,
remember...
Sir Nightmare...

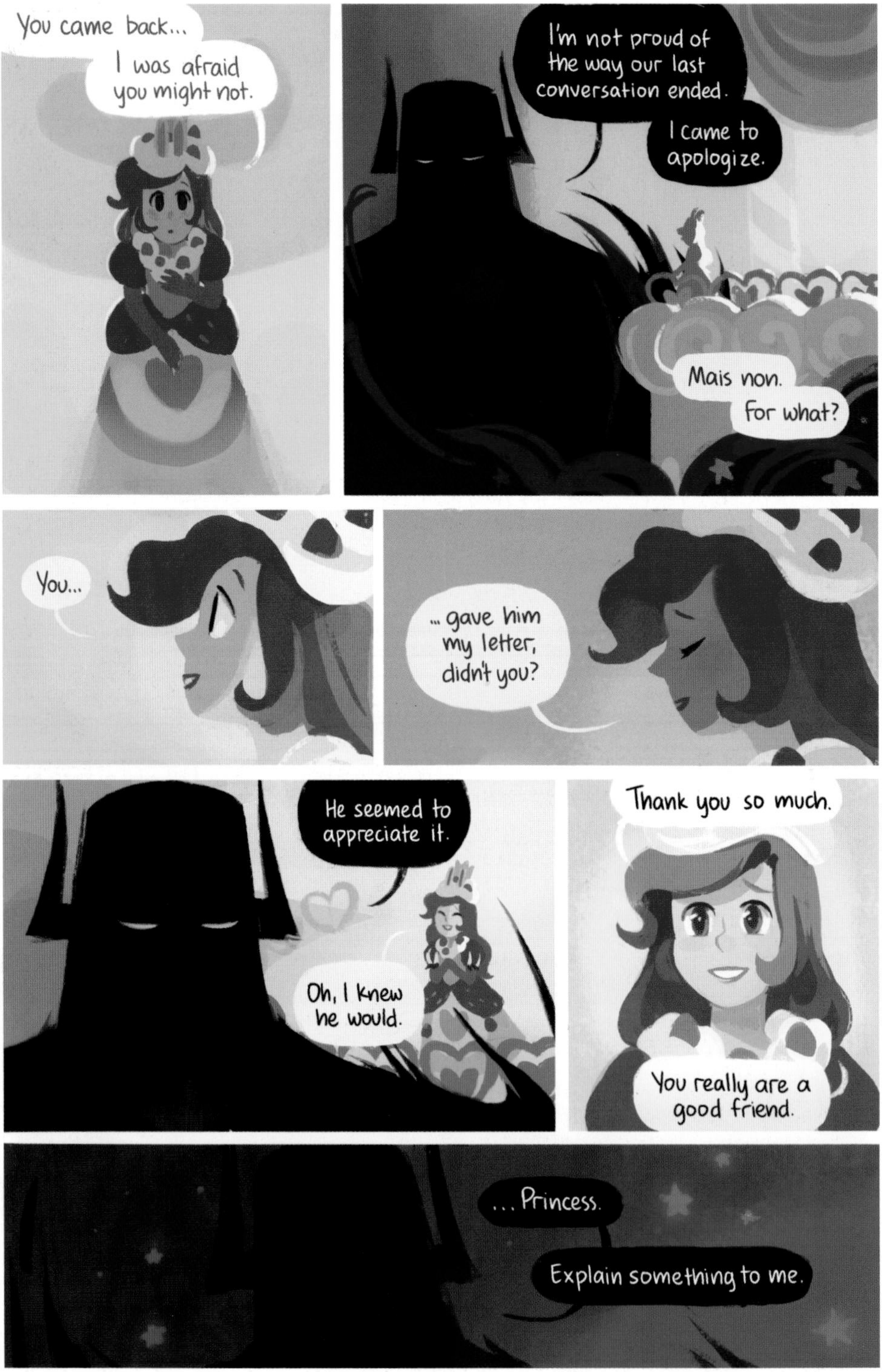
You came back...
I was afraid you might not.
I'm not proud of the way our last conversation ended.
I came to apologize.
Mais non. For what?
You...
... gave him my letter, didn't you?
He seemed to appreciate it.
Oh, I knew he would.
Thank you so much.
You really are a good friend.
... Princess.
Explain something to me.

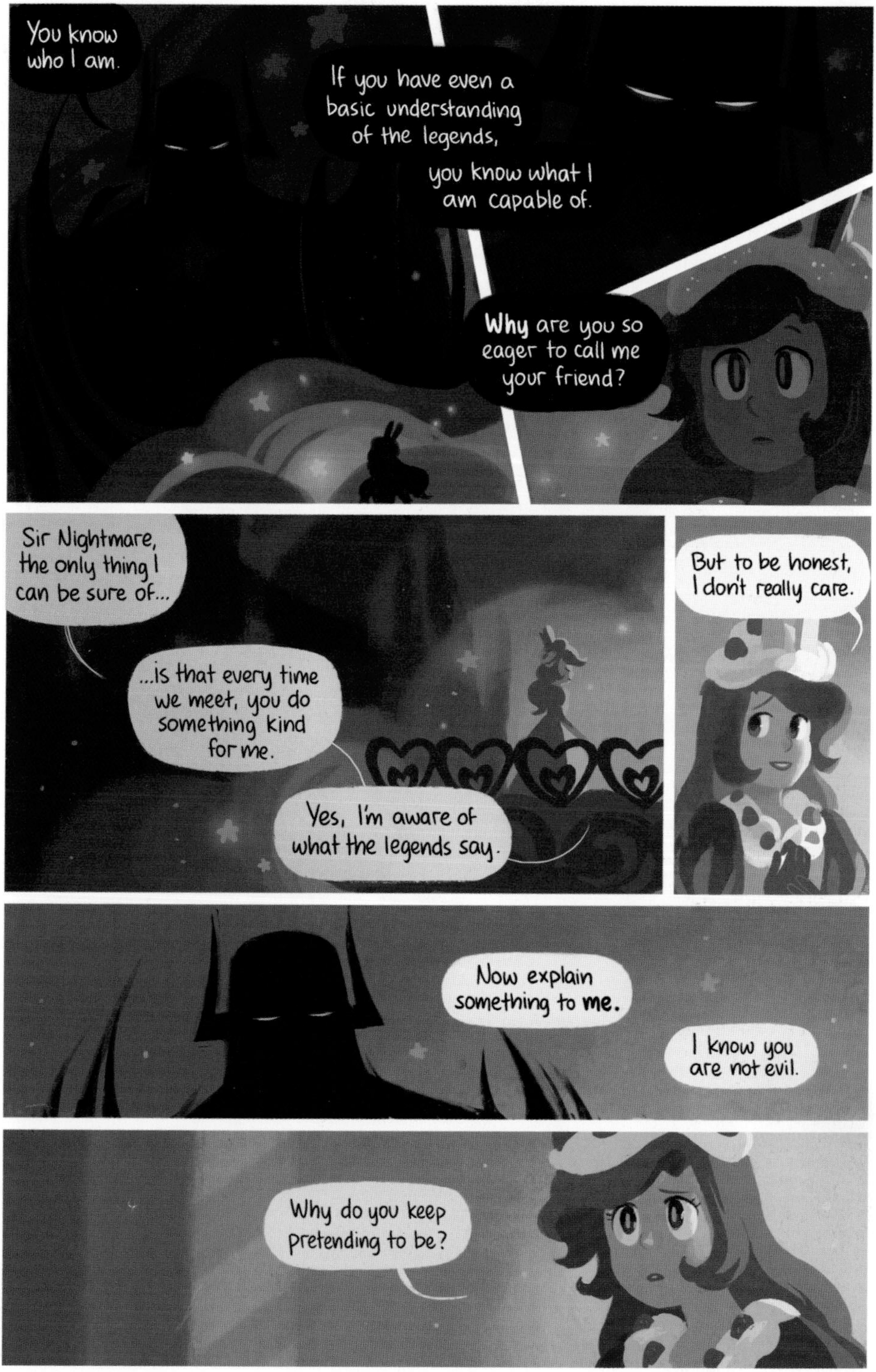
You know who I am.
If you have even a basic understanding of the legends,
you know what I am capable of.
Why are you so eager to call me your friend?
Sir Nightmare, the only thing I can be sure of...
...is that every time we meet, you do something kind for me.
Yes, I'm aware of what the legends say.
But to be honest, I don't really care.
Now explain something to **me.**
I know you are not evil.
Why do you keep pretending to be?

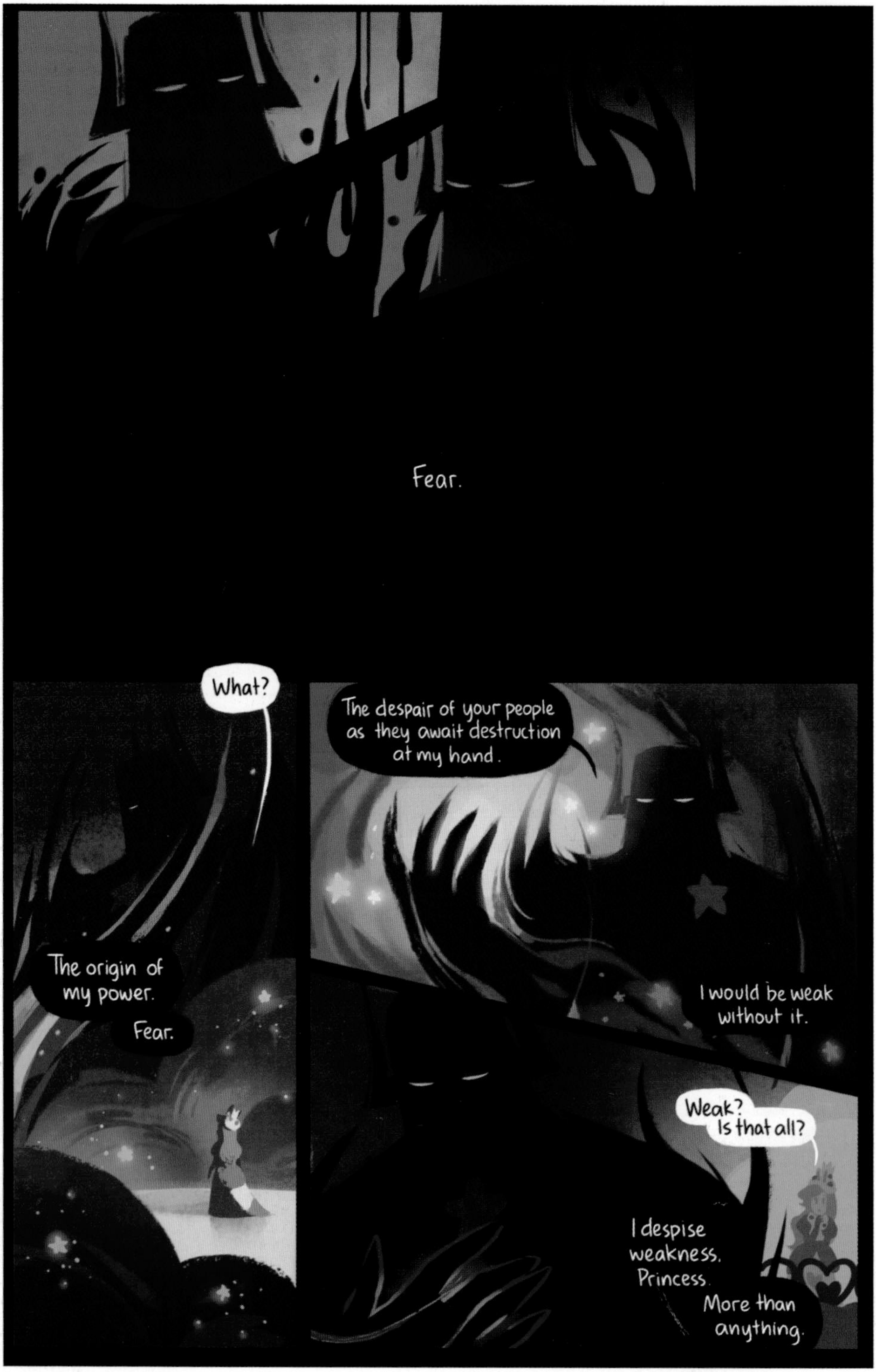
Fear.
What?
The origin of my power.
Fear.
The despair of your people as they await destruction at my hand.
I would be weak without it.
Weak? Is that all?
I despise weakness, Princess.
More than anything.

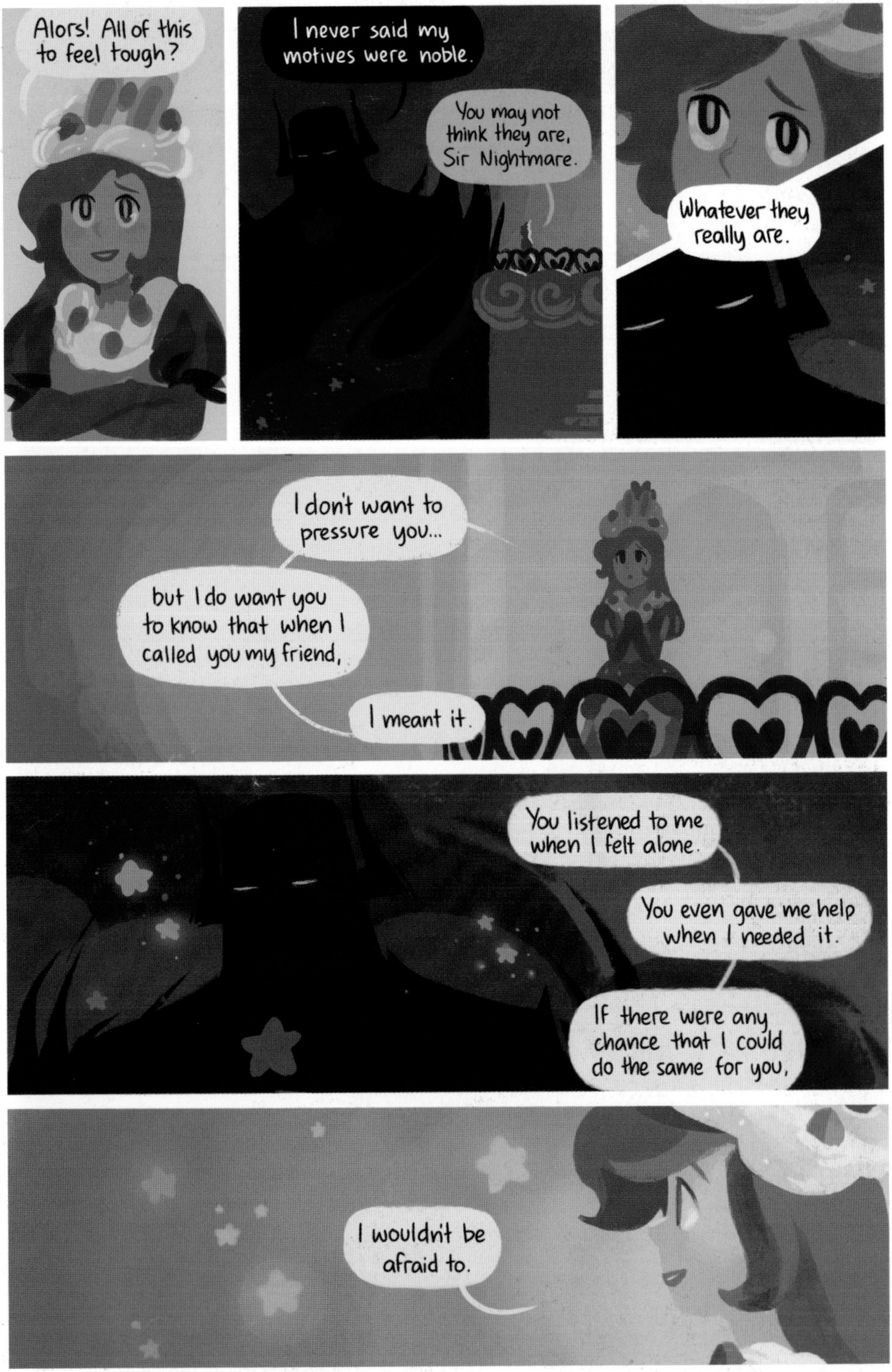

Alors! All of this to feel tough?
I never said my motives were noble.
You may not think they are, Sir Nightmare.
Whatever they really are.
I don't want to pressure you...
but I do want you to know that when I called you my friend,
I meant it.
You listened to me when I felt alone.
You even gave me help when I needed it.
If there were any chance that I could do the same for you,
I wouldn't be afraid to.

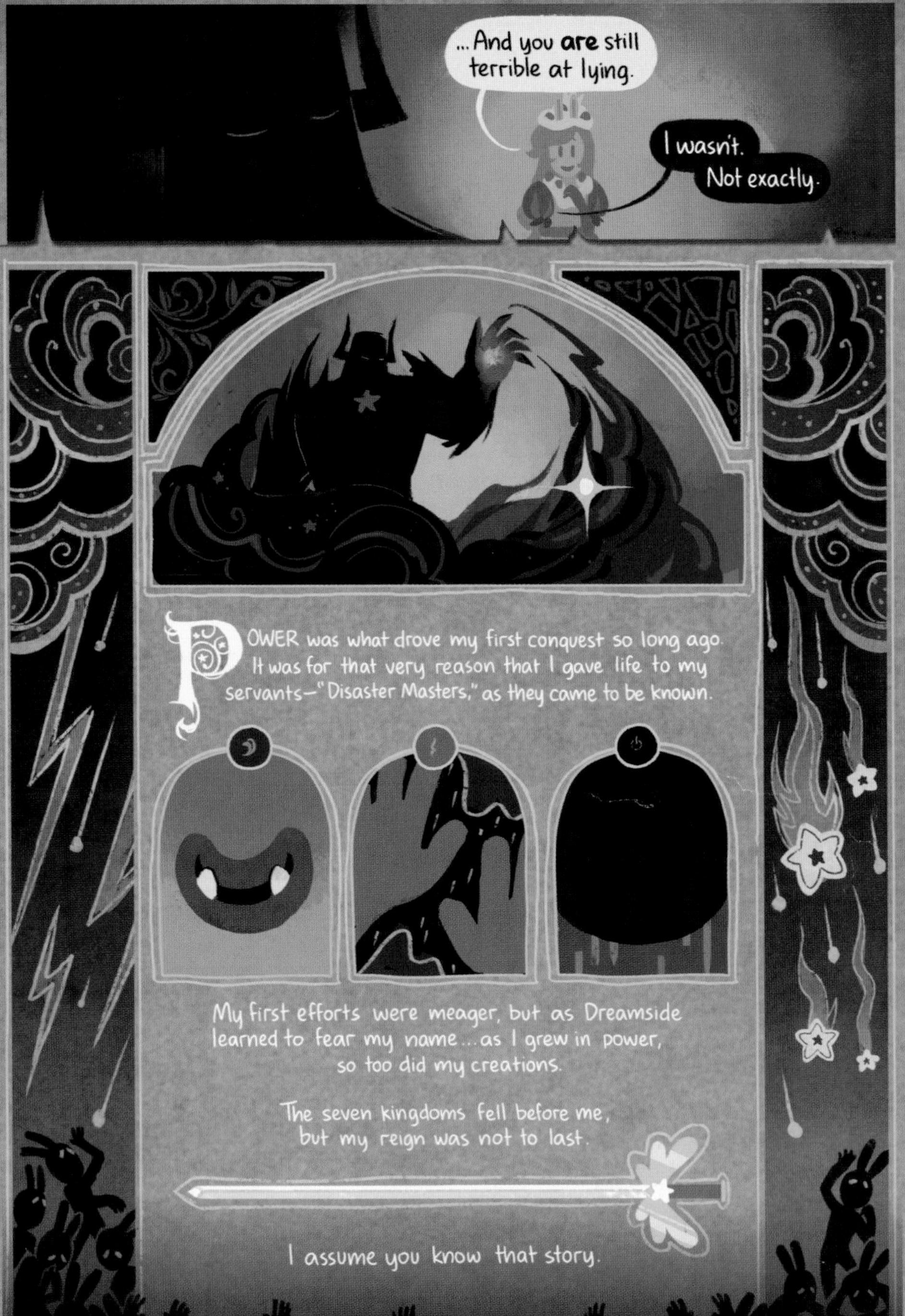
...And you **are** still terrible at lying.
I wasn't. Not exactly.
POWER was what drove my first conquest so long ago. It was for that very reason that I gave life to my servants—"Disaster Masters," as they came to be known.
My first efforts were meager, but as Dreamside learned to fear my name...as I grew in power, so too did my creations.
The seven kingdoms fell before me, but my reign was not to last.
I assume you know that story.

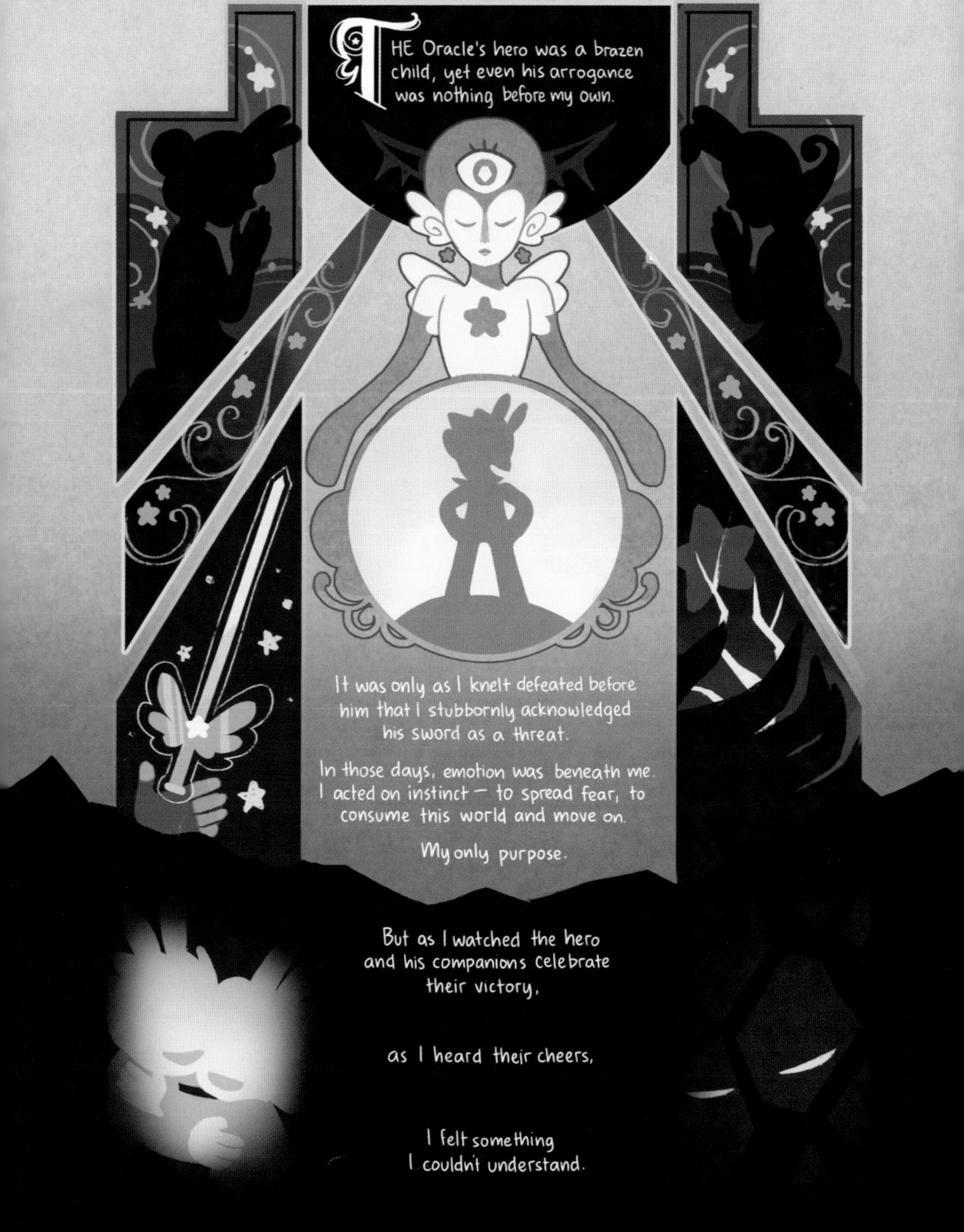
THE Oracle's hero was a brazen child, yet even his arrogance was nothing before my own.
It was only as I knelt defeated before him that I stubbornly acknowledged his sword as a threat.
In those days, emotion was beneath me. I acted on instinct — to spread fear, to consume this world and move on.
My only purpose.
But as I watched the hero and his companions celebrate their victory,
as I heard their cheers,
I felt something I couldn't understand.

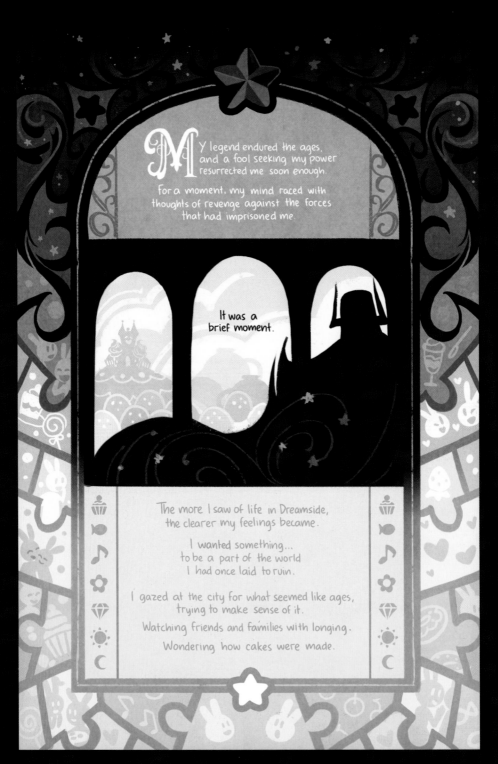

My legend endured the ages, and a fool seeking my power resurrected me soon enough.

For a moment, my mind raced with thoughts of revenge against the forces that had imprisoned me.

It was a brief moment.

The more I saw of life in Dreamside, the clearer my feelings became.

I wanted something... to be a part of the world I had once laid to ruin.

I gazed at the city for what seemed like ages, trying to make sense of it.

Watching friends and families with longing.

Wondering how cakes were made.

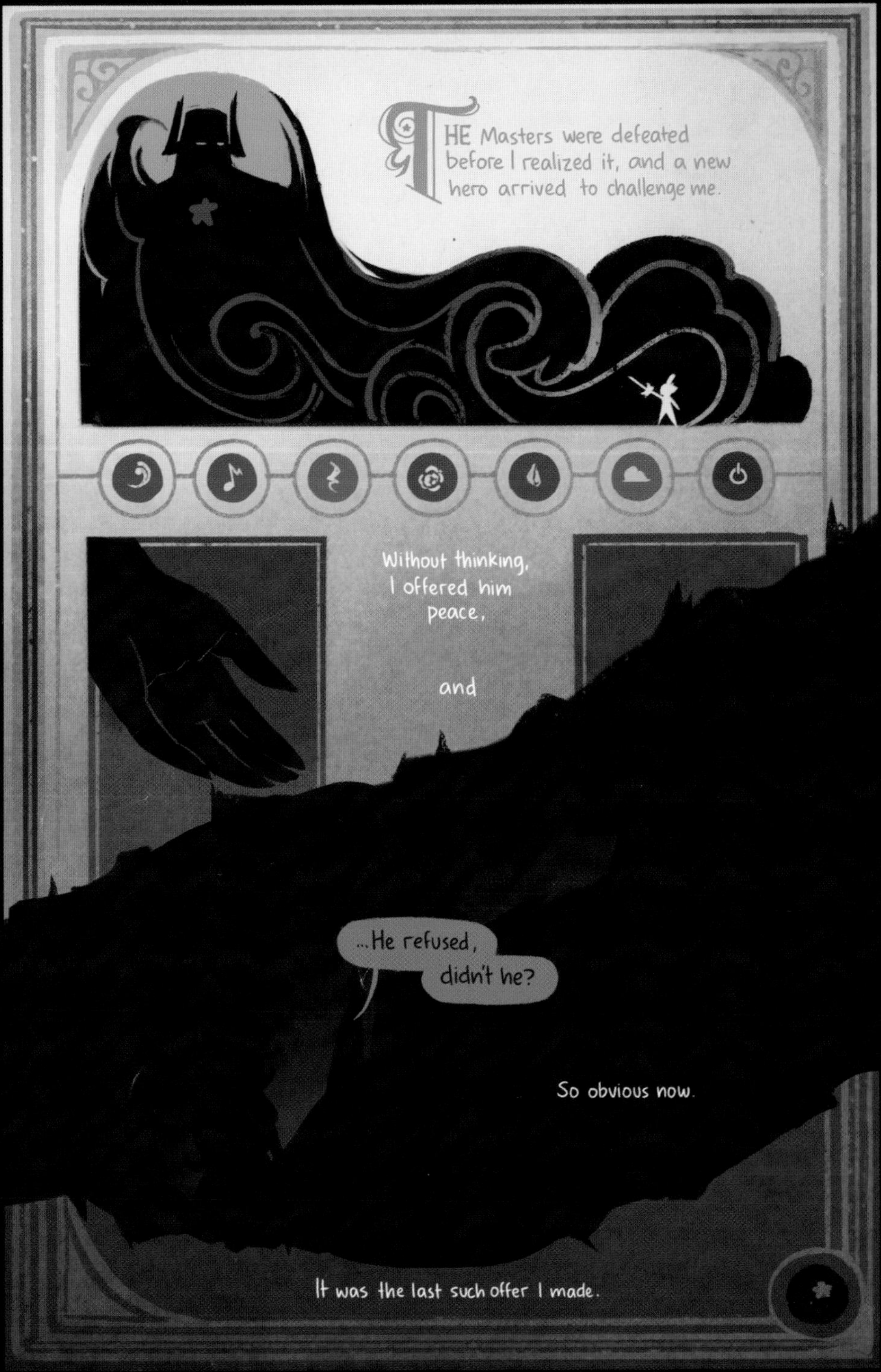
THE Masters were defeated before I realized it, and a new hero arrived to challenge me.
Without thinking, I offered him peace,
and
...He refused, didn't he?
So obvious now.
It was the last such offer I made.

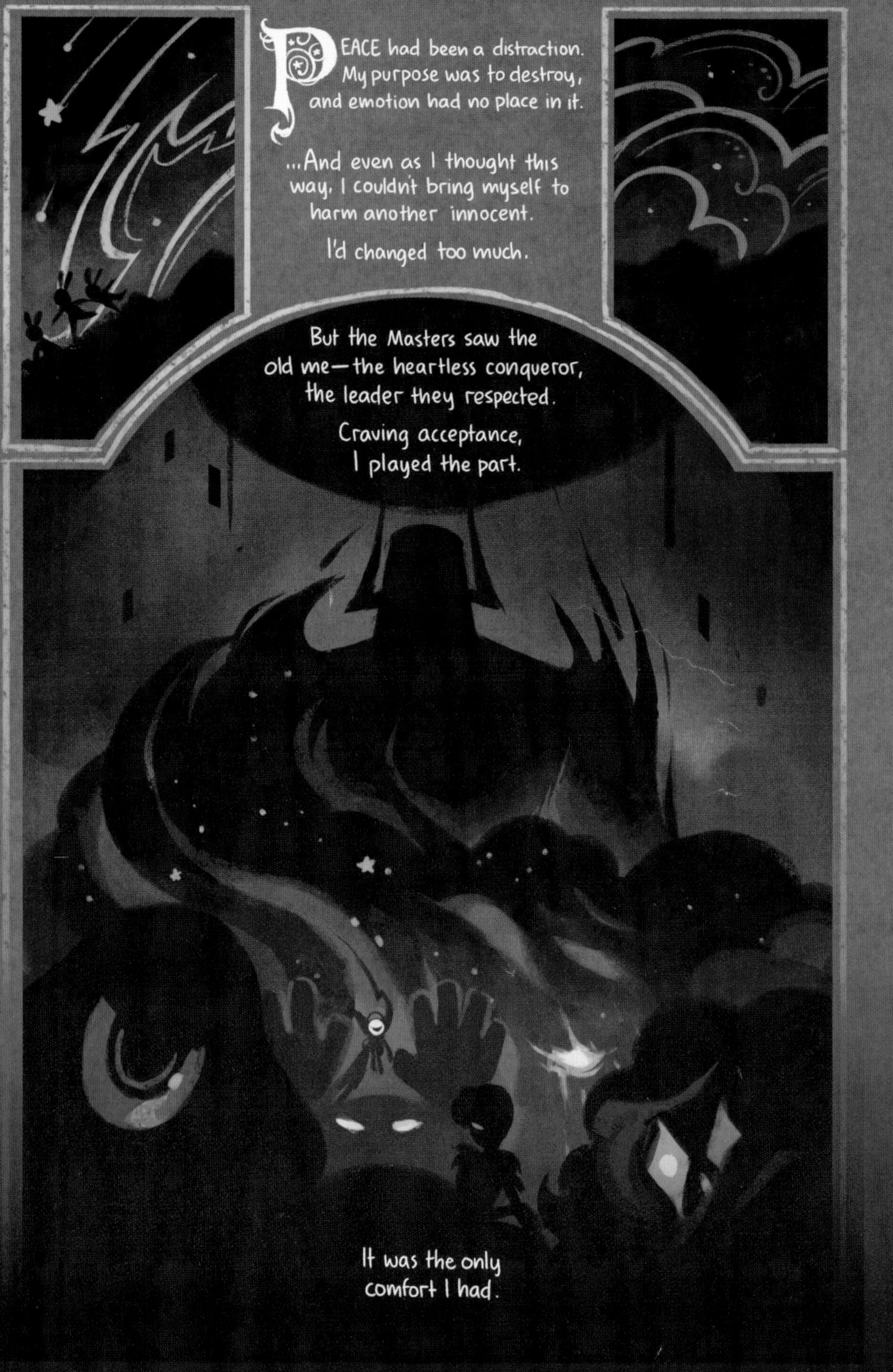
PEACE had been a distraction. My purpose was to destroy, and emotion had no place in it.
...And even as I thought this way, I couldn't bring myself to harm another innocent.
I'd changed too much.
But the Masters saw the old me—the heartless conqueror, the leader they respected.
Craving acceptance, I played the part.
It was the only comfort I had.

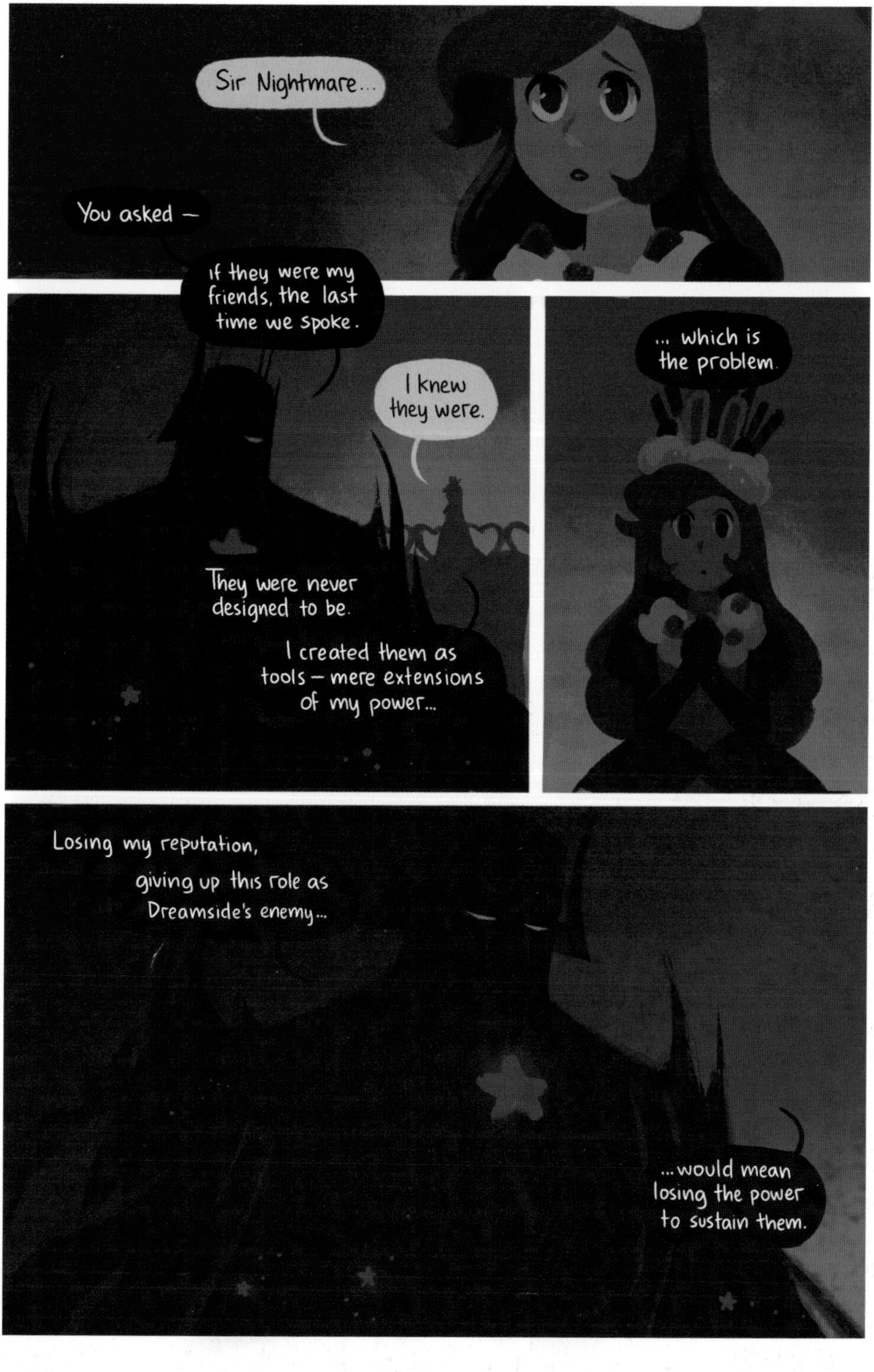

Sir Nightmare...
You asked —
if they were my friends, the last time we spoke.
I knew they were.
They were never designed to be.
I created them as tools — mere extensions of my power...
... which is the problem.
Losing my reputation,
giving up this role as Dreamside's enemy...
...would mean losing the power to sustain them.

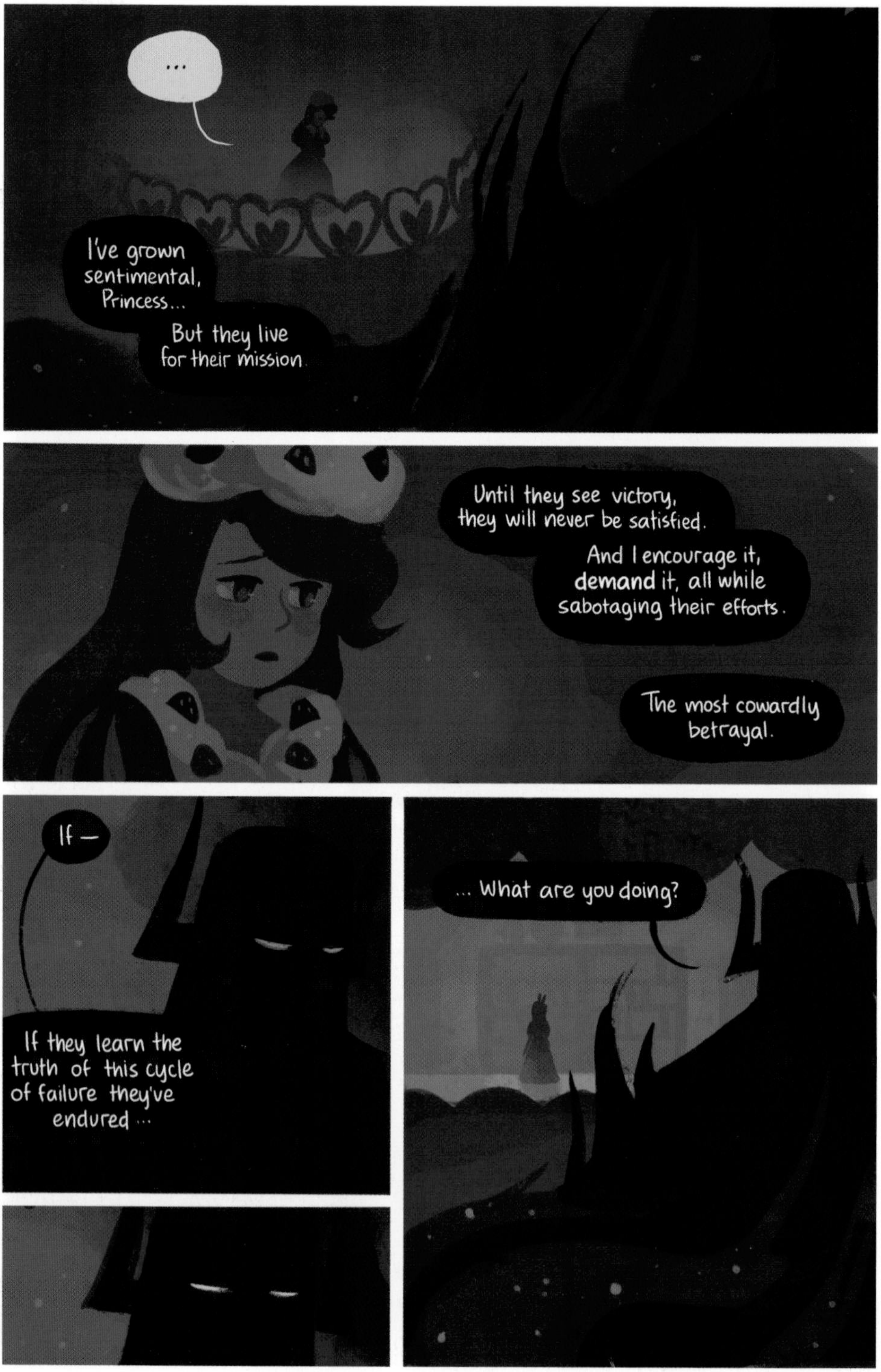
...
I've grown sentimental, Princess...
But they live for their mission.
Until they see victory, they will never be satisfied.
And I encourage it, **demand** it, all while sabotaging their efforts.
The most cowardly betrayal.
If—
If they learn the truth of this cycle of failure they've endured...
... What are you doing?

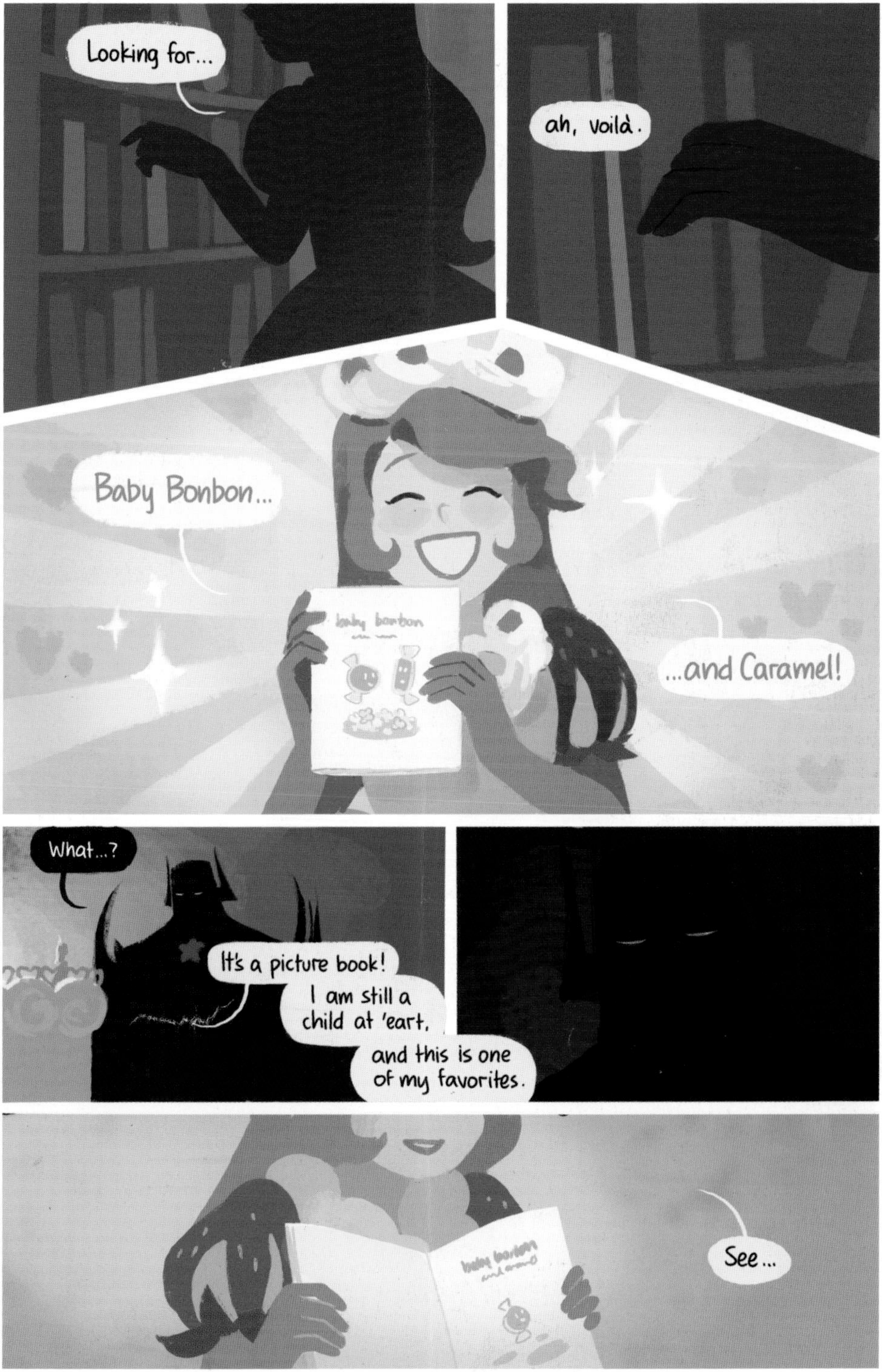
Looking for...
ah, voilà.
Baby Bonbon...
...and Caramel!
baby bonbon
What...?
It's a picture book!
I am still a child at 'eart,
and this is one of my favorites.
See...

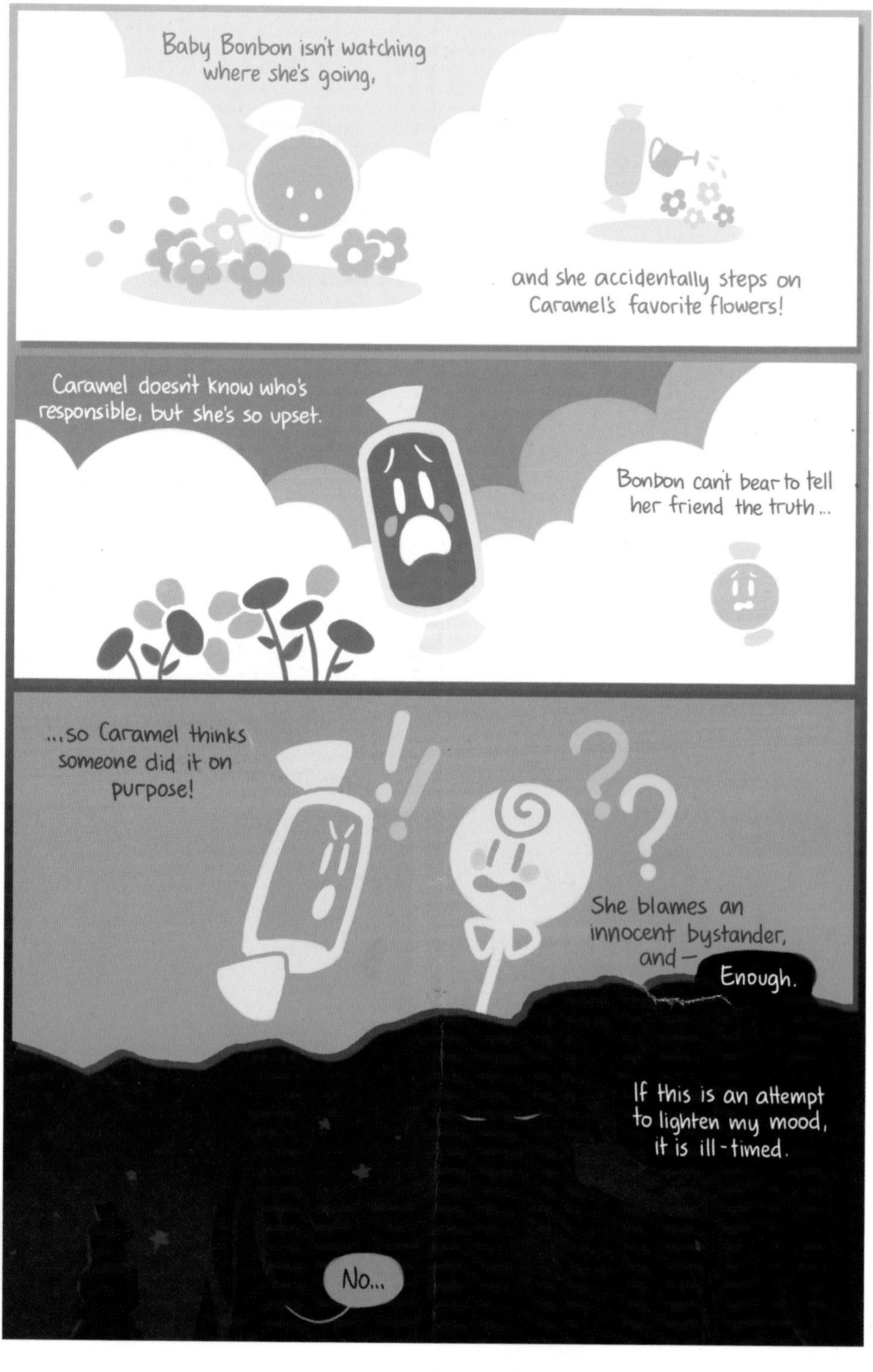

Baby Bonbon isn't watching where she's going,
and she accidentally steps on Caramel's favorite flowers!
Caramel doesn't know who's responsible, but she's so upset.
Bonbon can't bear to tell her friend the truth...
...so Caramel thinks someone did it on purpose!
She blames an innocent bystander, and—
Enough.
If this is an attempt to lighten my mood, it is ill-timed.
No...

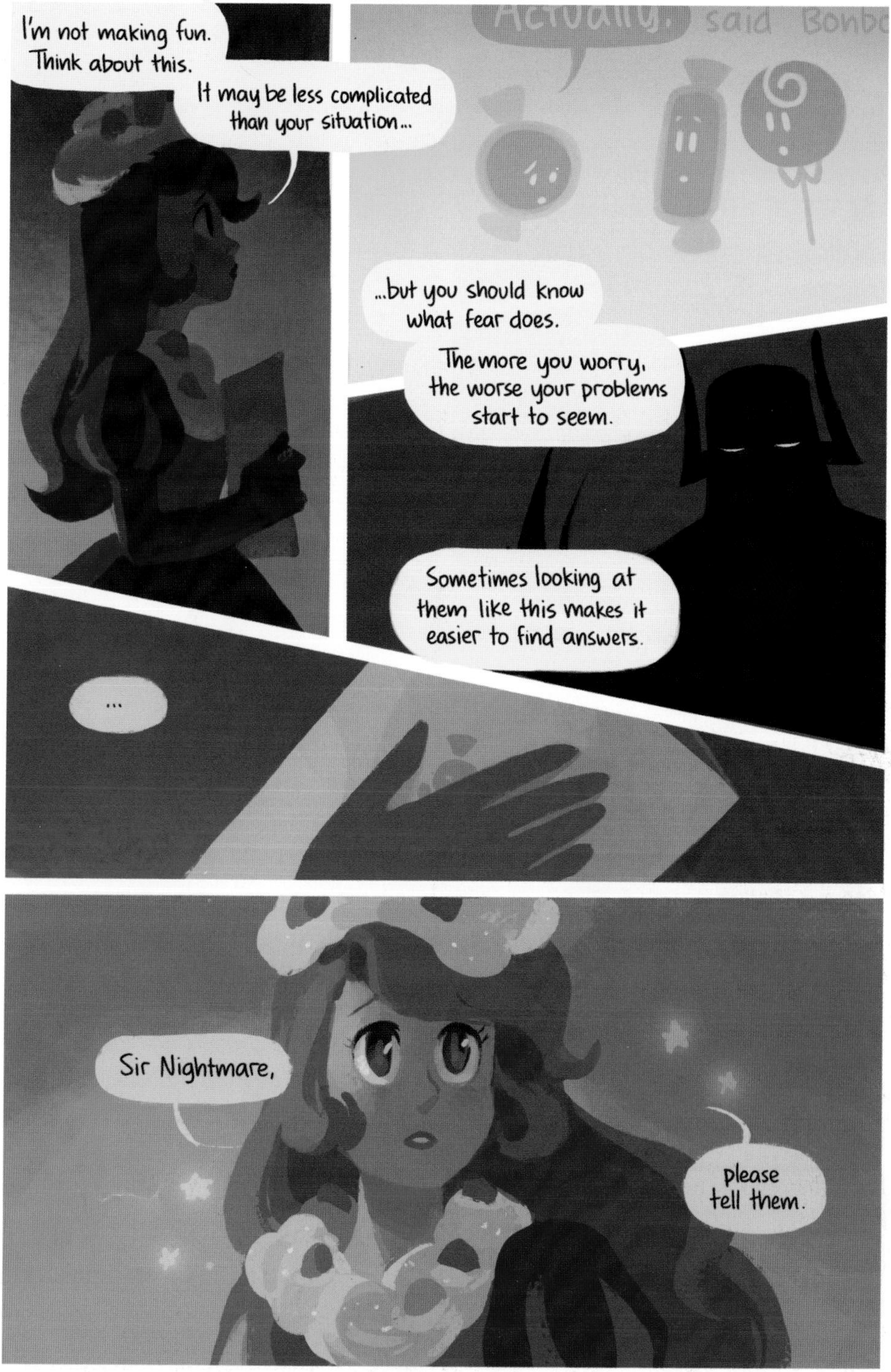
I'm not making fun. Think about this.
It may be less complicated than your situation...
Actually, said Bonbo
...but you should know what fear does.
The more you worry, the worse your problems start to seem.
Sometimes looking at them like this makes it easier to find answers.
...
Sir Nightmare,
please tell them.

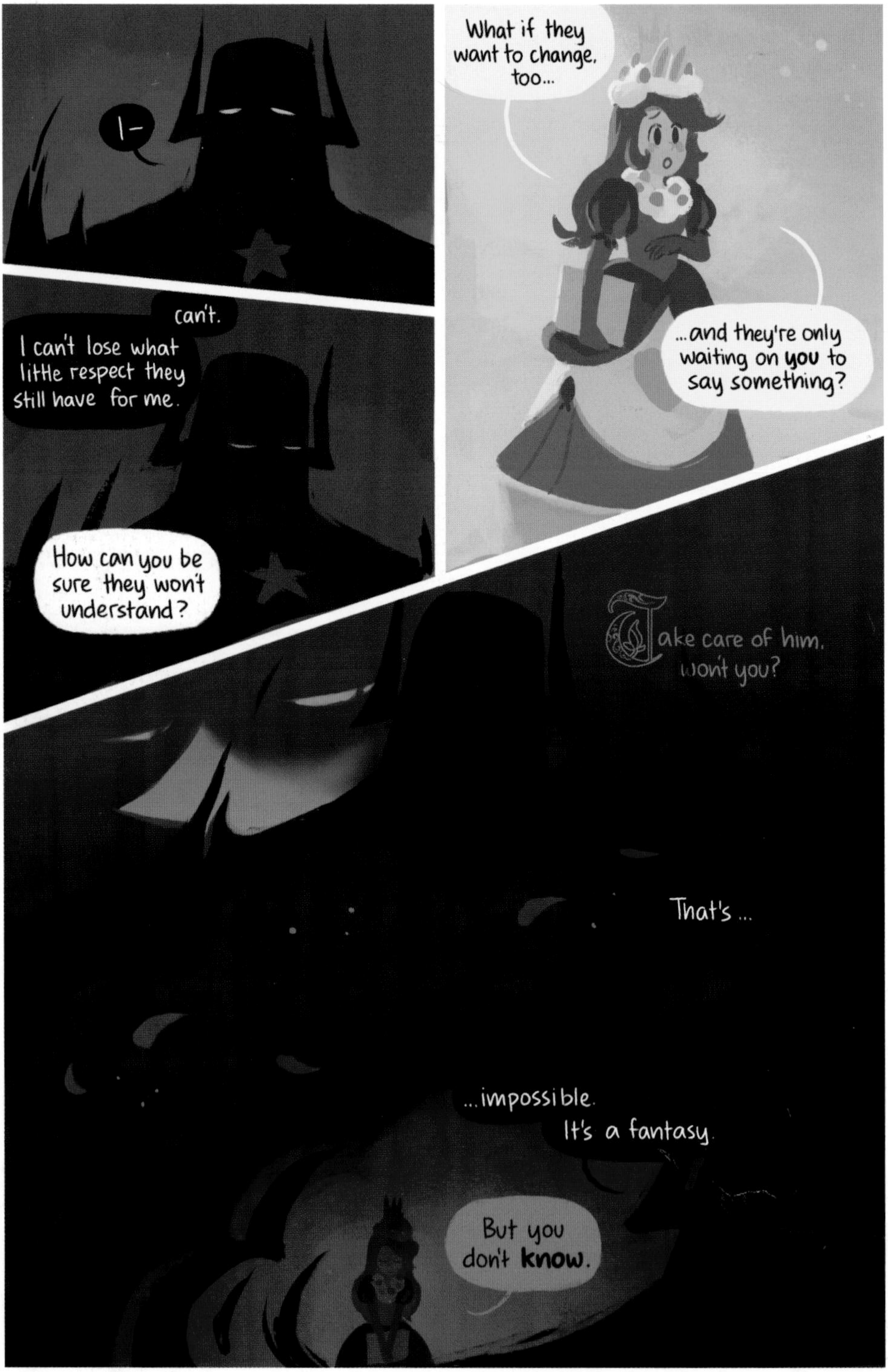
I-
What if they want to change, too...
...and they're only waiting on you to say something?
can't.
I can't lose what little respect they still have for me.
How can you be sure they won't understand?
Take care of him, won't you?
That's ...
...impossible.
It's a fantasy.
But you don't know.

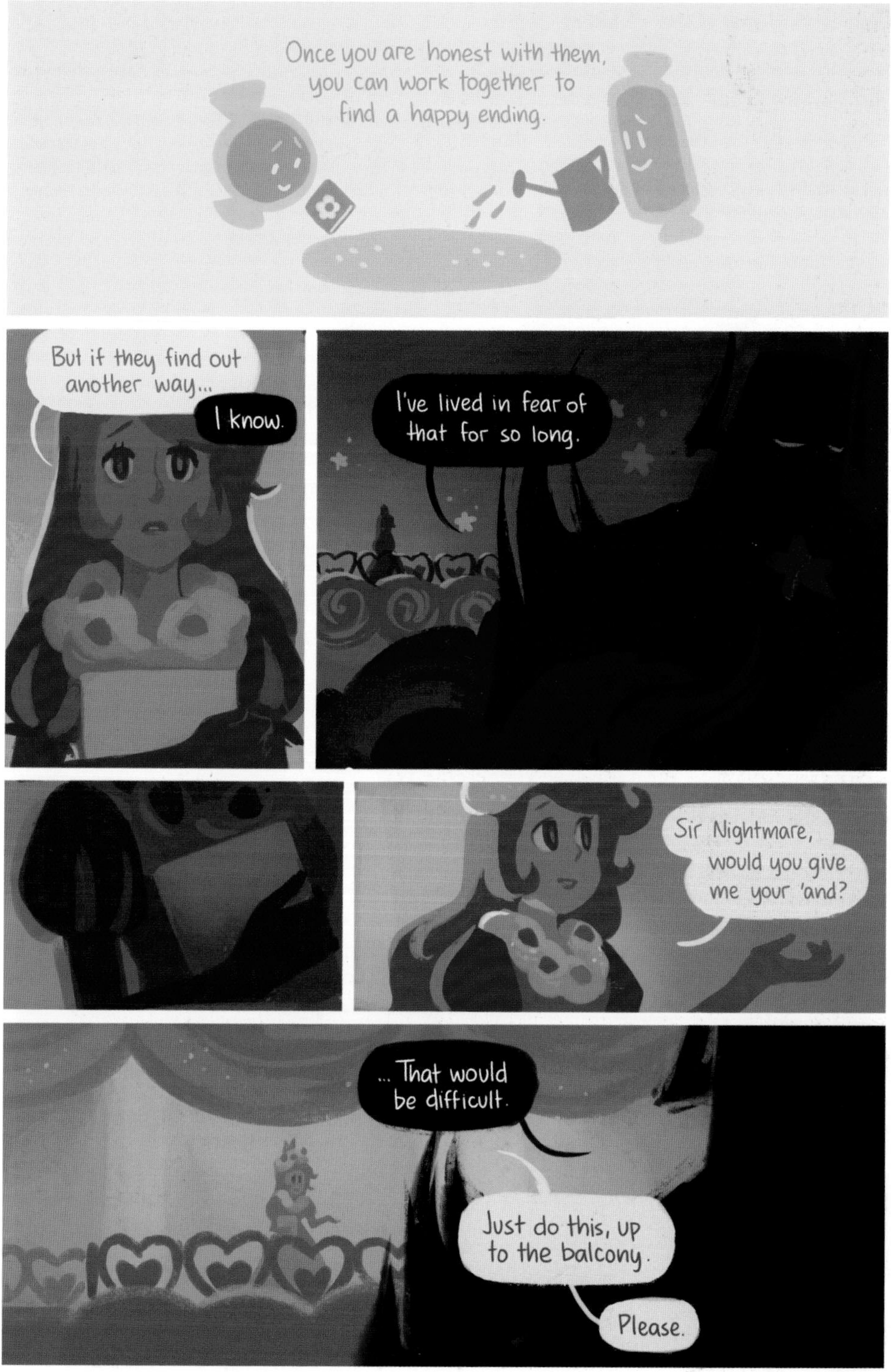
Once you are honest with them, you can work together to find a happy ending.
But if they find out another way...
I know.
I've lived in fear of that for so long.
Sir Nightmare, would you give me your 'and?
... That would be difficult.
Just do this, up to the balcony.
Please.

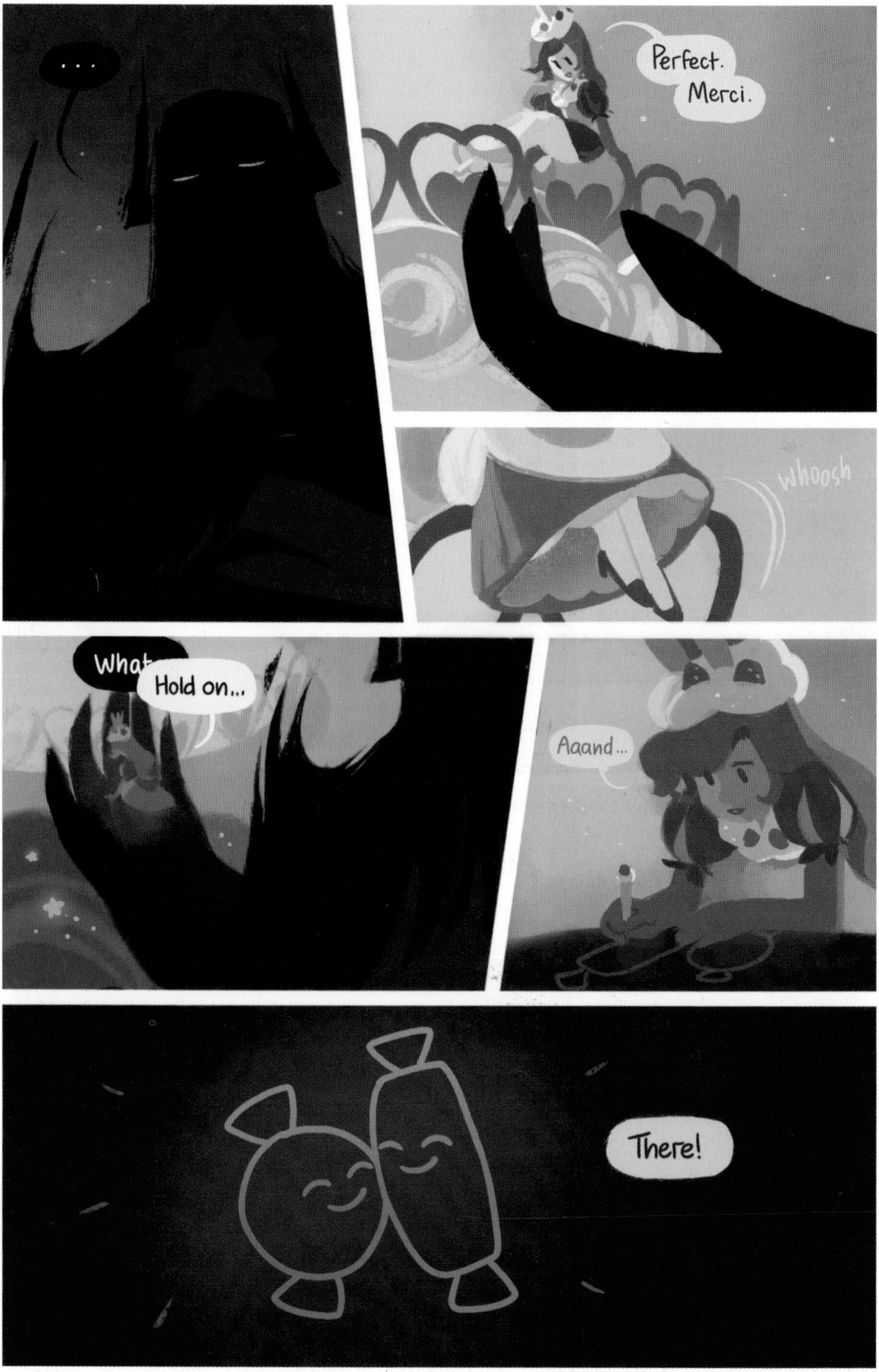
...
Perfect. Merci.
whoosh
What
Hold on...
Aaand...
There!

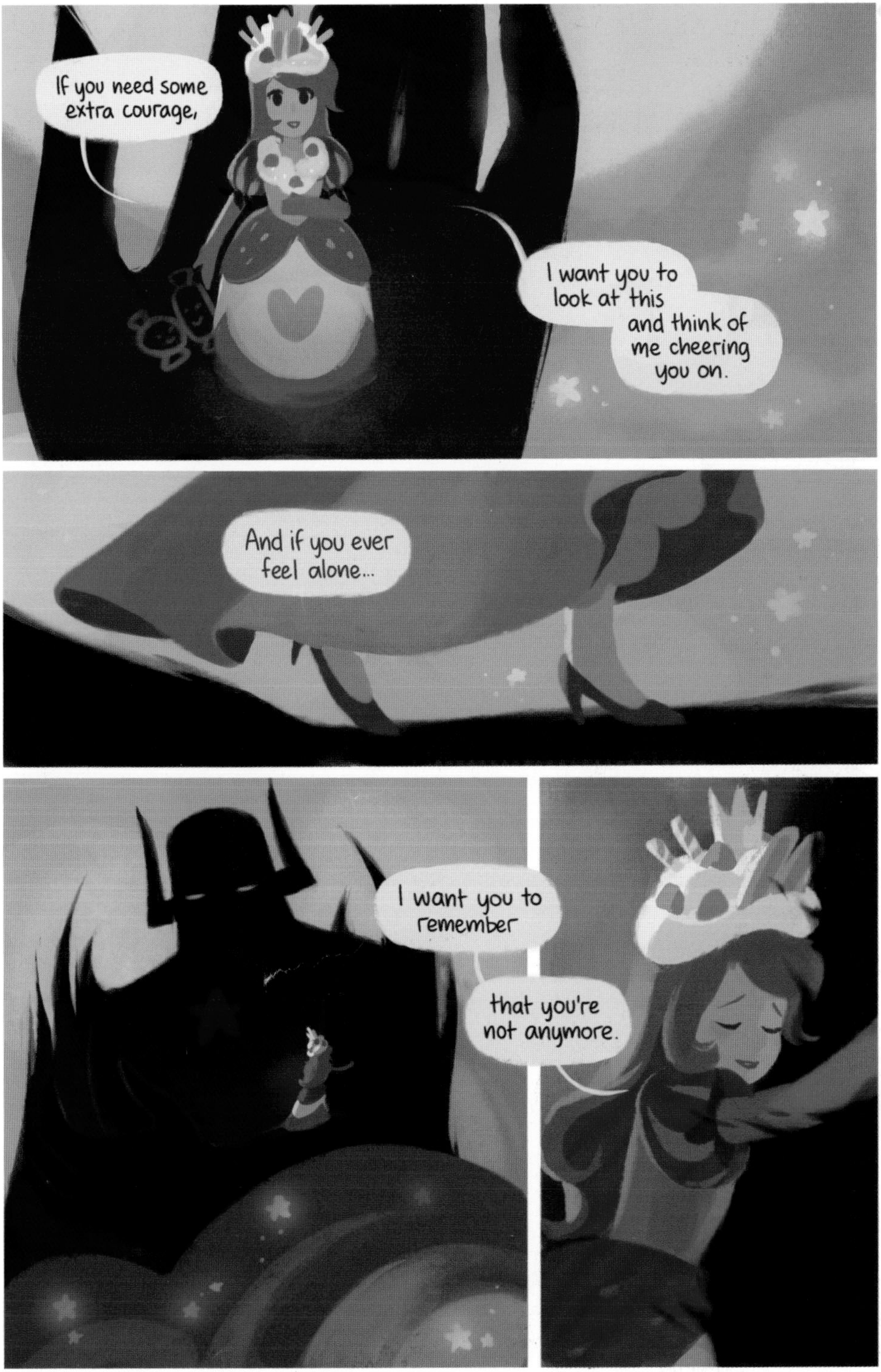
If you need some extra courage,
I want you to look at this
and think of me cheering you on.
And if you ever feel alone...
I want you to remember
that you're not anymore.

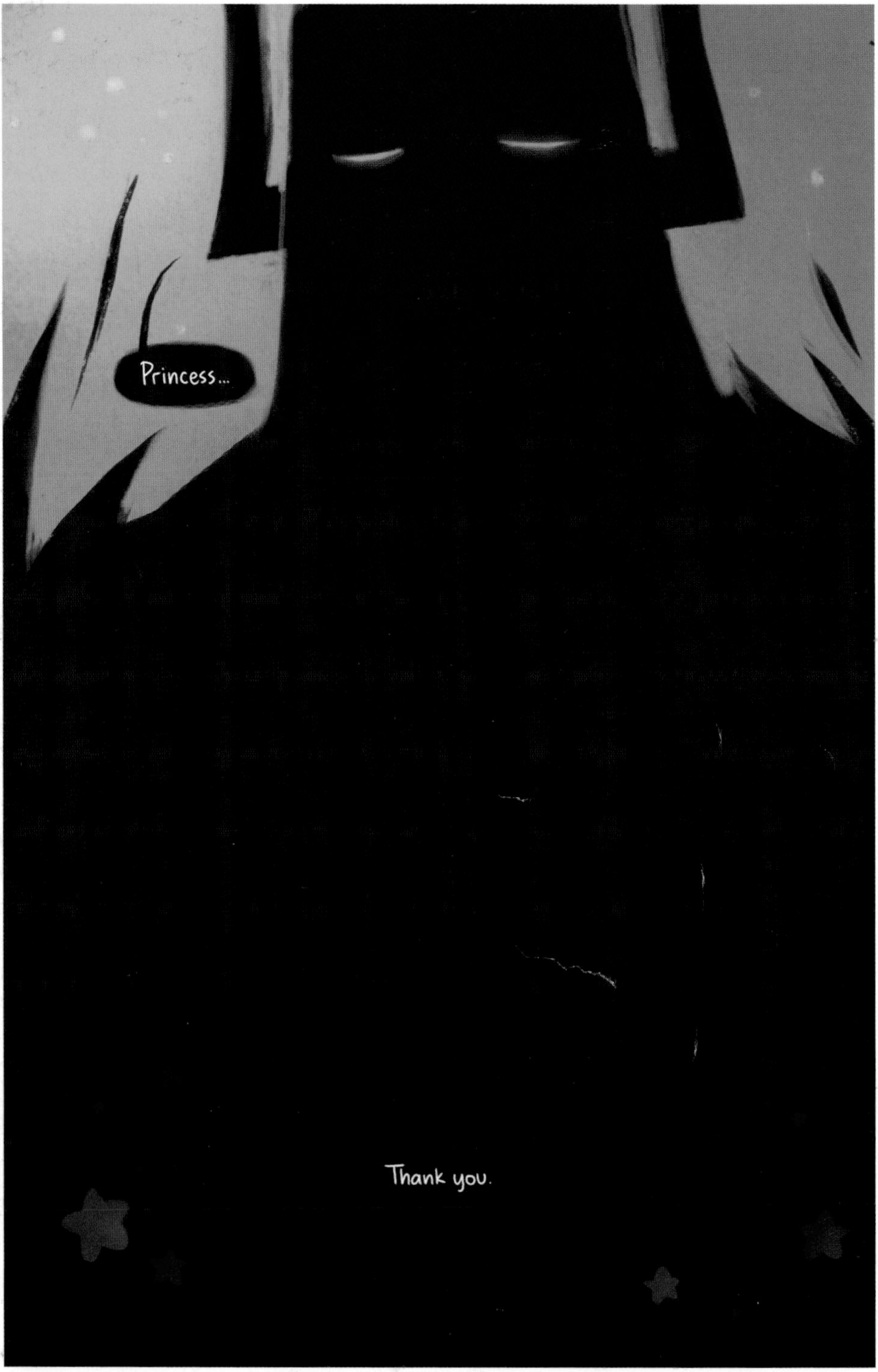
Princess...
Thank you.

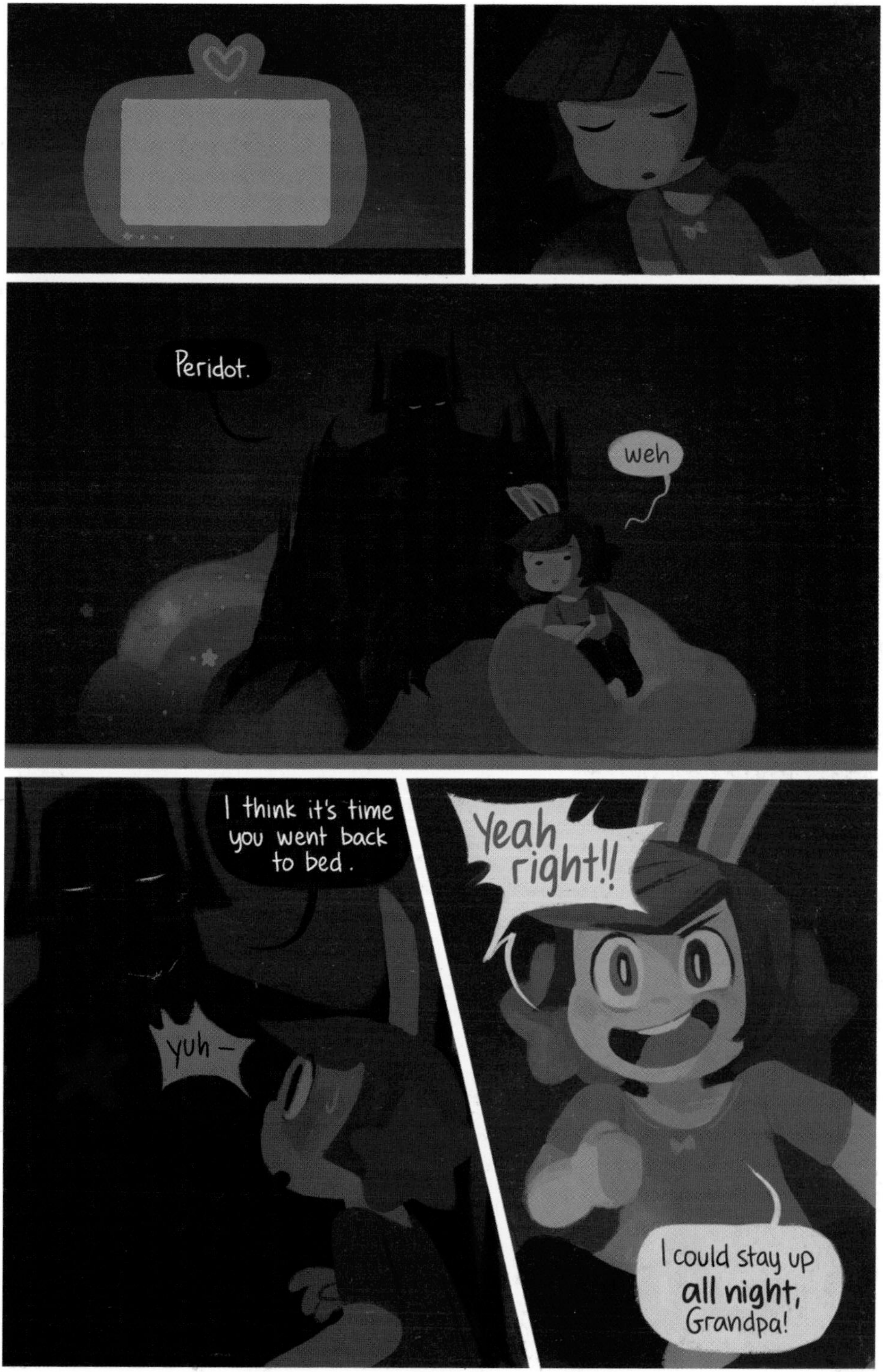
Peridot.
weh
I think it's time you went back to bed.
yuh—
Yeah right!!
I could stay up **all night,** Grandpa!

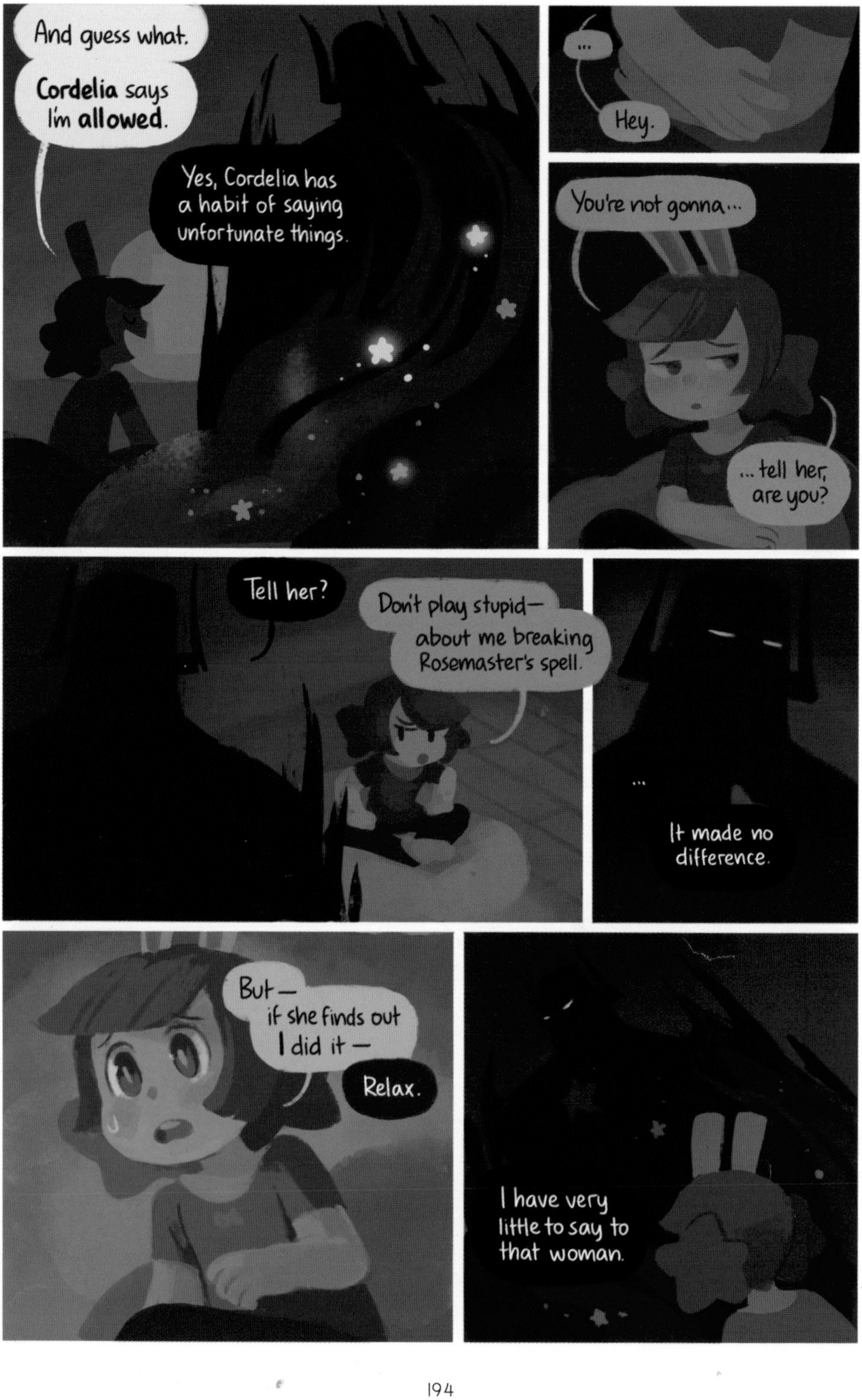
And guess what.
Cordelia says I'm allowed.
Yes, Cordelia has a habit of saying unfortunate things.
...
Hey.
You're not gonna...
...tell her, are you?
Tell her?
Don't play stupid— about me breaking Rosemaster's spell.
...
It made no difference.
But— if she finds out I did it—
Relax.
I have very little to say to that woman.

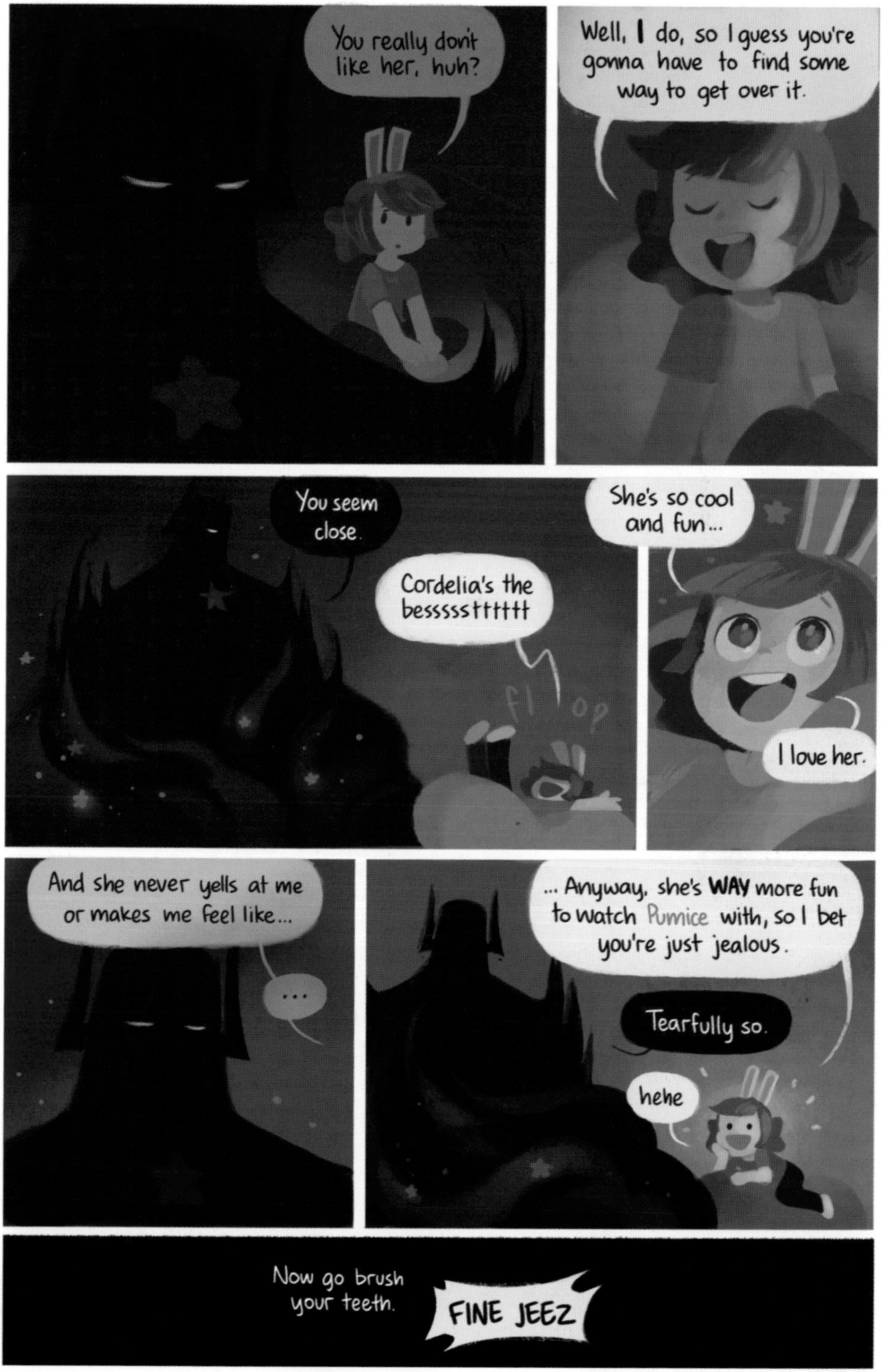
You really don't like her, huh?
Well, I do, so I guess you're gonna have to find some way to get over it.
You seem close.
Cordelia's the besssssttttt
flop
She's so cool and fun...
I love her.
And she never yells at me or makes me feel like...
...
... Anyway, she's WAY more fun to watch Pumice with, so I bet you're just jealous.
Tearfully so.
hehe
Now go brush your teeth.
FINE JEEZ

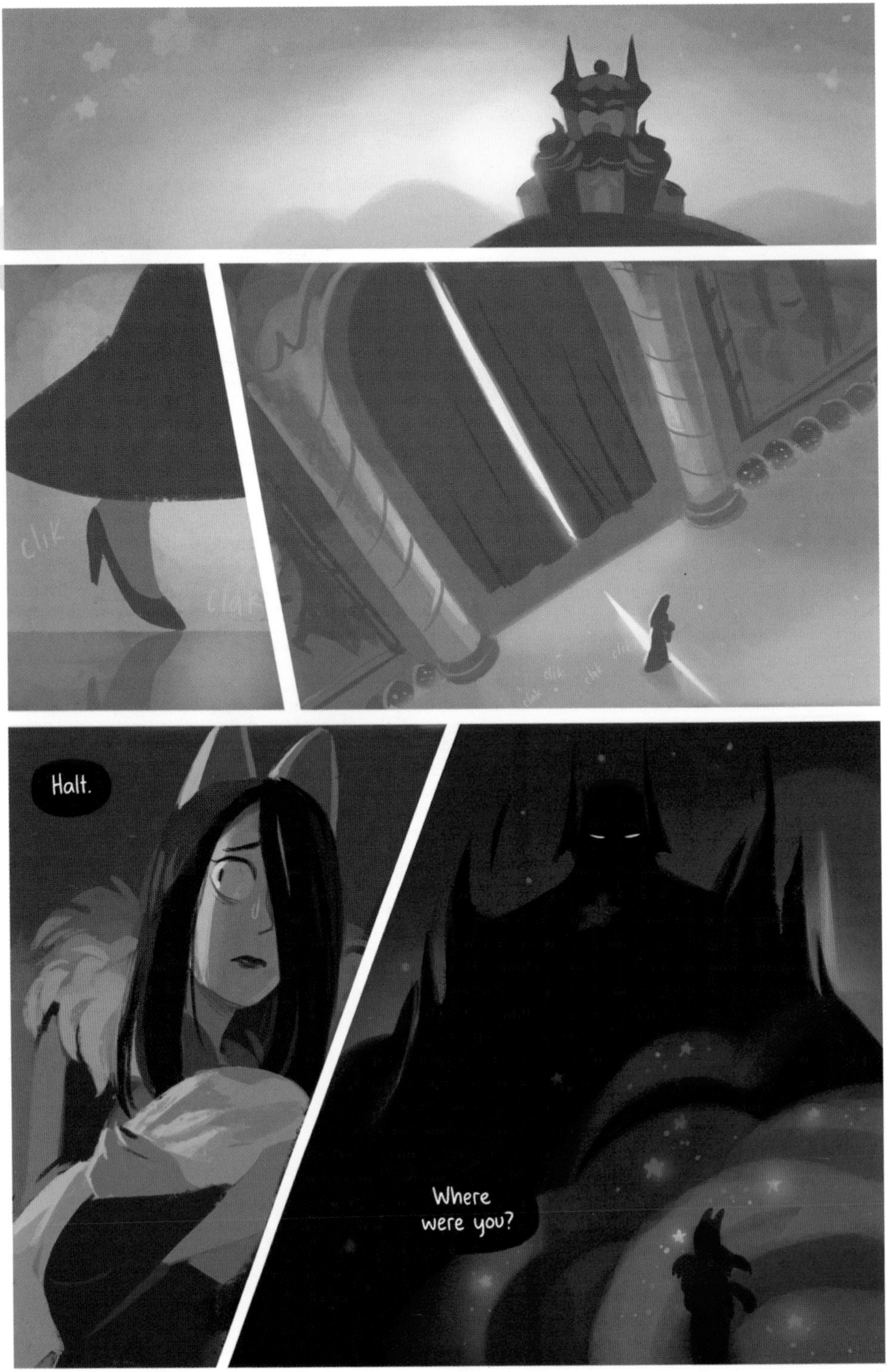
clik
clak
Halt.
Where were you?

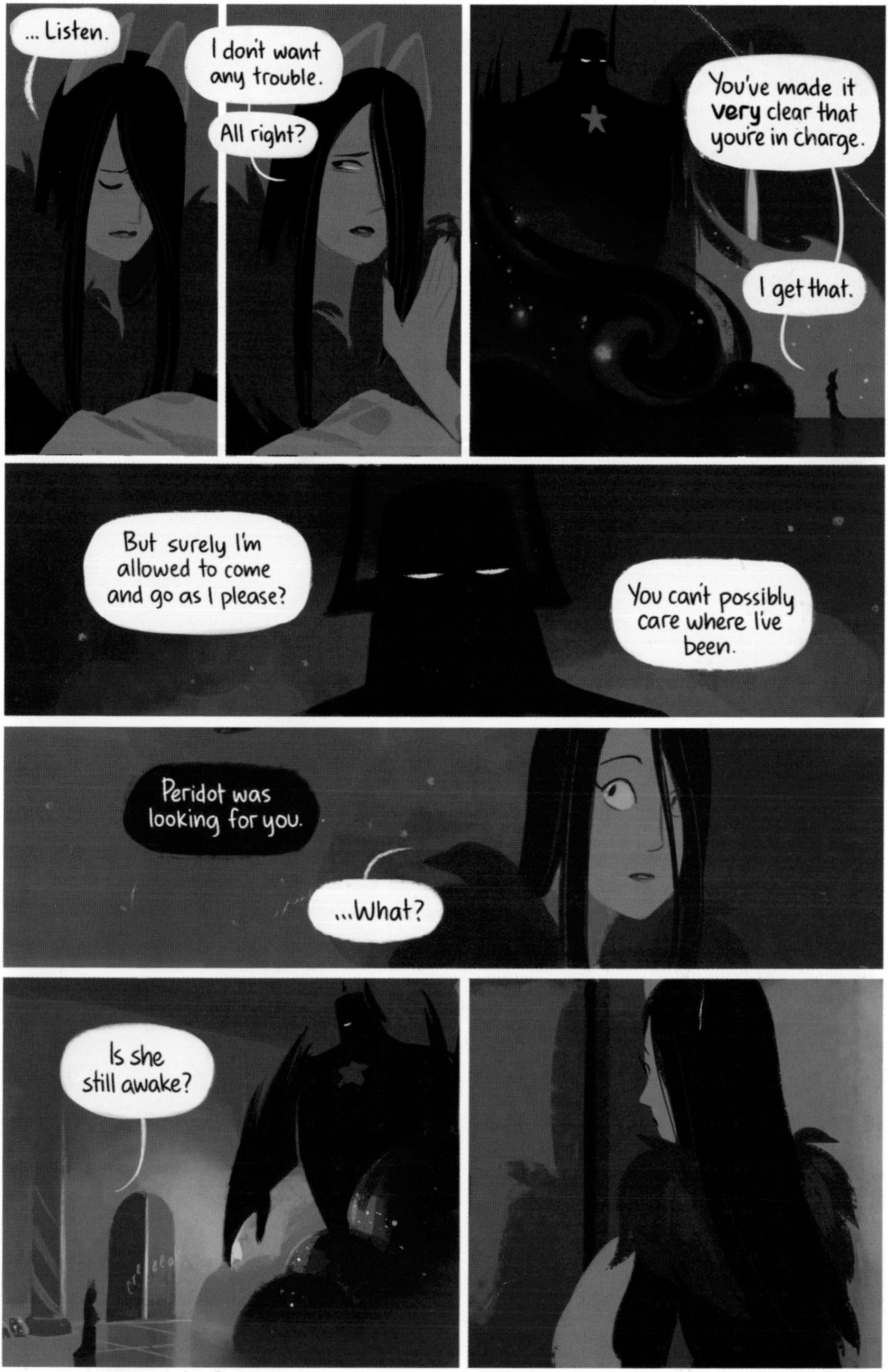
... Listen.
I don't want any trouble.
All right?
You've made it very clear that you're in charge.
I get that.
But surely I'm allowed to come and go as I please?
You can't possibly care where I've been.
Peridot was looking for you.
...What?
Is she still awake?

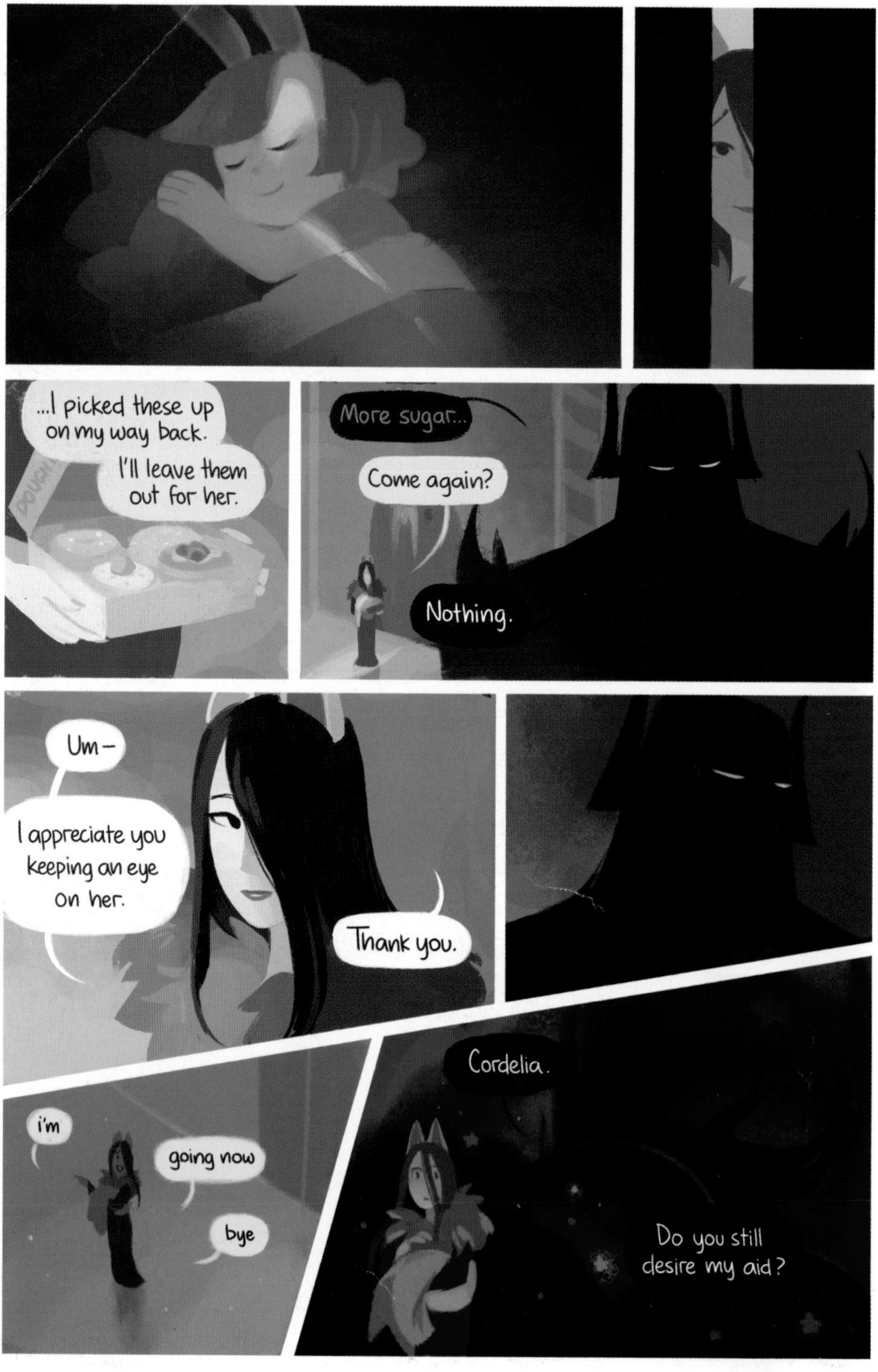
...I picked these up on my way back.
I'll leave them out for her.
DOUGH
More sugar...
Come again?
Nothing.
Um–
I appreciate you keeping an eye on her.
Thank you.
Cordelia.
i'm
going now
bye
Do you still desire my aid?

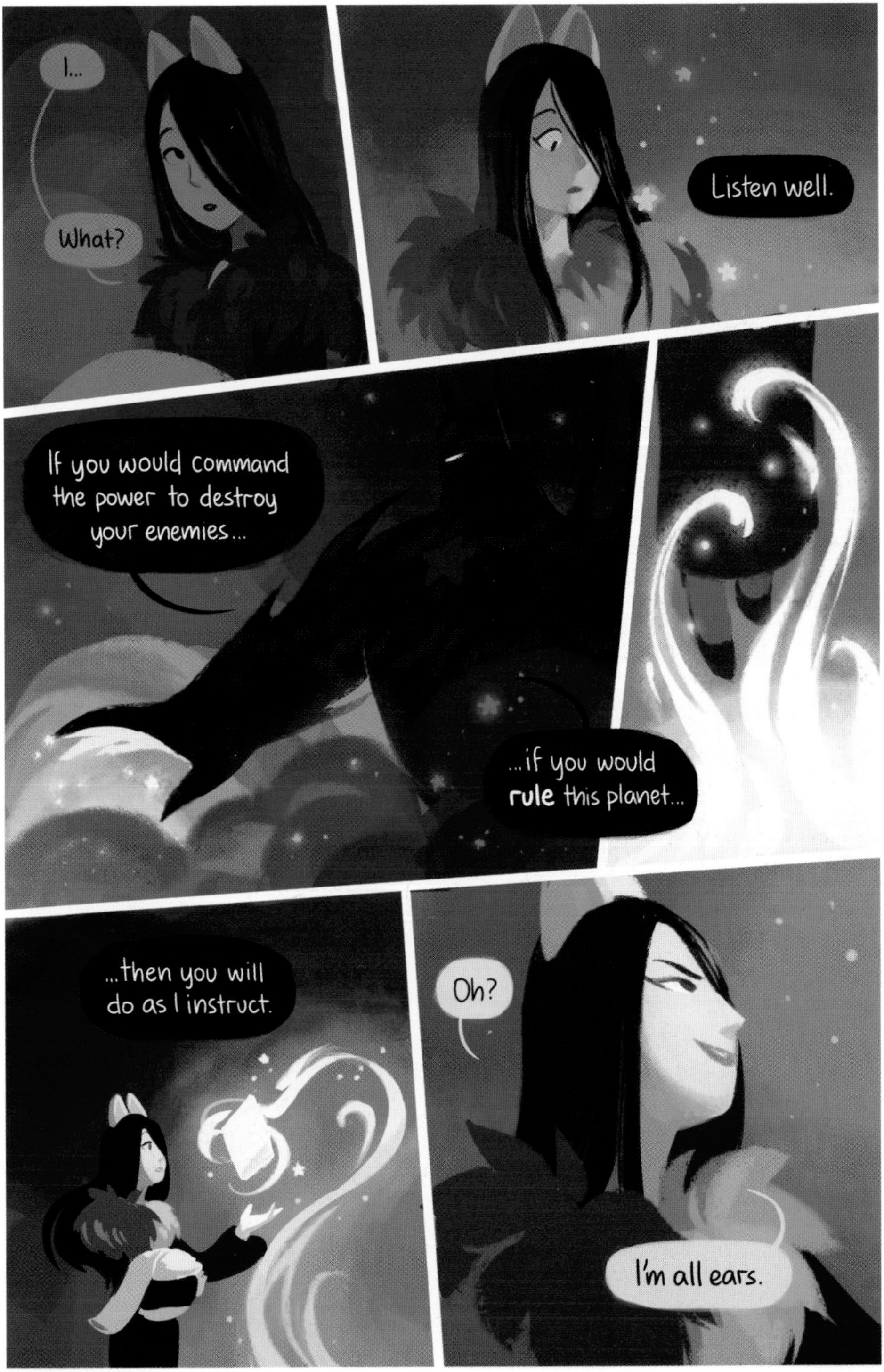
I...
What?
Listen well.
If you would command the power to destroy your enemies...
...if you would **rule** this planet...
...then you will do as I instruct.
Oh?
I'm all ears.

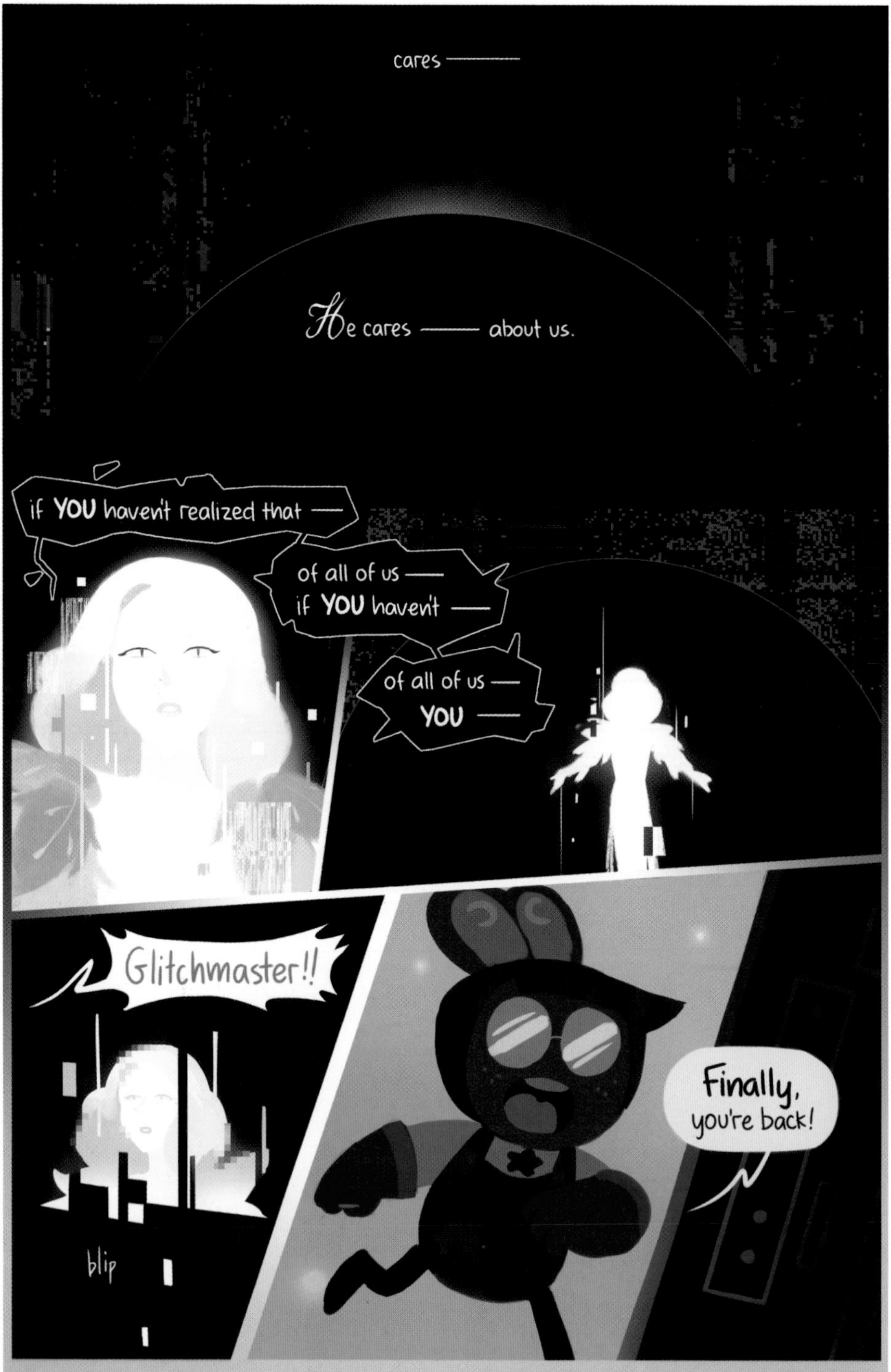
cares ——
He cares —— about us.
if YOU haven't realized that ——
of all of us ——
if YOU haven't ——
of all of us ——
YOU ——
Glitchmaster!!
blip
Finally, you're back!

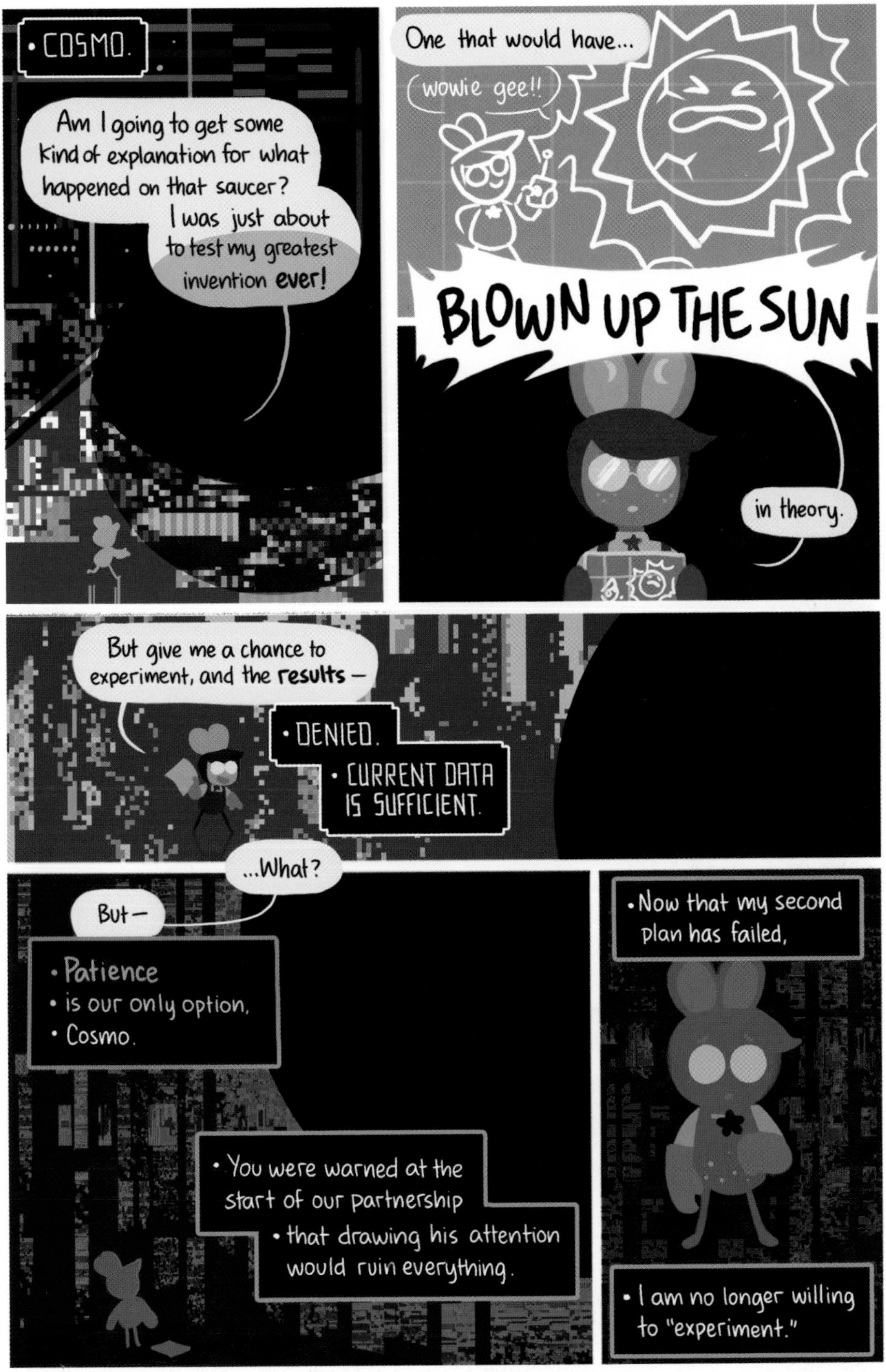
• COSMO.
Am I going to get some kind of explanation for what happened on that saucer?
I was just about to test my greatest invention ever!
One that would have...
wowie gee!!
BLOWN UP THE SUN
in theory.
But give me a chance to experiment, and the results —
• DENIED.
• CURRENT DATA IS SUFFICIENT.
...What?
But —
• Patience
• is our only option,
• Cosmo.
• You were warned at the start of our partnership
• that drawing his attention would ruin everything.
• Now that my second plan has failed,
• I am no longer willing to "experiment."

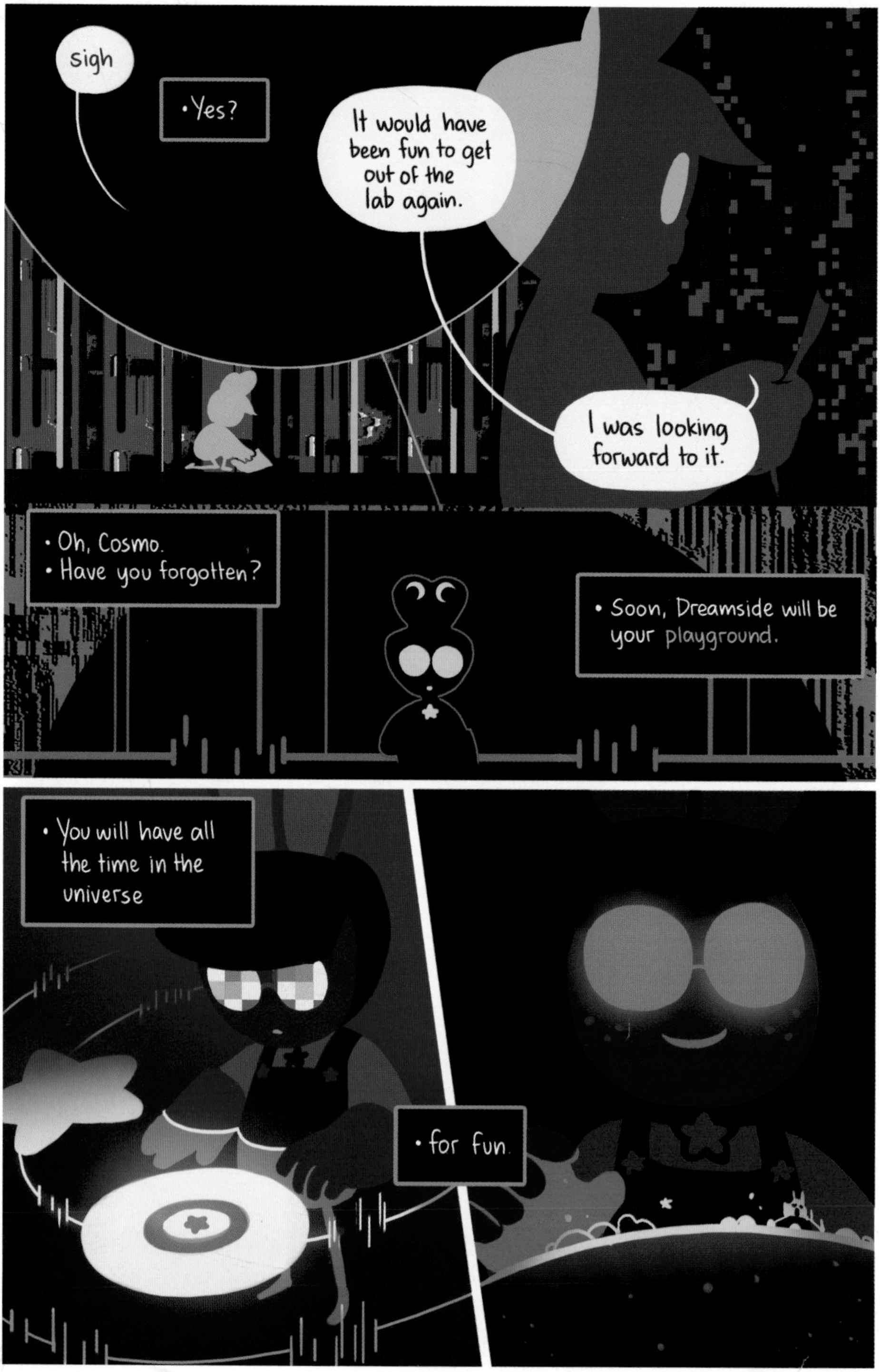
sigh
• Yes?
It would have been fun to get out of the lab again.
I was looking forward to it.
• Oh, Cosmo.
• Have you forgotten?
• Soon, Dreamside will be your playground.
• You will have all the time in the universe
• for fun.

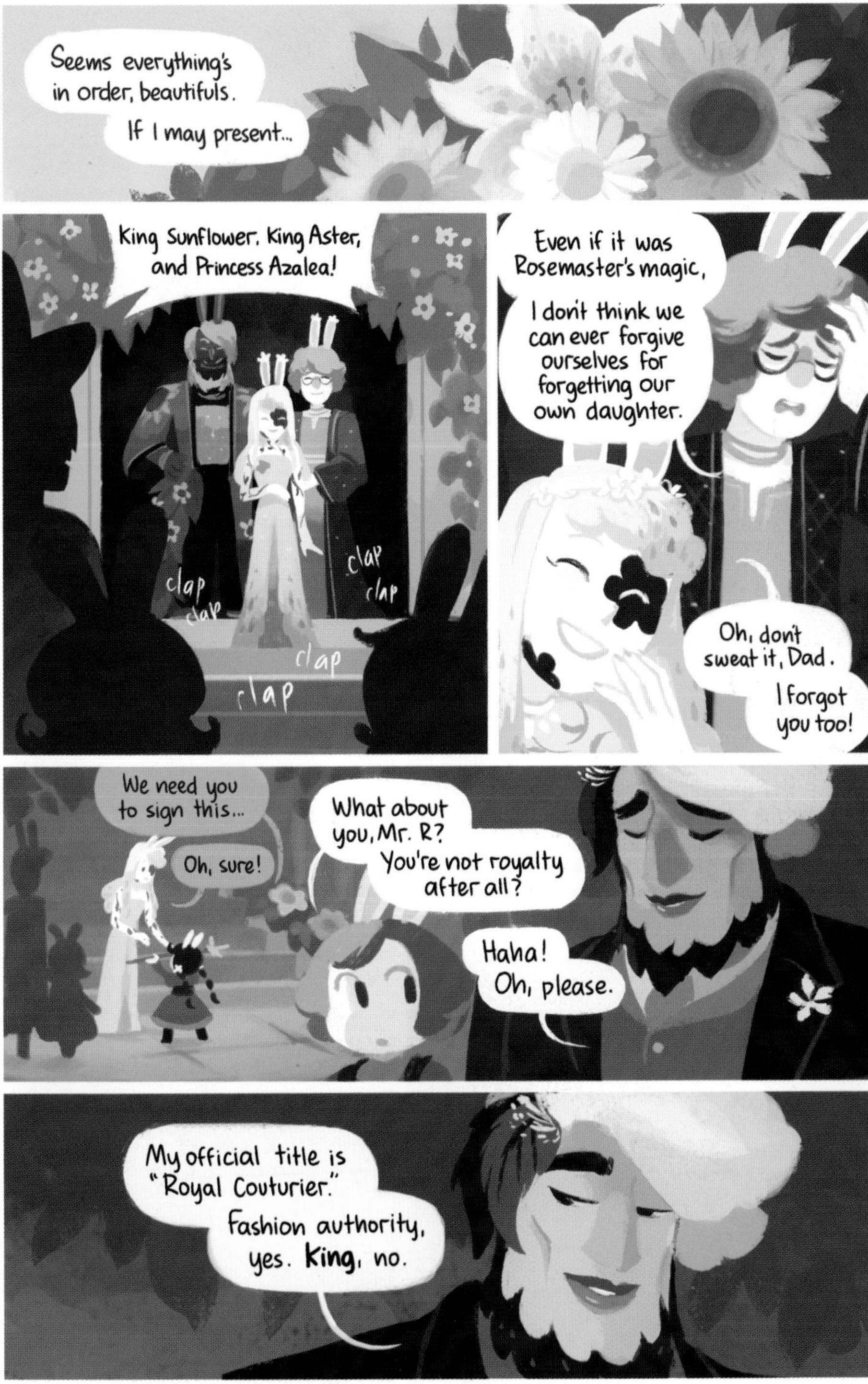
Seems everything's in order, beautifuls.
If I may present...
King Sunflower, King Aster, and Princess Azalea!
clap
clap
clap
clap
clap
clap
Even if it was Rosemaster's magic,
I don't think we can ever forgive ourselves for forgetting our own daughter.
Oh, don't sweat it, Dad.
I forgot you too!
We need you to sign this...
Oh, sure!
What about you, Mr. R?
You're not royalty after all?
Haha! Oh, please.
My official title is "Royal Couturier."
Fashion authority, yes. **King**, no.

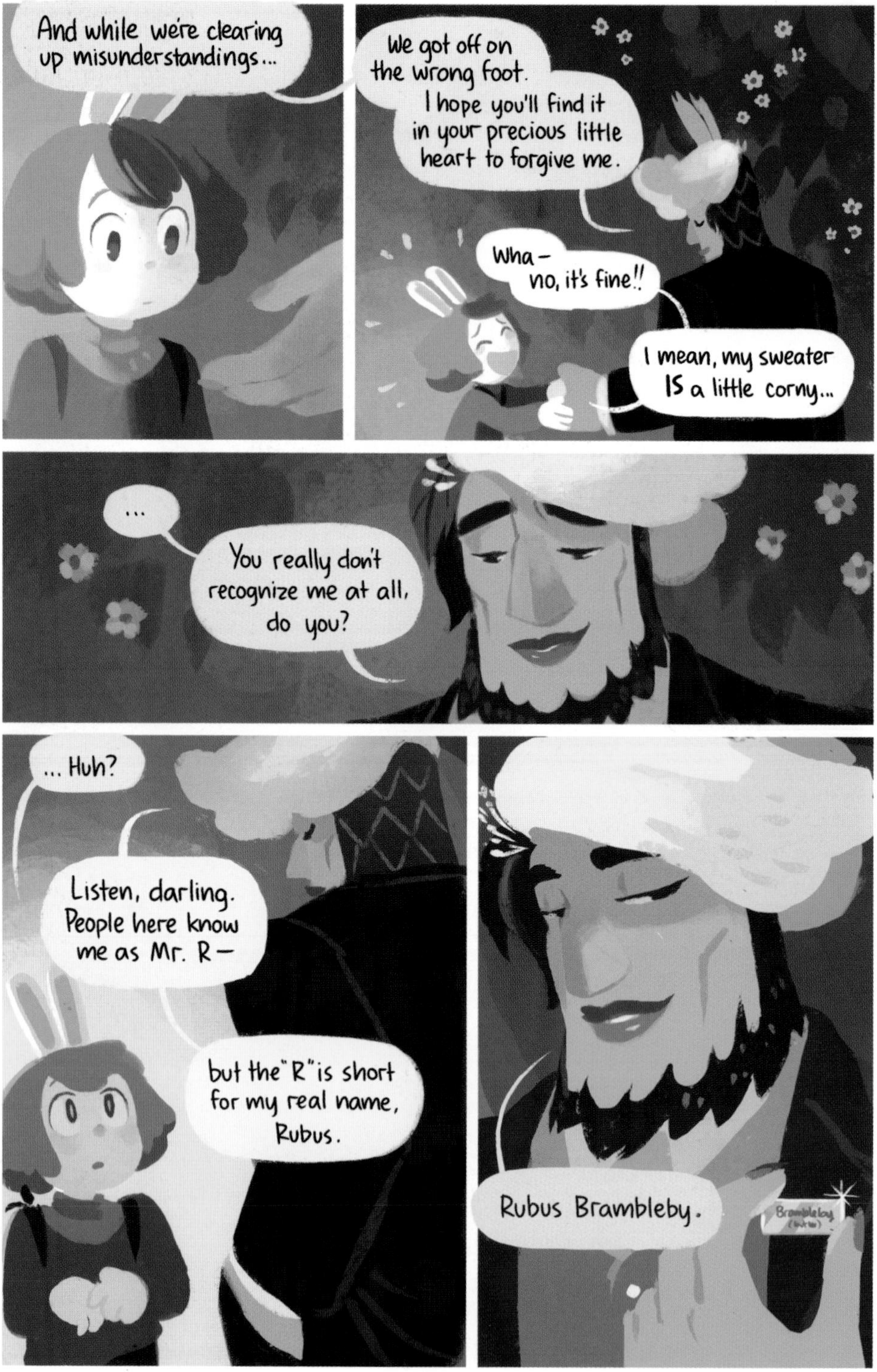
And while we're clearing up misunderstandings...
We got off on the wrong foot.
I hope you'll find it in your precious little heart to forgive me.
Wha– no, it's fine!!
I mean, my sweater IS a little corny...
...
You really don't recognize me at all, do you?
... Huh?
Listen, darling. People here know me as Mr. R–
but the "R" is short for my real name, Rubus.
Rubus Brambleby.
Brambleby

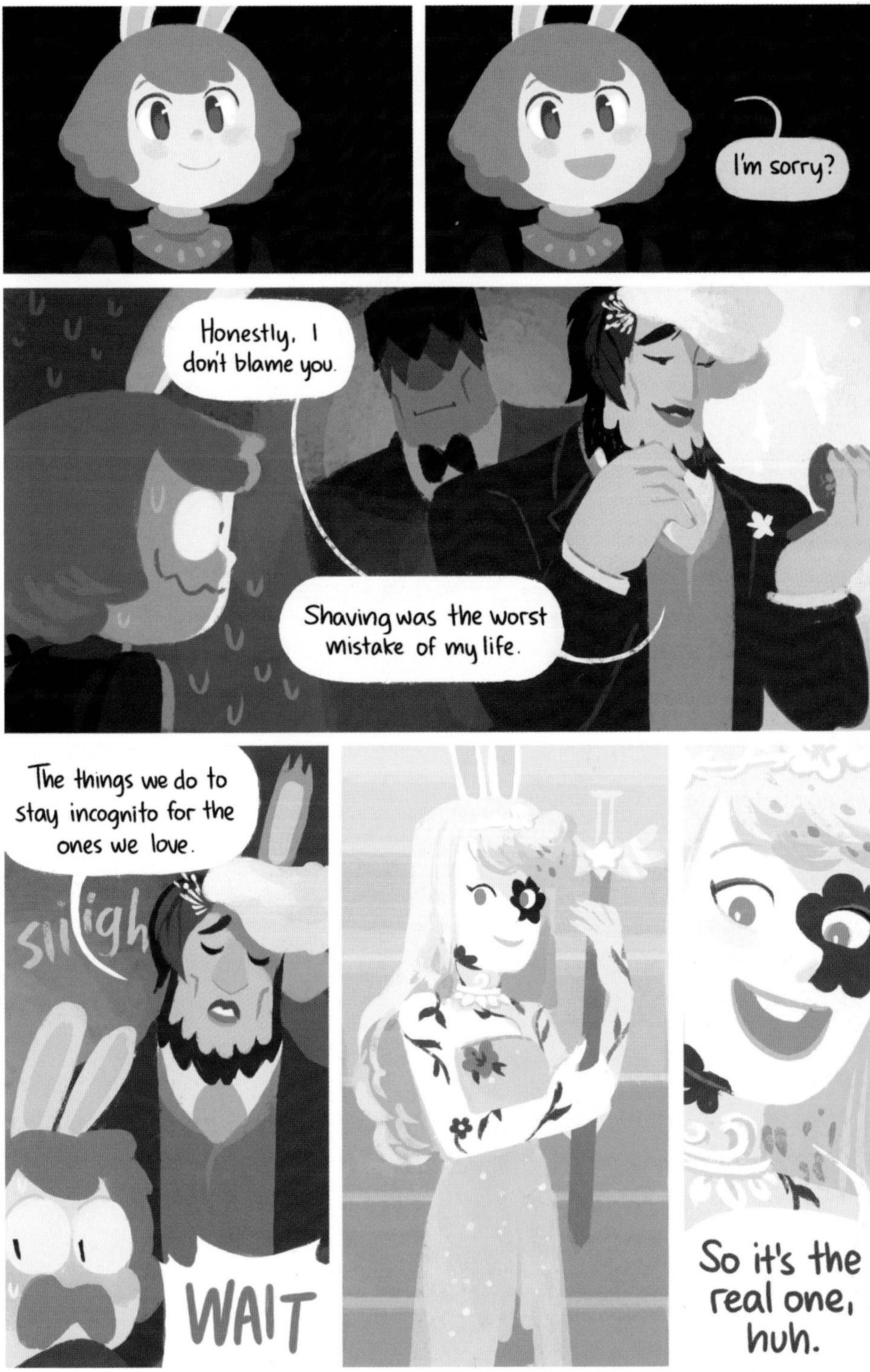

I'm sorry?
Honestly, I don't blame you.
Shaving was the worst mistake of my life.
The things we do to stay incognito for the ones we love.
siiigh
WAIT
So it's the real one, huh.

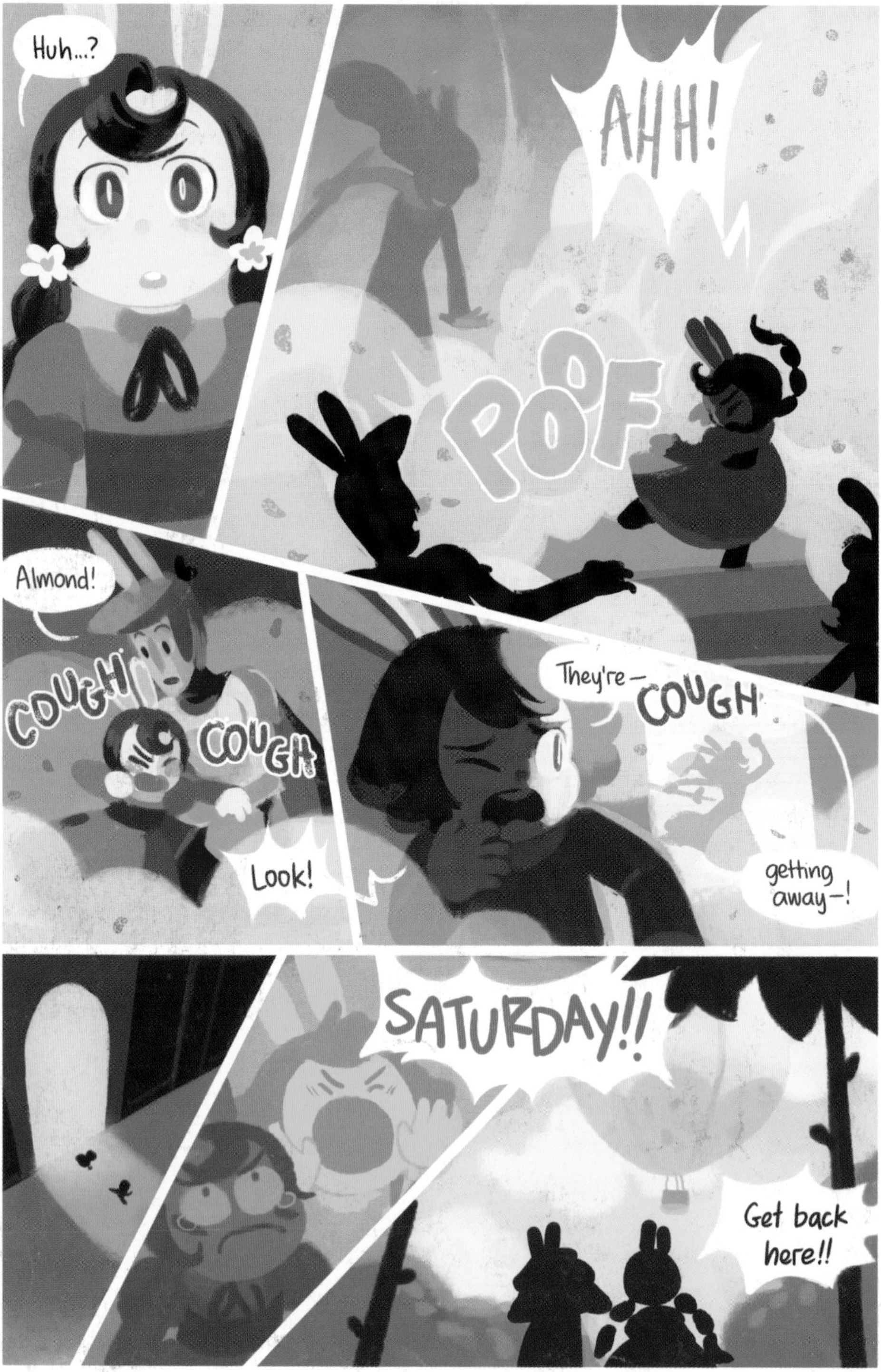
Huh...?
AHH!
POOF
Almond!
COUGH
COUGH
Look!
They're—
COUGH
getting away—!
SATURDAY!!
Get back here!!

Sorry, y'all!

Looks like I win this round!

HEA HA HUH HEH

You know... I've met her at royal functions before.

She's lively, certainly, but I never expected this side of her.

Please don't misunderstand!

Our daughter is no burglar.

Um, all due respect, sir, you **just** watched her burgle us.

Well... it's not exactly **dignified**, but she's going through something of a ... thrill-seeking phase.

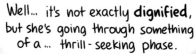

Azalea's had an interesting "hobby" for some time now— maybe that sword of yours is central to it?

You'd have to ask her, though.

We have to **catch** her!!

Need a riiiiiiide, kids?

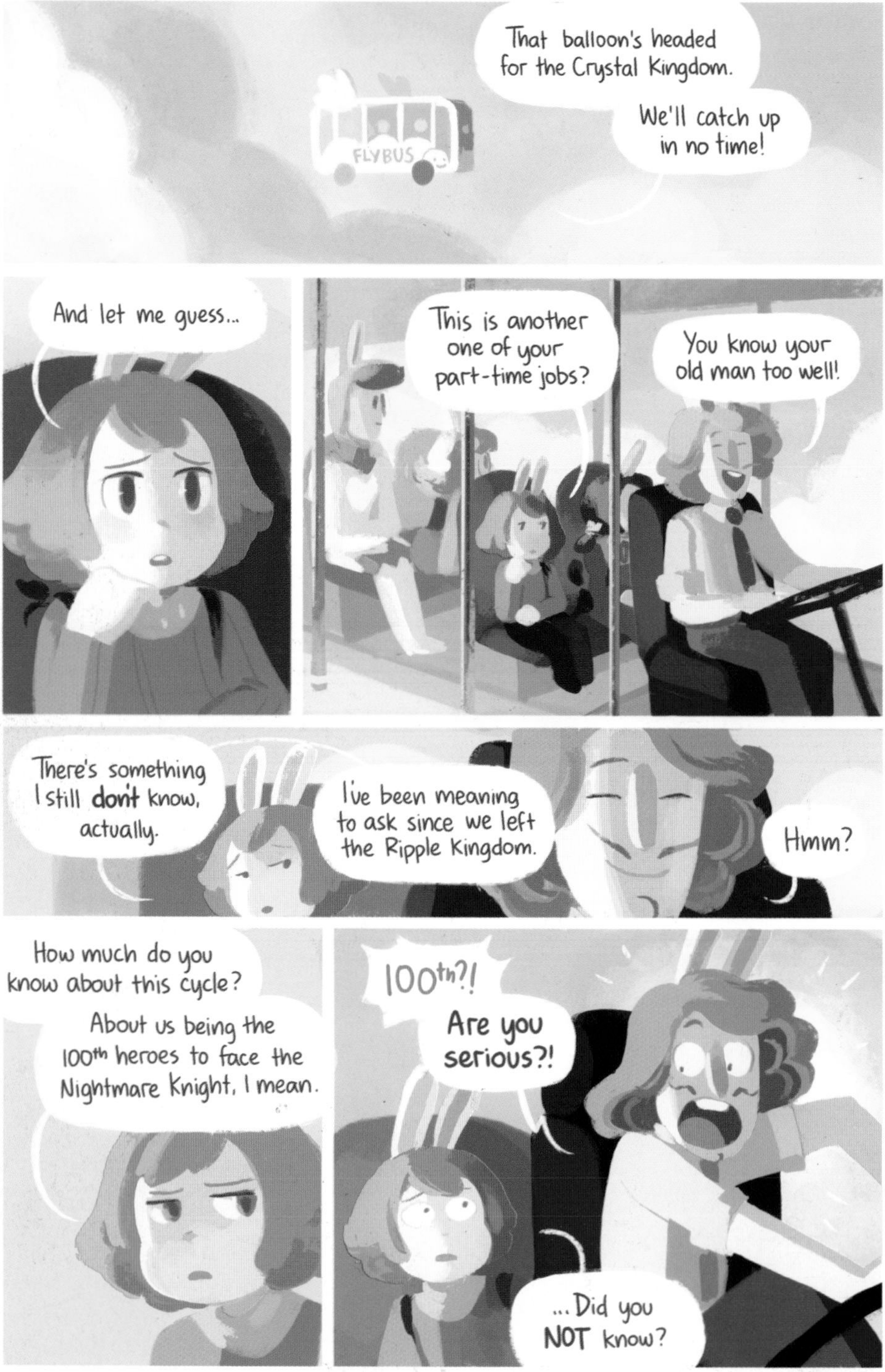

That balloon's headed for the Crystal Kingdom.
We'll catch up in no time!
FLYBUS
And let me guess...
This is another one of your part-time jobs?
You know your old man too well!
There's something I still **don't** know, actually.
I've been meaning to ask since we left the Ripple Kingdom.
Hmm?
How much do you know about this cycle?
About us being the 100th heroes to face the Nightmare Knight, I mean.
100th?!
Are you serious?!
...Did you **NOT** know?

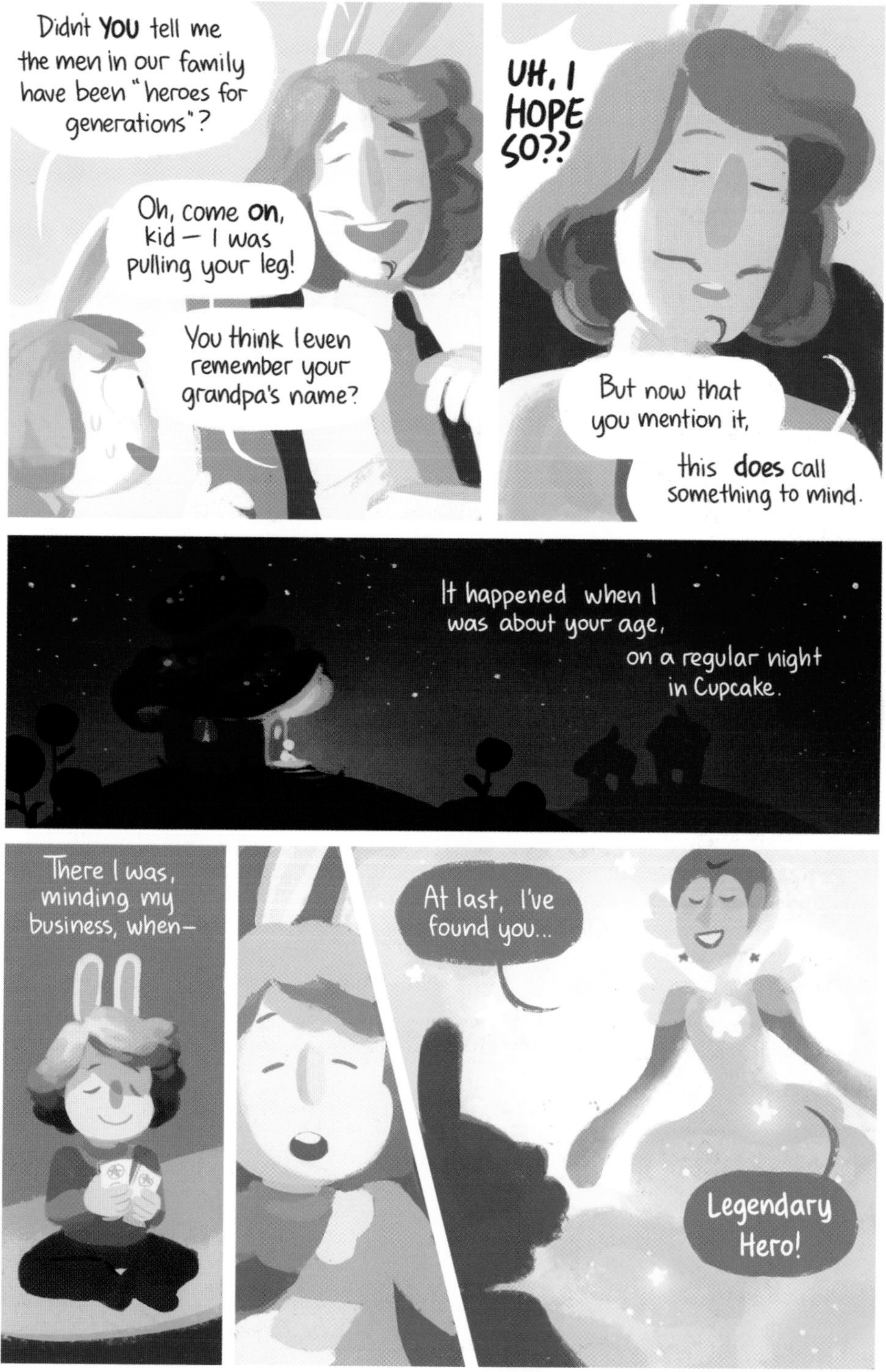

Didn't YOU tell me the men in our family have been "heroes for generations"?
Oh, come on, kid — I was pulling your leg!
You think I even remember your grandpa's name?
UH, I HOPE SO??
But now that you mention it,
this does call something to mind.
It happened when I was about your age,
on a regular night in Cupcake.
There I was, minding my business, when—
At last, I've found you...
Legendary Hero!

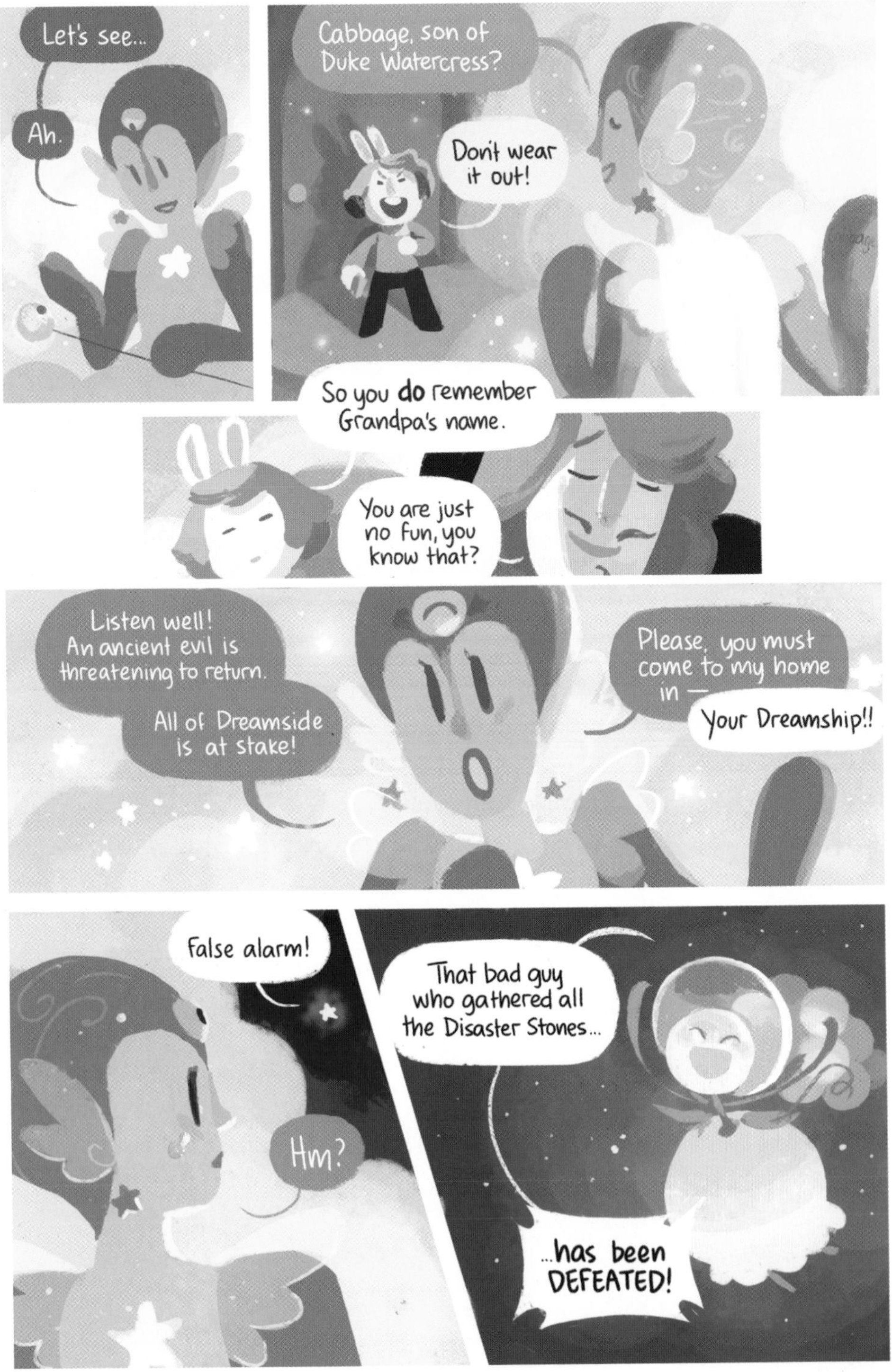
Let's see...
Ah.
Cabbage, son of Duke Watercress?
Don't wear it out!
So you do remember Grandpa's name.
You are just no fun, you know that?
Listen well! An ancient evil is threatening to return.
All of Dreamside is at stake!
Please, you must come to my home in —
Your Dreamship!!
False alarm!
Hm?
That bad guy who gathered all the Disaster Stones...
...has been DEFEATED!

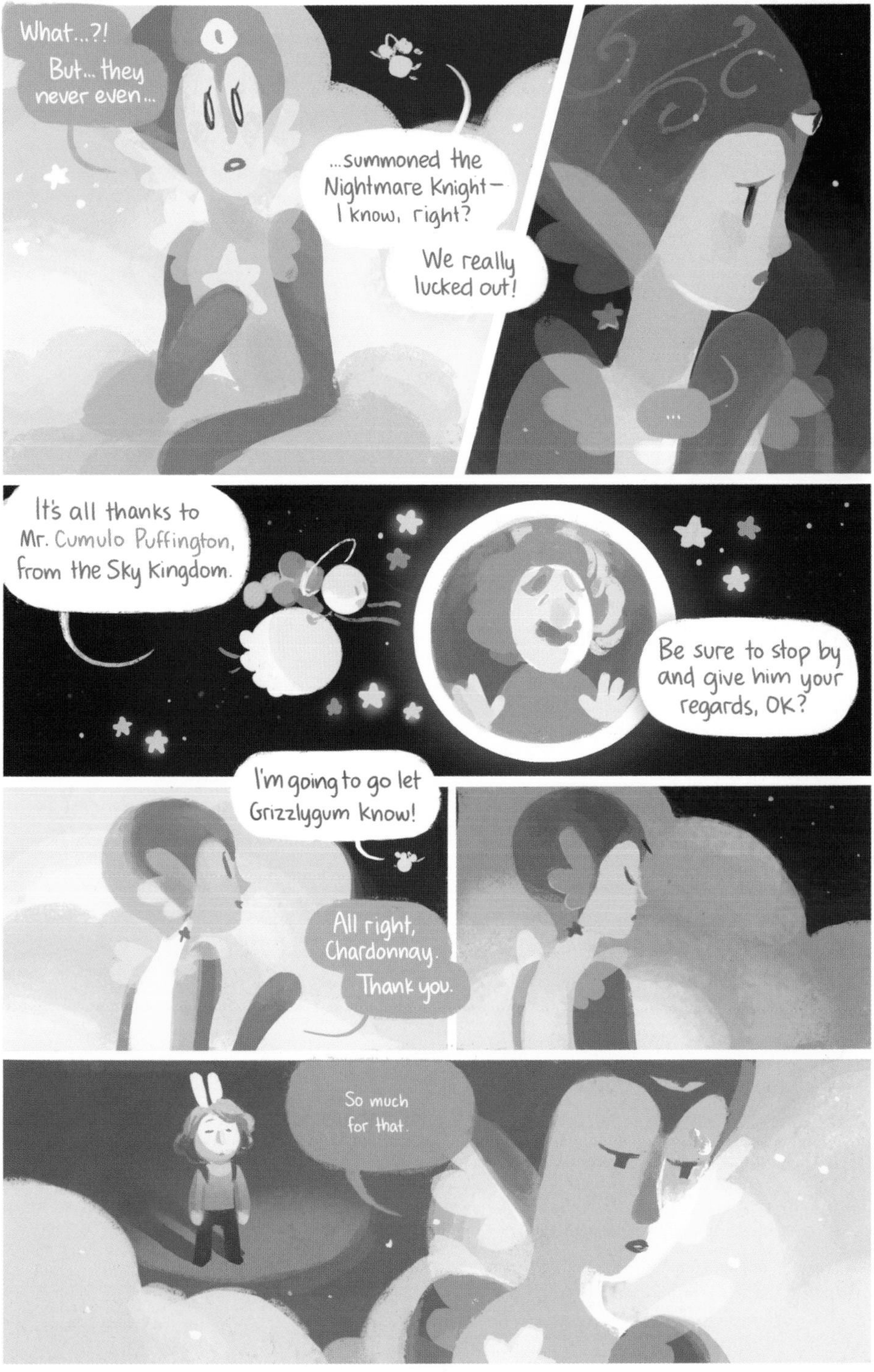
What...?!
But... they never even...
...summoned the Nightmare Knight— I know, right?
We really lucked out!
...
It's all thanks to Mr. Cumulo Puffington, from the Sky Kingdom.
Be sure to stop by and give him your regards, OK?
I'm going to go let Grizzlygum know!
All right, Chardonnay. Thank you.
So much for that.

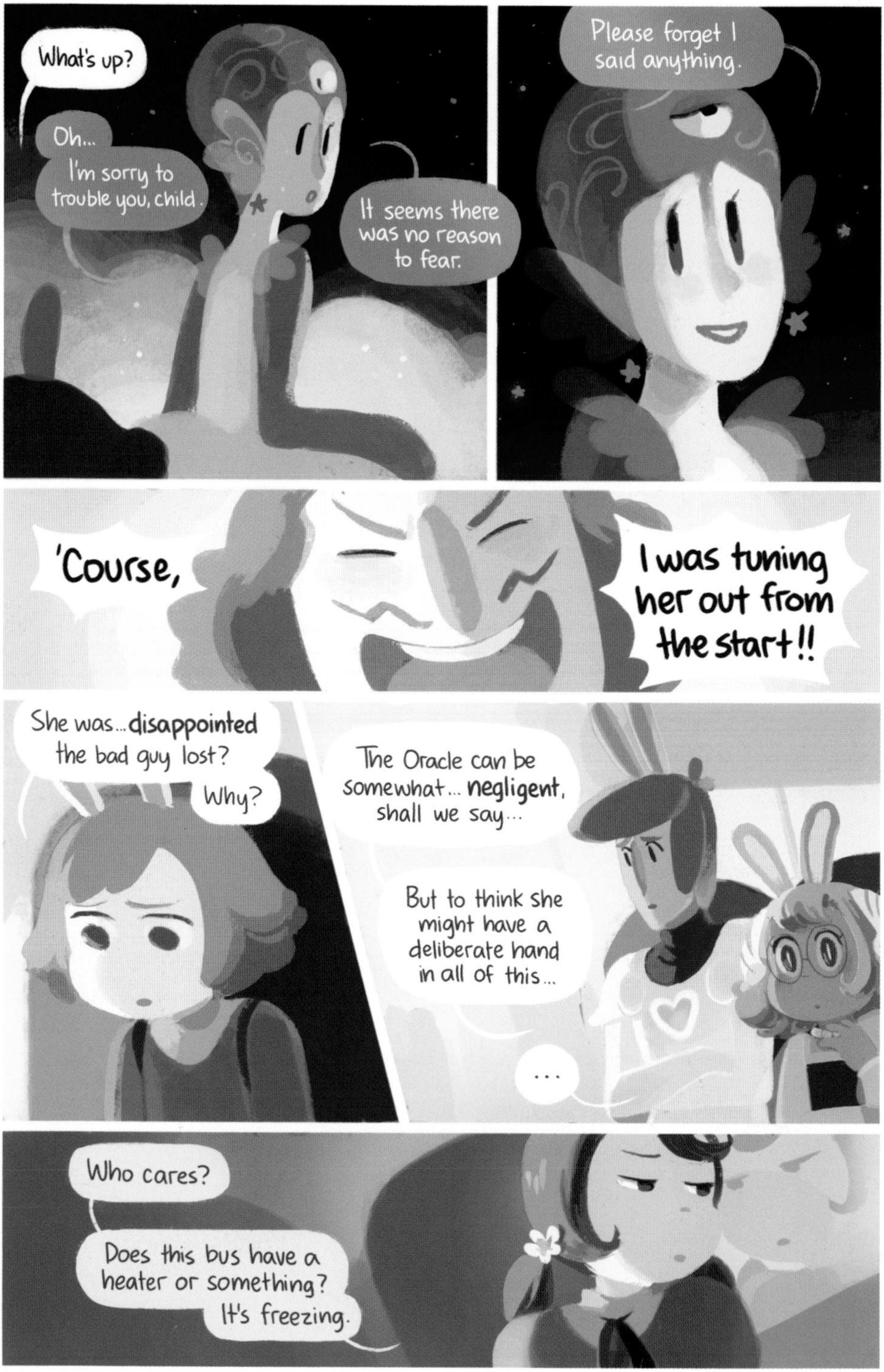
What's up?
Oh...
I'm sorry to trouble you, child.
It seems there was no reason to fear.
Please forget I said anything.
'Course,
I was tuning her out from the start!!
She was... disappointed the bad guy lost?
Why?
The Oracle can be somewhat... negligent, shall we say...
But to think she might have a deliberate hand in all of this...
...
Who cares?
Does this bus have a heater or something?
It's freezing.

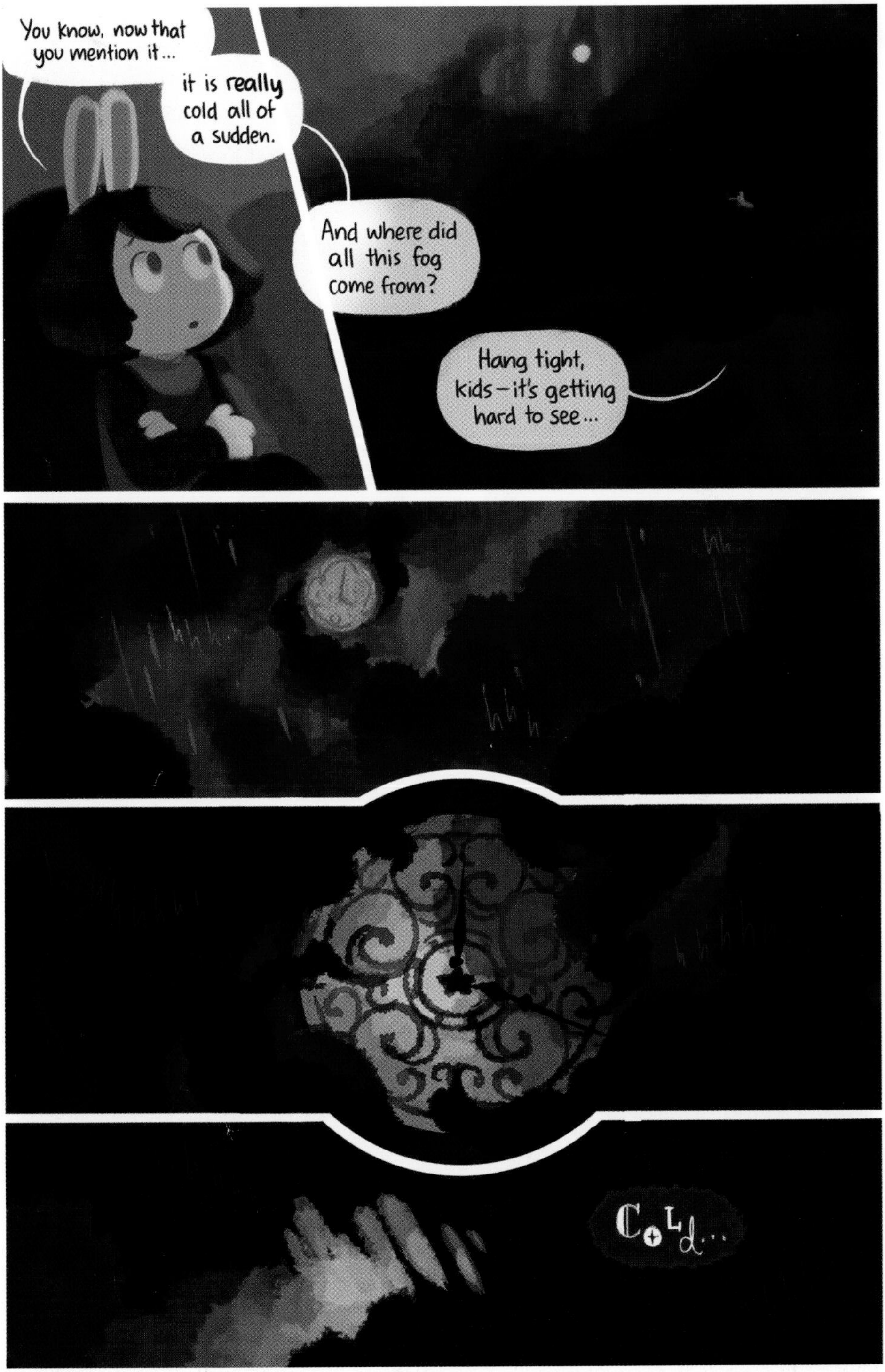
You know, now that you mention it...
it is **really** cold all of a sudden.
And where did all this fog come from?
Hang tight, kids—it's getting hard to see...
Cold...

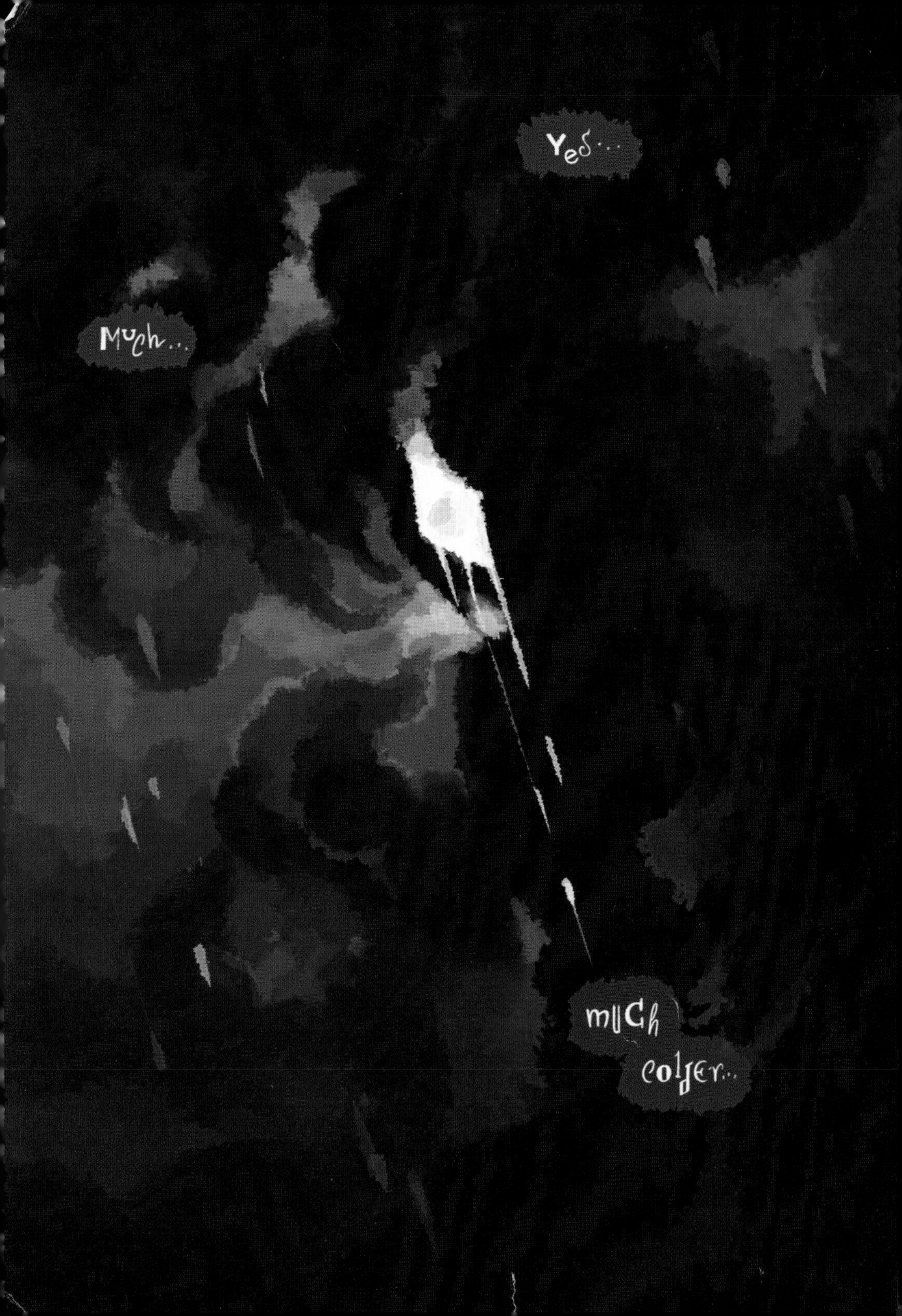
Yes...
Much...
much
colder...

To be continued

Cucumber QUEST

CUCUMBER.GIGIDIGI.COM

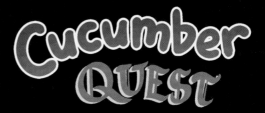

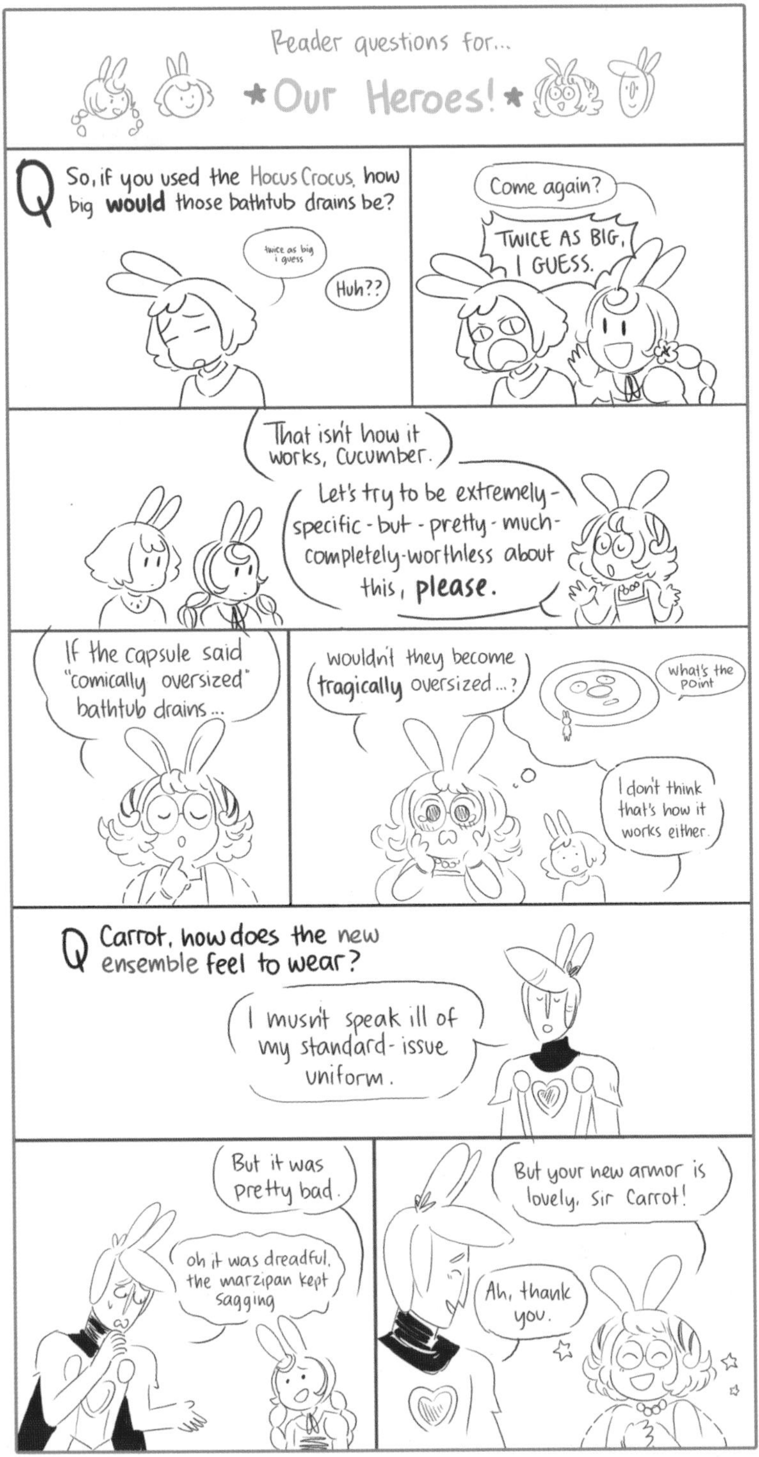
Reader questions for...
★ Our Heroes! ★
Q So, if you used the Hocus Crocus, how big would those bathtub drains be?
twice as big i guess
Huh??
Come again?
TWICE AS BIG, I GUESS.
That isn't how it works, Cucumber.
Let's try to be extremely-specific-but-pretty-much-completely-worthless about this, please.
If the capsule said "comically oversized" bathtub drains...
wouldn't they become tragically oversized...?
what's the point
I don't think that's how it works either.
Q Carrot, how does the new ensemble feel to wear?
I musn't speak ill of my standard-issue uniform.
But it was pretty bad.
oh it was dreadful. the marzipan kept sagging
But your new armor is lovely, Sir Carrot!
Ah, thank you.

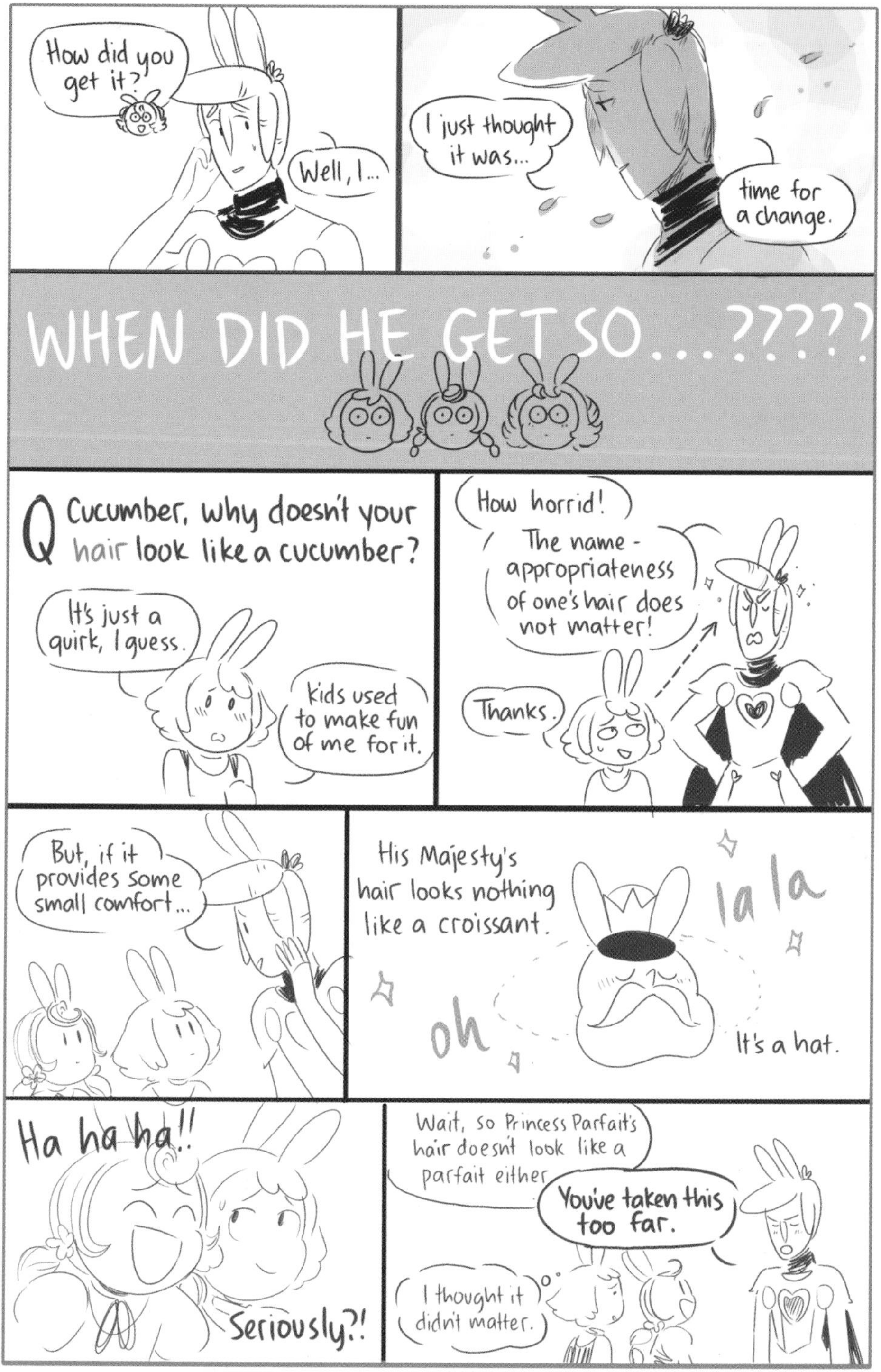
How did you get it?
Well, I...
I just thought it was...
time for a change.
WHEN DID HE GET SO...?????
Q Cucumber, why doesn't your hair look like a cucumber?
It's just a quirk, I guess.
kids used to make fun of me for it.
How horrid!
The name-appropriateness of one's hair does not matter!
Thanks.
But, if it provides some small comfort...
His Majesty's hair looks nothing like a croissant.
la la
oh
It's a hat.
Ha ha ha!!
Seriously?!
Wait, so Princess Parfait's hair doesn't look like a parfait either
You've taken this too far.
I thought it didn't matter.

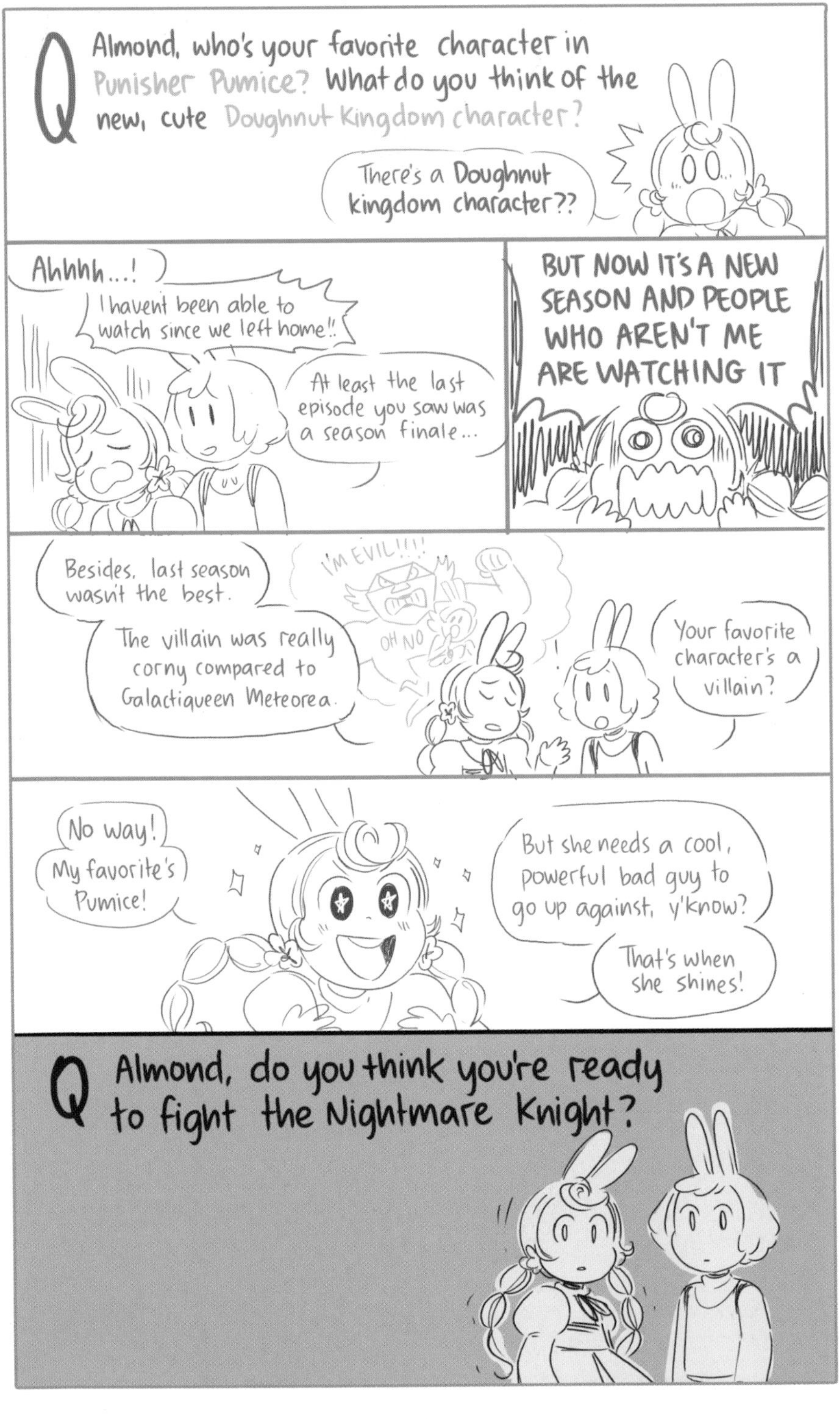
Q Almond, who's your favorite character in Punisher Pumice? What do you think of the new, cute Doughnut Kingdom character?
There's a Doughnut kingdom character??
Ahhhh...!
I havent been able to watch since we left home!!
At least the last episode you saw was a season finale...
BUT NOW IT'S A NEW SEASON AND PEOPLE WHO AREN'T ME ARE WATCHING IT
Besides, last season wasn't the best.
The villain was really corny compared to Galactiqueen Meteorea.
I'M EVIL!!!!
OH NO
Your favorite character's a villain?
No way!
My favorite's Pumice!
But she needs a cool, powerful bad guy to go up against, y'know?
That's when she shines!
Q Almond, do you think you're ready to fight the Nightmare Knight?

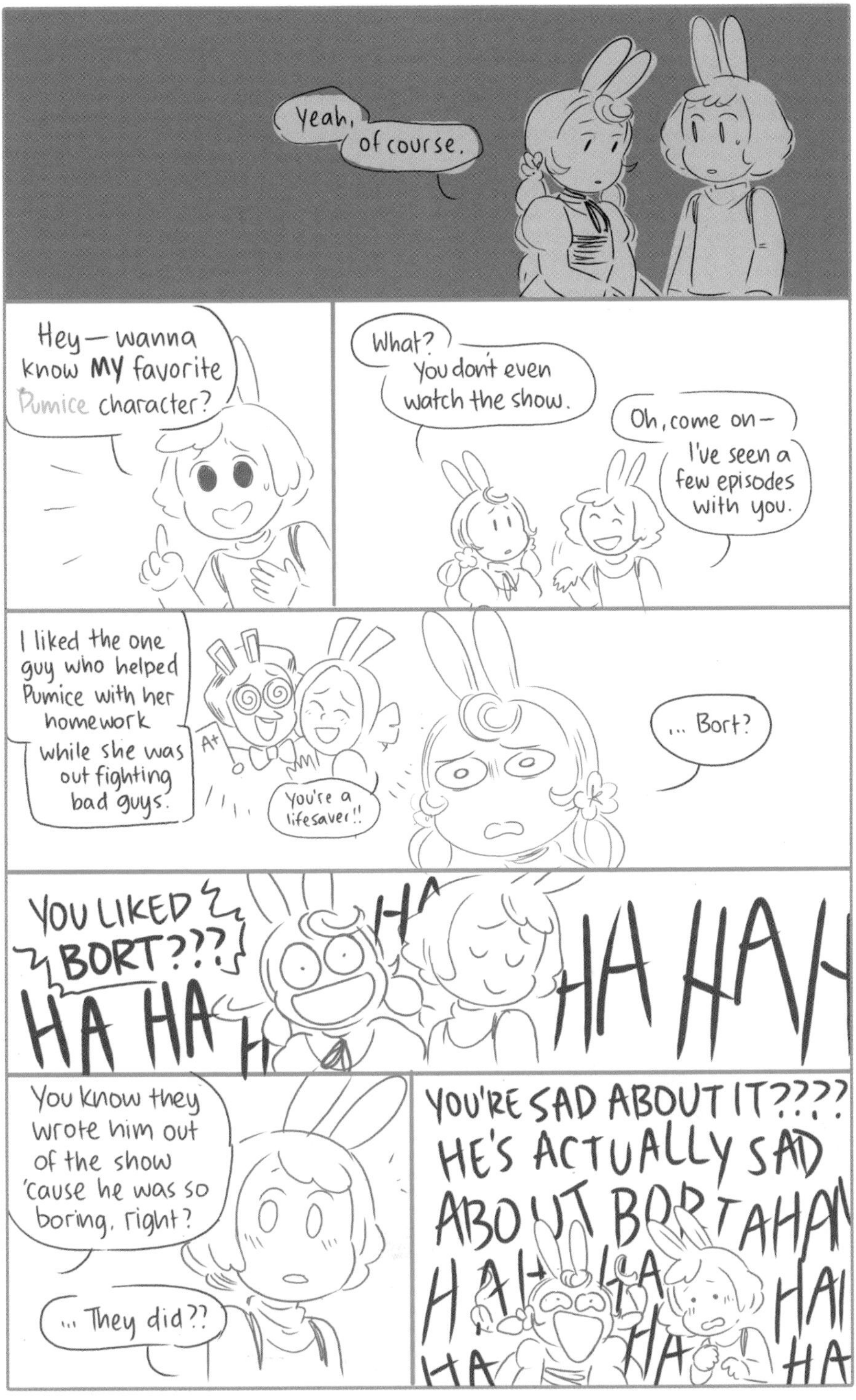
Yeah, of course.
Hey— wanna know MY favorite Pumice character?
What? You don't even watch the show.
Oh, come on— I've seen a few episodes with you.
I liked the one guy who helped Pumice with her homework while she was out fighting bad guys.
A+
You're a lifesaver!!
... Bort?
YOU LIKED BORT???
HA HA HA HA HA HA
You know they wrote him out of the show 'cause he was so boring, right?
... They did??
YOU'RE SAD ABOUT IT???? HE'S ACTUALLY SAD ABOUT BORTAHAH
HAHAHAHAHAHAHA

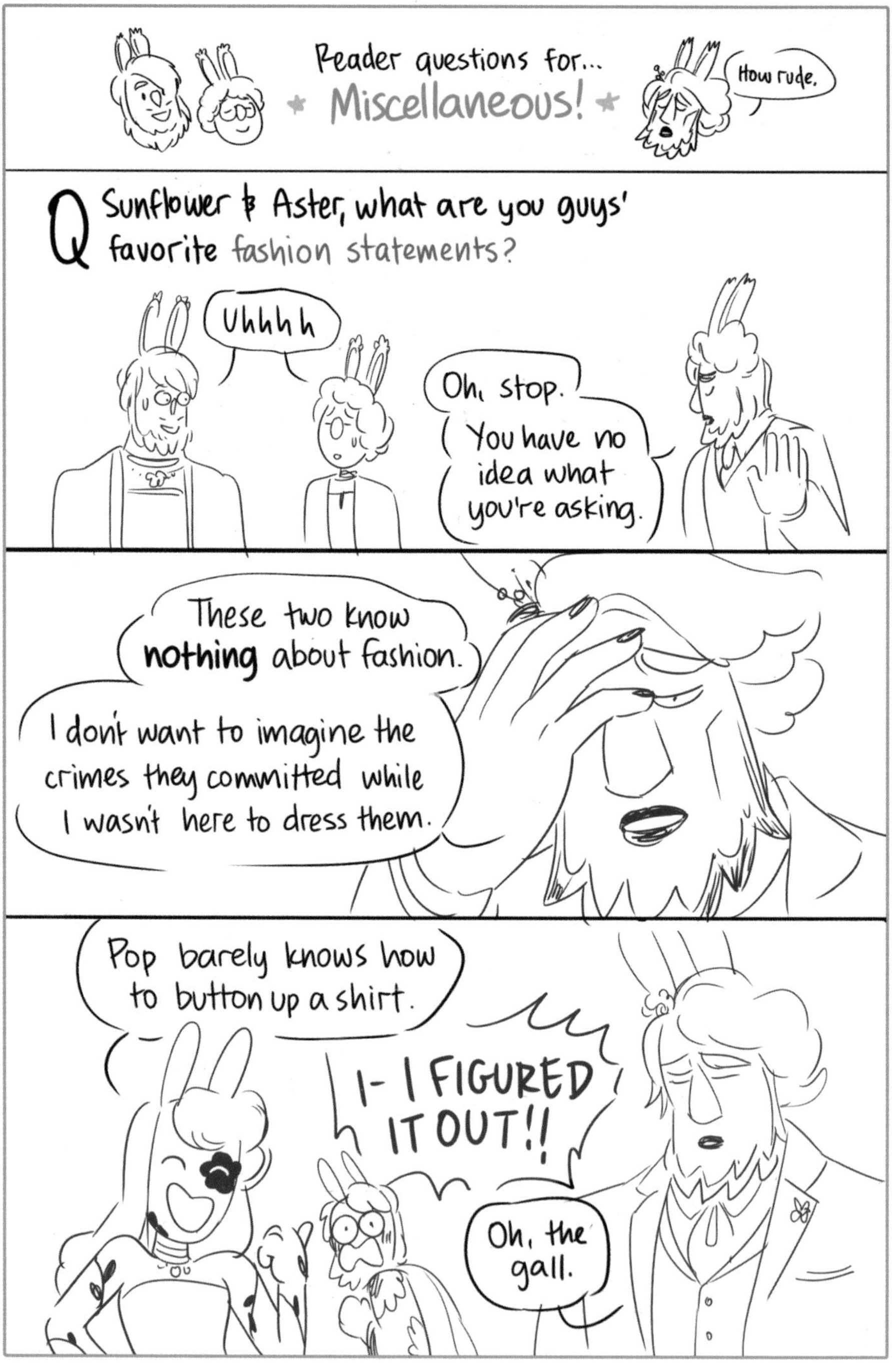
Reader questions for...
Miscellaneous!
How rude.
Q Sunflower & Aster, what are you guys' favorite fashion statements?
Uhhhh
Oh, stop.
You have no idea what you're asking.
These two know **nothing** about fashion.
I don't want to imagine the crimes they committed while I wasn't here to dress them.
Pop barely knows how to button up a shirt.
I- I FIGURED IT OUT!!
Oh, the gall.

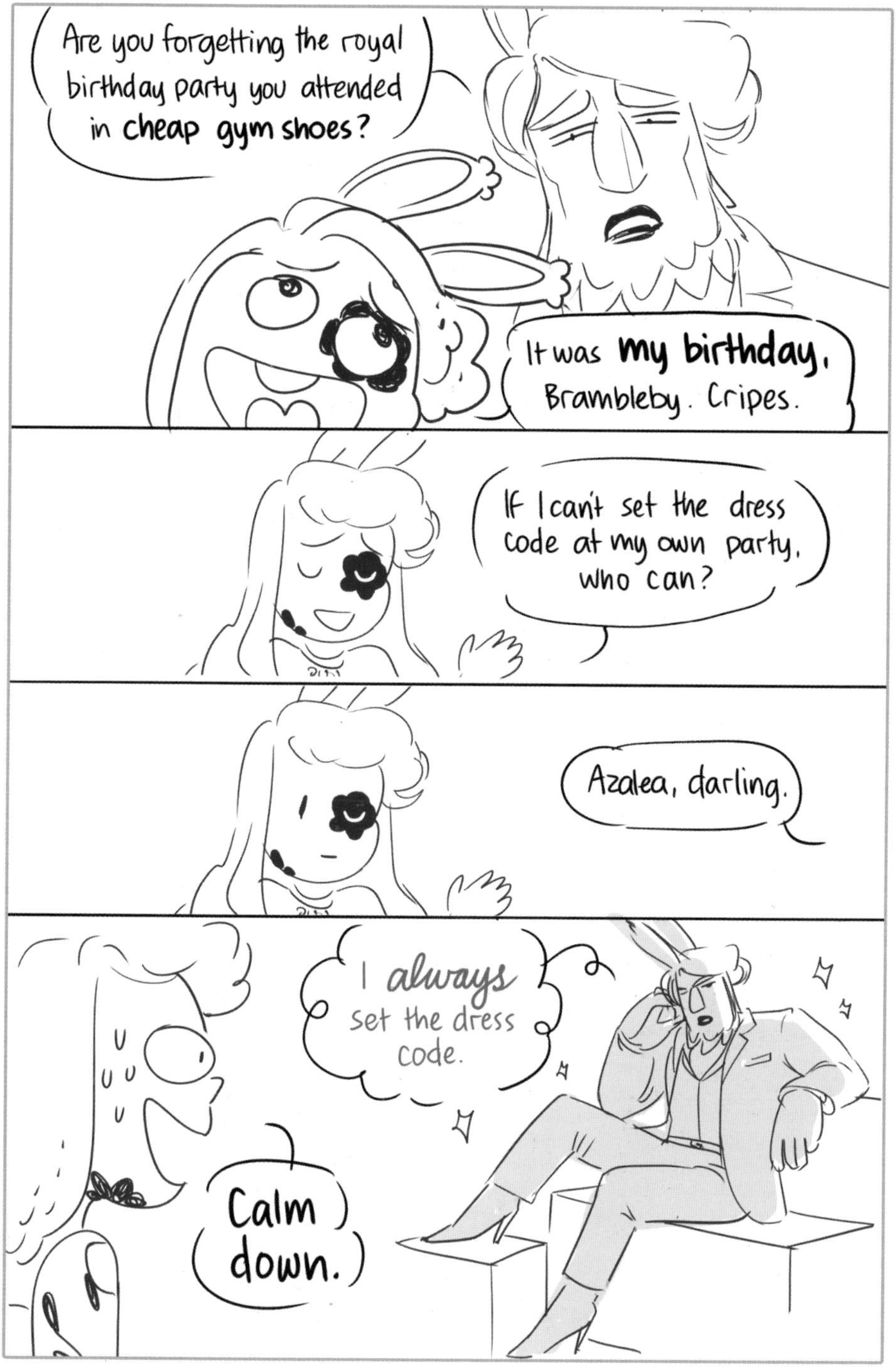
Are you forgetting the royal birthday party you attended in **cheap gym shoes?**
It was **my birthday,** Brambleby. Cripes.
If I can't set the dress code at my own party, who can?
Azalea, darling.
I *always* set the dress code.
Calm down.

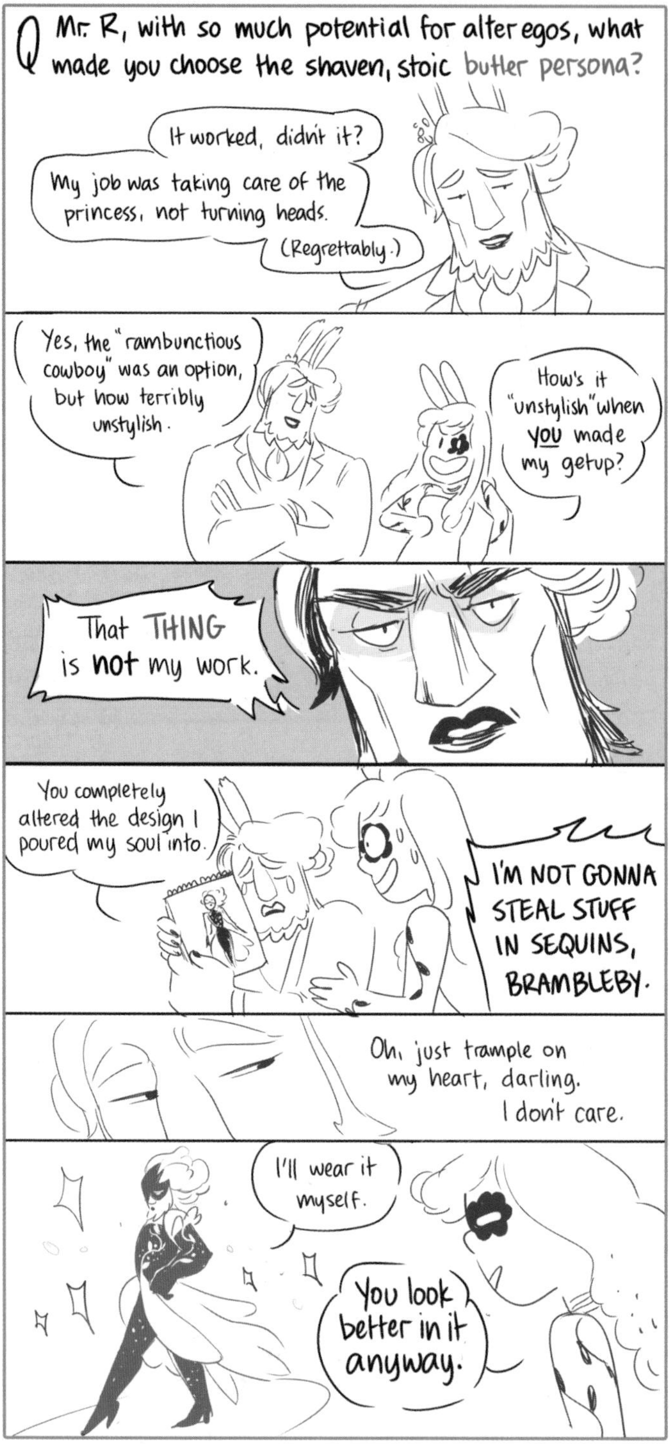
Q Mr. R, with so much potential for alter egos, what made you choose the shaven, stoic butler persona?
It worked, didn't it?
My job was taking care of the princess, not turning heads.
(Regrettably.)
Yes, the "rambunctious cowboy" was an option, but how terribly unstylish.
How's it "unstylish" when YOU made my getup?
That THING is not my work.
You completely altered the design I poured my soul into.
I'M NOT GONNA STEAL STUFF IN SEQUINS, BRAMBLEBY.
Oh, just trample on my heart, darling. I don't care.
I'll wear it myself.
You look better in it anyway.

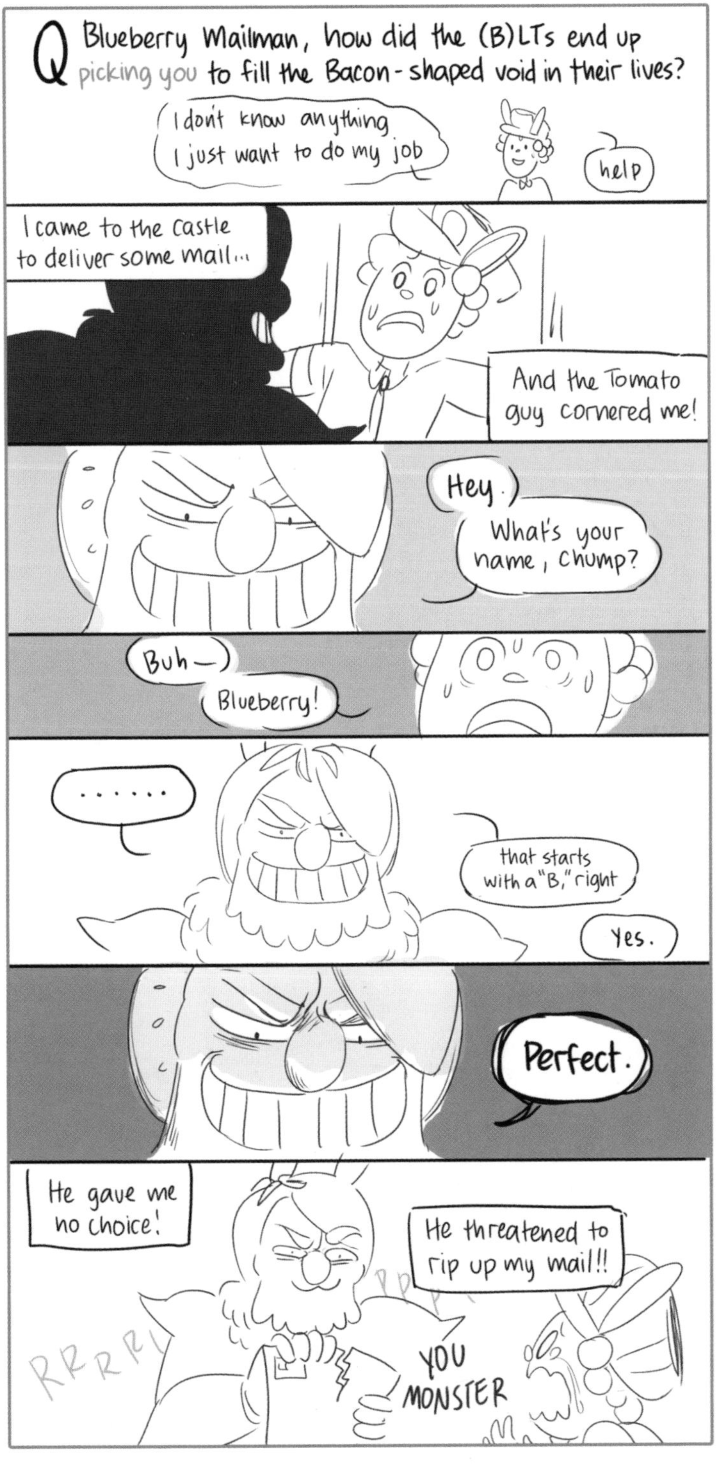
Q Blueberry Mailman, how did the (B)LTs end up picking you to fill the Bacon-shaped void in their lives?
I don't know anything
I just want to do my job
help
I came to the castle to deliver some mail...
And the Tomato guy cornered me!
Hey.
What's your name, chump?
Buh—
Blueberry!
......
that starts with a "B," right
Yes.
Perfect.
He gave me no choice!
He threatened to rip up my mail!!
RRRRI
RRRRI
YOU MONSTER

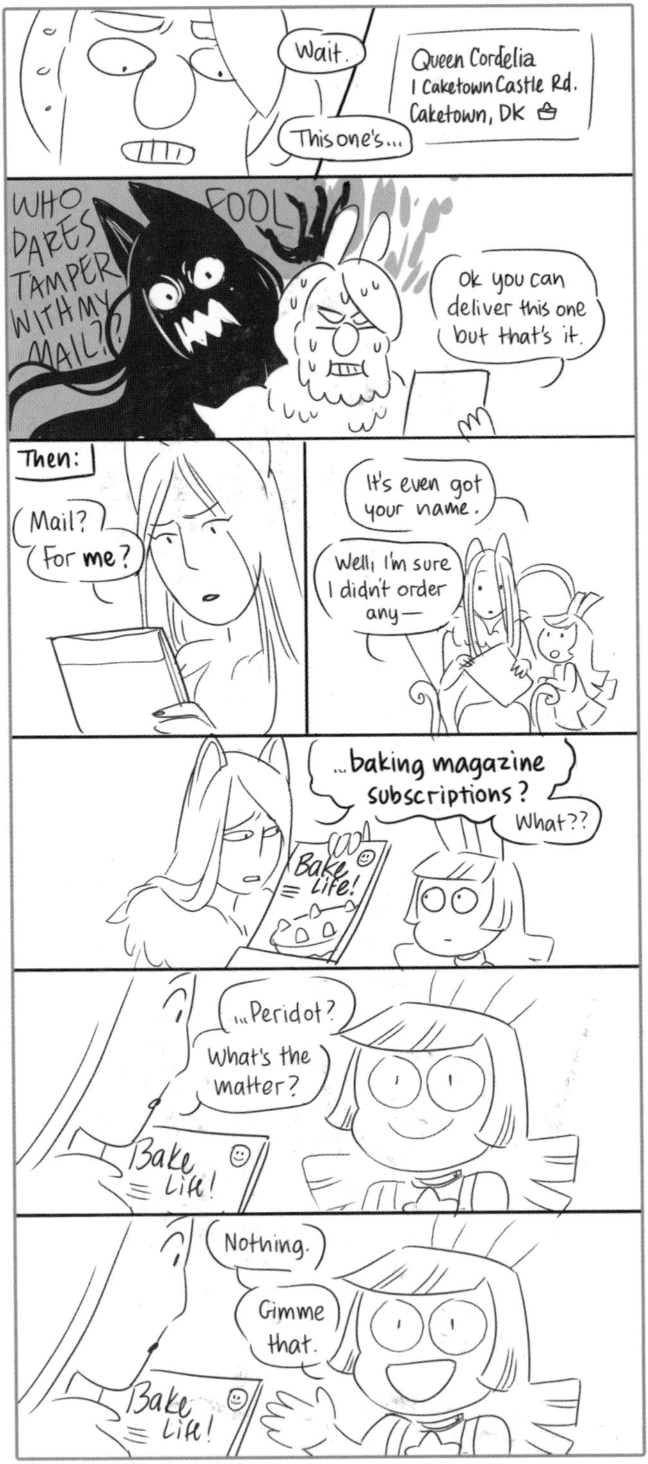
Wait.
This one's...
Queen Cordelia
1 Caketown Castle Rd.
Caketown, DK
WHO DARES TAMPER WITH MY MAIL??
FOOL!
Ok you can deliver this one but that's it.
Then:
Mail? For **me**?
It's even got your name.
Well, I'm sure I didn't order any—
...**baking magazine subscriptions?**
What??
Bake Life!
...Peridot?
What's the matter?
Bake Life!
Nothing.
Gimme that.
Bake Life!

 Reader questions for... **Peridot & the Nightmare Knight!**

Q Nightmare Knight, how do you taste-test your pastries without a mouth?

Q For that matter, how do you talk without a mouth?

 I'm not doing this.

HEY

You **have** to! I do it!!

Even if I showed you... **THIS?!**

You **enjoy** it. I have nothing to contribute.

 **Bake Life!**

A magazine.

YOUR magazine. And I'm gonna rip up a page for every embarrassing question you don't answer.

How tragic. So many cakes we could have enjoyed, lost forever.

......

ok i'm not gonna rip it **BUT YOU HAVE TO ANSWER SOME OR YOU CAN'T HAVE IT BACK**

Clearly I have no choice.

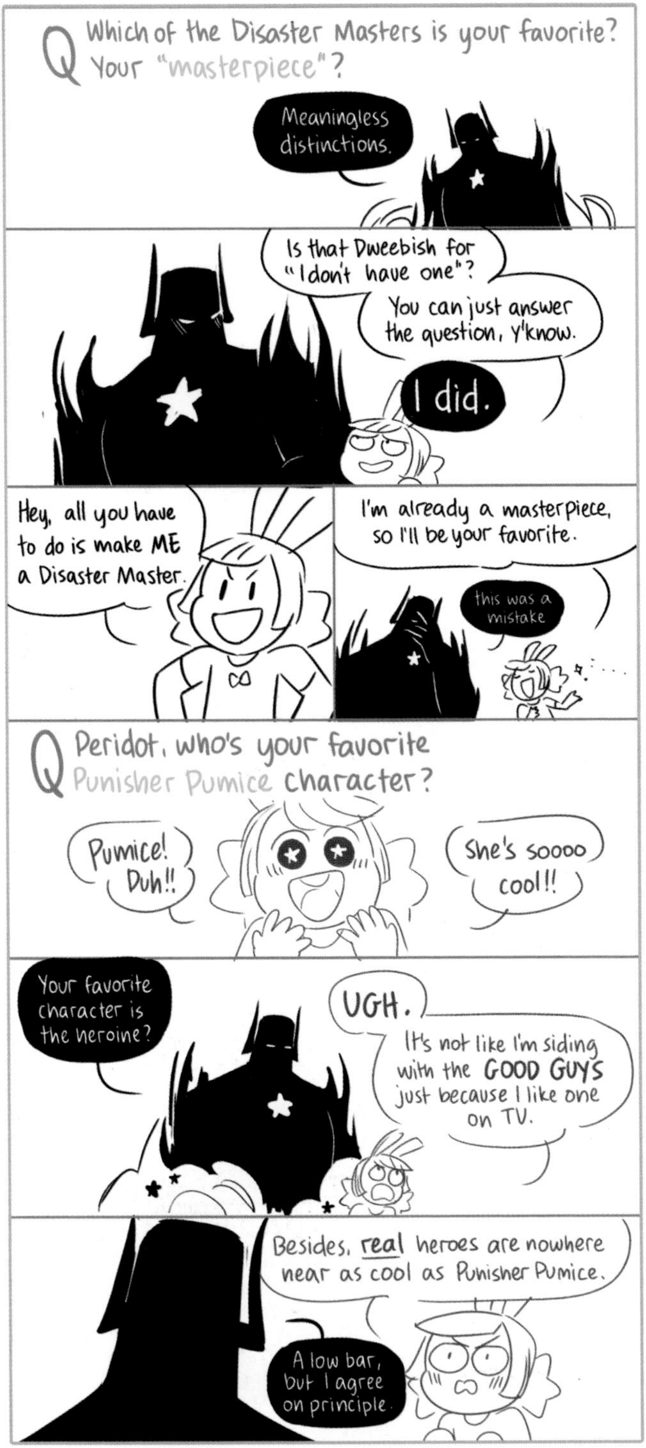
Q Which of the Disaster Masters is your favorite? Your "masterpiece"?
Meaningless distinctions.
Is that Dweebish for "I don't have one"?
You can just answer the question, y'know.
I did.
Hey, all you have to do is make ME a Disaster Master.
I'm already a masterpiece, so I'll be your favorite.
this was a mistake
Q Peridot, who's your favorite Punisher Pumice character?
Pumice! Duh!!
She's soooo cool!!
Your favorite character is the heroine?
UGH.
It's not like I'm siding with the GOOD GUYS just because I like one on TV.
Besides, real heroes are nowhere near as cool as Punisher Pumice.
A low bar, but I agree on principle.

Q Were the Disaster Masters just willed into being, or did you put actual thought into it? If the latter... why Splashmaster?

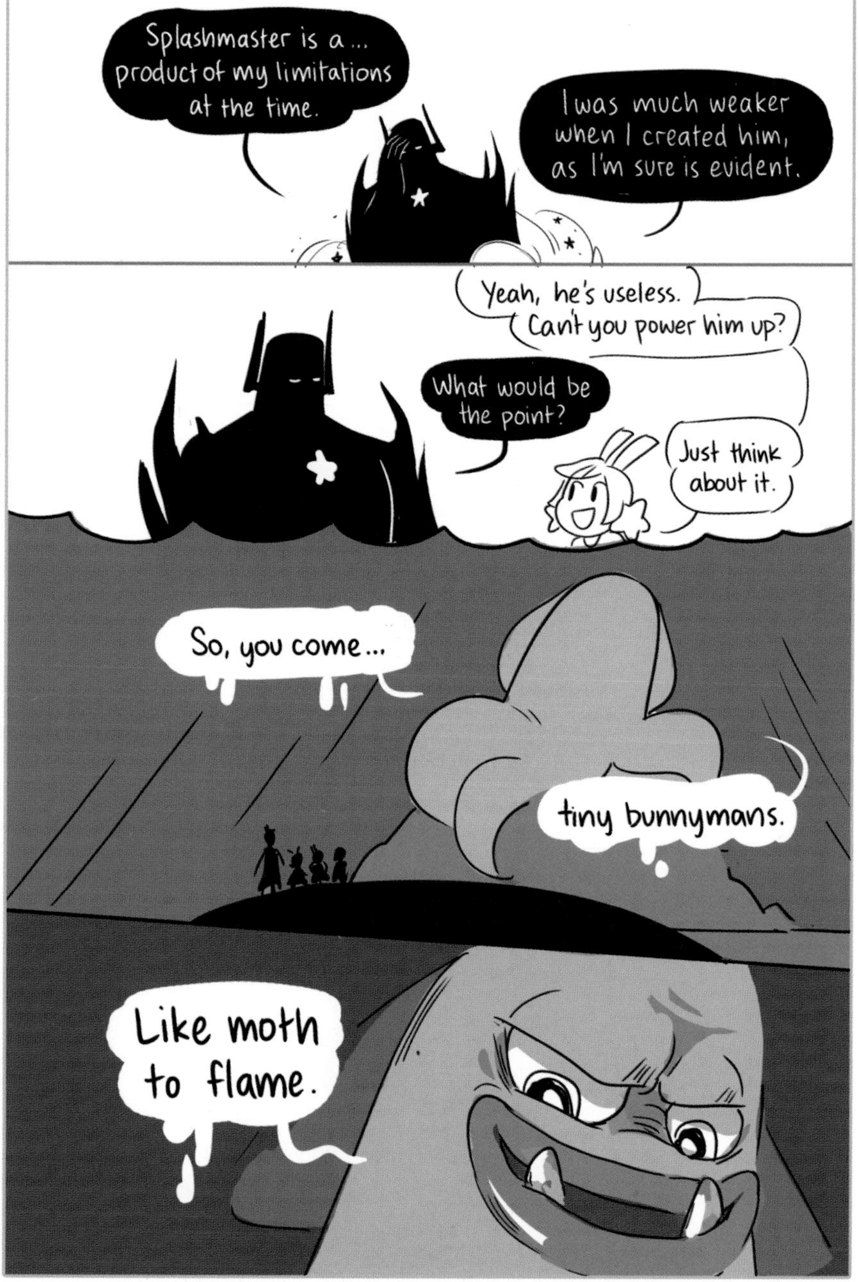
Splashmaster is a... product of my limitations at the time.
I was much weaker when I created him, as I'm sure is evident.
Yeah, he's useless. Can't you power him up?
What would be the point?
Just think about it.
So, you come...
tiny bunnymans.
Like moth to flame.

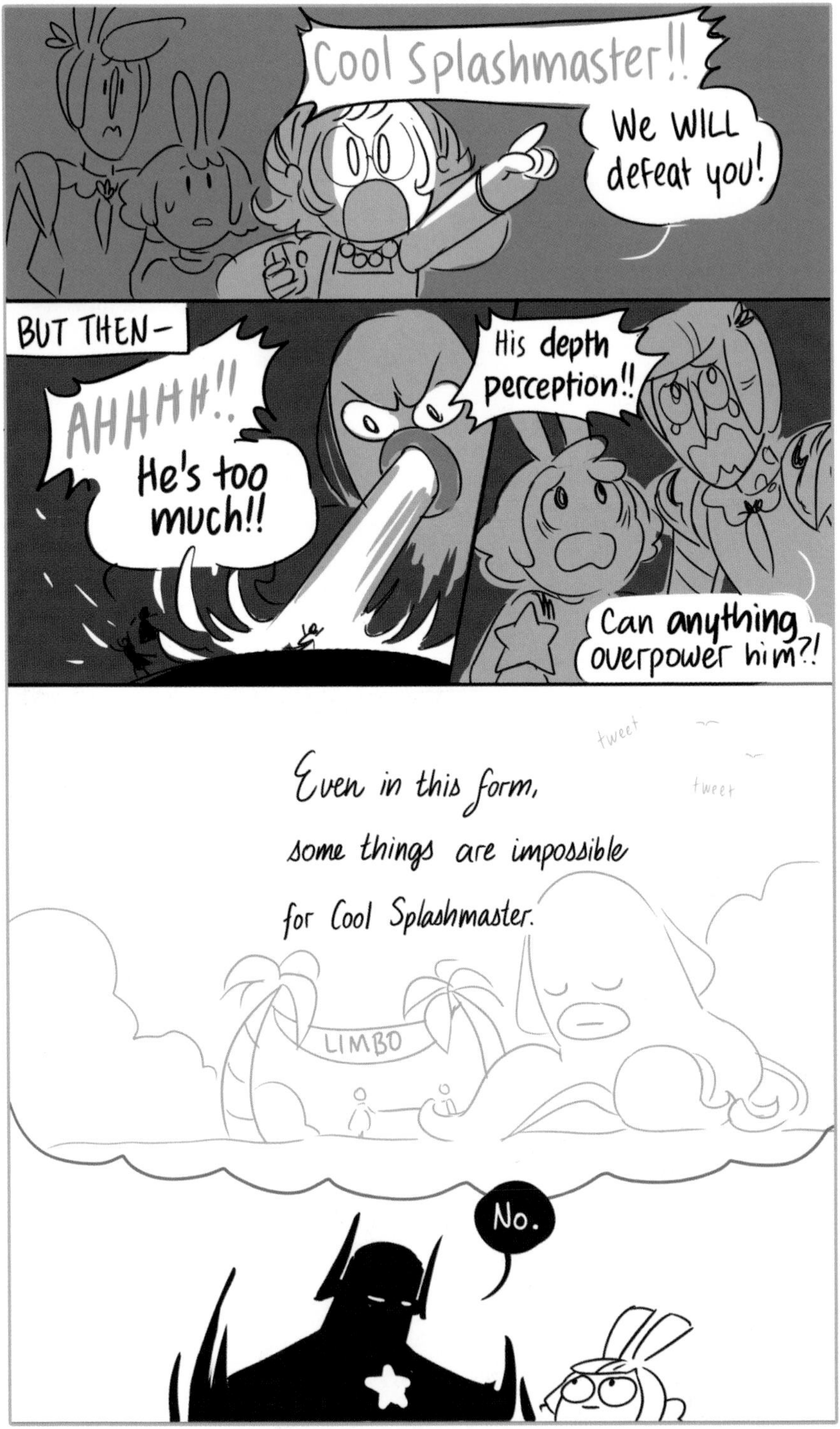
Cool Splashmaster!!
We WILL defeat you!
BUT THEN—
AHHHH!!
He's too much!!
His depth perception!!
Can anything overpower him?!
tweet
tweet
Even in this form,
some things are impossible
for Cool Splashmaster.
LIMBO
No.

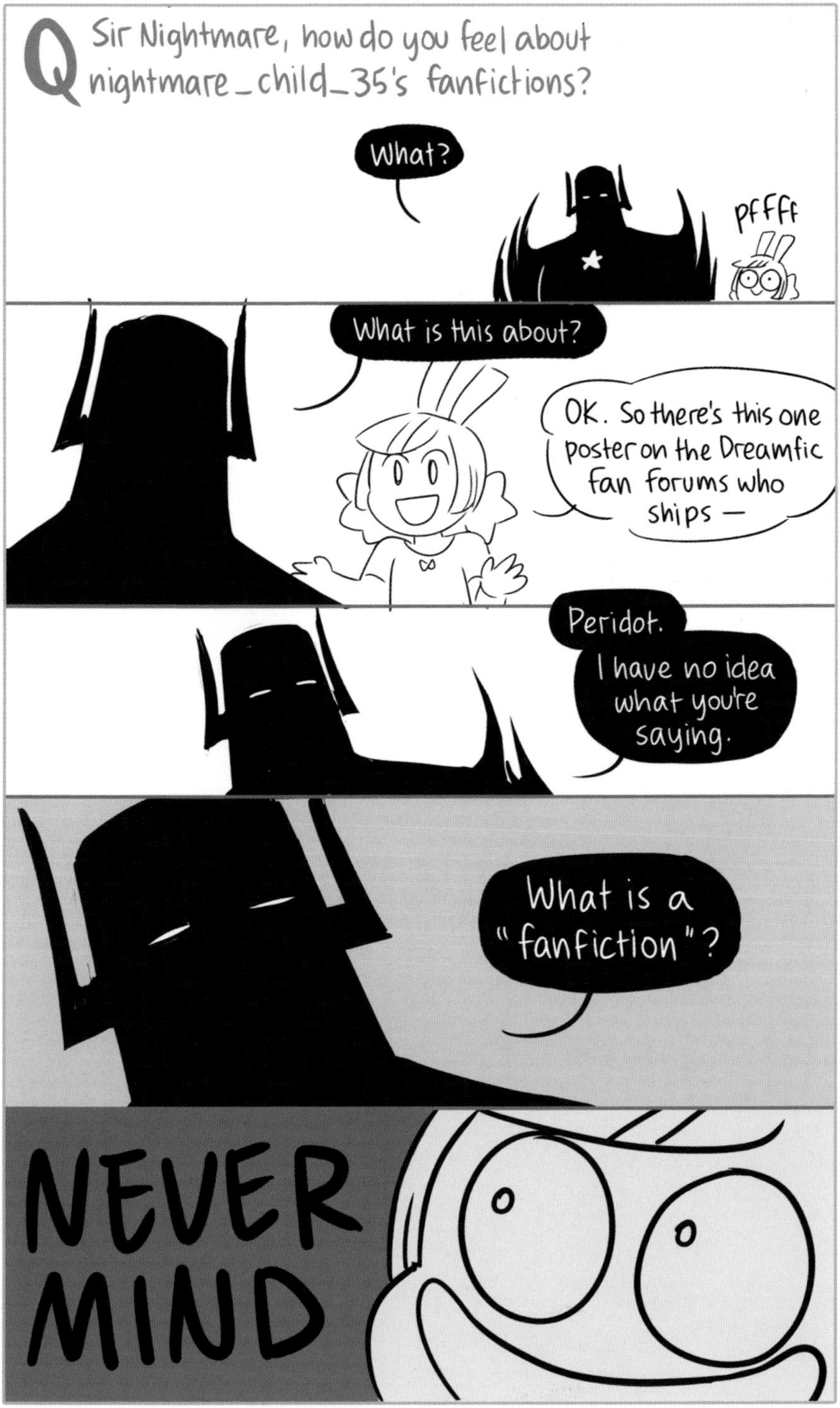

Q Sir Nightmare, how do you feel about nightmare_child_35's fanfictions?
What?
pffff
What is this about?
OK. So there's this one poster on the Dreamfic fan forums who ships —
Peridot.
I have no idea what you're saying.
What is a "fanfiction"?
NEVER MIND

Flower Kingdom

Dreamside's floral paradise also happens to be its smallest kingdom. Its population is centralized in Botanica Springs, while the rest of the island is untamed wilderness.

Botanica Springs is structured on a large tree with roots extending deep beneath the ground.

surface

ground level

Hocus Crocus is here!

The underground region is where you'll find remnants of the ancient Flower Kingdom, which was devastated by the Nightmare Knight and Rosemaster long ago.

The statue you saw here is a depiction of Queen Lotus, known for her charity and beauty.

By the way, King Sunflower is descended from her!

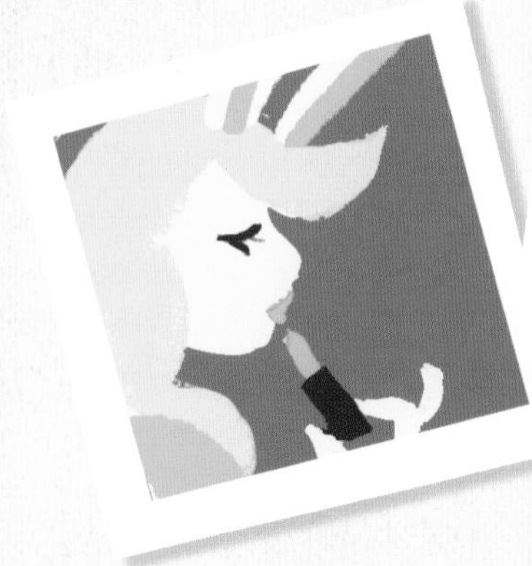

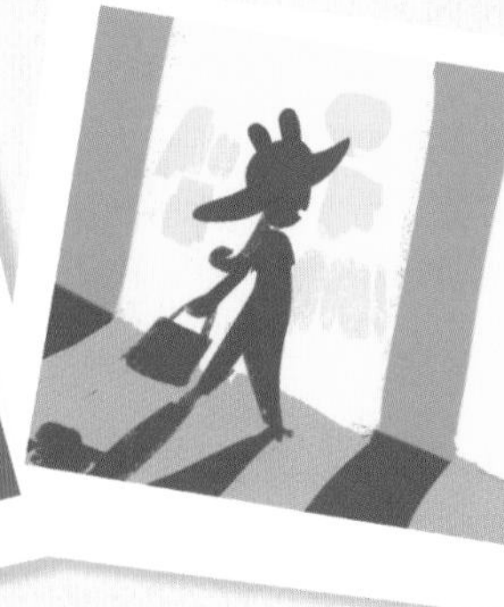

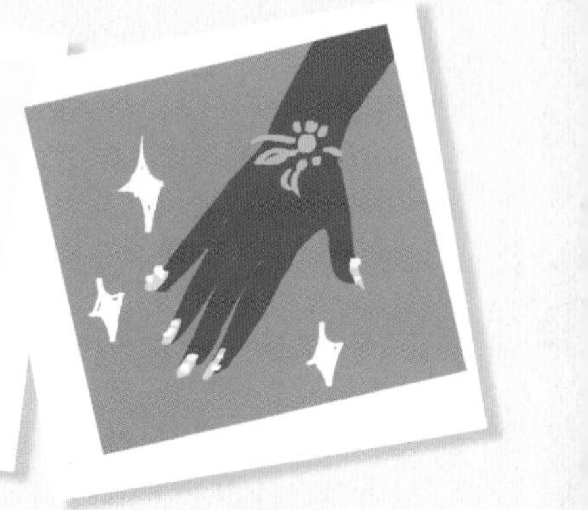

Modern Botanica Springs is a hot spot for trendsetters. You'll find no better shopping destination in Dreamside, except maybe the Galaxy Galleria in the Space Kingdom.

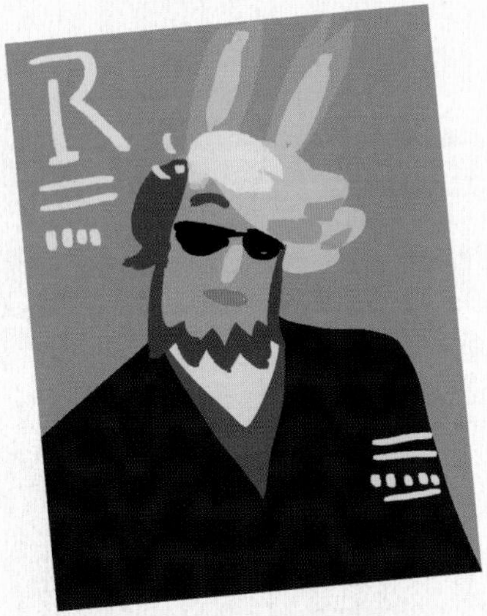
R

And who do Botanicals have to thank for their city's super-chic image? Well...you know the answer to that already.

He may seem untouchable, but Mr. R considers himself first and foremost a servant of the people.

He even worked with the police to design their uniforms!

(They had to talk him down from sequins, but still.)

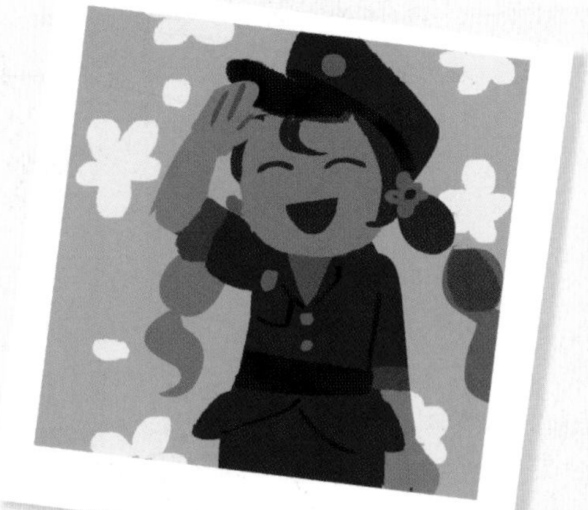

Okay, let's address the photo-realistic elephant in the room... What is the Guardener's deal, anyway?

No one can say for certain, but there are all kinds of rumors floating around about that guy.

Some say he was cursed.

Others say he was warped by the power of the Hocus Crocus.

Still others say he might be from a different world...

Nah, I'm just some guy.

It seems we may never know the truth...

Concept Art

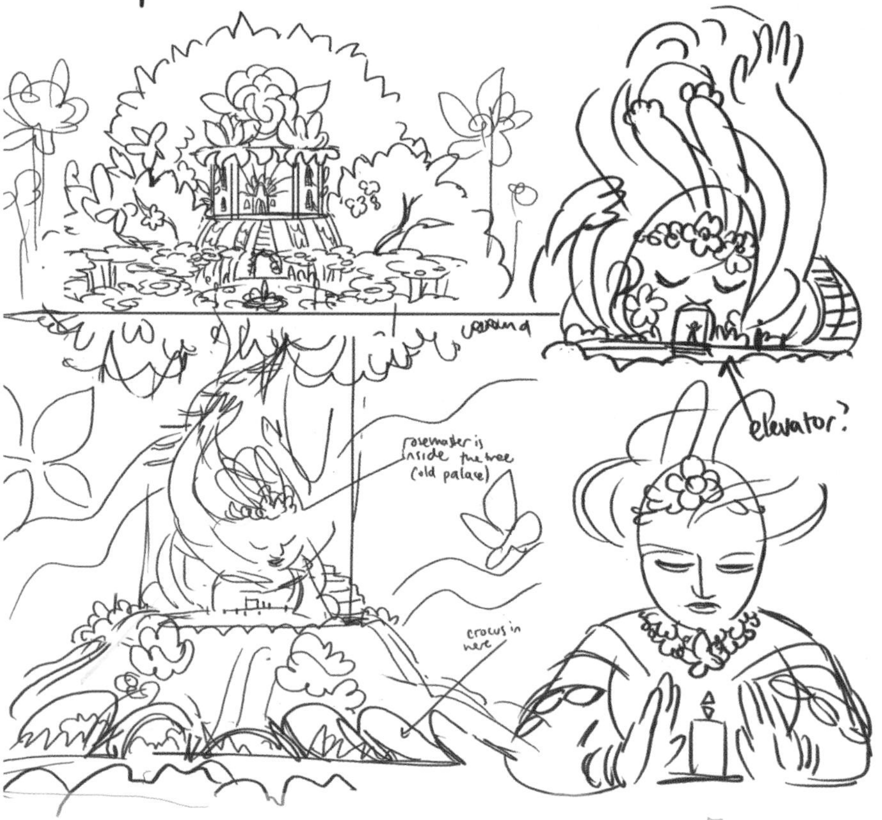
rosemaster is inside the tree (old palace)
crocus in here
elevator?

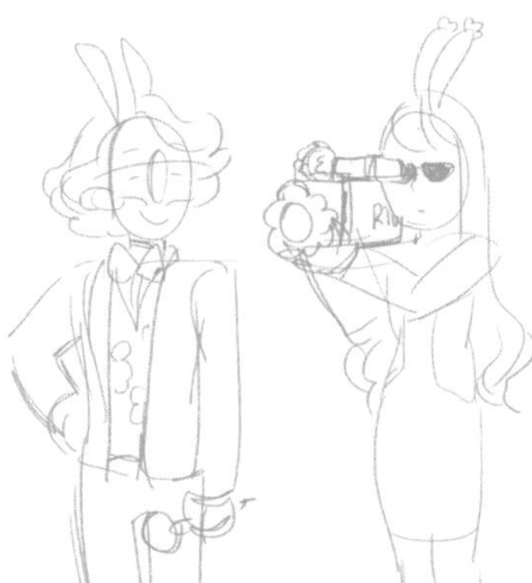

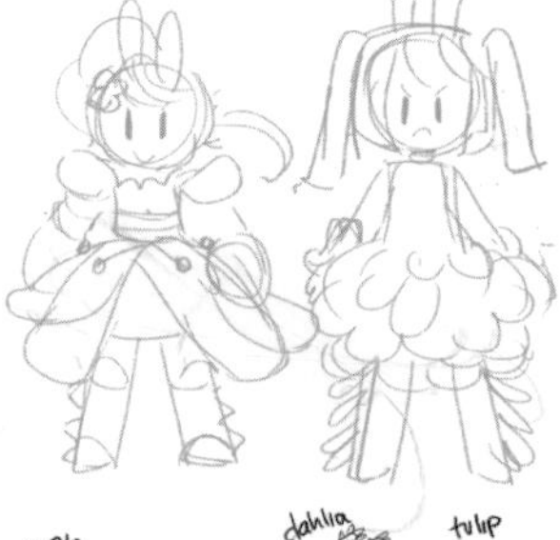

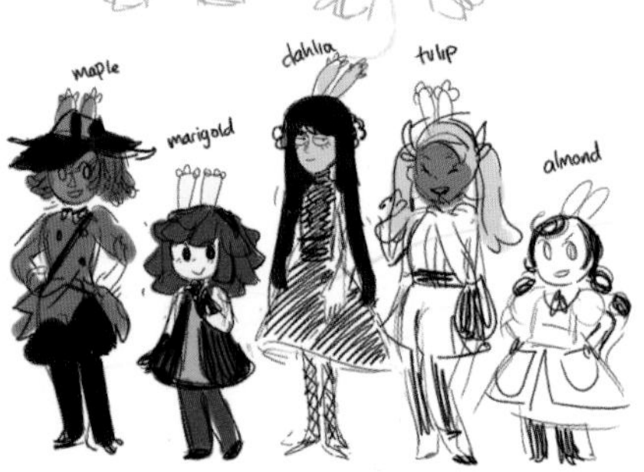
maple
marigold
dahlia
tulip
almond

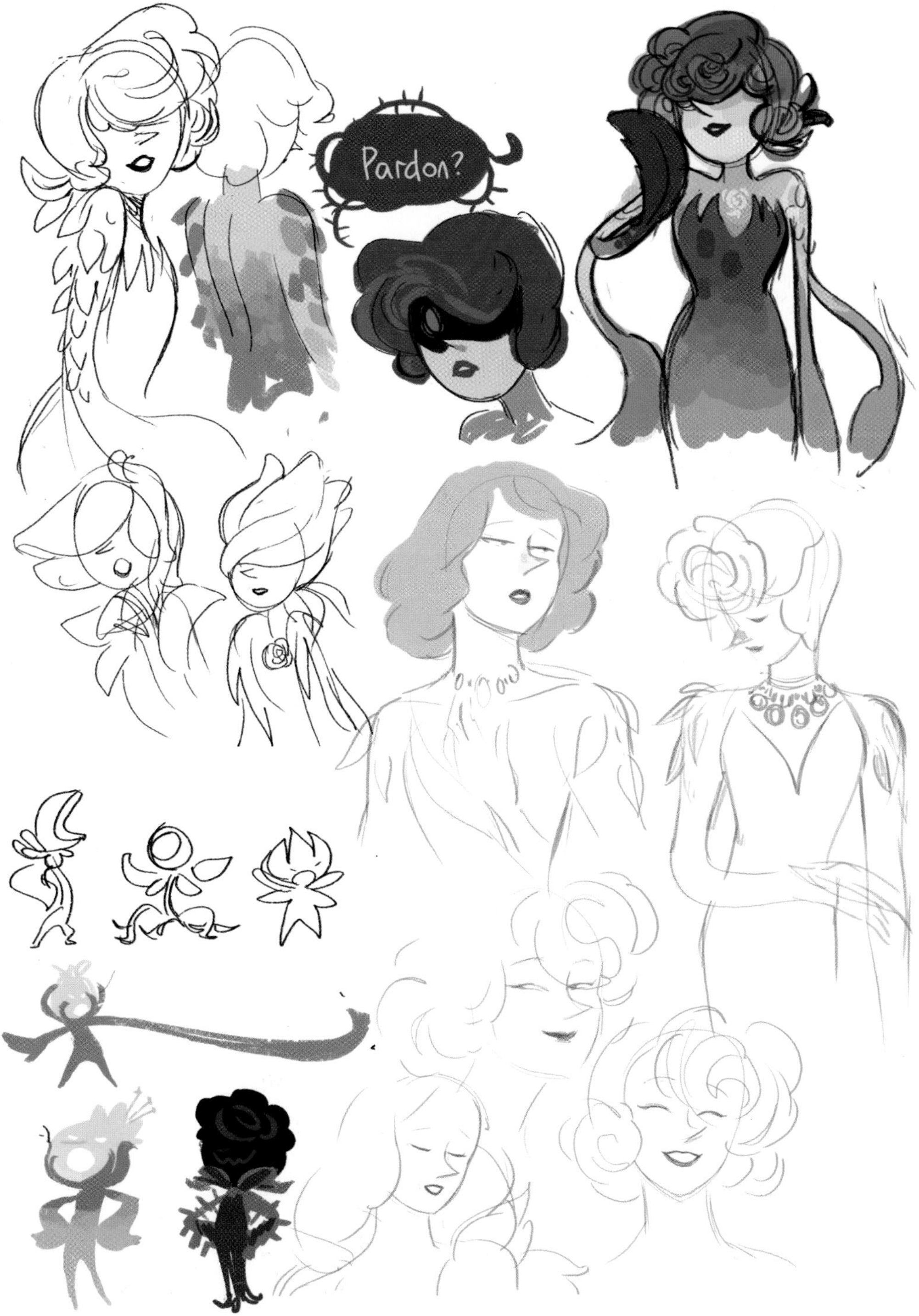
Pardon?

The Flower Kingdom

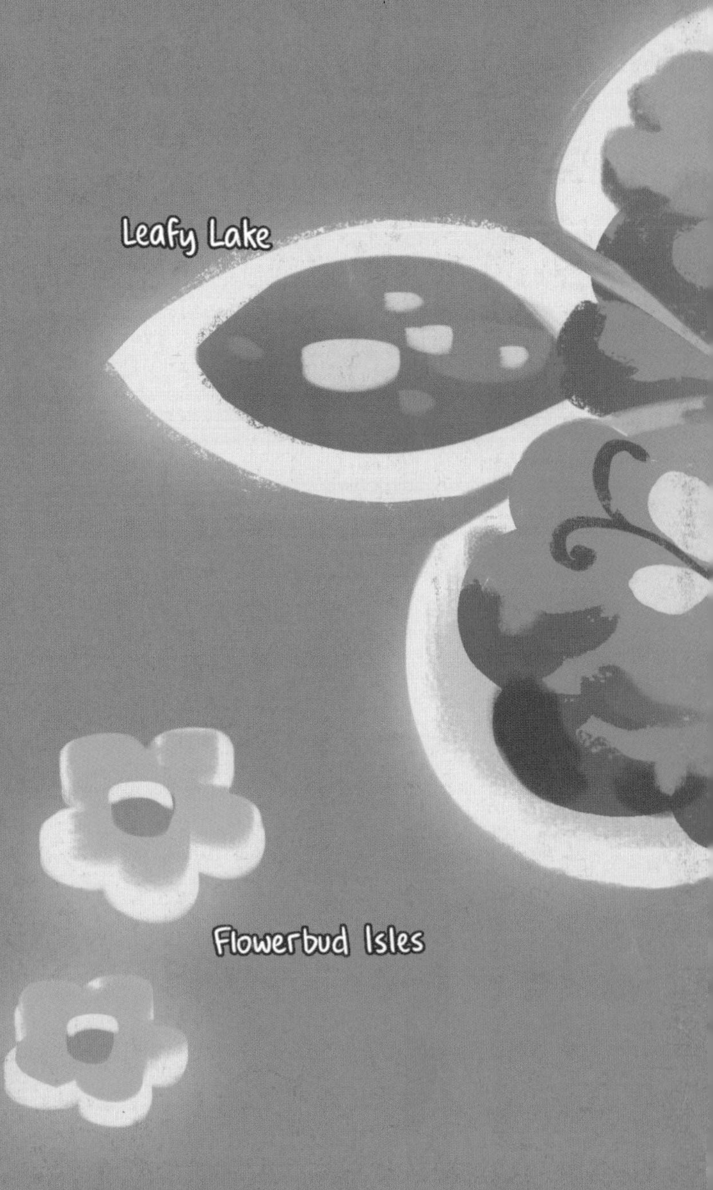
Leafy Lake
Flowerbud Isles

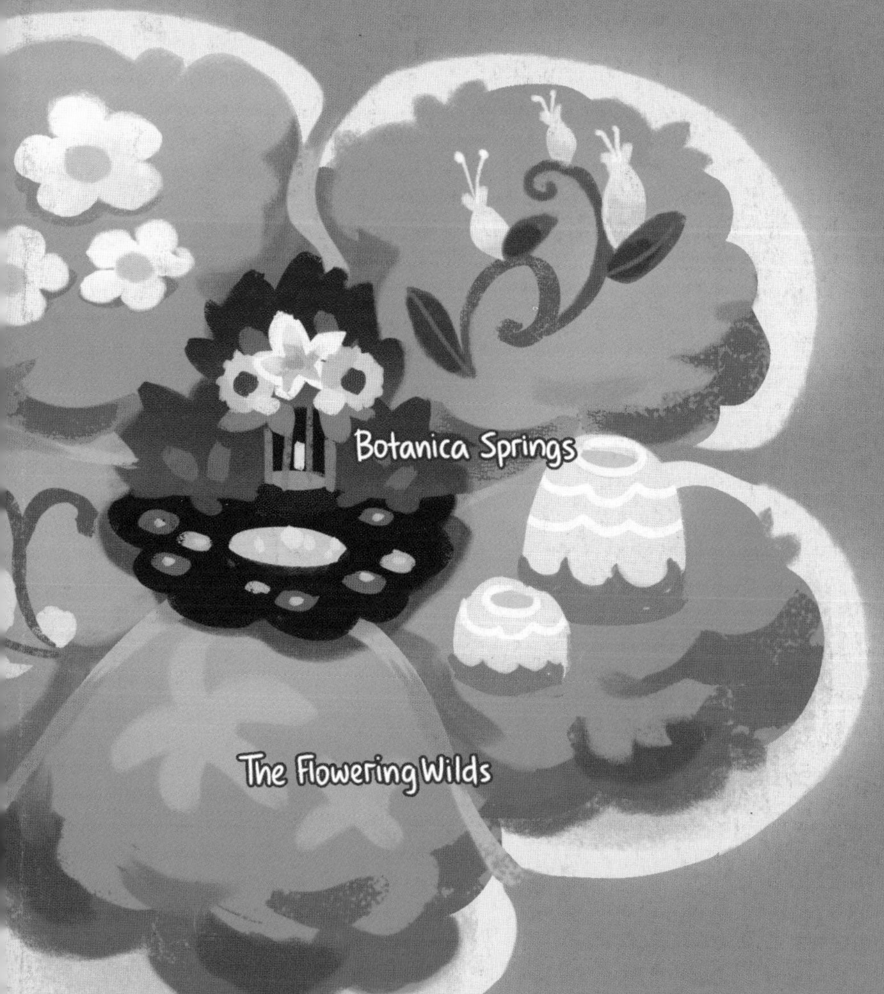
Botanica Springs
The Flowering Wilds

First Second

New York

Copyright © 2018 by Gigi D.G.

Published by First Second
First Second is an imprint of Roaring Brook Press, a division of
Holtzbrinck Publishing Holdings Limited Partnership
175 Fifth Avenue, New York, NY 10010

All rights reserved

Library of Congress Control Number: 2017957142

Hardcover ISBN: 978-1-250-16295-3
Paperback ISBN: 978-1-62672-835-6

Our books may be purchased in bulk for promotional, educational,
or business use. Please contact your local bookseller or the Macmillan
Corporate and Premium Sales Department at (800) 221-7945 ext. 5442
or by e-mail at MacmillanSpecialMarkets@macmillan.com.

First edition, 2018
Book design by Rob Steen

Cucumber Quest is created entirely in Photoshop.

Printed in China by RR Donnelley Asia Printing Solutions Ltd., Dongguan City, Guangdong Province

Hardcover: 10 9 8 7 6 5 4 3 2 1
Paperback: 10 9 8 7 6 5 4 3 2 1